I hope you enjoy

A VANISHING BREED:
The Gold Miner

A local gold miner

by
Jimmy Simpson

Jimmy Simpson

Be kind to your Neighbors and you will have better Neighbors

Printed in IMPRESORA NACIONAL
Ocampo 104 Tel. Fax 2-14-15
CD. SABINAS, COAHUILA MEXICO

THE VANISHING BREED
THE GOLD MINER

COPYRIGHT APPLIED JANUARY 1996
SIMPSON PUBLISHING BY JIMMY SIMPSON

ALL RIGHTS RESERVED INCLUDING THE RIGHTS
TO REPRODUCE THIS BOOK, OR ANY PORTIONS
THEREOF, IN ANY FORM EXCEPT FOR THE
INCLUSION OF BRIEF QUOTATIONS
IN A REVIEW

ISBN 0-9651227-0-0

Printing in Sabinas, Coahuila Mexico

SECOND EDITION 1999

Cover photo by Pat and Babia Morrow

Book cover designed by
Carl H. Dickerson Jr.
of Eagle Pass, Texas

I want to thank Duanne Gregg, "Duey", for her many, many hours and dedication on her computer<u>s</u> - she keeps updating them - while helping me with my book.

I'd also like to thank her husband "Radio Red", James Gregg, who helped as a sounding board, and for his many suggestions.

There wouldn't have been "A VANISHING BREED: The Gold Miner" without them, so Thanks to you both, friends of many years,

        Jimmy Simpson

OUR DEAR FRIENDS, DEWEY AND JAMES (RADIO RED) GREEGG.

This book is dedicated to Jadene Allison Simpson Magill, our dear daughter, born in Anchorage, Alaska, October 20, 1960. She works in the Medical Intensive Care Unit at Baptist Hospital in Nashville, Tennessee. She has a Bachelor of Science degree in Nursing, CCRN, BCLS, ACLS, and I don't know how many "S"-es she has, but she does love nursing.

Also, to Scotty Lynn Magill, her husband, born in Indiana, March, 1961. He's attending Austin Peay University in Clarksville, Tennessee, to become a veterinarian, and is on the Dean's List, cum laude, Phi Beta, and other organizations.

And to their lovely daughters, Jennifer Nicole and Tia Elaine.

JADENE AND SCOTT MAGILL WITH THEIR CHILDREN JENNIFER AND TIA ELAINE.

Carl H. Dickerson

We first met Carl while he was working for U.S. Customs at Poker Creek Border Crossing between the U.S. and Canada. Since then we have become close friends of him and his family.

We cherish the time that Carl and Rosie spent with us on gay gulch in the Yukon in 1989.

Our friendship brings us to Eagle Pass, Texas as often as we can fit in our schedule.

Carl and I have been working on some gold properties in old Mexico and hopefully some good will come from our efforts.

Carl is a man of many talents and has a memory like an elephant. Thank you C.H. Jr. for your cover design and for Michaels help. You just don't run into folks like the Dickersons .

When I first met Jimmy Simpson I was enthralled by his stories of gold mining and living and working in the "last frontiers" of our continent. Plus, he could tell a story as few people can, I "guess you had to be there". I offered to help him write his book and in doing so I've tried to leave his "flavor" on it rather than injecting mine. Anyone can learn to write grammatically correct sentences, but few of us can **really** tell a story that keeps your interest, entertains you, and teaches you things you probably didn't know. I hope you hear **his story** as you read his book.

Duey Gregg

A VANISHING BREED: The Gold Miner
by Jimmy Simpson

Prologue

It was a cold, windy March 24th, 1928, when I first saw the light of day. I was born to Nellie Evelyn and John Dudley Simpson. The house I was born in had four rooms and an outhouse, and was in Sullivan Hollow (pronounced "holler" in Tennessee), about 2-1/2 miles from Ashland City, Tennessee. My Mom and Daddy had one daughter 2 years old at the time of my birth, my sister Louetha, and in years to come our family would grow to eight children, six girls and two boys.

When Mama started having labor pains, Daddy walked the 2-1/2 miles to Ashland City to get Dr. Lockert. They rode back in Doc's "Tin Lizzy", a Model T Ford coupe, to the mouth of Sullivan Hollow, but then had to walk the remaining mile around back-water. In those days, the late twenties, the TVA Dam systems on the Cumberland River had not yet been built, so for about 6 weeks each spring, creeks that flowed into the Cumberland, Tennessee, and Mississippi Rivers backed up, and people living in those areas had to cope with skirting around the back-waters.

The fee for the house-call and delivering me was $20. Daddy argued a little over the price, but Doc said if I had been twins the fee would have been $40. Dr. Lockert had to accept a variety of items for his services from folks who didn't have money to pay him. Some of the things he received were chickens, eggs, pigs, and all kinds of vegetables and canned goods. He never turned anyone down, this "jolly man in his Tin Lizzy".

My parents were hard-working, honest and religious people. This was the depression era and we learned early in life to cope with hard times. Back then, there wasn't TV and we didn't have a radio, but we did have an old wind-up Victrola record player that played the old 78 rpm records, and that was our entertainment.

I'll never forget my first day in school, and there were lots of "firsts" to follow. For transportation we had mules and a wagon until I was about 12 years old; that's when we got our first car. I remember one Sunday, on the way home from church I went to sleep and fell off of the wagon, and a wheel ran over my foot and broke it. As I was hobbling up the road and crying, Daddy was laughing at me, and said, "I can't understand anyone that'd go to sleep and fall off of the wagon." We would ride the wagon to church on Bear Wallow Road (pronounced "Bear Waller").

One Sunday we heard at church that they were just beginning daylight savings time. That was a first, and it really confused everyone. We didn't really know what to think about it. Franklin Delano Roosevelt was President then.

The three most important things that my Daddy taught me were to work, to be honest, and to manage money. I remember my first pocket watch, I gave Billy Ray Jackson 10 cents for it. And I'll never forget my first 22 rifle, I got it from Daddy as a Christmas present. It was a single shot Winchester rifle. In those days, 1939, the price was $4.25 for a new Winchester single shot rifle.

I bought my first bicycle with money I received from my share of corn that I'd raised for Daddy on our farm on Boston Creek. I got $24 for the corn, and the bike cost me $18.50. I got so much money for my corn because I talked to Mr. Roos Tucker, who owned the flour and corn mill there in Ashland City, and he suggested that I shell the corn, then I'd get more money for it. So I found an old corn sheller and proceeded to shell all that corn and put it in burlap bags. Whether or not it was worth all the effort didn't really matter, because I did get more money for it and my time wasn't all that valuable anyway.

The first suit of clothes I ever owned I purchased from Mr. W. C. Bouldin at the dry goods store in Ashland City. It cost me $12 and I earned the money dragging railroad cross-ties out of the woods, with an old gray horse, at 3 cents each. The guy that I was working for in those days was Mr. Frank Haines.

One time, when I was about 10 years old, I cut several hundred bean sticks for a Mr. Hampton, and he paid me with tomato plants. It was a good lesson to have an understanding of what your pay will be before you start a job. I would like to add that Mr. Hampton raised vegetable gardens and things for the market in those days.

I wasn't able to get involved in sports in school as I had too many chores to do at home, and my number one job, of course, was to cut wood. We had wood stoves for heat and a wood cookstove for Mama's kitchen. It took quite a bit of my time just keeping them going. Also, I'd help Daddy cut timber on Sunday afternoons with an old crosscut saw. This was before they had chainsaws. Daddy was working, hewing the cross-ties by hand with a broad ax. He was working those "on shares", we called it in those days, getting so much for each tie. There were different size cross-ties and different prices. If I remember correctly, for one size my Dad got 10 cents for hewing, and for another, 15 cents, and one of the bigger ones was 20 cents. Lots of times I've seen Daddy's paycheck on a Saturday be just a little more than the grocery bill.

During the week, in the evenings, I'd go up and drag cross-ties out and bring them in to the log road, an area where we could drive the wagon back in to load up the cross-ties. I did that every Saturday morning. I'd take the wagon, hitch up the mules, and go load the cross-ties onto the wagon, then haul them in to Ashland City to the tie yard. Daddy would always go in on the second load to pick up his money from the owner of the timber.

My first movie to see was a great experience. It was named, "The Call of the Lonesome Pine", and I thoroughly enjoyed that movie. I went to Nashville with our school class on a school bus to see it and I'll never forget that one.

I was about 12 years old when I bought my first comic book. It cost 10 cents and I wore that sucker out reading it. I don't know how many times I read that first comic book that I bought. I do know that it was a western, I think it was written based on a Gene Autrey story.

I won't ever forget the first Coca Cola I went to buy. I went into Baxter Nicholson's Grocery Store in Ashland City, right next to the Klondike Cafe, and I asked for an orange Coca Cola, and I got a hot Coke. I assumed that all drinks were Coca Colas, regardless of what other flavor that you wanted, so that's where I made my mistake. I was so bashful that I couldn't tell Mr. Baxter that I really wanted the orange drink, so I tried to drink the Coke and it made me about half sick. To this day I really don't care for Coca Cola.

I used to ride an old gray horse most every place I went, and I was riding up Boston Hollow one morning when I rode up on a moonshine still sitting right there in the hollow. I got off the horse and started to look around, when someone told me to get back on the horse and get out of there. Even though I couldn't see the person, my hair stood up as I scrambled to get back on the horse. Needless to say, I hooked'em and got out of range of that moonshine still in a hurry.

Also on that old gray horse, I'll never forget the night my Dad took me over to Mr. Tom Naybor's house to listen to the Joe Louis-Max Schmeling fight on his radio (well, I'm almost sure that was the fight), but, boy, I thought that was something else.

Speaking of horses, a bunch of us boys got together in Ashland City, on a Halloween Night, of course, and we got ahold of a guy's horse, it was a great horse, too. We took the horse and led him down to the cross-tie yard, where the railroad bought the cross-ties, and we made stair-steps out of those cross-ties. Us boys flat worked hard that night; we stacked up a bunch of those cross-ties making the stair-steps, and we walked the horse up on them. We put up a cardboard sign and wrote on it, "Living high", and we also penned the horse in, put cross-ties all the way around him. I never did hear what the man who owned the horse had to say, but I can imagine what his thinking was.

Also, on our way back through town we made a pass down by the Chevrolet place, which was almost across from Cliff Hagewood's Ford place. In those days you didn't have to worry about leaving your cars unlocked, because there was no crime as we know it today, and no one hardly ever touched anything. So, us boys moved all the cars from the Chevrolet lot over to the Ford lot and "switcheroo'd" them. We'd take one at a time, move a Chevy over across the road and move a Ford back to the Chevy lot. And we'd keep doing that, watching for the Sheriff, or the Sheriff's Deputies, we'd make sure no one was coming. We didn't have all the traffic back then that you have today either. Needless to say, we got all the Chevys over on the Ford lot, and all the Fords over on the Chevy lot, and they had a nice little time unscrambling them the next day.

I used to enjoy trapping in the wintertime. I was always up early, making rounds to the traps and rabbit boxes. Daddy taught me to trap and to make the rabbit boxes. One morning as I came out the front door, a rabid dog bit my arm, we called them "mad" dogs. We shot the dog, had his head checked, and sure enough, he was rabid. I had to take 21 shots in my stomach, and to this day I don't care for mean dogs.

I quit school when I was in the eighth grade. Daddy gave me a choice; he said, "Okay, you clear this 4 acres of hillside up here, everything except cedar and pine, or go back to school." I cleared the land with an ax and a briar hook. After I finished the clearing job I hitchhiked to Houston, Texas. Later, while I was in the Navy, I took a GED test, passed with flying colors and got my high school diploma, but I'd like to tell some of my experiences along the way.

Down in Mississippi I thought I'd try a little hoboing. I caught a freight train, and boy, after we got rolling down the tracks a little way, my side started acting up and hurting, really, really hurting. So I figured the next town I came to I would bail off. It was pouring down raining, but I had to get out of there, I couldn't stand it in that boxcar. We came into a little town and I bailed off the boxcar, walked around and found a guy's garage to get in out of the rain and sit down. This was about 11 o'clock at night. I sat down in a corner of the carport/garage and the pain in my side got a little easier. After awhile I dozed off. When I woke up the next morning, the light was on in the kitchen, so I figured I'd better get up and get out of there before that guy caught me out there in his garage by his car. So I took off out on the road, this time hitchhiking.

I caught rides and got into Lafayette, Louisiana. I'll never forget it, I had 35 cents left when I went into this little restaurant type of affair. In those days, they had slot machines in all of the restaurants and different places, around the country. It wasn't illegal to have them back then in Louisiana, and Tennessee I might add. Anyway, I put coins in a machine and got 3 dollars-something out of it. I got all "cherries" I think, or something to that effect. Boy, I thought I was rich, so I bought me a Greyhound bus ticket to Houston, and still had some change left.

In Houston I went to work for a riding stable out at the end of South Main Street. I also worked on a ranch owned by a Mrs. Redding up near Waller, Texas. I enjoyed my stay there, but it still wasn't what I was really looking for, so I returned to Tennessee and got a job working on my first big-inch pipeline. Williams Brothers, from Houston and Oklahoma City, was the company installing a 24-inch pipeline from Texas to Pennsylvania. After the pipeline job, I went to South Dakota and worked in the wheat harvest. I returned from South Dakota and joined the Navy. After my hitch in the Navy I worked pipelines about a year before joining the Army, the 82nd Airborne Division. I got discharged from the 82nd Airborne in January 1950.

I met my wife, Marcene, in San Antonio, Texas, during the time I was in service and going to medical and surgical tech school at Fort Sam Houston. We were married August 14, 1949.

Marcene Olivia Best was born in Bronte, Texas, April 12, 1926. On October 6, 1942, she changed her birth certificate to read "1920", and enrolled in the W.A.A.C. - later called the Women's Army Corps - and served in the South Pacific. She was a Sergeant with the Recruiting Service. Marcene ("Boots", I called her) had learned to fly in Fort Worth, Texas, at Meacham Field, on the G.I. Bill. She took her flight test to be an instructor, but got transferred to Fort Sam Houston before she took the written part and didn't follow through for her instructor's license.

We met in the P.X. at Fort Sam Houston. Two weeks later I was driving to Tennessee and Marcene was on leave up in Austin visiting her sister. I told her I'd come by her sister's place and pick her up to go with me. But I got to thinking about it, and wasn't sure it was such a good idea, so I flipped a coin, "heads, I get her, and tails, I don't." It came up tails. By the time I got to Tennessee I missed her and knew I'd made the wrong choice, so I called her from Ashland City and sent her a plane ticket, which at that time was around $55. We got married the day after she arrived in Tennessee.

On December 24, 1949, we bought our first new car from Cliff Hagewood, in Ashland City, and the total price of that car was $1795.

Upon discharge from the Paratroopers, we went to Robert Lee, Texas, where I got my first oil rig job. I kept looking for jobs and getting turned down. They'd say, "Do you have any experience as a roughneck?", and when I'd say, "No.", they'd turn me down. Finally, one day in a cafe, I asked a driller for a job and he asked me, "Are you a roughneck?" I said, "Yes." So he said, "Okay, I'll pick you up this evening and take you out to the oil field, you've got a job."

That first night on the oil rig was a 3-ring circus. Coming up out of the hole, I kind of stumbled, slipped in the mud, and the driller said to me, "You've never been out on an oil rig in your life."

He never said another word about it to me that night, but on the way home the next morning, he said, "If you hadn't of busted your butt so hard last night, I would have run you off, but I'm gonna keep you because I think you'll make a good hand."

We moved up to Snyder, Texas, in the summer of 1950. That was the big oil boom of Scurry County, and during the peak of that boom, you could count 479 oil rigs out across the landscape if you were standing up in the derrick at night. It was no problem to get a job on an oil rig in Scurry County during that oil boom. All you had to do was help the driller run pipe into the hole, or help him bring it out of the hole, or help him make the round trip, and you'd get 8 hours for it. The procedure was, the driller would send one of his hands around to other rigs, rounding up enough people to help him bring the pipe out of the hole, and/or make the round trip. That's the way it was in the oil fields in Scurry County in 1950.

I got my back hurt on a drilling rig in 1952, and during my recuperation I got into music, eventually playing bars, clubs, radio and TV. I recorded several songs during my travels in music. My first disc jockey job was at KERC in Eastland, Texas, and there were several other D.J. jobs to follow during my chasing the music business. I'd like to add that my first appearance on the Grand Old Opry was in August 1954. It was really a great thrill to stand out on the stage where all the greats had stood over the years, and be introduced by my dear friend, Mr. Ernest Tubb.

My first TV show was KTXL at San Angelo, Texas. We'd trade time for talent. We wanted to make it in the business, so we didn't really have to get paid for going on TV in those days. I'll never forget the first time I met Elvis Presley. It was on a show that we played in San Angelo. The two headliners were Jimmy Lee and Johnny; they had a song called, "If You Don't, Somebody Else Will". Billy Walker was also a star on the show; Billy, and Joe Treadway, had booked the show. I was on the show, and Elvis was also on the show. It was one show, and probably the only one, where Elvis got paid less than any of the other people on the show.

In the summer of 1954 I had a sad experience with a bank in Nashville, Tennessee. I owed only $1400 on a 1952 Cadillac Fleetwood. We had just gotten back to town from playing in Texas, Colorado, and Oregon, and I had a note to contact the bank. I was about 5 weeks in arrears on the car payments, and after paying for a new set of tires, paying the band members and the insurance, I only had food money left.

I went by and tried to talk to the banker, tried to talk him into giving me a couple of days to get money from my folks, but he was kind of greedy, I guess, and I was young, and he won. I was naive and just didn't understand how to deal with a banker. The car was equipped with air conditioning, which was a prize in those days, and the car was in immaculate condition, so right away I knew he wanted it. I don't remember his name, but I won't ever forget how he looked when he dumped Marcene and me out at our apartment on West End Avenue in Nashville.

Marcene and I walked in the rain down to Oliver McGee's car lot across from the Sears building on Murfreesboro Road. Oliver was a dear friend of ours and he sold us a '52 Kaiser for $500. Just a note, Oliver McGee was also a songwriter, and he traded a song to Hank Williams which became one of Hank's biggest hits, for Hank's western wear store on Seventh Avenue and $4000. That night I wrote a song: "Standing on the corner of Eighth and Broad, smoking a cheap cigar, my baby left with my money, and the bank took back my car". I suppose if I get enough lessons like these I'll have a good education someday.

We'd wanted to go to Alaska to homestead for quite some time, so in March of 1957 we finally got underway. I'd like to add that the last performance I made on our way to Alaska was on TV with Willie Nelson. Willie was a disc jockey at KVAN in Vancouver, Washington. His TV show in Portland, Oregon, was sponsored by Northwest Ford. I'd also like to add that Willie had a flat top haircut in those days, and he was a real nice guy. I haven't seen Willie for some time now, but I would assume that he's changed a bit, at least in the way of the hairdo.

In April we were still on our way up to Alaska. We slept in sleeping bags and cooked over an open fire. We did make an exception the first night that we were in Alaska. Even though we only had $82 left, we spent $4 for a nice, cozy cabin at the Tazlina Lodge. That's about 150 miles east of Anchorage.

Our first night in Anchorage I fronted a band, played guitar, and sang, at the Montana Club for Norm Dahl. After singing, talking and picking from 9 p.m. to 5 a.m., Norm told me that I did good. He said that last night was an audition and I could go to work tonight. I told Norm that I would look for something else, thank you.

The first paying job I had in Alaska was with Anchorage Gas and Oil, on an oil rig at Houston, Alaska. The owners were George Tucker and Ralph Peterson, and the pay was as follows: $1200 a month for a driller, and we had to take 20 percent of our pay in stock. I eventually gave all of my stock away as Christmas presents. I gave stock in Anchorage Gas and Oil to Ernest Tubb, Grant Turner, Mrs. Carrie Rogers, different friends throughout the music business. There was one good thing that came from me working that job, we were able to file on, and prove-up on, a 160-acre homestead. We had to build 2-1/2 miles of road into the homestead and clear and plant 20 acres. The homestead was about 3 miles from the oil rig, and the site of Houston, Alaska, today.

My brother, Buzz Simpson, came up and worked for me on the oil rig at Houston. Buzz helped me cut the trail into our homestead the summer of 1957. We were able to drive my old Army 6-by truck all the way in to the site on the lake where we planned to build our log house. Buzz came back the next year and worked as a derrick man on the oil rig. In the evenings we set up a portable sawmill, but we never could make it pay.

The summer of 1957, the cook in our camp at the oil rig accused some of the guys of stealing food from the kitchen. One day I saw a bear coming out of the back door with a ham and that ended the argument right there.

In the fall of 1957, I killed my first grizzly bear on the old winter sled road adjoining our homestead. I was moose hunting at the time and just came around a curve face to face with that critter. I had a 35 Marlin and was in doubt as to whether it was enough gun. There were no trees or anything right there that I could climb, so after I took two shots and the bear went down I took off and got away from him a ways to see just what he was gonna do. Later, I sneaked back up to him, taking a few steps at a time, with my trusty little 35 aimed at him, and sure enough, he was all done in.

While I was working on the oil rig and trying to prove-upon our homestead, Marcene was driving 55 to 60 miles every day into the Co-op in Palmer, Alaska. There was 35 miles of gravel road with the remainder pavement. She'd make that trip every day, 5 days a week, and very seldom she'd make the round trip without having at least one flat. We didn't have fancy tires in those days like the good ones we have today. They were those old rayon tires.

In all the years, I've only missed being with my folks in Tennessee for Christmas twice, once while in the Navy, and the first year on our homestead. We built our first log home in the winter of 1957-58. It never got above zero while we were building our home, and that's why we named the lake it was on Zero Lake. For building our log house I used an ax, a draw knife, a hammer, hand saw, and a small rope, block and tackle. I dragged all the logs to the building site with a rope over my shoulder. The logs would slide pretty good on frozen snow after they were peeled and left overnight.

For the first three years in Alaska I worked part-time as a disc jockey at KBYR. I used to have to drive 69 miles into Anchorage to do a 5-hour show each Saturday night. Over 30 miles of it was gravel. Lefty Frizzell came up and played the summer of 1957. The sun was up when he got there, the sun was shining when he went to work, and it was shining each morning when he got off. He spent a week and said, "Jimmy, this has been the longest week of my life, I've never seen anything like it."

During my stint there I also had the pleasure to interview Tex Ritter, who was a grand man, and Johnny Horton, a real nice guy who I'd known from "Louisiana Hayride" a few years back. George Morgan, another super nice person from Nashville, came up. Cowboy Copas was up to see us and he was a real nice one. Carl Perkins came up too. I always liked that guy; he did "Blue Suede Shoes" like no one else ever could.

One February night, while doing my D.J. job on KBYR in Anchorage, I got a call from a writer with *National Geographic*. He explained to me that he wanted to get a story on the big and the small homesteader. I had agreed earlier in the evening to front the band for Doc Holiday at the Buckaroo Club. Doc's Mom had passed away and he had to go outside (to the "lower 48") that night for her funeral. So the writer went to the club with us, and at 5 a.m. we were on our way to our homestead. When we got to our house the water bucket was frozen, the linoleum was rolled up on the edges, and outside it was 42 degrees below zero. He took one look at the inside of our house and asked if we planned to sleep here tonight. I built a big fire in our barrel stove and it only took about 20 minutes for things to get cozy inside. We also had a shop there that had a wood heater in it for our Edsel. We'd pull the Edsel inside, build a fire in the heater, and that way it would take care of our car and keep it from getting so cold.

The following day was Sunday and we had company come, by plane on skis, by dog sled, and one couple in a pickup. We always kept our vegetables in the lake, down below the ice. We'd cut a hole in the ice, put the vegies in a burlap bag, tie a rope onto the bag and drop them down through the ice. They wouldn't freeze because the water was about 35 to 36 degrees below the ice.

The other person he interviewed while in Alaska was Mrs. Kellogg, who was a large homesteader and the owner of our local telephone company in Palmer. The writer left, all smiles, but we never got to read the story.

The fall of 1958, long in September, on my way to do the radio show in Anchorage, we saw a guy and his wife and kids on our homestead road. He had a California license plate on his station wagon, and he had an illegal cow-moose down in the middle of the road. The guy said, "Sir, we're hungry and I had to get the moose." I felt sorry for him, he didn't have the slightest idea how to dress the thing out, he didn't even know which end to start at. I helped him quarter the moose, and I sure kept my fingers crossed while dressing out that moose. Then we went back to the house, had to wash up and change clothes, and we let the folks clean up at our place. We often wondered what happened to them. When they left, they did leave us a quarter of the moose, and it was nice of them to do that.

My first movie to be in was "The Alamo", starring John Wayne. The Duke's double was Chuck Roberson. Chuck's brother, Danny, was working for me on the oil rig in Alaska. Danny kept telling me that he could get me in the movies and I thought he was just pulling my leg. Danny left for California in late August of 1959, and again, before leaving, he told me to come see him in Anaheim and he'd get me in a movie. So, when we left Alaska in the fall of 1959, we drove our Edsel down the Alcan Highway and west coast into California, where it broke down on the San Fernando Valley Freeway. We called Danny to come get us, and when we got to Danny's house, he called Chuck in Brackettville, Texas. Danny had already told Chuck about me and Chuck said, "Come on down." It was okay for me to work in the movie.

The movie business was okay, but too much sitting around and waiting. We'd get up in the wee hours of the morning, go over and get our horses, get them all fed, then sit around and wait, build fires and wait. Then, maybe in the afternoon we'd do a 15 to 30 minute stint, and that would be it for the day. It just wasn't my cup of tea. Also, while I was there Chuck did offer to get me in a movie with Glen Ford over at Tucson, Arizona, called "Cimerron". But I never looked back and I don't ever regret not staying with the movie business.

During that trip out the winter of 1959, I stopped in Bakersfield, California, to try for a disc jockey job for the winter months at KUZZ. I've had friends around Bakersfield for years, Red Simpson, Bill Woods, to mention a couple. It took me 3 days to get the job, and the job lasted 8 minutes. I had to drive down to L.A. to get it, then come back up to Bakersfield. The reason I left the job so quick was this engineer trying to tell me which records to play. Of course I didn't like that and I figured that I was looking for a job when I found this one, so "Adios to you". I figured I'd just hook'em on back north and go back to work part-time for KBYR there in Anchorage.

In the spring of 1959, I worked a short while for John C. Miller. We called him "Tennessee" Miller, everyone who knew him well did. He was a true pioneer. John C. took the first Cat train to the North Slope for an oil company in the spring of 1960. Now, there are enough stories about John C. to fill a book. At one time, during the big boom on the North Slope, it took 2 accountants 2 weeks trying to figure just how many pieces of equipment that "Tennessee" Miller actually owned.

I can well remember my first dozer, it was a D6 Caterpillar and I bought it on a bid auction at the Air Force Surplus in Anchorage for $2500. I talked my boss, George Tucker, into putting up the money, and he said, "Okay, Jim, I'll let you have it, but you're gonna have to get it refinanced within 30 days." So I went to Kyle Turner at the Matanuska Valley Bank in Palmer and explained to him what I had done. He went along with me and came up with the $2500, and that was how I got my first dozer.

Talking about firsts, here's a doozy for you. My first moose kill was a disaster. I shot that sucker in a swamp, and two other guys and I worked all night cleaning and dressing that moose. Never again will I ever shoot a moose in a swamp; that's boggy ground and the water and muck was about knee deep. We had a 3-ring circus with that one.

The first job that I could find after moving into Anchorage in the spring of 1960 was with Ramstead Construction. And, Mr. Joe Ramstead was also responsible for me getting a superintendent job with Rod Cherrier at the Inlet Company. Rod had a saying, which I didn't believe in all that much, but he'd say, "Don't worry about it. If it blows up you don't have to hunt the problem." Rod came out on the job in Anchorage one day, about 3 sheets in the wind. It was about 4 o'clock, and he didn't like the way that we were lowering the pipe down in the ditch. He jerked his hat off and began stomping on it, so I climbed the ladder up out of the ditch and told Rod that I'd help him stomp his hat. After the hat was beyond wearing, we shook hands and laughed it off, and got on with laying our pipe.

The reason I first went into business for myself was because Rod suggested I do it. We were doing a major water project in Fairbanks in July of 1963, and Rod told me I should be in business for myself, so I took his advice. I bought my first backhoe, a new one, from Yukon Equipment in Fairbanks, for $500 down. The total price was $9400.

We had a chance to buy our first airplane in 1960, it was a Taylorcraft with an 85-hp engine in it. We decided we could afford it, since it was only $1800, and Marcene was a pilot. By that time she was working at the FAA in Anchorage. We enjoyed that little airplane, but one time, in June of 1960, we broke a bungee on the plane flying into Willow Airport. Boy! You talk about a hassle, I tried to tie that bungee back up, but once you break a bungee you're gonna lose a wrap for sure. Anyway, I got it wrapped back with one less wrap than it was supposed to have had, and that airplane looked like a little ugly duckling, it had "droopy drawers" on one side. The people who worked with Marcene at the FAA sure teased her about the way she came in and landed, but the landing was perfect. They didn't realize that she had a broken bungee. Once she hit the ground that weak side almost gave way, but she held the wing up and everything worked out fine.

Also in June, we were on our way to Fairbanks, Marcene flying the Taylorcraft. We hit head winds just north of Nenana, and the oil gauge started to fluctuate. I didn't want to alarm Marcene so I held a tight one and was looking for anything to set down on. We finally flew over the last ridge and saw Fairbanks about ten miles ahead. When we got on the ground we had one quart of oil left in the engine. This was our first real test with the little Taylorcraft.

In the fall of 1960, Marcene flew us into Shorty Bradley's oat field west of Talkeetna, near where the new Fairbanks Highway runs today. Shorty had oats stacked on sharp sticks; he had them in neat rows and we thought we could make it down in between stacks. One stick got in the way and sliced the fabric on the right wing. No problem though. After visiting Shorty, we duck-taped the wing and flew on back to Anchorage.

On a brisk February morning in 1961, Marcene was going to fly us up to Talkeetna. The day before we took off we had loaned the plane to a guy who worked for the FAA, Danny Burns. The Taylorcraft had 2 wing tanks and a main tank up front. The switch that controlled the wing tanks was backwards, and this was fine as long as we were the only ones flying the plane. We didn't know that Danny had used the avgas in the left wing tank, and left the switch turned one half round open. Marcene taxied over to pick up fuel and we filled all tanks. We took off down the runway and were airborne leaving Anchorage, and just about halfway across Cook Inlet, when I discovered the leak. The switch was "on" and gas was draining from the left wing tank, right through the center tank in front of the windshield. The windshield was icing over and we had gasoline sloshing around on the floor of the plane. I got the switch shut off but the gas kept coming. Of course, it would until it all ran out of the line coming down to the main tank in front of the windshield. We had 3 choices: we could go back to Merrill Field, land on a rough beach with ice chunks, or the Knik Missile Site. We took the latter. We landed, used up a roll of paper towels, and let the plane air out about 2 hours. Not one person ever came out to check on us this Sunday morning at that missile site. We did take off and make it back to Anchorage just fine; we didn't go on to Talkeetna that day. The airplane smelled a little "gassy".

In May, 1961, while I was superintendent for the Inlet Company, we were digging sewer lines in Spenard, on the outskirts of Anchorage. We were working a double shift, from 3 a.m. until 9 o'clock at night. About 3:30 a.m., Frank Rotter, our backhoe operator, was digging behind a house in the alley, and unaware, of course, that there was a lady in that house using it's commode. He dug into the log crib cesspool and it almost killed the backhoe's engine. Frank did the normal thing and slacked off the bucket. The lady on the commode didn't know what was going on, but needless to say, the backlash through the sewer pipe literally blew her off the commode. It took a fancy nightgown, new curtains, new cover for the commode, new paint, and two days of peace-making by our P.R. man, Roy Cantrell, to finally appease the lady. We were fortunate not to have been sued.

During the summer of 1962, Jadene, our daughter, used to ride with me in our pickup to jobsites. One day it was warm out so I left her in the pickup with the windows partially rolled down. I looked over my shoulder and was surprised at this little 2-year old girl running up to me, smiling. Evidently she had climbed through the window of the pickup and dropped herself, or fell, to the ground, but she wasn't hurt so everything was fine.

In 1963, after I purchased the new backhoe in Fairbanks I had plenty of work with Rod Cherrier and Earl King to carry me through for the rest of the construction season. But the winter of 1963-64 was slow in Alaska. I took a job on an oil rig in the Sand Lake area about 8 miles south of Anchorage, to help pay the bills. I applied for, and recieved, my General Contractor's License in February, 1964, and the number on my license was 39. I was the thirty-ninth one in the state to get that license.

On March 27th, 1964, Marcene, Jadene and I were in Kenai, Alaska, during the big earthquake. I'd gone to Kenai to bid on a water and sewer job, and stopped by to see my old friend, Frank Kempton. He was a contractor and doing a sewer job in north Kenai at the time. Frank's pipelayers were having trouble getting the pipe on grade, etc., so I went down in the ditch and gave them a hand. About the time we got the joint of pipe set and wrapped up, the bank slid in. One guy was covered with sand up to his chin. Another was covered to his shoulders and I was covered to just above my waist. It was a hair-raising experience. All our shovels were covered up and Frank wanted to maneuver the backhoe around to try and dig us out, but I told him not to start the backhoe because the vibration would cause the banks to slide in worse. I finally got through to him to go after shovels. Frank's oiler and I were digging around the other guys with our hands. Frank got back with the shovels, we got dug out, and quit for the day.

Just as we were driving up to Frank's apartment where Jadene and Marcene were, the earthquake hit. The weirdest thing happened; we could see the ocean, the tidal wave about 40 feet high, and it was coming right in to the beach. The trees were swaying, the ground was moving, and we thought that someone had dropped an atomic bomb on Anchorage. Unless you've gone through an earthquake, it's hard to describe. After the quake subsided, we drove back to Frank's jobsite and everything was level in the ditches. We were saved by about 15 minutes. All bridges between Kenai and Anchorage were down, so I had to fly my pickup to Anchorage with Bobby Sholton's Northern Air Cargo. He flew a flying boxcar and charged $300 per vehicle for flying pickups and cars from Kenai to Anchorage during the quake period.

Marcene, Jadene and I flew up the morning after the quake with a bush pilot. It seems every time Alaska gets in a slump, along comes a natural disaster. With my experience in utility construction, and there was a great bit of damage done to the utilities in the

Anchorage area, I stayed busy. Most of my work was negotiated, as most of the engineering firms were well acquainted with my previous work. After the earthquake I got so busy I felt I needed some help. That's the reason for taking Dean Briski in as a partner. Two weeks later his brother Jerry joined us to become BB&S Inc. After two seasons I sold out to the Briski brother.

I did some joint venture work with Bill Prosser, Prosser Excavating, and we never had any problems. Bill and I got along and everything worked out great. The summer after the earthquake I did a $57,000 job for Tex Kaiser, just a handshake, no contract. That's the way old-time Alaskans used to operate.

It was long in the fall of 1964, after the earthquake, and Johnny Garrett and I had been operating a road boring machine. That's a machine that bores under railroad tracks, under highways, and under airport runways. We'd been operating as a partnership all summer, but we came to a parting of the ways. We had some accounts receivable and a couple of pickups in the venture, and also a flatbed truck to haul the boring machine, casing, auger, etc. When we got to an attorney's office to settle up, Johnny said, "Jim, do you want the business, or do you want the accounts receivable?" I told him to flip a half dollar off the wall. The attorney looked at us and said, "I've never seen anything settled like this before, but if that's the way you want it, that's the way it'll be". So, there went the Alaska Road Boring Machine Company down the tubes with Johnny. Eventually he lost the company.

In the spring of 1967, I helped Joe Giamavia, with Joe's Trucking, get his bonding. Joe used my bonding his first four jobs, and after the insurance company saw the work that Joe did they let him have his own bonding. While working with Joe, I met a guy by the name of Mike Hayden. Today Mike is still my friend and a very successful paving contractor in the Anchorage area. The name of his company is Quality Asphalt Paving.

It seemed as if I was always getting involved in some weird thing or another. In the fall of 1967, I got a call from an insurance agent, Carl Jones. He told me that he had a doozy for me. Some guys hauling a load of registered sheep from Montana to Kodiak Island rolled their rig on Johnson Pass. My job was to take my Peterbilt, lowboy, and dozer to Portage, and unload the dozer and lowboy at the Portage garbage dump. The next move was to get a wrecker to upright the sheep trailer, haul the 8 dead sheep to the dump and bury them. Next, we went to the top of Johnson Pass and backed the trailer into the bank. Before leaving Anchorage I got a roll of snow fence to use as a temporary corral and chute to the trailer. We found one sheep that someone had butchered out. There were tales of people all the way from Homer to Talkeetna taking these sheep. We had difficulty finding the sheep, so we had to get a helicopter to locate them. We finally got the sheep loaded up. Of the initial 400 sheep, I believe we loaded 321.

Wet and smelling like sheep, we headed south, drove in rain all the way down to Homer. The guys in charge of the sheep called Kodiak and we were instructed to take the ferry that night for Kodiak Island. I drove out to the ferry terminal on Homer Spit. When the purser checked the length of my rig, he said I would have to back my load of sheep out of there, as my rig, tractor and trailer, was 6 feet too long for the ferry. We had a long night in the Peterbilt, Dick Eadie and myself.

We got instructions the next morning to find a fenced pasture for the sheep. The owners were to send a landing craft over to Homer from Kodiak to pick up the sheep. We dropped the sheep off on East Road, the friendly Barber's farm. This was a guy I had met last year while doing the water system there in Homer, a real nice guy. I sure was glad to get back to Anchorage and, oh yes, the insurance company paid up. I could just imagine how much money they had in each one of those sheep when they finally got to Kodiak.

It was in the winter of 1967 that I acquired my first subdivision. I had installed water, sewer and services in Windsor Village subdivision for the owner, H. A. Burnett. He couldn't pay me for my work so he offered me the remainder of his subdivision as payment of the debt, minus 12 lots that he'd built homes on. Marcene and I talked it over, and went for it. It worked out real well for us.

We built our first coin operated laundry on Jewell Lake Road, right near Four Corners in Anchorage, and named it Four Corners Laundrymat. We were proud to see the doors open on that little jewel.

In February of 1969, a pilot by the name of Serge Amundson came by my shop and gave me his story. He'd crashed his plane on a mountain west of Crosswind Lake. Now, Crosswind is located aproximately 180 miles east of Anchorage and about 20 miles due north, then about 20 more miles to the crash site. He asked me to get my equipment and go up there to bring his plane out.

I hauled a Cat and a sled on the lowboy, and took along a snowmobile. We had to walk the dozer about 44 miles each way. Bob Brinkley, an old friend of mine, and his sidekick Lucky went along with us. Serge had snowshoed out 3 days before, and I've got to hand it to him, he led us right to that plane, even through the dark of night. We got a caribou on the way up, Lucky's first one to get. We took the wings off the plane and stood a wing on each side of the fuselage, then padded between sideboards of the sled and the wings. It was a hairy trip back to Anchorage. Boy! It was glare ice. I don't know whatever happened to Serge Amundson, but he never paid me a penny. I paid Bob and Lucky for their trip though. I thought it a little weird when Serge said, "I'll make it well worth your time. I really need you to go get my airplane out."

I first met my old friend, Art Fields, in Kotzebue, Alaska, in the spring of 1970. Tom Courtney and I were in Kotzebue for the 250-mile cross-country snowmobile race. We asked Art if he knew of a restaurant where we could buy something to eat. Art, being the nice guy that he is, invited Tom and me to his house for supper. He served us caribou tongue and crackers.

Art Fields is an individualist and definitely one of "a vanishing breed". He is part Eskimo, Russian, and Irish, and a very friendly person. Art was the first Eskimo to receive his Big Game Guide License. He flew and guided many celebrities in his time, Roy Rogers, Bobby and Al Unser, A.J. Foyt, just to name a few, and many, many more benefited from his expertise. Art was an enterprising guy with many holdings. He owned a liquor store, pool hall, cab company, restaurant, mining ventures, and of course, his guide business. One winter Art traded a case of whiskey to an Eskimo for his house and lot, after the guy bugged him for about 4 hours.

The night we met Art we had a blizzard and snow was up over a lot of houses in town. The next morning I got my machine at Tommy Sauer's shop and took off for the beach and the starting line. I got about 300 feet from the shop and heard a funny sound. I looked back and saw a stove pipe with smoke coming out of it sticking up out of the snow. I've often wondered what those poor people thought was happening to them when I drove over their home.

Long in March of 1970, the night before the annual Kotzebue 250-mile cross-country snowmobile race, we met some racers that seemed a bit out of their element. The guys with me, Rodney Jackson, Jim Rerick, and Ellis Smith, were all seasoned snowmobile racers from Anchorage. The other racers were Al and Bobby Unser and A.J. Foyt, who were in Kotzebue for a polar bear hunt. Rodney Jackson tried to persuade A.J. to enter our race. Just before A.J. had enough and got fed up with Rodney, Jim Rerick and I hustled Rodney outside and finally conned him into going to bed.

I got my Arctic Cat snow machine dealership in 1970, and for the next 7 years I was to be the top Arctic Cat dealer in the state. The reason I got the dealership was to help with my racing, and the business just kind of snowballed on me. Also, I practiced something that I always preached: you give people a bargain and then give them service. Service what you sell and take care of your customers; in turn, they will take care of you.

In March of 1974, while in Nome during the Nome-Golovin snow machine race, I had the pleasure of introducing Governor Keith Miller to the folks attending the banquet, and the band. I think it surprised everyone how well the Governor sang country music. On our flight back to Anchorage the weather got consistently worse. As we crossed Cook Inlet, approaching the runway at Anchorage International Airport, it really got rough. As Governor Miller was a Republican, I couldn't resist telling him that the pilot just had to be a Democrat, the way the plane was dippy-diving around. Just a note, Governor Miller had homesteaded not too far from our place, and came up through the political ranks in the state of Alaska. He was a very well read man, and he could think awful fast on his feet.

Also, in 1974, after a year of going to planning and zoning meetings, we finally got the approval and go-ahead on our Green Belt Camper Park, on Old Seward Highway, just south of Airport Road, by Campbell Creek. For that, we owed thanks to Joe Wells and his much needed help on the project. All the years that I dealt in property, in construction, in any business around the Anchorage area, I basically dealt with nice people. I used to tell people who wanted to sell me something, or buy something from me, to go ahead and fill out the paperwork, and if I liked it I'd sign it. This was my way of both parties being satisfied.

After I bought my first backhoe and began sub-contracting to larger construction companies in 1963, a contractor friend of mine advised me to get a tape recorder and keep it with me so that I could make notes, record what deals I made, remember conversations, etc. I tried that for awhile, but the recorder would be in the way on my pickup seat or dashboard, or get lost under stuff, or get dirty, whatever. Anyway, I got a diary and made notes in it. I just found that easier. Since then, and to this day, I've kept diaries about my business and personal life, and they've been useful many times.

Several years ago when a friend of ours suggested that I could write a book about my gold mining experiences, I wasn't so sure, but those diaries sure made the difference. I used them as the basis for this book, sometimes just the entries themselves are included. They certainly helped me recall the many adventures we've had, and I hope that I entertain, or at least educate you a little.

A VANISHING BREED: The Gold Miner
by Jimmy Simpson

April 1974

Early in 1974 I decided to go gold mining. I'd met Art Fields a few years before while snow machine racing in Alaska, and he and I became partners in my first gold mining venture out of Kotzebue, Alaska.

I'll start my story with moving our equipment to Kotzebue, a small city north of the Seward Peninsula, inside the Arctic Circle. In order to get it up there I had two choices: I could fly my stuff up with Bobby Sholton, of Northern Air Cargo, or go in with a barge, but wait until summertime to go up. So, I chose to go up in April of 1974. When I first contacted Bobby it was near the end of March, but I'll skip over here a little bit and tell how we finally got into Kotzebue, got our equipment up there, got all ready, and started a journey cross-country.

I had a guy by the name of Bob Kirsch working for me at the time, a former pilot for Hughes Air West out of McCall, Idaho. Bob was going up to the mine with me as my mechanic, and he was helping me get things ready to go and get them shipped out from Anchorage. I first met Bob Kirsch when he came by my Arctic Cat shop on Jewel Lake Road in Anchorage. He worked on snowmobiles and was a whiz at it, just about the fastest mechanic on snowmobiles I'd ever run into. Also, he was a heavy and light duty mechanic, and a good welder, and I felt he would make a good hand. I thought he was just the man I needed for a mining venture.

I bought a van load of groceries from a guy who came up from Arizona and California. He'd bought them down there on auction sale and was going to put in a grocery store in Anchorage until he found out we already had supermarkets. So I bought everything he had in the van for 10 cents a can, regardless of what it was, large cans of peaches, whatever. I shipped those up by Alaska Airlines. Art Fields's daughter was working for Alaska Airlines at the time and needless to say, we didn't have to pay any freight to get it shipped from Anchorage to Kotzebue. I sent up 4 El Camino loads!

It was April 15, 1974, when we flew our first load of equipment to Kotzebue with Bobby Sholton. Bob Kirsch went up with the dozer and some stuff that he had to get assembled when we got to Kotzebue, putting the blade back on the dozer and such. I flew to Kotzebue April 17th.

When we got to Kotzebue we needed to rent a big heavy sled to haul our diesel fuel and various parts, a welder, cutting torches, etc., to take on our "Cat train". We were going to go 187 miles and figured it would take about 3 or 4 days. We acquired a large sled, 35 feet long, from Steve Salinas, who was a local businessman in Kotzebue. It took Bob and me all day to clean it out. Steve had used the sled to haul "honey pots" and all kinds of garbage. "Honey pots" were what Eskimos used in their toilets. They were lined with heavy plastic bags. This sled was used to haul off all this sewage and garbage, because Kotzebue didn't have a sewer system in 1974. To say it was "ripe" would be an understatement.

April 20th, a Saturday, the weather was nice and we finally got underway about 9 o'clock. We had a toothless Eskimo with us by the name of Benny, and another native Eskimo from Deering, Alaska, we called "Roy-the-reindeer-herder". He was riding a 400cc Skidoo snowmobile.

We left Kotzebue in the morning and went around Kobuk Lake. The first problem we had was when the Skidoo blew a bearing about 20 miles out, so we loaded it on top of all our other gear on the sled. The weather was nice until we started to leave Kobuk Lake and the wind started blowing. It got colder as we headed for Elephant Point Bay. We stopped about 18 miles from Elephant Point and Benny, the toothless Eskimo, said there was a cabin at Elephant Point, so we decided to let him take my snow machine, an Arctic Cat, and go on to build a fire for us in the cabin. At that time of year it was awfully cold, around 40 below. I drove a D4 Cat, and didn't have my longhandles on. My legs sure got cold with the wind blowing and the Cat tracks throwing snow all over me. We really had it rough going across Elephant Point Bay, with the ice heaves, and winds blowing 60 miles an hour. At one point, I really got shook up because I saw water squirting up behind the tracks of the dozer Bob Kirsch was on just in front of me. Bob got stuck several times in icy cracks while crossing the Bay.

We got across to Elephant Point about 1 a.m. Sunday morning, and stopped. All but one of the cabins had been washed out by high water the year before, and it was filled with muktuk (whale blubber) and stunk to high heaven. The only thing we could do was put up a tent. We had a new Eddie Bauer tent, but it was so cold that we couldn't take our mitts off to put the tent up. Our hands would just get like rocks right away, so finally what I did was just level off a place and use the sled and Cats for a wind break. We took the sleeping bags out of the plastic garbage bags we'd put them in to keep the ice and snow from getting on them, and crawled inside.

I laid there and rolled around all night until about 6 in the morning. Old Benny, the toothless Eskimo, rolled over about 5:30 that morning and said, "I'll have my coffee in bed this morning, Jimmy." Not a drop of water anywhere, it was so cold. I didn't want to dig out the coffee pot and start thawing snow for water and stuff like that. We'd fueled up the Cats when we first got there and then left them running, because we couldn't shut them down in that cold, so we fueled them up again and just headed up Kotzebue Sound coast. About 3 o'clock in the afternoon we came to a reindeer herder's cabin, an old one. We stopped there, fixed a fire, and got us a bite to eat.

When we'd left in the morning, I put a beer inside my Arctic Cat suit, just above my belly, and when we stopped by the reindeer herder's old cabin, I thought for sure I'd have a beer to drink. So I pulled the pop-top and the ice just rolled out. It was that cold! The wind was really cutting and there was no way you could get away from it; it was right out of the north and it felt like we were heading right into it.

We stopped at a little place called Kiwalik where there were about 5 or 6 little cabins. Last winter some of the seismograph crews from Western Geophysical had been there, and they'd had a stove going in one of the cabins. So I took my Arctic Cat, went out and rounded up some boards and old shoes and stuff from the other cabins, and got a fire going. And, boy, it was nice just to sit back, take your snowsuit off, and really get warm for a change. If you've never been out on a trail in 30 and 40 below, and the wind blowing 40, 50, 60 miles an hour, you don't really know what just a regular old wood stove fire will do for you.

Monday, April 22nd. We got into Deering last night. Spent the night before last in Candle, which was 14 miles out of the way. Benny, the Eskimo, told me we could go up the Candle River, then go over the hill to Utica where our gold mining claims were. Utica is on the Inmachuk River, about 18 miles upstream from Deering.

We got to Candle along about dark, pulled down onto the Candle River and parked the Cats there on the ice. It was below a bank, a windbreak of sorts. The town of Candle is an abandoned gold mining town, and we were able to find a cabin there where we could spend the night. To get water we cut a hole through the ice on the river. We slept by a wood stove. We'd scrounged enough wood to get a fire going to carry us through the night, so that was a real break for us, and we were able to get a pretty good night's rest.

On the way into Candle we saw lots of ptarmigans, the Alaska state bird. It's a bird that is brown in the summer and turns white during the winter months. The ptarmigan is plentiful in Alaska, and good eating. A little red fox followed along with us for about 4 or 5 miles. He was like a dog, he would just run along with us, so finally I stopped. I figured that the little feller had slim pickings out there. I got out some crackers, cheese, and a piece of lunch meat, and threw it out to him. Boy, he really enjoyed that.

A note about Candle: Art was telling me about Archie Ferguson mining by the airstrip there, just over the hill from where we were mining. He was going in under the bank, had about 90 feet of overburden (which is material you have to move and/or stockpile to uncover gold bearing sand, gravel, and bedrock), and they were washing it with a giant, also called a monitor. One native he had working for him would run the loader and go back in under there, going about 40 or 50 feet back under the ice and overburden. He was in real good gold and just wouldn't quit. Archie paid that operator $10 every time he'd run back in there and get a load with that loader after they'd monitored it down. Finally, the Safety Inspector from Nome (actually out of Fairbanks) came over and shut him down. He said, "You're gonna have to start at the top and take all that down, otherwise don't send that loader operator back in under there again." So, Archie shut down, as 90 feet of permafrost was a bit too much for him to move.

The next morning, Benny told me the hill was too steep to take the Cat train over. Guess what? We backtracked 14 miles to the coastline of the Kotzebue Sound. That's 28 miles out of the way with the Cat train. The reason Benny took us through Candle was to check on his house there, but that's alright, we did get a good night's sleep this way.

This time we took off and went around the coast to Deering, Alaska. That's right at the mouth of the Inmachuk River. When we were about 8 miles out of Deering, the natives (Eskimos) saw us coming because the headlights on our equipment were on, and they came out to meet us on their snowmobiles. They were glad to see us, but until we got into town I didn't realize just how glad they really were - their airport had been weathered in for about 3 weeks.

We rented a place upstairs at the old general store there, and it left something to be desired. The window panes were broke out, so we took some of our old work clothes and stuffed them in where the window panes were supposed to be. There was a stove, but no wood, and no way to get any wood around there, so we rigged up a 5-gallon can of diesel with a piece of copper tubing, put a little valve on it and started it dripping in the stove. Pretty soon it got pretty nice in there.

The mayor of Deering, Mr. Barr, came over and had a meeting with us while we got a little bite to eat. He wanted to know if we'd make a deal; he wanted us to clear the airstrip for him tomorrow and he said he'd pay us. I said he couldn't pay us, but we'd trade our work for diesel, if they had some, we were running pretty low. He agreed to that, and I'll tell you how we found the diesel, and where the supply came from.

Tuesday, April 23rd. We got up early after a pretty good night's sleep. We'd left our bulldozers running all night again, because it was so cold. So after we ate some breakfast and refueled the dozers we went down to clear the runway. After we'd finished, the natives showed us where the fuel barrels were. We had to dig out about 6 or 7 feet of snow to find them. When we finally got into them, we fueled our dozers again and then filled up the barrels on the sled. The natives told us that the fuel was left there by the Navy a few years back. Of course, it didn't really matter all that much one way or the other at the time, because, gosh, we needed fuel and we were doing those guys a big favor by clearing their runway. Anyway, the Weins Air plane didn't get to make their run in that day either, because the winds in Kotzebue were too high for them to take off, and needless to say, the strip at Deering blew back together that night.

When we got up the next morning, April 24th, gee whiz!, the airstrip was all closed, blowed in, so we cleared it off - again. Late that afternoon the wind died down a little bit in Kotzebue and the plane came in. Everybody was really happy to see the mail, food, and other necessities that it brought.

The reason the natives in Deering hadn't been able to clear their airstrip was that the D7 Cat dozer that the FAA had for them there was broke down. My mechanic, Bob, fixed their Cat and got it going, so when we left they at least had their own bulldozer to clear their runway if it closed in again.

Friday, April 26th. We were still in Deering. The weather was really cold and the wind blowing like all getout, but we were getting acquainted with all the natives around there. We got to know the mayor, of course, and the rest of the Barrs, and the Karmuns, who were reindeer herders there. We just kind of sat back and enjoyed the visit with them. Some of the natives came over and we had a nice poker game.

Saturday, April 27th. We were finally able to get underway to Utica. We went up the Inmachuk River, and by skirting around some high water, we got onto a high ridge and ran into a whiteout. A whiteout is a weather condition that limits your visibility to zero. It's caused by a combination of wind, snow and frost. Driving, or flying, in a whiteout is like driving in a big balloon. You can't see up, down, or to your sides.

We kept climbing up onto higher ground to get away from the overflow from the river, and we wound up about 9 miles farther upstream than where we were supposed to be. We thought we'd drop off the mountain and come back to the Inmachuk River right above where we were heading. Once we started down the hill we couldn't go back and had to go on to the bottom. Bob went through the ice on one D4 Cat, and it went right under. I mean, it got his feet, legs, everything wet, so we had to stop and build a big fire and dry Bob out. Then we had to drag the Cat out, and we had one heck of a time getting it drained out and back up the mountain.

We knew we were too far upriver, so decided to go back to Deering on the snowmobiles. Bob and I took my Arctic Cat and the natives, Benny and Roy, were able to use the Skidoo since we'd had it repaired while we were in Deering.

We called Leon Shallabarger, a bush pilot, to come over in his Cessna 206, and take Bob Kirsch and me back to Kotzebue. That was $90. Bob stayed in Kotzebue with my partner, Art Fields, working on his cabs, doing welding, and flying Art's Super Cub, etc., while I went back to Anchorage for parts and various things.

Thursday, May 9th. Bob Kirsch called around 2:30 in the afternoon and said that I'd better come on up to Kotzebue right away. The weather was warm at Deering and we had to get our equipment in, like tomorrow, or forget it. The river was going to break up and everything would be flooded for a month or 6 weeks - it was spring breakup. So Bob and I flew to Deering, and went out to tow in the old 6x6 to the airstrip at Utica, near our mine. It needed work on it.

The next day we went up to get our equipment and take it on in to camp, and, oh, what a mess that was! Bob got on a side hill, and of course, when you're on a side hill with Cats and snow and ice, you've got problems. We had around 10,000 pounds of gear on the sled and it slid off the hill pulling the D4 Cat with it. Bob tried to make the best of it, but he had problems. He went in the creek - again. The dozer dropped into about 6 feet of water. He left it running, and lucky he did. I was watching and would have bet $1000 we couldn't get the D4 out of this here hole. I went back, tied on to the sled, pulled it back uphill, then tied on to the D4 and, between us, we made it. The D4 was sputtering, as it was about to run out of fuel at the angle that it was sitting.

We got to camp alright, drained oil, water, everything from the D4 and replenished it with new oils. Bob said that if we could make it to Deering in one hour, we could fly back to Kotzebue tonight. So, Bob and I took off on our Arctic Cat and headed for Deering. We made it in 45 minutes, a trip that took the Cats 9 hours to make. Bob was driving the snowmobile; he ran through overflow one foot or more. He acted like a guy in a snow machine race, all the way, but we made it back to Deering and then on to Kotzebue just fine.

On Saturday I was going to drive my little Ampicat over to Deering, going across the bay on that silly thing. It's a 6-wheeled rig, open air, with flotation tires, and is designed for driving over tundra (grassy, uneven, or boggy terrain). It was about 95 miles to Deering, and I only got about 12 miles out when I decided this was not the way to go, so I went back. Bob and I flew the Super Cub plane off Kobuk Lake, and changed from skis to wheels on Art's airplane. Art Fields, my partner, was still in Whitehorse, Yukon Territory, attending a meeting over there.

Sunday, May 12th. We spent the night at Art's house and watched TV. Sure was nice of him to let us just move in. When we got up this a.m., the weather sure was pretty. Harold Lee came over for about an hour; he's a bush pilot and a Yamaha snowmobile dealer in Kotzebue, and a nice guy. Art called today and said he'd be back Tuesday or Wednesday. I called Marcene tonight and gave her a parts order. No work today, just goofing around.

On Tuesday Art and I flew into Nome, spent the night, and saw Stan Sobozinski, "the Pollack", about staying in his cabin in Utica. He said it was okay and gave me the keys. We met with Stan and Roscoe Wilkie about the Nenana to Nome snow machine race. Jim West gave me a car to use while we were there in Nome, and he wouldn't charge me anything for it. It snowed hard today. Art has to go to Homer, Alaska, leaving tomorrow, his uncle died. We're going to let him use our motorhome to go from Anchorage, and take some of his kinfolk with him.

May 15th. Bob Kirsch and I were weathered in in Nome 'til about 1 p.m., then flew to camp and landed safely. The strip was in good shape. Art's still gone. Parts for our 6x6 and the pickup got in, but still no work at the mine.

Friday, May 17th. Bob and I left Kotzebue this a.m. and flew to camp. We packed our bags, groceries, and guns, etc., in from the airstrip to camp, then flew on up to where we took the dozers and sled last week. Bob landed on top of the hill and I went down and got my 450 dozer. I started pulling a small sled all loaded down, but I broke the sled on the way back to camp, so I had to tie everything onto the dozer. I looked like a gypsy going out across the tundra on my dozer with all the gear tied to the canopy. That was the roughest trail I know I've ever seen, either too much snow, or not enough, and clumps of grass protruding through the snow called niggerheads, making the trip very difficult.

Wein Air didn't bring over my dredge and other equipment today, but we did manage to get set up in Stan's cabin. Not too bad. We scrounged fuel oil for the heater, melted snow and washed "mice pills" out of the dishes. I'm tired and think I'll go to bed. It's 10:30 at night and still light out.

Saturday, May 18th. Bob and I flew back to Kotzebue, just not ready at Utica yet. We'll have to wait about another week or so.

Monday, June 3rd. Clark, Art's son-in-law, called me in Anchorage today and said we could probably go to work next Monday. Bob Kirsch is still working on Art's equipment. We put $450 into Bob's account today and made a $151 pickup payment.

For the next week and a half we were stalled, not able to begin mining, but we used the time to work on equipment and fly supplies, etc., up to Kotzebue to be ready.

Thursday, June 13th. I flew from Anchorage to Kotzebue today and Art met me. We went right to Deering, over to camp with Shallabarger Airlines. Then Art and I went back to Deering, looking for Moto, and he'd just left for Kotzebue, so we came back to camp. We needed to get ahold of Moto regarding ground on Old Glory Creek that we also wanted to work. Art took off to catch Moto. He had to go on to Anchorage, and I spent the night at camp.

June 14th. Huckle, the reindeer herder, and I went to Moto's claim, clearing about 7 miles of road. Roy Fields, Art's son, and Bob Kirsch caught up with us as we were about halfway back to camp. We got the D4 stuck and worked 'til 1:30 in the morning before we got back to camp. The track came off in the creek. Oh, boy! By the way, it was snowing this morning; here it is, June 14th, and we're having snow.

Saturday, June 15th. Bob, Roy, Huckle and I are working, trying to get an anchor pin off of the old gold dredge, but it turned out to be too heavy duty and just too heavy. We'd planned on making a metal sluice box out of that big anchor pin, but it was too thick and just wasn't feasible, so we gave up on that. I took the 4x4 to Deering this p.m., tried to call home, but no answer. Our tent didn't get in so I went back to camp. Still no word from Art. Shallabarger is flying in fuel for us in a Cessna 206.

June 16th. Bob and I flew to Deering. I called Marcene and she finally found Art. He said we would be working Moto's claim on Old Glory Creek. We went back to camp, took off and got our other D4 and gear, pumps, etc., at Mindenhall's (an old abandoned mining camp around 8 miles above Utica). To top everything off, Huckle got stuck coming up the hill from Mindenhall's. We got in about 1 o'clock; the boys like to sleep late, so we'll just work late. Kind of equals out okay. The swing frame on the D4 that Benny, the Eskimo, drove over from Kotzebue was broke and it will take half a day or more to weld it up. Seems there's no end, but I still have patience and believe in Art.

Monday, June 17th. Got word from Art to go ahead on Moto's claim, and we're in the middle of constructing a 30-foot sluice box, a good one, with parts and pieces that we've scrounged from over a radius of about 15 miles. I got it bad today, got my eyes burnt welding. Tonight I had to scrape potatoes for my eyes, but I still had a case of the "pains", just laid awake in bed all night. Bob and Huckle flew over the reindeer herd to check on them, and killed another grizzly bear. This makes 2 of them. The grizzly bears like to get into a reindeer herd and kill the little ones. They can kill as many as a dozen or two at one setting.

June 18th. My eyes started to ease up about 2 p.m. We're still working on the sluice box, building it on skids so we can handle it easily with a Cat. Roy, Leo (a friend of a friend of Art's), and

Huckle went to Deering for some special rod for welding. Bob and Huckle are working on the box and we should go on up to Moto's claim tomorrow with both D4s, the 6-by and the 4-by, loaded with fuel and pumps.

June 19th. We worked last night 'til 12:30 and got up this a.m. about 9 o'clock. We had breakfast, then Roy, Huckle and I went up to the big dredge and got some more plating for the sluice box. Bob and Roy Fields are welding. Shallabarger's plane brought 8 cases of airplane fuel called avgas. We loaded the 6x6 with diesel, gas pumps, etc., for Moto's claim. Art's not back yet. Marcene got me some welding rod and we received it tonight about 9:30. Bob flew into Kotzebue, and Roy's wife, Pat, and Debbie came back with him for the night. After he got in, Bob flew the reindeer herder, Mr. Karmun, out to see his reindeer herd. Huckle and I put the pad on the D4 and built a gravel bridge across Old Glory Creek, and a ramp so we could get trucks across. Sure was nice today. We quit work at midnight. Tomorrow we'll set up at Moto's on Old Glory Creek, after Roy gets the swing frame welded on the D4 dozer wide pad.

June 20th. We got all loaded out and Roy got the swing frame welded about 10 o'clock. We had so much stuff loaded onto the old 6x6 we looked like gypsies. About a mile from where we were going to be working we stopped and built an airstrip about 600 feet long, plenty for a Cessna Super Cub. I took Huckle's Cat, rather than trying to keep him lined out. Bob and I worked 2-1/4 hours, with 2 D4s, building that airstrip.

Afterward, we went up the creek most of the way and got to our location about 6:30. We built a dam and it broke on us. Oh, yes, we diverted the creek with a ditch running about 600 feet downstream, and we'll use the water for our sluice box. This way, we won't have to use pumps for the water supply. We rebuilt the dam and it looks like it's going to hold - - got water going down the ditch. Huckle got the track off of his D4 and Bob helped him get it back on. I ran the other D4 and finished the dam. I looked at my watch and it was 12:15 (after midnight), and we still could see the sun. We went down to the tent, about a mile downcreek, cleaned it up, and it was about 1:45 a.m. when we got to bed. We're all tired, wet, and muddy.

June 21st. We slept a little late this morning, and had some C-rations for breakfast. We tried our 4-inch dredge today, it was quite a workout with very little results. So, that's $1195 shot. Everything went pretty good 'til I dropped my 450 Case dozer through about 6 feet of icy water, and we had the rest of the day cut out for us. What I was doing, I was stripping the bank and slid 60 feet downhill, off of the bank onto ice on the creek, and right through it. Just before I got to the creek there was one willow standing out there, and I grabbed that willow and swung onto it. The dozer just went bye-bye, hit the ice and went in. I walked down to the tent, about a mile away, got a big heavy choker and dragged it back. We decided to break the dam and get rid of the water, part of it.

If you've ever broke through ice and dropped a dozer in 6 feet of water, you know it's one experience you only need once in a lifetime. We had a problem getting it out; we broke the tow hitch off of it, and I didn't really want to do it, but we had to tie around the blade in order to get ahold of it. We had to go down under the water to get the choker around the blade, and that water was just like ice. But we finally got it out that way. We got back to the tent at 12:30 tonight.

I guess God knew what he was doing when he hid the gold, because it sure doesn't come easy.

When we finally got back to the tent, we got the oil heater going and put up a wire to hang our wet and muddy pants, shirts, socks and boots up to dry. It's bad when you have to dry out hip boots. We drained water out of the dozer, the oil and everything, changed everything, filters, the diesel fuel, the whole bit. Then we ran it for about an hour and dropped everything out of it again. Tomorrow morning we'll fill everything back up. I think the dozer will be alright.

June 22nd. Our dam is still holding okay. We started the 450 dozer and moved our sluice box into position upstream from where they worked last year on Old Glory Creek. We stripped the overburden off, enough ground to carry us for about a week. We worked hard with the shovels and dozers. Taking one joint of 12-inch flume pipe, about 12 feet long, we set it up so we could block it off as needed, and supply the sluice box with water. We were so tired we didn't feel like unloading the 6x6, so we took off on my Case 450 dozer. We needed to take it back to the Utica camp anyway, about 8 miles, to get it all fixed after the dunking. The fuel pump did start messing up, so we needed to change that, get a new one. One day without problems would be nice. I'm going to celebrate somehow if that ever happens. We got to Utica about 7 o'clock, dirty, tired and hungry.

Art flew us into Kotzebue tonight in his new Super Cub. It started acting up, so I figured my luck was still holding when we made it okay. I called Marcene and Jadene, sure was nice talking to them.

June 24th. Got up this a.m. in camp to nice weather. Bob and I fixed the washing machine and washed our clothes. Art came in this morning and he and I went to see Jack Hoogadorn. Jack took us into his tunnel where he'd tunneled under the lava beds upriver from camp, and we really enjoyed it. You could actually see gold in the bedrock. I could hardly believe it. Jack had 4 sluice boxes that hadn't been cleaned up, the gold was still in them and just sitting there for 2 or 3 years. I asked him, "Why didn't you clean that gold up?" He took us around and showed us another area, and said that the gold was so good he just made a big room in there. He'd left a little too much frozen gravel on the lava up above, and all that lava and stuff fell down, hitting his pump, sluice box, wheelbarrow, different things. He said that when he came in the next morning and saw it, he figured that the Good Lord was trying to tell him something, so he just gave it up and hasn't been back in there to do any work since. He just goes in there to look at things from time to time.

Jack told me that over the 7 years he'd worked there, he figured he had made a very good living (when gold was $35 an ounce) from those tunnels. He could work in the winter same as in the summer, because it was about 29 degrees year round in there. But you can't put meat in his ice cold cave as it will mold for some reason.

Jack told me where to strip and work on the property that we had there at Utica, and it was a big help to us. Art and I are going to Fairbanks on Thursday to file on some more claims here, and check on some other properties. After flying to Kotzebue to pick up parts, Bob put the fuel pump on the Case, and I went to our claims and started stripping. Bob and Art flew down to check some ground, and we'll move the sluice box down there tomorrow and get it started. I'm tired and 'tis 1:30 a.m. You don't need lights in the summer up here, the sun shines just about all night. Oh, yes, I cooked supper tonight: chicken, gravy, beans, and peaches. Huckle didn't show up today. Typical!

Tuesday, June 25th. A good friend, Jim Keaton, got killed today at Kiana. He was flying the twin engine plane for Shallabarger, and he tried to take off with one engine from the Kiana airport.

June 26th. Got up about 8 o'clock and Art and I fixed breakfast, then we went down and set up the sluice box while Bob and Roy went to Kotzebue in Art's plane for groceries. Weins is supposed to send up my Max, which is that little machine I tried to take off from Kotzebue with, but only made 12 miles before I had to turn around and go back. I went to Deering at 6 o'clock and waited 'til 8:30. The plane finally came in, but no Max. I can't believe it. Bob told them to be sure to put it on and they said they would. Same old story up here. Taylor Moto, who's working for us, is a councilman in Deering. He's half Japanese and half Eskimo. Mr. Karmun brought us one quarter of a reindeer, and that's good meat. Those Karmuns are sure nice people. That's the reason we fly over their reindeer herds to check them, and kill the grizzly bears and wolves that get into their herds.

Art and I are to fly to Fairbanks tomorrow to file on some claims where we're working, and different properties. We got a little kid in from Kotzebue today, Art brought him in and he's going to work with us. We call him Duffy. He's one of 11 kids of alcoholic parents. He can drink more pop than anyone I've ever seen, and of course, he loves fruit cocktail. Once I told him he could have a bowl, he could eat all he wanted. So, he ate the whole works. He drank about 2 quarts of Coca Cola this afternoon, and I told Art that I thought that it might hurt him. Art said, "Well, he never gets anything like that." So the poor little feller is just in hog-heaven over here at the mine.

June 27th. We ran the sluice box today and stripped overburden by number 2 dredge on property that Art and I staked. We have 2 dredges on our properties up here, big dredges. Art also ran the Cat for about an hour and we checked the riffles. Looks like we'll have quite a bit of gold.

Art and I went to Fairbanks with bush pilot, Lee Staley ("Barefoot Staley") out of Kiana. He's quite a guy, and a good pilot, too. Took 3-1/2 hours flying time. We went out to the University of Fairbanks, checking on the mining claims we're after and it looks like everything will be a "go". We found out what we needed to know, so we'll record them in Nome, the local district for recording. Actually, the claims were open, so we'll go back and stake them, then file on them in Nome. I called Shorty (Al Mentkin) in Fairbanks, and went over and slept in his camper awhile.

June 28th. I note here that things are awful scarce around Fairbanks due to pipeline construction. These small gas pumps that we're using are just not gonna get it, so we'll have to rig up a large diesel pump for the mine. I looked for a good used 6-inch pump in Fairbanks, but couldn't find one.

My ATV came in today. Art and I went to Deering to get it and got back to camp at 11:30. When we got back to Utica they'd had bad luck. Gibson Moto stuck a D4 Cat, got it off the track, and the pump quit working, shaft or something. I guess Bob really had a rough day. Didn't keep Moto and "little kid" on the job. Bob and Roy got the Cat up to camp and pulled the big diesel pump down to the sluice box. Tomorrow we'll get it going.

Sunday, June 30th. I flew over to Kotzebue with Bob this a.m. to meet Marcene. We rounded up parts, shopped for groceries, had a good time in town, then caught Shallabarger's plane to Utica. Showed Marcene around the camp, and then Art and I went to work stripping and picking up the giants. (A giant, also called a monitor, is a large nozzle with high pressure water going through it to wash down a frozen soil bank.) Bob and Roy are working on a pump from a blown-up engine, and a diesel engine from a worn-out dozer.

We had a seagull in camp at Utica, there at the mine. If we didn't get back into camp just on time, at noontime, or in the evening, either one, the seagull would come down to the mining operation and squawk and fly around, wanting us to come to camp so we could feed him. One day Art fed him some peanut butter and crackers. He took off squawking and didn't come back for about a week. We thought he'd got done in, or something, but he finally came back. We named him Jack-the-Seagull.

Tuesday, July 2nd. I'm dozing on our ground and getting it prepared for sluicing today. Roy and Bob are still working on the pump. Shallabarger's plane brought gas, parts and groceries this morning. Roy went back into Kotzebue with Leon, and Bob went in this p.m. in Art's Super Cub to pick him up. My little ATV needs work, just doesn't get it. The claims we are filing on include the airstrip in the town of Utica, 2 by the old dredge on Black's leases, and 5 claims on Clear Creek. Oh, by the way, Bob lost his nice nuggeted watch that I had made for him while putting in a culvert today. We spent about 4 hours looking for it, and I told Bob, "We can't look for it anymore, you can look for it on your own time. But I'll replace it, I'll get one made just like it and replace it." And I did.

We set up the giants today, 2 of them, and we're going to run them off of a 10-inch pump. That way we'll start thawing gound pretty fast and see what happens. We have a 10-inch pump now, a diesel engine, which we genuinely need. We took an engine out of an old International TD24 dozer, about a 1941 model. It saved us about $6000-plus, for it. A guy named Leo just drifted in up here and Art kind of let him hang around. He's a ding-a-ling, and is sure getting to me and the rest of the crew.

This is Thursday, the Fourth of July. Art went in to Nome to file claims today. Bob, Roy, and I are moving the pump and sluice box down to our property. Mr. Hoogadorn came down today and told me that we were dozing in the wrong place. We wasted 3 weeks stripping overburden in the wrong place, but I hope we're finally on the right track. He kind of lined me out and showed me which way to go.

July 5th. We got our sluice box set up on Black's property, our claim now, about 2:30 p.m. Art got in about 4, we got the sluice box going about 6, shut down at 7, and went into camp and ate, then went back to work for about 2 hours. The color (gold is called color) in the riffles looks good. Marcene got 3 nuggets and we put them in the bottle. We had company come in with Shallabarger, a guy and his wife, the Greens, with 2 dogs and 6 pups, and all their gear. They have a little dredge, 2-1/2 inch, and they just don't know what they're in for. Lots of work. Ha! Duffy came back to camp today. He's the little feller that stayed over for awhile and worked with us, then went back to Kotzebue. He told Leon Shallabarger that he should bring him back over to camp, that we were gonna rehire him, so he came back to see us.

Sunday, July 7th. We worked the sluice box today for awhile and then cleaned up. We took about a pound of gold out, so that isn't too bad. We're just getting started here in this pit and think it's gonna work out good for us.

July 8th. Bob took Art's plane to Kotzebue to get it fixed, but will have to take it to Fairbanks. We're having to pay $67 for a 55-gallon drum of diesel, and gasoline costs a little more yet. The old diesel TD18 International engine hooked up to the 10-inch Jaeger pump is doing okay, just temperamental about starting. Bob got in as we were eating supper tonight. I ran the dozer and helped Roy run the sluice box. Art ran a dozer 'til about 3 p.m., ran it off the track, then came down and helped on the sluice box. I'm tired tonight from jumping off and on the dozer.

July 9th. Art took off real early this morning for Fairbanks to get his airplane worked on. We got up about 7, the weather was bad and starting to rain. I cooked breakfast and Marcene cooked dinner and supper. We're getting pretty good color at the mine, our bottle we keep nuggets in is getting heavier.

July 10th. We're working the sluice box today. I was running a dozer and Bob and Roy were raking rocks. Leo's cousins came up today, getting too many people around here. We put about 3 or 4 ounces, from the first 3 riffles, in the bottle today. Just taking some gold out was fun, we're getting some real nice jewelry nuggets. It's sure raining, and our kitchen roof needs fixing.

"Raking rocks" is using a large heavy rake, and pulling the rocks to the end of the sluice box, the ones that hang up on the riffles. If they hang up in the box, the water will whip the gold right out of the riffles, and as the rocks eventually move down, they just keep whipping the gold out, takes it right on out the end of the box. If you get onto the rocks right away, get them moving and on out, everything's cool. Now, this raking rocks is connected with a straight sluice box where you do not have a shaker to separate the rocks. I found out early in my mining career that number one was to get rid of your rocks and wash them good, because gold sticks to clay that hangs onto rocks.

July 11th. It's still raining this morning and cold. We went to work in the rain about 9, and when we came in for lunch Roy and Bob fixed the roof of the kitchen. Duffy went to work with us this morning and fell in the pump pit, up to his arms, poor little feller. He about froze so I sent him back to camp. It was raining cats and dogs when we went back to the mine, but we worked about 1-1/2 to 2 hours, then I discovered a hydraulic leak on my dozer. Bob and I took the line off, quite a chore. We were all soaked so we just came on in to camp.

Marcene, Duffy and I went to Deering tonight and I called George Lott, the manager of our camper park in Anchorage. He got the package okay that I sent containing a mastodon tusk. Marcene called Foster's Air in Nome to pick us up Saturday at 5 p.m. Art's still in Fairbanks. I called Clark in Kotzebue, and told him to check on freight that was supposed to be in Deering today.

July 12th. Bob and Roy are working the sluice box and I'm running the dozer. Bob and I put the track back on the D4 that Art ran off on Monday. We're in some real good ground now, looks like our summer will be okay yet. Art's still in Fairbanks getting his plane fixed. Marcene made a good supper: fried chicken, biscuits, gravy, corn, and peach cobbler. Marcene and I took a ride on the Max and the chain came apart. I fixed it and we made it back to camp. Guess it's just not in the books for this darn thing to run for me.

We're anxious to go to Nome tomorrow. The Greens, the couple with the dogs, gave us a list about a mile long of things to get them when we go to Nome, but only $60. So, I'll spend their $60 and that's it. Don't really like the guy anyway, he's goofy, and so smart that he's stupid.

Saturday, July 13th. Marcene and I flew with Foster Air to Nome this afternoon. The weather was nice today and a nice trip into Nome. When we got ready to leave camp we buried our gold, and I carried a map of where the gold was buried in my billfold in case the plane went down and I didn't make it.

Monday, July 15th. We spent two nights in Nome, and got back to camp about 1 p.m. today. We brought a batch of groceries, etc., for the Greens staying down the road in a tent with their dogs. We call them "the dog people". Boy, howdy! Never again! This morning, in Nome, I went to the Magistrate's Office and filed our claims on Old Glory Creek, eight 40-acre claims; also wrote up a claim just south of Pinnell River by Inmachuk River.

July 16th. We got word by radio today that Jenine, our niece, was dead, and we don't know the circumstances yet. Brock, the engineer, is still around looking for Art, but he went back to Fairbanks to get his plane and don't know when he'll be back. Marie came over and went back this afternoon on Shallabarger's plane. We got a letter from Jadene, 'tis hot in Philadelphia where she's visiting Marcene's niece and her husband. We worked the sluice box 8 hours today, looks pretty good. We're getting some pretty nice gold, just hope it holds out. Little Duffy is real good about carrying water for Marcene. She taught him to play solitaire.

July 17th. It rained a bit today, but I didn't mind at all. As we started cleaning up the sluice box I found a 2-ounce nugget. (Gold is measured in troy ounces; 12 troy ounces equal a pound, rather than standard measure ounces which are 16 to a pound.) We were all worked up over it, tickled Marcene. We didn't finish cleaning up, we'll finish tomorrow. We have approximately 5 to 6 pounds of gold so far, and just hope we can keep working like we've been doing. Art didn't make it back yet, so Brock left today for Kotzebue looking for him.

July 18th. We finished cleaning up today and have 8 pounds of gold (96 ounces), as of tonight. We have it in the Wells Fargo safe. We went up the Inmachuk River to where the Pinnell River intersects and got pretty good showing there. We worked the sluice box in our pit about 7 hours and got some nice size nuggets. It rained today and we're having trouble with frost. The pump is doing okay, but it sure is hard to start. Art's not back yet.

We cut Duffy's hair today. I told him this morning, at the breakfast table, that we had clippers in camp. He said, "Oh, no, you don't have a barber in camp." I said, "Yeah, I got barber's clippers in camp." And he said, "Oh, no!" So I said, "I'll make you a bet. If we have the clippers, and I can show them to you at noon, I cut your hair. And, if not, you owe me all your work over here for free." He said, "Okay, okay."

I came in at noon, with my overalls on, and the little guy's sitting there looking at me. Duffy kept looking at me, and pretty soon he started laughing. I went over to our cabin, got the clippers and stuck them in my bib pocket, and didn't say anything when I came back in, but he's laughing yet. When dinner was over, Duffy was still eating something, and he looked up at me as I brought those clippers out of my pocket. His eyes just fell, he looked sad. But, we sat him outside in a chair, and I said, "Well, when you make a deal you've gotta stick by it." Bob started cutting his hair and I finished it up. The haircut made him self conscious, and he felt bad for a few days around there, but then he looked a lot better, and he got to where he accepted it pretty good.

Art's still not back from Fairbanks. It was kind of cold today, rained a bit. We'll go to Deering tomorrow for mail, and make phone calls. It's 18 miles down the road and takes better than an hour to get there, more like 2 hours.

Sunday, July 21st. I stripped overburden down on our claims at Black's old property, and we tried pumping on the hill. Roy and Bob rigged up the pump, got the monitor set up, and it's washing a lot of dirt down. I think it's going to do quite well. It's raining again today.

July 22nd. Duffy lost his cap in the sluice box early this morning, and also his shovel. We found his shovel, but never did find the Arctic Cat cap that I had given him. Roy, Bob and I staked nine 40-acre claims on Old Glory Creek and one on American Creek. We did lots of walking and packing posts, 4 x 4s. I carried the 4 x 4s and a shovel about a mile and a half over niggerheads, muck and creek. Sure was tired tonight when we got in about 11 o'clock from that staking. We had supper and needed no one to rock us to sleep.

July 23rd. We got started at 9 o'clock this morning and broke a hose on the Case 450 dozer, then lost an hour for welding a fitting. Marcene and I went to Deering this evening to check mail and make phone calls. We went in a pickup; it rides better, but we had to drive in second gear 'cause it was missing so bad and the road was so rough. We called George at our Camper park, and everything was fine, talked to Art and he may be over tomorrow. He has to get x-rays first thing in the morning. We got a letter from Mama, from my sister Faye, and Jadene today. Shallabarger came in tonight about 10 o'clock and brought groceries. Duffy went back to Kotzebue with him. The sluice box worked about 4-1/2 hours today and we had a good showing, the riffles looked good (yellow). I found a big nugget, about an ounce and a quarter.

July 24th. Shallabarger came in today and brought more fuel. He went up on his price for flying in fuel, $150 per trip, and that's $50 per barrel for fuel and oil for the dozers. It's a 90-mile trip over here and he hauls 3 barrels at a time for $150. Bob went back to Kotzebue to get Art's Super Cub. He brought it back to Utica and brought Roy's wife and daughter back with him, got in about 6:30 p.m. We didn't get to work the sluice box much today, paydirt is real spotty. Can't quite figure out just where we're gonna dig next. Marcene and I went down the road about 3 miles and visited the Greens. We took them some canned goods, eggs, and so forth. The weather was nice today and we'll sleep good tonight.

July 25th. Bob and Marcene flew to Nome today for parts, supplies, and to make telephone calls, and got weathered in. Roy and I worked almost all day stripping and ran the sluice box for about 2 hours. The wide pad D4 dozer broke down -- again, hydraulics this time, and the cooling system's leaking real bad. Both D4s are broke. My poor 450 has caught it all summer. Sure hate to beat it like this, but just got to do it. Wein Air is to fly their Twin Otter in tomorrow with 15 barrels of fuel, so we have to drag the airport, put up barrels at the ends of the runway, and on both sides, for markers.

July 26th. Didn't sleep good at all last night, kept waking up and looking at my watch. I got up this morning at four and went down to the creek and panned for awhile. It was sure nice out, sun shining. Tonight I panned the pit from one end to the other and found good spots, and we got some nice nuggets. We heard on the Tundra Telegram, that Marcene was in Kotzebue and wants someone to pick her up at Deering tomorrow. Bob had left her in Nome, telling her he was weathered in, then took off without her. She had to get to Kotzebue, then to Deering, on her own. That wasn't nice of him, he has his dark side.

The Tundra Telegram is where people can call the radio station with a message for someone, and at certain hours the messages are aired. It's done all over Alaska, which is good, because there aren't many phones.

Saturday, July 27th. The Greens stopped me on the way to Deering and wanted to go in with me. They took their 2 dogs and rode in the back of the pickup with the dogs. Green also paid for groceries that Marcene picked up in Nome for them. We got into better gold today at our mine, larger stuff. It's still windy and raining out, just miserable. We're low on gas 'til the plane comes back, and I want to save it in case of an emergency.

July 28th. Roy's wife stepped on a nail and had to be flown back to Kotzebue. I stripped at the mine about 3 hours. Weins brought 4 barrels of gas and 4 barrels of diesel over today in the Twin Otter, and landed on the strip below camp.

July 29th. The wind is blowing hard. Roy and I worked the sluice box about 5 hours. We set up a little dredge on the creek and worked about 40 gallon buckets of material by the hygrade shack, and got about 1 ounce of nuggets. The hygrade shack is the old gold shack left over from the dredge era. Marie came over this evening with Bob, and Art's coming over tomorrow.

August 3rd. This is Saturday and Bob flew me into Kotzebue this morning where I caught the plane into Anchorage. I had 10 pounds 8 ounces (troy) of gold and took it to Anchorage, carrying it in a plastic gallon jug. An inspector dude at the airport in Kotzebue wanted me to pour it out so he could look at it. I laughed at him and told him to go get the station manager. The station manager knew me and knew what was happening, so he told the guy, "Don't worry about it."

Tuesday, August 6th. Marcene was operated on today for a hiatal hernia, and everything went okay. I went by 2 times to see her, she looked good, and I'm glad there were no complications.

Friday, August 9th. Bob called and said that the pump engine had blown up, and gave me a big list of parts to get for it. I called Art, and also called Ron Ingstrom in Nome, where he has a gold dredge. We may get a D9 Caterpillar from Ron and his dad, but it's just in the talking stage.

Monday, August 12th. I called Art and he's going to buy a pump from Bobby Miller in Fairbanks, and have him send it right away. Carrington Company is going to ship parts direct to Kotzebue for the International TD18 pump motor and bill me later.

Thursday, August 15th. I went to Nome today and met Art, he'd flown in from Fairbanks. We stayed at Alaska Airlines' hotel there. The rooms had a wood sidewalk running along them, and the windows overlooked the sidewalk. You had to go around kind of to the side to come in the door of the room. I didn't want to stay out too late with Art, running around, so I went to the room after I made a few rounds and ate a little supper.

With nothing to do, I was just lying there about half asleep. The wind was blowing real hard. I heard some feet walking down that boardwalk and there were 2 guys, Eskimos. One walked up and tried the door and it was locked, of course, but I had the window raised up as it was hot in the room. One guy said to the other, when the door wouldn't open, "Hey, let's go round and try the window, I think it was up." So I just lay stretched out on the bed there, and set one foot on the floor over on the right side of the cot (it was kind of 2 cots that we were sleeping on in that motel), got a real good brace, and when that guy started climbing through the window, I let him have it right in the kisser. He fell back and hit the floor, and I heard footsteps of the other one, taking about 3 steps a jump, going back down the sidewalk. I didn't hear anything out of the guy that fell and hit the floor.

Pretty soon, as I kept lying there I thought I'd look out, and when I did, the one guy was still lying there laid out cold, I guess. Then pretty soon I heard footsteps creeping back; he'd take a few steps and he'd stop, and I sneaked a peek out. The other guy came walking back, got his buddy, and dragged him down the wood sidewalk. I don't know where they went. Anyway, Art was roaming around town just about all night and got in sometime in the wee hours of the morning.

Coming back from Nome, the weather was bad and we got lost, or the pilot who was flying me thought he was lost. He took me about 40 miles too far east and I told him I thought so, but how do you go about telling a short, ex-Navy pilot he's wrong. We finally came to Buckland River, and after him getting almost hysterical because he couldn't see the ocean, I finally told him where we were and that he had to head northwest to get back to water. He climbed up quite a ways and we could see a hole right over Candle, so we had to turn around and go to Deering, then come back up the Inmachuk River. He bounced about 10 feet when he hit the ground in Utica, and he was flying a Cessna 206. When he hit the runway, he said, "Boy, what a crosswind!" And the windsock was hanging straight down.

What a ride, 2 hours and 37 minutes from Nome, which is almost double the time it should take. When he got ready to leave he had the nerve to ask me, if I was flying to Nome which route would I take. He started to unfold a map and I told him, "Man, if you don't know your way to Nome, you better just hang 'er up right here." Well, he did; he got killed about 2 weeks after that. I knew that that guy was gonna get it because he just wasn't the pilot for this country up here. It takes a special breed to fly in this north country, where there are no landmarks, or anything else to speak of.

Monday, August 19th. We're still working on the pump engine. We've got a lot of material ready to go. Bob flew to Kotzebue at noon to carry Roy's sister and her daughter. The weather was a bit better today.

August 20th. We finally got the pump engine together and running about 3:30 p.m., and worked the sluice box for the first time in over 2 weeks. Roy and Benny went into Deering at noon to catch Weins to Kotzebue, but they missed the plane so they came back. Bob was going to fly them in tonight, but got fogged in part of the way over and had to come back. I went to Deering tonight and called Marcene and Jadene. Marcene was doing good and I was happy to hear that as I've been worried about her. The weather was nice today, but fog tonight, guess it will rain some more. Leo's not talking to anyone around camp, so, whoop-de-doo! "Just another rock in my shoe."

August 21st. Today wasn't our lucky day. The pump engine wouldn't start so we tried jumping it with my dozer battery and blew up the batteries in my dozer, both of them. Bob, Roy and Benny flew to Kotzebue; Roy and Benny stayed, and Bob got back about 1:30. He ordered 2 batteries and George is to pick them up at Husky Battery in Anchorage and send them up by Air Alaska.

Roy Scott, ("Huckle") came back with Bob and he's going to be working with us 'til freeze-up, I guess. I don't know what else can break. I left my dozer running all night; there's no way to start it without batteries, it has an automatic transmission. We ran the sluice box an hour and a half after supper.

August 22nd. We got up early and were on the job by 7:45, but the pump wouldn't start. We worried with it for 2-1/2 hours before finally getting it started. We ran the sluice box for an hour and then a freeze plug blew out of the pump engine. It took Bob an hour and a half more to scrounge another one and replace it. So, we ran the sluice box 6-1/2 hours today. Can't hardly believe it. The weather is beautiful, not a cloud in the sky. Bob had to fly to Kotzebue tonight; a message on the Tundra Telegram just said, "Bob, come to Kotzebue."

August 23rd. Huckle and I ran the sluice box 8 hours today. Bob and Roy are both in Kotzebue. The wind blew all day, weather was really bad. Bob, and the rest of them in Kotzebue, got into camp tonight about 9:30. A friend of Art's, Mr. Hugh Chatham, came with them - 2 planes. Mr. Chatham owns Holiday Hotels, and is partners in mining with Art. I told him tonight, in the bunkhouse, "Well, the new guy in camp has to cook breakfast." He said, "Don't worry about it, don't feel bad about that, I'm a pretty good hand at making sourdough pancakes." Then he read his *Wall Street Journal* and got all ready for bed. He was walking around in his little boxer shorts. He said, "You don't believe that I can cook breakfast in the morning, do you." And I said, "Oh, yes, I believe."

August 24th. Last night, when Hugh Chatham came in, he said to me, "I've heard a lot about you." And I said, "Well, I've heard a lot about you, too." He said something like, "Well, I'm not much of a miner, or operator, or anything, but I'm willing to get my feet wet." I told him, "That's about the first thing you'll do when you hit that sluice box." This morning he got his feet wet, also his shoes, boots and britches wet, the whole works, but he was quite a sport, a real nice guy. We ran the sluice box about 8 hours today, and Hugh was down on the sluice box raking rocks. Art and I were running dozers while Roy, Huckle, Bob and Hugh worked the sluice box. Then Bob took Hugh flying this evening.

Sunday, August 25th. Roy, Bob and Huckle ran the sluice box 6 hours today. We ran both D4s for 6 hours and got good showing in the first few riffles. We raised the end of the sluice box up about 3 or 4 inches. It rained most all day, kind of miserable.

August 26th. We ran our 2-inch pump about 9 hours cleaning the sluice box. This is cleaning gold from the big box, and we got quite a bit of gold, but don't know for sure yet just how much, we'll have to weigh it up. We don't have gold scales, we're using baby scales - 16 ounces instead of 12 troy ounces. Hugh is still here, he's going to leave tomorrow. We thoroughly enjoyed him here at the mine. It was cloudy and we had some rain today. Buck Matson flew 2 diesel, 3 avgas, 80-87, and some other stuff on his trip in today, $200 from Kotzebue. Roy, Bob, Art and I worked 9 hours today.

August 27th. Hugh took 2.8 pounds of gold with him back to San Francisco, as he is Art's silent partner, and Art flew him to Kotzebue to catch the plane back home. While he was in Kotzebue, Art picked up ham and bacon that Marcene had sent last week. We worked the sluice box 8 hours today, Huckle worked on the sluice box and I ran a D4 dozer. We were going to start the sluice box on Old Glory Creek tomorrow, but didn't get Benny, or Karmun, a couple of Eskimos, to help.

August 28th. My 450 Dozer broke down and we're waiting on parts for it. The 10-inch pump is running. A track came off the D4 at quitting time, we'll put it back on tomorrow. We're just about out of material to work with 'til we start to strip some more, or run the monitors and wash it down.

Stan Sobozinski and his son came in today by Foster Air, and that little son's a squirrel. He got in our sluice box and started picking nuggets out and putting them in his pockets. I let Stan know what I thought. The boy's about 14, and knows better.

August 29th. Art and I flew into Kotzebue, picked up parts, ordered fuel, etc., to be flown over by Buck Matson. Bob and Huckle worked on the D4s about 4 hours today. First they put the track back on the narrow pad, then had to put a pin back on the wide pad track. Boy, this wore out equipment sure is costly in parts and downtime. Sure wish we had just one new piece of equipment, bigger than my little Case 450 dozer - it's a good dozer. The sluice box ran about 5 hours today.

August 30th. Art's daughter is going to pull out all checks for the mine for this season, and get copies made of them, and all receipts she can find, also statements, etc. I asked her to do this to make sure that all our expenses for this mining venture were paid, or being taken care of. Also, Marcene is sending paid bills, etc., up this week. Shallabarger will have them up to her this weekend. We worked the sluice box about 7 hours today. We fixed the Case 450, had it running at 10 a.m., first time it's been broke down all year. Can't beat new equipment. Bob and Roy went to Nome in the Super Cub this afternoon. They took off while I was bulldozing on the hill. They supposedly were going after 2 track pins for a D4, which we didn't need. Guess it's okay when you're using other people's money, but Bob never said a word to me about going. I stripped 'til 10 p.m. with the Case 450. Huckle went to Deering tonight and I guess he won't be back.

Saturday, August 31st. The weather was good today. Art and I ran the sluice box about 6 hours today, alone in the morning, then Marie came down in the afternoon and helped. Bob and Roy got in from Nome about 2:45 p.m. and came down to help about 3 p.m. I washed up my Case 450 dozer after work with the 2-inch pump, and then Art flew me to Deering this evening so I could call Marcene. The mayor of Deering gave us salmon, and that was nice of him.

September 1st. Art and I flew over to Candle to see an old miner, Freddie Weinard, about a mastodon tusk, and we agreed to buy his gold for $125 per ounce. He's 69 years old and has been in Candle since he was a little kid. Art and I got back to camp at noon and gave Bob and Roy a hand working on the D4, got the wide pad sections on and the track adjusted, and got the extension on the sluice box. We're getting things ready for Roy and Bob to go to Old Glory Creek tomorrow morning.

September 2nd. Bob and Roy took off for Old Glory Creek this morning, left camp about 9, and Art had to go to Kotzebue. This afternoon Art, Marie and I worked the sluice box for 2-1/2 hours, then I stockpiled material for tomorrow while Art and Marie flew up to Old Glory Creek to check on Roy and Bob. He took some meat and cookies to drop for them. One time, Art flew over camp, dropped posts (we finally found them) and supplies, but of all things, 2 frozen chickens went through the roof of the outhouse and fell in the hole.

September 3rd. The weather was good today and the sluice box ran about 5 hours. Art and I worked the pit and had a pretty good showing. Bob and Roy got the sluice box on Old Glory Creek going and ran it about 2 hours. They also built a dam and diverted the creek. Art made Leo unload a bed and mattress that he took from one of our log cabins in camp.

September 4th. It was nice out today, the sun was shining all day. Art and I went to Candle early this morning to see Freddie regarding his gold and the mastodon tusk, but we didn't get to see him. There was frost on the wings of Art's plane, so we took a rope, threw it over the wings, and with one of us on each side of the wing, we pulled the rope back and forth to rid the wings of frost. We checked on Roy and Bob on the way back, and everything looks good on Old Glory Creek. Later, Art and Marie went to Kotzebue; he has to be at a Town Council meeting tomorrow as he's a member of the Council. He'll be back Friday. I stripped most of the day and ran the sluice box about an hour by myself. In the evening I went up to Old Glory Creek to check things out. Looks real good. Had lots of rainbow trout right in the sluice box, up to 18 inches long. Bob and Roy and going to cook the ones we caught. They said they don't need any help on Old Glory Creek, everything is just fine. I drove back to camp in the dark with no lights. Everybody should try that some time. It's 10:30 p.m., and being it's dark this early I'm going to bed. It's September, getting into the fall time, so the days are getting shorter.

September 5th. The weather was beautiful and clear today. Buck Matson's plane came over this morning and brought a load of diesel, antifreeze, avgas, and all kinds of goodies, 2 cases of groceries, 2 cases of beer, and 2 cases of pop. Also got a half case of eggs, 5 loaves of bread, and a case of antifreeze that Marcene sent up yesterday. We buy day-old bread in Anchorage because it can be 3 or 4 days before we get it anyway. Art and Marie are in Kotzebue, Bob and Roy are working Old Glory Creek, and I worked Black's pit by myself, ran the sluice box 4 hours. I sold 5 gallons of blazo, fuel you use in Coleman stoves, to the Greens, "the dog people" downstream from us, and they paid by cash. I drove into Deering this evening, called Marcene and everything's fine in Anchorage.

September 6th. I took antifreeze up to Bob, we have enough to put all equipment down to zero, so that should do us the rest of the season. I used the 4x4 to go up to Old Glory Creek, picked up Bob and Roy and they're taking it back, along with tools, in the morning. It's a World War II relic, but runs good. Bob will tear the John Deere loader-backhoe combination apart and we'll see what we need to get it going. It's broken down.

September 7th. Art and I staked another 40-acre claim at Mile 16 Bench this morning on the Inmachuk River, between our camp and Deering. I took my 450 dozer down and stripped overburden, the Greens agreed to work this claim that we staked for 50% of the gold. We're furnishing the 4-inch dredge and fuel, and the good paydirt there. We're going to set up a sluice box there next spring. Art and I also staked one 40-acre claim on Arizona Creek at the Inmachuk River. Bob and Roy went back up to Old Glory today, took the 4x4, welder, and so forth. They plan on a cleanup about Monday.

Sunday, September 8th. Art and I went to Candle and bought $2500 of gold from Freddie Weinard, paid him $125 an ounce for it. It was about 30% jewelry gold, which was worth a bit more, but by taking it all he got his price that he wanted, so everybody was happy. We worked the sluice box about 3 hours today. The Greens are working at our Mile 16 Bench claim. We're going to move the sluice box down there in about 2 or 3 days because they just aren't getting it there. Ice is getting bad on Old Glory Creek, we're gonna have to shut down there pretty quick.

September 9th. Art and I went to Candle this morning and bought 70 ounces of gold at $125 an ounce from Riney Berg, and 3 more ounces from Freddie, for a total of 23 ounces from him. We had to pay Riney Berg by check for the 70 ounces because he has partners and didn't want cash. Very seldom that you ever see a miner who won't take cash for his gold. By the way, Riney was part owner in that Red Dog Mine up out of Kotzebue, the one that's operating up there today, and Art was one-third owner of it. Riney, Art, and the other owner, whose name I forget, decided that they'd go in there and do some assessment work and so forth, and they dug a shaft. It looked good. Art liked the air sled that they had, an airplane engine on a sled, and he said he wanted to sell out his portion of the mine, and would take that air sled as payment. So, that's what Art got out of what's known today as the Red Dog Mine out of Kotzebue. It's a big, big, super-big mine, lead and zinc.

Art and I cleaned up at Black's pit today, not too good. We got a total of 7 pounds. Roy and Bob got in tonight from Old Glory Creek and their cleanup looks real good. They do have nuggets up there.

September 10th. We got moved from Black's pit down to Mile 16 Bench and got set up and running about 1:15 p.m. It took 3 hours to move a mile and a half, then set up the pump, sluice box and hopper. Things look real good, lots of coarse stuff. We hired John Green to help on the sluice box. He works pretty good when he's working the sluice box.

September 11th. The sluice box ran 6 hours today on Mile 16 Bench. We moved about 150 yards and got real good color and nuggets. John Green told me that he was quitting this morning. It was a little too rough for him, and maybe good riddance, whatever. The pump blew a bearing this evening, just at quitting time. Bob said we have a bearing and he'll fix it in the morning. Art had to fly to Kotzebue for a special Council meeting and got back about 6:30.

We boxed up 2 cartons of Cat parts tonight to be shipped into Kotzebue. These were new parts left in the shop from the previous miners.

September 12th. Buck Matson picked me up at 7 a.m. and we went to Kotzebue. He brought 3 empty barrels in with him. I caught Alaska Airlines to Anchorage, taking gold with me. So far, we're doing okay.

Saturday, September 14th. I got the head, rings, etc., for the John Deere backhoe-loader at Craig Taylor's today and will carry them back with me on the plane tomorrow.

September 15th. It was raining today when I flew back to Kotzebue. I flew on to camp in Utica with Buck's pilot who was flying in 2 drums of diesel. The guys were running the sluice box when we got to Utica.

September 16th. Well, this isn't news, but the D4 Cat was stuck for 3 hours, then off the track for the rest of the day. Art was running it. Roy and Bob went up to Old Glory this morning, took the John Deere parts along, and are going to use the loader to do the rest of the work there this year.

September 17th. It was cloudy all day and light rain. The sluice box ran 7 hours. We're working in bedrock, large boulders, and permafrost, so only had small yardage - 150 yards. The color and nuggets look good. Art flew into Kotzebue for parts and groceries. Bob and Roy are working Old Glory.

September 18th. Today was clear and warm. We cleaned up at Mile 16 Bench and will have a tally on the gold tomorrow, as we didn't get all concentrates panned out today. Roy came down from Old Glory to get a belt for the John Deere backhoe and left Bob sluicing.

Dan, a native from Deering, got 2 moose this morning and spent most of the day cleaning and hauling them in. We hired Dan the other day. He came down to the pit one morning looking for a job. I'm used to having to show the Eskimos what to do a half dozen times, and then keep reminding them what to do, but this Dan guy came down, saw that water was in the pit and went to work. He checked the oil in the pump, filled the little 3-inch pump with gas and got it started and running, then cleared the suction and started the pump to pumping water. I walked over to him and said, "Hey, where did you learn your construction? Have you ever been in the service, or any place other than Alaska?" And he said, "Oh, yeah, I was in the 82nd Airborne Division, I was a scout. Me and another Eskimo were talking Eskimo in Europe and the Germans never figured out what the language was, so it worked out real good for us." Needless to say, he's one of the better hands that I have working for us.

The sluice box ran 3 hours at Mile 16 pit. We spent most of the morning checking ground, and pumping water, panning and putting riffles back in the sluice box. We had a real good showing this afternoon after we shut down, one half-ounce nugget and other nice nuggets from the first 3 riffles. Art and I flew into Deering at 11 a.m., and I called Marcene. Everything is fine in Anchorage. Marcene goes back and forth between Anchorage and the mine, as our daughter, Jadene, is only 14 and doesn't need to be left alone a lot. She's a real good girl, though, a cheerleader at Diamond High School in Anchorage, also in the Swing Choir, and plays piano for the choir.

Friday, September 20th. It's partly cloudy and we had some ice this morning, about a quarter inch. The sluice box ran 6 hours today and when we checked the riffles it was the best material that we've had this season. This material is just above and in the top of the bedrock. Roy and Bob came down from Old Glory tonight and they say there's lots of gold up there.

September 21st. It was foggy 'til noon, then fair the rest of the day, nice and warm out. We put the narrow track back on the D4 this morning, and ran the sluice box for 5 hours. Looks like we're just about out of pay 'til we get something to rip the frost here with. We should have about 2 hours work left in the pit. Bob and Ray went back to Old Glory this afternoon and will be ready for a cleanup there about Monday or Tuesday. We'll clean up at Mile 16 Bench Monday, and that's the way that one goes.

September 22. Cloudy and light rain today. We loaded the cabin out for Old Glory Creek where Bob and Ray Snyder are working. Buck came over and brought 7 drums of diesel, and groceries from Marcene. We dug a test hole north of Mile 16 pit where we are set up and it looks real good. We didn't run the sluice box at Mile 16 today, but we did assessment work at Arizona Creek. Roy got stuck in the process.

September 23rd. Cloudy and rain again today. The sluice box ran 2-1/2 hours. We cleaned up this afternoon. Bob and Ray came in with the wide pad dozer to help pull the cabin up to Old Glory, help us clean up and get the sluice box and pumps, etc., put away for the winter. We got about 4 pounds of gold at Mile 16 on this cleanup, 16-1/2 hours. No work at Old Glory today, Bob and Ray were helping us at Mile 16.

September 24th. It's a cloudy day. We finished cleaning up at Mile 16 and put away all equipment, then took off for Old Glory with all 3 dozers, the 2 D4s pulling the cabin. Dan, Ray, Roy, Bob and I went up, and we made it there about 6 p.m. No major problems. It'll be nice to have a cabin to sleep in here on the creek, instead of a tent.

We got up at 6 a.m. this Wednesday morning, September 25th, and it was raining. We got the sluice box going and we'll run all thawed material. Bob ran the backhoe while Roy, Dan and Ray worked the sluice box. I stripped some overburden and will finish tomorrow. Looks like we'll finish sluicing tomorrow about noon. It sure is muddy up here. We caught a bunch of rainbow trout in the sluice box last night and we'll have them for supper tonight. Art flew over and dropped a package for me, a box of cigars Marcene had sent up. I really appreciated that.

September 26th. We had freezing rain today. We finished sluicing at 1:30 p.m. and started cleaning up. I finished stripping overburden for next year's start. Looks like we'll have about 4 or 5 pounds in cleanup, and we do have nuggets. We should finish cleanup and get out around noon tomorrow.

September 27th. Today it was cloudy, cold and raining. I took the Case 450 and went about 5 miles up Old Glory Creek, digging test holes. I dug 15 and panned each hole, got the best showing at the junction of American Creek. Bob and Roy finished cleaning up and were ready to go when I got back. Ray and Dan put a roofjack on the cabin and moved the stove in. Roy took off with the 4x4, and Ray Snyder took off with a D4 pulling the sluice box. Bob was running the backhoe, and Dan and I got stuck. We finally got out and off for beautiful Utica. Sure was a miserable trip, cold freezing rain and snowballs.

We got to camp and Art walked up, he'd cracked up his Super Cub. I knew right away when I saw him coming that something was wrong because Art's pants and clothes were wet up above his waist. He'd walked about 8 miles up the river from where he'd crashed. We got thawed out and went down to flip his plane over, then pulled it out of the Inmachuk River over to the road. Today was supposed to be "caboose" at the mine (the end for this season), but we'll have to take his plane apart tomorrow, load it out and haul it into Deering. The right wing tank cap didn't have an air vent in it, and the tank collapsed. It came from the factory that way. Boy, was he lucky it didn't happen over water (Kotzebue Sound).

September 28th. Cold, cloudy and a little snow this morning. We took the wings off Art's plane, loaded the disabled Super Cub on a trailer and took it to Deering, then we all took Weins Air to Kotzebue. I paid the fare for all of us, Art, Roy, Bob, Ray and myself. Art is having Weins fly his Super Cub to Fairbanks in a Skyvan plane.

Sunday, September 29th. It was clear and nice in Anchorage today when Bob and I got in from Kotzebue. It's sure nice to get back to civilization, a different world.

Tuesday, October 1st. The weather was cold and windy. Roy Fields came to Anchorage today, and he and Bob separated the gold tonight. Art can pick whichever jars he wishes, he can flip a half dollar, or whatever he'd like to do. Roy separated all the nuggets. Art, Roy, Bob and I are going to San Francisco Wednesday night at the invitation of Hugh Chatham, who's opening a new Holiday Hotel at Van Nuys Boulevard, on top of the hill in San Francisco, and we should be back Saturday. I won't take my gold.

We got to San Francisco, and Hugh had us meet with one of the "biggie-biggies" at the Wells Fargo Bank, and another big financial guy. They got us in the conference room there in Chatham's big new hotel, and they had all kinds of ideas on how to produce gold and how to get things done. But I saw right through them. They wanted to buy a new D7, a 966 loader, and a Cessna 206 airplane for hauling fuel. Bob said, "I'll fly the plane."

Everything was going good, but when we got ready to leave, I talked to Hugh and to each one of the guys. I said, "Well, you know it's one thing when you're putting all the money up and got the equipment, and it's another thing getting the gold out. You have to have the people in order to do it, and same way with flying the airplane, you have to have somebody to look after it and so forth." Anyway, we kind of let it go at that.

I knew what they wanted, to get their hooks into all those claims that we had chased down and staked. They saw that we were getting quite a bit of gold there, so they envisioned that with more money and equipment, we'd get even more gold. In other words, if you got a little dozer and you get 10 ounces, you get a big dozer and you'll get 20 ounces. If you have one person working you'll get x-number ounces of gold, and if you have two people working you'll get twice as much. But things don't work thataway. You've gotta have your men, you gotta pick them and know how to go about working the ground and so forth.   So, with the way they were thinking, I was a little bit leery that things weren't gonna work out all that good with Hugh Chatham and his people, and myself. I can work with Art Fields 'til everything freezes over, but these guys were just playing in a different ball league.

Saturday, October 5th. We drove down to Monterey, California, and checked into the Holiday Inn. We stopped and toured the Winchester House; wish Marcene and Jadene could have been along to see it. Then we went down to Pebble Beach and Hugh showed us his home right on the golf course. We drove around, and he said, "When you go into the hotel there on the beach, just sign your names and in front, put 'Hugh H. Chatham'. I've instructed them to accept that." That's what we did, and it didn't cost us anything in Frisco, or down there in Monterey.

Monday, October 7th. Hugh had a special little Jeep station wagon that he just loved, and he let Roy, Art's boy, do the driving. Art, Roy, Bob and I got into the Jeep on the parking floor of the hotel, Roy driving. We were heading down through there, hit one of those speed bumps, bounced up and hit overhead, and bent the top down on that Jeep, Hugh's favorite vehicle. We felt bad about it, but Hugh kind of overlooked it.

He showed me one of those fancy cars he bought, it was a Mercedes 450SL convertible. He said the way he bought all his new cars was to save his change. When he went out, eating and so forth, whatever change he had he threw in a bottle and saved it that way. And that's the way he bought his new cars. His favorite hobby was picking up golf balls there at Pebble Beach.

October 8th. After having a meeting with Hugh, Jay and Brock, it looks like I may be just biding my time to sell out on the claims, or something, because I don't feel that it's going to work out for us there.

Monday, October 14th. Art called today and said that my shirts and belt that Hugh sent were in, and he'd send them on down to me. He said that Bob found a D7 dozer in Fairbanks for $30,000. I guess Bob is going up to help with Art's Super Cub. Oh, by the way, I also found out that Bob found a Cessna 206 for sale, $32,000, but didn't bother to tell me, or have me look at it before he called Art. I've just got a hunch that Bob is going to go behind my back and try to finagle something out of Hugh and the guys down in Frisco.

I found out that Mike Hamlin, my shop manager in our snow machine shop, has gotten together with Bob, and it looks like they're going to try to go to Kotzebue. Bob is thinking about taking over the mining operation there, Art's part of it. Mike is figuring on taking over the liquor store, cab company, and the pool hall. George Lott, the manager of our camper park, is going to go up with them and use the gold that they get out of the mine to make jewelry. What a nest of worms this thing is turning into. But, my old saying is, you give a guy enough rope and he will eventually hang himself.

Thursday, October 17th. I lost Mike, the manager of my snow machine shop, Bob, my mechanic, and George, my manager of the Green Belt Camper Park, all at once. I told them it's like pulling your thumb out of a glass of water, the hole will fill up. Here I'd helped all 3 of them, a lot, and no "thanks" from any of them.

Wednesday, October 23rd. I called Art today and he told me that Bob, Mike and Illa Jean, Mike's wife, are with Roy and Marie, at camp over at Utica. I could see the handwriting on the wall there.

Saturday, November 2nd. Art called from Kotzebue and I told him about a letter from Steve Salinas, the Mexican we borrowed the sled from, to use on our move over to Deering. Art told me not to worry about it, that he would talk to Salinas and take care of it. He also said I was not to send the big nugget to Marie as per our agreement, that it was mine, per an agreement with Hugh in San Francisco. My portion of the gold that Hugh took down to San Francisco would go to Art in exchange for the big nugget.

It sure is bad how Mike and Bob are doing Art. There is one thing for sure, if you don't lie, you don't have to worry about what you've said. I sure hate to see Art get beaten out of what he's worked so hard for.

Thursday, November 7th. Bob Kirsch, Roy Fields and Mike Hamlin came out this morning, and Roy tried to get me to sign some papers, but I refused. I told him I didn't think they were legal, but would meet Art anywhere he wished and sign my half of the claims to Fields Exploration. I told Roy that he was welcome to be with Art, but I didn't want Mike or Bob around. I had talked to Art and agreed to assign my half of the claims to him, but with instructions to keep Bob, Mike, and George Lott out of the picture.

I picked up Hugh's watch today, the gold nuggeted watch that I had George make up for him, and also sent one to Art in Kotzebue.

1975

Wednesday, January 1, 1975. Art Fields is down and spent the night with us. He and I went to Alyeska today, and went by the cab company to see Howdy Foster. We talked things over regarding the mine, how things were going, and what we were gonna do next year. Looks like we'll be back up there, make a few changes, but everything will be alright.

Monday, March 10th. Art and I just flew into Galena this evening. We're covering the Top of the World 1000 Snow Machine Race, from Nenana to Nome. I'm the Race Marshall and Art's flying cover. We stopped in Hobo Benson's and walked inside the bar. There was a payphone on the wall that was all tore up, looked like the cats had got ahold of it. I asked Hobo what in the heck had happened to his phone, and he said, "Oh, there was a drunk Indian come in here the other night and tried to make a phone call. He didn't get through, or something, maybe got cut off. He pointed at the phone, shook his fist, and said, 'I'll take care of you!' Then he went home and got his shotgun and just blew it all to pieces." I said, "Well, what're you gonna do with it, you gonna get it replaced?" He said, "No, I'm gonna leave it there for a conversation piece."

While we were in there that night, two old Swedes, old miners - they had to be in their eighties - were talking about the moon and stars. Astronauts had just recently landed on the moon. Anyway, one old boy said, "Hey, you know, a billy goat goes out in the pasture and does his thing, and a cow does the same thing, and it's different, splatters all over. A horse does his, and it's different. How come?" The other old boy said, "I don't know." The first one said, "You mean to tell me that you know all about them stars and the moon and everything, and you don't know shit!" They got into a fight and were rolling around on the floor. I thought one of them would have a heart attack. Finally they went back to the bar and started laughing and drinking.

Friday, April 11th. Art got in town today. We picked him up and he spent the night at our house. We had a nice visit.

Friday, May 30th. I met Art at the airport and we went to Fairbanks. Shorty (Al Mentkin) met us at the airport and took us over to where they keep all the mining claims records. The records show that all our claims are valid. Sobby hasn't filed his assessment work since November 1973, unless the office in Nome goofed sending the records out to Fairbanks. I came back to Anghorage tonight, and it was a long day.

Tuesday, June 3rd. I called Art today and he says everything is about "go" at the mine. Shorty's going to check over everything, see what we need to get our equipment going, and call me after checking things out. I called Art back to tell him that Shorty would be there and to be looking out for him. I first met Al Mentkin racing snow machines, and hired him to sell them for me. He was married to a native.

June 4th. I took Shorty, Bert and Vicky (his wife and daughter) to the airport; they're going to Kotzebue.

June 5th. Art called today and said he is in agreement with me on the letter I wrote Hugh Chatham, so that's good. My letter said that I would work with Art and Hugh, but no way with Mike Hamlin, Bob Kirsch, or George Lott.

Tuesday, June 10th. I left today for Kotzebue and got there okay, but stuff we had sent up didn't make it. As usual for Weins, their freight got all crossed up. Shorty met me at the airport and we found Art at the new hotel, the Nunukluvick. I got my bags, and then Shorty, Bert, Vicky and I, and the baggage, headed for Deering. Not much had changed at camp, about everything was broken down except one old D4 Cat. This was caused from Mike, Bob, George and Roy working after we had shut down last fall, without our permission.

June 11th. Shorty and I put the steering gear in the old 4x4 and got it going. It drives pretty good. We ate dinner and headed for Deering, and had a heck of a time getting into Deering, lots of snow. We had to take to the tundra and drive around it. I visited the Karmuns, called the shop in Anchorage, and tried to call Marcene, but her phone was busy. We picked up the D4 wide pad and Shorty drove it back to camp. It had a track pad missing, also top roller and bottom roller missing, we'll try to fix it tomorrow. We got back into camp about 9:30 p.m., sure tired.

Shallabarger's plane brought over 2 barrels of fuel, 2 cans of avgas, and groceries today. He took back 4 empty barrels. Mr. Karmun said he'd give us some reindeer meat as soon as the engine got in for his pickup. Well, that'll be nice. Love that reindeer meat! It's better than caribou.

June 12th. We got the top roller fixed on the wide pad D4 Cat, but still have no tools and can't fix my dozer 'til we get tools. The right steering clutch is out of the narrow pad D4 dozer. What a pile of junk! Shorty and I went down to Mile 16 Bench and started lowering water in the dredge pond. Digging a ditch across the road lowered the water about 2 feet today. No word from Art, guess the weather's bad in Kotzebue, but it's pretty good here.

June 13th. Shorty and I spent about 2 hours getting the washing machine going for Bert, and we rigged up a pump for water. Then we went on down and worked on the ditch, and started stripping by Mile 16 Bench. One D4 can't steer but one way, and the other won't stay on the track. I wish I had my Case 450 dozer going. When we went back to camp to eat, the plane came in with my tools and baggage. Shorty and I started to work on my dozer and lack about 2 hours of having it ready to go to work. The Karmuns came up to visit today and it was nice visiting with them. Shorty and I got 3 graylings (similar to rainbow trout) today, and we had fish for supper.

Saturday, June 14th. It was cold out this morning, wind blowing and cloudy, but it cleared up about 1 p.m. and was nice the rest of the day. Shorty and I worked on my dozer again, there were lots of little things wrong with it after the boys used it last fall, after we'd shut down. Of course, it's always nice to hop on a good dozer. We went down and got the pump to wash off the dozer, and we lowered the ditch at the dredge pond at Mile 16 Bench. The 3 guys who told Art they had water rights on Old Glory dropped their little rig through the ice into the river today and spent most of the day getting it out.

We took off about 3 p.m. for Deering and, boy, what a drive. The truck acted up and we were lucky to get back. I got through and talked to Marcene and Peanut (my daughter, Jadene), and it sure was nice to talk to them. A lady in Deering had a heart attack, so I had to cut my call short so a doctor could be called from Kotzebue. The Karmuns' son-in-law flew her to Kotzebue. Herbie's engine came in today, so we'll probably have some fresh reindeer meat pretty soon. No word from Art today.

June 15th. Art got into camp this morning. We finished my dozer, then went down and finished lowering the water in the pond. We put in a culvert, stripped, and we're getting ready to set up the sluice box. It was pretty nice today, so Art and I flew up to Old Glory Creek this afternoon. Looks pretty good up that way. We went to Deering, but the circuits were busy when I tried to make calls so I couldn't get through.

June 16th. We were up early today and went down to Mile 16 Bench. We got the pumps, sluice box and hopper set today and got ready to start sluicing. A rock got down in the hydraulic line on my dozer and cracked a fitting. Shorty tried to fix it, but couldn't, so Art flew into Kotzebue for a new hose and fitting, oil and hydraulic fluid, also groceries. I just don't see how we can do too much good with the equipment that we have, as the frost is so bad. I cooked breakfast, Art and I cooked dinner, and I cooked supper.

I think I'll give it the rest of this week and see what happens. Maybe we'll sell my dozer to the City of Deering and try something else. I hate to be a quitter, but this is very frustrating.

June 17th. Shorty and I worked on the pump about all day, never did get it started. Art came in this evening and we got the hoses hooked up. I did some stripping and pushing material, about half a day's work. I got a letter from Marcene, also 8 boxes of groceries. The Karmuns brought it up to me. Nice of them.

June 18th. Art and Shorty flew in to Kotzebue this morning for a starter and parts for the International pump and motor. I stripped overburden and got ready to sluice.

June 19th. Art, Shorty and I ran the sluice box about 4 hours total, there was lots of frost and rocks at Mile 16 Bench. We had a pretty good showing in the first riffles. The weather was good, but kind of cold. Art flew Herbie Karmun over his reindeer herds this p.m., checking for wolves and bears in the herds.

June 20th. This morning we cleaned half of the sluice box and got about a pound of gold. Shorty started working on the wide pad D4. I sure wish we had a ripper Cat and a rubber tire loader. Art flew me into Kotzebue this p.m. and we did our shopping: grease, oil, groceries, etc. Then I caught Weins' plane for Anchorage this evening, it's sure good to be going home.

Wednesday, July 2nd. I caught a plane to Kotzebue this evening, and went from Kotzebue on over to Utica with Shallabarger. When I got into camp, Shorty and I went down to look at the pit. It sure was a mess! We'll try to clean it up tomorrow. Art has 2 guys over at the camp here, and we really don't need them. The weather is good and it was mighty pretty today. Shorty killed a moose yesterday, so we have lots of meat now. We have it in a screened-in meathouse, sure hope we don't have any of it spoil.

July 3rd. We got up early this morning and went down to Mile 16 to try and clean up the mess with my dozer, but there was just too much mud. I guess Art has a thing about water and pumps. I worked 'til 2 p.m., then went up to Black's pit where Shorty and the other 2 guys were trying to put the track on the D4. They'd spent about 4 hours trying to get that track on. I pushed overburden for about an hour before we went in to eat lunch, and after lunch I helped the guys with the track - it took about 20 minutes. Looks like we'll move back up to Black's pit, as we have about 2 to 3 days' sluicing there. The weather sure was nice today, light winds and not many skeeters.

July 4th. I went to Deering today and tried to phone home. The battery was down on the phone and no one could start the light plant. I finally got it going after about an hour's work. Dan Barr said that he thought the phone itself wasn't working, so I blew this trip after all. Seems when you go to Deering anymore, you just about have to carry along a battery. Art came in late this p.m. His back's been bothering him, but he's feeling a bit better.

Sunday, July 6th. Our hired hand, George, filled a gas stove with diesel, and we sure had a hard time trying to figure out what was wrong, the stove wouldn't generate. He finally told us what he'd done. Art and I flew to Kotzebue to pick up a foot valve for our 6-inch high pressure pump. On the way to OTZ (Kotzebue Airport) we flew over white whales, saw about a thousand of them. That sure was something. We got to Kotzebue around 11 p.m. and went by Art's house. It just isn't the same there anymore. I rented a room at the new hotel and we both took a shower. Marcene should be up tomorrow.

July 7th. I called Wes Hamrick, our new shop manager in Anchorage, and he's to send up parts for Art's D4 dozer. Marcene came in today with Forresters Aviation, from Nome, in their 180 Cessna. Sure glad to see her. We got our sluice box going and worked about 30 yards through it.

Where we were pushing tailings at Black's, I ran across an Arctic tern's nest with one egg in it. It was only a half nest, they don't make a real nest. Terns are white birds with red bills. The tern and its mate tried to run me off and Art got to laughing at me. They were trying to get me to leave by diving at me and squealing, and each time they dived they would shit right at me. Art laughed so hard he had to hold his sides. I tried to hit them with rocks, but they are so fast I couldn't hit them, and they'd come within inches of me. They sure are brave, but it was a real eerie feeling. They're real bad on a reindeer herd. What they do is they peck the eyes out of the little baby reindeer.

July 8th. This morning I slept in a bit because my watch was wrong one hour. I went down to Mile 16 with my Case dozer and stripped. On my way back to Black's I met George, the hired hand, coming after me. Art had got stuck and I had to go pull him out. We got things all straightened out and managed to get in about .3 hours on the sluice box, then Art went into Kotzebue this p.m. His back was really hurting him, and he may go on to Anchorage to the hospital. We did get a little showing in the sluice box this afternoon, a few small nuggets. It was windy and kind of cold today, but no skeeters.

July 9th. We worked Black's pit 'til noon, but it rained so hard we took off the rest of the day. It rained all afternoon and into the night. Our bed and sleeping bags got wet, the roof on the cabin leaked, and the kitchen has a few leaks also. Mr. Karmun came by and said that they'd bring a roll of roofing paper to us tomorrow. He told Marcene, "Now you gots a water bed in Utica." He had been to our home on Campbell Lake in Anchorage and knew we had a water bed there.

July 10th. We worked the sluice box 6 hours today and it looked fair. The Karmuns brought up the roofing paper today. We'll have to do something nice for them one of these days, other than just flying over their herds checking for wolves and bears. We got a message on the radio that some parts for us were in Kotzebue, and I told Wes to send them on to Deering. Well, so be it.

July 11th. Our sluice box ran about 6 hours again today and we had a fair showing. The wide pad D4 broke down at noon, blew a seal on the crank. That makes 2 of the darn things down. They both should be in the junk yard. The weather was cold and cloudy all day. George, the hired hand that we've got over here, is about the laziest guy I've ever used. I'd send him to Kotzebue, but Art's in Anchorage or Fairbanks with the Super Cub.

July 12th. We tore down the narrow track D4 this morning. The bearing was shot on the steering clutch, and the arm broke on the starter. Guess we'll have to wait about a week for the parts. We ran the sluice box about 3-1/2 hours today and it looks like we've worked about all we can in this pit for now. Shorty went to Deering this evening and called Wes for groceries and parts. Our food sure was good today, Marcene is a good cook!

Sunday, July 13th. I stripped at Mile 16 Bench, Shorty and Cliff tore down the narrow pad D4 Cat, and we have George working on the roof. I'm going to have to take a couple of pads out of the track on my Case 450 because they're getting bad. Marcene, Al, Bert and I used the sluice box today and did we ever goof up. We were running material we got by the old cleanup shack and got into a batch of mercury. It messed up our gold and we won't do that again.

July 14th. We took 2 pads and links out of my Case 450 and it sure works better. We ran the sluice box about 2 hours, panning all of the pit at Black's, and it still looks good. Harold Lee flew over this morning but didn't stop. We got a message from Wes that packages for us would be in Deering tomorrow. Art sent a message that he'd try to come over tomorrow, weather permitting. The weather was nice today.

July 15th. It was raining this morning. I sent "lonesome" George home today, gave him $100 and took him to Deering to catch a plane. I called Wes, got cut off 5 times, but finally got my message through. This phone at Deering is something else. Then I talked to Ben Walsh, manager of our camper park, and he talked to me like I couldn't fire him, or make him move from the camper park. I met the plane but no parts or groceries that were shipped last week got here. I wish the mighty politicians would just have to spend at least a month up here, and have to go through what we have to go through, trying to get mail, parts, and so forth. They'd do something about it, I'm pretty sure. They'd break Weins' monopoly up in a hurry.

Shorty and Cliff worked the sluice box about 3-1/2 hours, but didn't get very much color. Shorty and I cooked off mercury from gold we got by the old hygrade shack. Mercury is very dangerous to handle.

July 16th. We ran the sluice box about 2-1/2 to 3 hours. We have some good paydirt right in the center of the pit and tomorrow we'll try to water-thaw it. A barge came into Deering today, so Shorty and Cliff went in to bring back our pickup and a load of fuel. Art's still in Kotzebue, I guess, haven't heard from him. I was panning by the river tonight and had 7 or 8 nuggets in a bottle. Shorty's little puppy, Peanuts, came along and spilled them in the rocks. I started to throw him in the river, the little stinker!

July 17th. We cleaned up at Black's pit today and got about 4-1/2 pounds of gold. The weather was fine and Art came in this afternoon. Also, Shallabarger brought over groceries, parts, and one barrel of gas. Art and Shorty flew to Candle this p.m. to see how Freddie Weinard's pump was set up.

Saturday, July 19th. Marcene and I went to Anchorage this afternoon. Art gave me 5 signed checks on Fields Exploration to take along, in case I ran into something down there that we really need for the mine.

Monday, July 21st. We chased parts all day. Boy, Anchorage is sure a mess with all the traffic and the "ding-a-lings" running around town. Makes you want to get back up north again. Ha!

July 22nd. I caught a plane for Kotzebue, and it was late as usual, so I missed the plane to Deering. It left 30 minutes before we got there. I was mad and got onto the Station Manager. He dug out a load of freight going to Deering and I rode on top of the freight. The Karmuns took me up to camp from Deering this evening. They sure are nice people. Art's girl friend, Edna, and 2 kids were at camp, also Taylor Moto, from Deering, and our new hired hand, Cliff, is still around. Shorty hired Taylor Moto because Cliff took off with the pickup and all of Art's booze, and was gone for 2 days. The natives wouldn't think of touching your gold, even if you let it sit out on the table, but you can hide the booze wherever you want to, and they'll find it, one way or the other.

The pit looked good, they did a good job on it while I was gone. When I got back to camp the propane fridge was out, meat all thawed, and no one seemed to really care. So I got out the ice boxes and went up the river to Pinnell River and filled them with ice. I was able to save that meat, and the 40 pounds of meat that I had brought back with me.

July 23rd. We're still working the monitors at Black's pit and they're sure doing a good job. I built a dam in the river and diverted clear water to our pumping pond. That way the water is running over gravel about half a mile down the backside of the river, and it has a tendency to warm up during the day. We have too many people here in camp. Edna and a couple of kids are still here. Things should change a bit.

July 24th. I told Cliff that he couldn't work drunk on the job, so we paid him off and Art flew him into Deering. We stripped some at Mile 16 today and it's looking good down there. Art's pickup runs horrible. Shorty tuned it up and I guess that's the reason it runs horrible.

July 25th. Art went to Fairbanks this morning, took Edna, her 2 kids, and their gear. Oh, boy! She's from Fairbanks. Shallabarger came over and brought oil and some parts. Taylor Moto is working the monitors, cutting down lee and permafrost at Black's pit. Shorty's doing mechanic work and I went up river to get ice. I panned 2 buckets by the cleanup shack, but skeeters were so bad I had to give it up. Got a few small nuggets, though. We heard a message on the radio that Cliff had arrived in Kotzebue, so I guess he's in the Ponderosa Club by now. Too bad, he's such a good hand, but just can't hold his booze.

July 26th. Shorty, Taylor Moto and I ran the monitors at Black's pit today, then this p.m. I drove into Deering to meet the plane and pick up Marcene, Jadene, and the mail. Cliff was trying to get on a plane in Kotzebue to come back to camp when Marcene and Jadene were there, and she gave him $20. She didn't know I'd fired him. The weather was good this morning, but got windy and cold later. No word from Art today, don't know if he made it to Fairbanks or not.

Sunday, July 27th. We had fried chicken, biscuits, cake, and all kinds of goodies today. It sure is nice to have Marcene and Jadene up here. They're helping to run the monitors. We got ice from the creek for the meat in the ice boxes. Art's still in Fairbanks.

Tuesday, July 29th. Marcene, Jadene and I went to Deering for mail, and Jadene drove the stick-shift pickup most of the way in and all the way back. I called our camper park and everything's okay down there. We have a new manager at the park, a woman named Shirley. I also called Wes for parts and everything's okay at the shop. The weather was warm today, the ground really thawed good at the pit. Art got back this evening and we flew over Old Glory. Dahlenbach is working on our claims, guess we'll have to talk to him. Jadene flew in her first small plane today with Art and me.

We did our washing today and I put all my clean clothes in a basket inside the kitchen. Shorty's little dog, Peanuts, was out in the mud - it had been raining and he had mud all over him. He came running in the kitchen and jumped right up in the middle of my basket of clean clothes. I felt like shooting that little fart. Duffy, the little Eskimo boy, is staying with us again, and I noticed that his little shorts were pretty dirty, so I conned him into letting me have them to put in the wash. After washing and bleaching them, I saw his little shorts folded up on top of a couple pairs of his pants and some shirts. I asked him how come he didn't put them on. He said, "Oh, I don't want to get them dirty again, they're nice and clean now."

Thursday, July 31st. Art is in Kotzebue, I suppose he's weathered in over there. We ran the monitors from 9 a.m. 'til 7 p.m. The color looks good today and we should have a good cleanup after this run. Shorty took Moto into Deering this evening and I took Marcene and Jadene up to Jack Hoogadorn's to show them through his cave. They sure enjoyed that. You could see the old burnt wood where the old creek channel was, and the lava overflowed and burned the wood as it came over it. Some of the logs were still to be seen along the walls, and there were frosty icicles all over inside there, it was just beautiful. He gave us a piece of petrefied palm tree from his cave. At one time that was the tropics.

We met a guy just as we came out of Jack's who had walked about 25 miles carrying a 50-pound pack and a shotgun. He was pooped. He said he had been on an archeological dig and got ticked off at his buddies. We took him down to our camp, fed him and fixed him up a bed. He seemed like a nice guy.

August 1st. Shorty worked about 6 hours today getting the old wore out D7 running, he thought we could use it down at Mile 16 and at Black's pit for stripping. After he got it running he ran it down to Mile 16 and it conked out on him, blew up, so we're gonna bury it. Always did want to bury a D7 anyway. I'm tired of looking at it, tired of seeing Shorty work on it. So, we'll bury it and someday somebody will find a D7 Cat under all this gravel and wonder what the heck happened. Bert says she's going to Kotzebue tomorrow, so I hope she stays, another alcoholic. Dahlenbach is working on our claims at Old Glory Creek, guess we'll have to go up and see him about moving on up the creek.

August 2nd. The weather was good today and the ground's thawing good. We're melting away about 35 feet of black muck overburden with the monitors at Black's pit. We brought Chuck Karmun over from Deering. It's good for Jadene to have someone her age for company here, and the Karmuns are real nice people.

Sunday, August 3rd. Art and Shorty went into Kotzebue this a.m., and I ran the giants all day. They didn't make it back today, weathered in, I suppose. Weather was bad and they didn't get parts, but they sent a message that they would be over tomorrow. I got real good color from the pit today. Marcene and the girls went up and got ice. I checked in Shorty's cabin and he had quite a few nuggets hidden there, but I just left them there. I try my derndest to keep the hands out of the riffles, but it's hard to do.

Tuesday, August 5th. I was able to buy for Art a pump, hoses, foot valves and sluice box from a Mr. Friend today for $1050.

It was brand new and worth about $1400, not figuring freight, so it wasn't a bad buy. Taylor Moto came back to work for us again today, he's good help, and Shorty was there to get us in the pickup. We ran the monitors about 3-1/2 hours this p.m. The weather is lousy, cloudy, cold and drizzly. Art is still in Kotzebue, said he'd be over as soon as weather permitted, but don't know about Art. We can make it just fine without him though. He's a fine pilot, we gotta hand that to him.

August 6th. I stripped at Mile 16 Bench, ran the giants from 8:30 a.m. 'til 9:30 p.m. The water was cold and didn't thaw too good today, but Mile 16 looks good for this year yet. Shorty worked about 8 hours today. Weather was good today, but cold. Got a message the big 6-inch pump would be in Kotzebue tomorrow. Art's still in Kotzebue.

August 7th. Ran the giants at Black's pit from 8:30 a.m. to 7:45 p.m. today. The sun was out, it was warm and the muck melted good. That's the 35 feet that we're washing down. We had good showing in panning. Shorty cleaned up the yard, picking up tools and junk. Shallabarger came over this p.m., brought hose for the pump, and Ray Snyder. I didn't get to listen to Muckluck or Tundra Telegram, but will start listening tomorrow. They are programs on radio that relay messages.

August 8th. The weather was beautiful today, and we ran the giants about 10 hours. The river sure is getting low, no rain, but that's good for us, the water is warm and it thaws better. Art came over today for about 2 hours and went back to Kotzebue. He brought over a welder with him, Charles, and he started to work at noon. Shorty's been working on the D4 Cat all day, and Ray started to work this a.m. I brought my dozer back to Black's pit this p.m.

August 9th. We finished with the giants today and will start sluicing tomorrow. Shorty got the D4 narrow track running. What a pile of junk! The boys, Ray, Taylor, and Chuck, the welder, moved pipe, etc., setting up for sluicing. Chuck spent about 2 hours working on my Case today. I drove into Deering this p.m., tried to call Marcene, but the phone wasn't working. I got mail and right on back.

Sunday, August 10th. Art's still in Kotzebue. We got the sluice box running about 9 a.m. at Black's pit. Had a fair showing at 9, and a good showing this evening, about like Mile 16. We used the narrow pad D4 to push tailings and it worked okay. My Case 450 sure has sick tracks, pins and bushings; they're shot and it's just a matter of time. As soon as we can get more sent over, we're gonna "switcheroo 'em", change them out. As of today, we have 15 drums of diesel left. Chuck is cutting a sluice box, and is getting ready to make up one for Old Glory Creek. Moto went to Deering in the pickup to get a tetanus shot, as he stuck a piece of cable in his arm yesterday, and we felt he should take precautions.

August 11th. Art came in last night at 11 p.m., and left today about 1:30 p.m. He said Steve Salinas, the businessman from Kotzebue, was very interested in going partners with us, and shipping his equipment over in September. Also, Art will be sending over the 6-inch high pressure navy pump, with the pipes and so forth, that Marcene bought from Studniks Construction in Anchorage. It should be getting into Deering tomorrow evening and that'll be nice. The weather was good today, kind of hot. The tracks, pins and bushings are completely shot on my 450, but I'm still running it, just biding my time until we can get more. The narrow pad D4 is working pretty good now, both steering clutches are working.

August 12th. Shorty got the track off of the narrow pad D4, and I let him put it back on himself. He ran it off, so I just let him put it back on, and I figured he'd be more careful with it from here on out. He finally got the pickup fixed and it runs good. We had no real problems today. Whoop-de-doo! I sent Shorty into Deering tonight to pick up the pump and pipe. I panned for gold from the old cleanup shack for the dredges from years ago. Got about a quarter of an ounce.

August 13th. Shallabarger flew in today, brought oxygen and groceries. My tracks on the Case 450 are just about gone; I've mentioned that before, but thank goodness the narrow track D4 is still running just in case my 450 completely walks out of its shoes. Chuck, the welder, is working on the big sluice box this p.m. Shorty is running the Cat, Moto and Ray are working the sluice box. Looks like we have about one-third of the material we had monitored down here in Black's pit run through the box.

August 14th. Our 26th anniversary today, Marcene's and mine. I called Marcene this a.m., and she's sending tracks, idlers and sprockets for my Case 450 by Weins. She's also sending an electric impact wrench so we can speed up the changing of the pads, and the bolts on the undercarriage of my dozer. Art came back to Utica (the mine). We ran the sluice box 6-1/2 hours today and had a pretty good showing.

August 15th. We ran the box again today and found a real nice nugget this noon. Art, Ray, Shorty, Moto and I are working the pit. Chuck's welding on the new sluice box, the big one.

Saturday, August 16th. The weather was good, but cool today. Art went into Kotzebue this a.m. and took Shorty's wife and daughter, Bert and Vicky, with him. Guess they're going back to Fairbanks. Later, I got a message from Art and he'll be back tomorrow. Also, Buck should fly the pump engine and pipe over to Deering tomorrow. We didn't go in for mail today, maybe someone will bring it up tomorrow. We ran the box 7 hours, looks okay, but we're just about out of material here. Shorty went prospecting this p.m. after supper, and the boys were panning tonight from the old cleanup shack. Mr. Dahlenbach came by this p.m. He broke his John Deere loader and wants us to weld it. We'll do it for him tomorrow morning.

August 17th. We're running the box again today at Black's pit. Art came in just after noon with a big batch of groceries. My poor tracks are just about gone on the Case 450. Charlie's still welding on the new sluice box, don't know where Art finds all these guys. Shorty and I went up to Old Glory Creek tonight, took the narrow pad D4 and the 4x4. We got the dam finished at 12:30; I was holding the lantern while Shorty ran the Cat. The cabin was in good shape and the heater worked fine. We didn't have covers, so just turned up the heater and slept in our clothes on the cots. Beats the tent.

August 18th. Weather was good today. Art flew over Old Glory this a.m. to check on us. We tried to start the John Deere backhoe, but will have to carry up another battery. It looks real good up here. Shorty and I went on back to the Utica camp. Art and the boys were working the monitors at Black's pit. The sluice box ran about 3-1/2 hours today. Weins was supposed to come over this p.m., but cancelled out. I guess Buck will bring the engine over tomorrow. Art went back to Kotzebue this p.m., Shorty and I went to Deering tonight. I finally got through to Marcene, it was nice to talk to her and Peanut.

August 19th. Chuck, Moto and Ray got drunk last night. They found the booze Art brought over earlier in the grease shack where I had it hid. When Shorty and I got back from Deering about 11:30 p.m., the boys were all setting around the table drinking Tang. They said, "Boy, we can make betta OK Tang dan Shorty." I asked Moto, "Moto, how in the world did you find that booze?" He said, "Found it accidentally." I said, "You don't accidentally go looking for work, and the only thing in that grease shack would be concerning work." Anyway, they kept setting there playing cards, they were playing "Eskimo Poker". They'd put a card, face out, right on their forehead, and hold it up there with their hand. They could see everybody else's card but their own. Then they'd bet that their card was better than everybody else's. In a way it was kind of comical and funny, but at the time, the bunks where we were sleeping were in the back of the cook shack there, and I finally asked them to go to bed about 12:30 because we had to get up in the morning and go to work. But they just kept setting there, so Shorty and I went over to Marcene's and my cabin. We slept over there and got up about 6 o'oclock in the morning, came back over, and 2 of them were still going. One was passed out on a bunk, but the other 2 were still talking and mixing Tang and vodka. So I told them, "Just get all your stuff and put it in your duffel bags, Shorty's taking you to Deering."

They loaded up, and unbeknownst to me they had gotten several bottles of Art's vodka out of the case in the grease shack. I never thought to check their baggage. We poured water on the one sleeping Eskimo to get him awake and up and going, and finally got his bag all packed, and Shorty took them to Deering. They got several of the people in Deering drunk because they had all that vodka with them, but we didn't realize it. Then they chartered Shallabarger's plane, charged it to Art and me, and went into Kotzebue. Of course, the mayor and some of the people around Deering got a little ticked off at us in camp for furnishing those guys with booze. The natives in Deering are very nice people, and most won't drink at all.

August 20th. The weather was nice today. Shorty and I ran the sluice box about 3 hours, and Art came in from Kotzebue and helped finish the cleanup. We got quite a bit of gold, about 10 to 12 pounds. Kind of nice not to have the "squirrels" around, and when I say "squirrels", I'm talking about the 2-legged ones. You have to tell them everything to do, and so forth, but actually, they're nice guys, they're just like little kids at times. Marcene sent a message today that the tracks were in for my Case 450. Buck brought them over to Deering this p.m., and we'll pick them up in the morning. She ordered wide pads, they sent narrow ones, but that's okay.

August 21st. Art left for Kotzebue this a.m., and Shorty and I went to Deering to pick up pipe, the dozer tracks, and etc. I called Marcene and also Wes Hamrick, and everything is okay in Anchorage. We came on back and started work on the dozer. We finished panning and got about 1-1/2 to 2 pounds of gold in this final cleanup. We also got between 9 and 10 pounds on the Old Glory cleanup up above. Shorty and I went up and got ice in the willows near the Pinnell River. There's lots of ice left yet, maybe enough to last 'til freeze-up. Shallabarger brought over a drunk native Eskimo, and some oil and etc., this p.m. Art sent him over to do some welding on the sluice box. Boy, oh boy! He said he'd be sober by tomorrow a.m. and everything'd be alright. I heard "Kiana Kid" this evening on the radio, sure is nice to hear requests for it. That's a record that I recorded, and it's about a guy at Kiana by the name of Vince Shirk. It's all about a snow machine racer up north. Also many other racers and other races. A hit in Alaska.

It's August 22th, Friday, and the weather's good today. Art's still in Kotzebue. We're working on my dozer today, got one track back on and just about ready to go on with the other, and the rollers should come in tomorrow. Shallabarger came by and dropped off filters, Bars-leak. The welder that Art sent over worked today and looks to be a pretty good welder. He's welding on my Case and the sluice box. I went into Deering and called Marcene. I picked up

Reggie Barr and took him back to camp. He went to work at 3:30 p.m.

August 23rd. The weather's nice today. We're working on my dozer still, putting new pads and rails on. Art came back over today and brought the rollers for my dozer, also got my impact wrench so that we can speed up putting the pad bolts in. Looks like we'll finish it by noon tomorrow, I hope. The new sluice box is getting a little closer to being. We got a bull moose this p.m., sure was tired when we got him out and loaded. I drove into Deering and got mail, and picked up 6 drums of fuel and gas. I talked to Dahlenbach and he said he's giving up on Old Glory Creek. Ed Barr gave me a real nice salmon today, sure was nice of him. Tried to call Marcene, but no answer.

Sunday, August 24th. We finished with my dozer this p.m., and got the sluice box and hopper moved to Mile 16. Art's in camp today and the welder's working on the new sluice box.

August 25th. It rained today, the weather was just miserable. Art went to Kotzebue this p.m. and took the welder back with him. The welder was here 5 days and that's caboose for him. We got the new pump going and set up, except putting pipe together and about 1 hour welding. It runs real good. I built a ramp for the pump and pipe, and we should get the sluice box going tomorrow around noontime. I dug across the road and lowered the water in the pond at Mile 16, and spent most of the day stripping.

August 26th. It rained again today, blowing rain, blowing sideways. We're stripping at Mile 16 and building a ramp for the sluice box. Art and I tested ground with the little Denver panner and it looks good. (A Denver panner is a trommel that helps clean gold from dirt, etc.) Shorty and Reggie put the new 6-inch pump together. Oh, yes, I got stuck good this p.m. With new tracks and cutting edges on my dozer, it didn't know how to act. Neither did I, so I guess everyone's been stuck at least once in their lifetime. Art and I drove into Deering tonight and I got through to Marcene. Nice talking to her. We brought back 5 drums of fuel.

August 27th. The weather was kind of icky today, cloudy and cool. Art's in Kotzebue and sent a message that we bought a D7 Cat from B & R Barge and Tug with less than 100 hours on it. They'll bring it over on a barge the 13th of September. We got the sluice box and hopper set up and I pushed up a stockpile of material. We had just enough 6-inch pipe for the new pump. Sure are in good ground here, but awful rocky.

This just wasn't my day. The impeller on the pump that we bought from Studniks was cracked around the shaft, but we think we may fix it enough to run 'til we get a new one. We took it down to an old machine shop at camp, got all the pieces and put them together. We took a bronze bushing and it fit right over the outside.

We squeezed them all together, filled in the cracks and brazed it up, and got the keyway all filed down and everything. So, I think it'll hold up for awhile. Shorty and I worked 'til 9:45 p.m. on the pump. I spent about 2 hours just filing that keyway, getting it perfect inside that impeller. I got a message from Marcene that everything went good with her operation. I can sleep okay now knowing Marcene is okay, and also, knowing that we'll be able to run the pump tomorrow.

August 28th. Art Fields is still in Kotzebue and no word from him today. Our pump is fixed and runs beautiful. The weather's good today, partly cloudy. A Fish & Wildlife guy, Scott Brundy, came over from Fairbanks, and we're gonna have to get permits this winter. Everything's okay as far as right now is concerned at Utica, the mining here at Mile 16 and Black's pit. Reggie Barr finished today. He's lazy, just about quit work when he got his belly full, then started thinking about going to Deering. They're usually good for about one week, maybe. We visited with Jack Hoogadorn this p.m., he's sure a nice guy.

August 29th. It rained about all day today. Shorty and I were working the sluice box at Mile 16, but we didn't have quite enough water today. We'll tie in the 4-inch pump tomorrow. We didn't run much yardage through today, and we were just getting into good gold at quitting time. I tore out part of the dam by Black's that the Fish & Wildlife guy asked me to do until after the salmon run is over. Art's still in Kotzebue, I guess, and no message from anyone today. Shorty's little dog, Peanuts, came in the kitchen this p.m. and went under my bunk and crawled up in my freshly washed clothes. He was all wet and muddy and had grease on him. He messed up 3 pair of shorts, 4 undershirts and 2 pair of socks. Shorty and I worked on material by the old shack from about 7 o'clock 'til 8:30, not too good tonight.

Saturday, August 30th. Art's in Kotzebue and no word from him. The weather was nice today and I took the dozer back to Mile 16. Shorty didn't feel good this a.m., back hurting, and I worked the sluice box 'til 10:45. I got good color in the first 3 riffles, think we'll have a good cleanup here. I sure would like to work Old Glory. Maybe we can get Herbie Karmun to go up with Shorty and work out something up there. I called Marcene tonight, she's home from the hospital and feeling okay. Shorty's arms and back are sure bothering him, so he may have to go into Anchorage.

August 31st. The weather's pretty good today. Shorty and I ran the sluice box at Mile 16 about 4-1/2 hours today. Looks like we have about 2 weeks, or more, work left at Mile 16. I'll be glad to get the new D7 that we're getting from B & R, so we can strip ground for next summer. Art's still in Kotzebue, no word from him, nothing. We're out of bread, eggs, and gloves, but we have enough beans, moose meat, and other goods to keep us going. We sure could use one other guy on the sluice box, and 2 guys up at Old Glory Creek. When I need people I don't have them around.

September 1st. Weather's cloudy and chilly today. Art's still in Kotzebue and no word from him. Shorty was feeling bad and I let him sleep in this a.m. He went to work at 2 p.m. 'til six. The sluice box ran 6 hours today, we're in real good pay, quite a few nuggets in the front riffles. We're having to run the 3-inch pump together with the 6-inch pump in order to have enough water. My Case 450 runs great and we had no problems today. We sure need some help though, but if we don't get any in the next 2 weeks it'll be too late to get people over here before freeze-up.

Wednesday, September 3rd. We had our first ice today. The pumps froze up, caught us with our pants down. Art, Shorty and I worked Mile 16, and the color's real good. We ran the sluice box 6 hours. Woody, Art's mechanic, came over with him and is going to help out for a few days. A guy was supposed to fly Art's plane over today, but didn't show. Art and I went up to Old Glory tonight and drained water out of the narrow pad D4 dozer. The new D7 will be over on B & R Tug this week.

September 4th. The weather was lousy today. We worked the sluice box for 5-1/2 hours and got real good color and nuggets in the 2 front riffles. We could have worked longer, but it just rained so hard we had to quit at 2:30. Art and Shorty flew to Kotzebue this p.m. with Shallabarger. Art went in to get his plane, and Shorty was going to fly home to Anchorage, said he was going to see a chiropractor and would be back this weekend. Don't know. Marcene gave Shorty $200 cash tonight. Isaac Kinsley came over today to go to work at noon on the sluice box. He's quite a little guy. His marbles aren't in one circle.

September 5th. Art's in Kotzebue today and no message from him, guess he's weathered in. It rained most all day, just plain miserable out. We ran the sluice box 8 hours today and had real good showing, got about 4 ounces of big stuff. But Woody, the mechanic, is done in, he can't take it, so he's going back to Kotzebue tomorrow. Shorty's in Anchorage, I guess. I must be tough; all these guys just come and go, and I'm still here, keep plodding along each day. Shorty couldn't find his wife, so he borrowed our company pickup and went to a massage parlor. Marcene told him it looked bad, as our company logo was on the truck, but he said it was okay because he parked in back.

September 6th. First snow this morning, and ice. The showing was good at the sluice box, ran it about an hour and a half this a.m. Marcene came in to Deering today, sure glad to see her. Art and Shorty came back to camp from Kotzebue with Leon Shallabarger's plane. Woody, the mechanic, went home, and good riddance. He was a nice guy, and helped around the kitchen, etc., but he couldn't do anything else right. Marcene bought Shorty's ticket to Deering and back, $220.51.

Sunday, September 7th. Old Isaac had been picking rocks out of the hopper, and he was slinging the rocks right down the side of the hopper. So I told him to "put a little more 'oompf' into it, and swing 'em out a ways to where I could get the dozer in there and push the rocks away." They were those kind of square rocks, about 2 or 3 inches thick and pretty heavy. Anyway, he would wring his gloves out everytime after he'd reach down in there to pick one out. His gloves would get wet again, and he'd wring them out again, and he'd do that process over, and over, and over.

A little bit later I had made 3 or 4 more passes, and I saw that the sluice box had gotten plugged up. I had a couple of Eskimos working on the sluice box, and invariably, every time it gets plugged up they keep raking stuff down, and it just keeps plugging worse. I bailed off of the dozer, ran down to the lower end, and started releasing the rocks, letting things clear out and clean out. When I got all through there I walked back up and set the shovel down by the rockpile up by the hopper. When I started to turn around, Isaac was still throwing rocks out of the hopper and he caught me right on the jaw. I went down to my knees, saw stars and everything, and I thought for a split second I was still in the boxing ring. I was light heavyweight with the 82nd Airborne at one time. That evening, when I went to eat, of course I couldn't. You can't eat anything with a broke jaw, you just have to drink fluids and stuff. Isaac said, "If I'd a had a little bigger rock, I'd of knocked old Jimmy out." I couldn't even laugh though, it really hurt.

We're getting ready to go to Old Glory Creek. Art is in camp today and he's working. Taylor Moto went back to work today at noon and worked 5 hours. There's snow on Asses' Ears Peak (between here and Nome) today. We had real good showing in the riffles.

September 8th. It rained most of the day. Art's in camp. We went up to Old Glory today and I got Shorty and Moto started sluicing. It looks good, we got the pit all lined out. I took my Case 450 up and brought it back to camp, and Art drove on back to camp in the old 4x4 army rig. Marcene is doing the cooking. A Fish & Wildlife guy, Paul, came by and is spending the night with us. He brought his big white dog over with him, it was a real nice dog, a clean one. The guy's gonna cruise the river, fly over in his plane, and count the fish for Fish & Wildlife. He said there are more fish in the river during mining than before. Stirring up the water gives the fish something to eat.

September 9th. Art went back to Kotdzebue today with Shallabarger, and Paul, the biologist with Fish & Wildlife, left today to go back to Nome. We got Isaac believing if he eats hot peppers he'll not have colds, so he's eating 2 jalapeno peppers each meal. He eats them and just sweats like all gitout. After Isaac finished the jar, I asked him, "Hey, Isaac, how's your cold?" He said, "Cold alright, but hot on de udder end."

September 10th. Art came back to camp and brought Ray Snyder this p.m. We ran the sluice box 'til about 5 p.m. Art went to Deering and called Forrester Aviation in Nome to pick us up tomorrow morning. Marcene and I went up to Old Glory and got Shorty. He came back to camp and picked up stuff, and Ray and Isaac. We sure had trouble starting the old International pump motor this morning. It was just too cold, I guess, for it's getting to be that time of the year.

September 11th. Forrester Aviation came by to pick us up this morning. Shorty and Isaac, Ray and Taylor Moto were working at Old Glory Creek. We had a bunch of gold in camp and I didn't know quite what to do with it. We didn't want to take it with us on the plane, so, again we buried it and made a map to carry in my billfold. In case the plane went down, at least the gold wouldn't be lost forever. We had about a quart fruit jar and 2 pint fruit jars full. We got into Nome about 1 p.m., got most of our running around done today. We went out to Ron Ingstrom's mine, but didn't get to see him. That's the dredge that he's running out east of Nome. Jim West let us have a new car to get around, no charge. Sure was nice of him. We went out for dinner and really enjoyed it here in Nome.

September 12th. Art called and woke us up this morning, the dirty dog. The weather's bad today, almost didn't get to go back to camp. Forresters flew us back though, and I dropped Shorty a note to bring Ray and Isaac down, and he did. The weather was nice in camp and it sure was good to be back. Art was going on to Anchorage today.

September 13th. Art is still in Anchorage. We ran the sluice box about 8 hours today at Mile 16 and had a pretty good showing. Weather was rainy all day. Marcene and I went to Deering to check on the barge tonight, to see if it came in, but it didn't. No word on the Tundra Telegram.

Sunday, September 14th. Shorty came down to Mile 16 about 5 o'clock this evening. He got the D4 stuck up at Old Glory Creek, so we'll have to take up another Cat tomorrow and pull him out. Maybe the D7 will get in tonight on the barge, and Shorty and Taylor can go in tomorrow morning and pick it up. We also have a load of fuel coming in. Marcene worked at the sluice box this afternoon. Isaac is ready to go to town, he's got his belly full and enough made for one night at the Ponderosa Club in Kotzebue. We had a nice visit tonight with Mr. Jack Hoogadorn, the miner up the creek from us. He's been here all of his life, just about, ever since he was a little kid 8 years old.

September 15th. Art is in Anchorage or Fairbanks, one of the two. I think we'll shut down tomorrow and start getting things put away. Shorty and the crew up at Old Glory Creek can clean out the box and bring concentrates down in buckets.

September 16th. No word from Art yet. Marcene, Ray and I started cleanup at Mile 16 and got about 8 or 9 pounds of nice gold, quite a few big nuggets. Then Ray and I finished staking this p.m. I staked 2 more claims down by the old dredge, about Mile 15. I think Parker, the previous miner, probably wouldn't have stripped it if it hadn't been good ground. We heard that our D7 and fuel was in Deering, but Shorty, Moto, and Isaac aren't back from Old Glory Creek yet, at 7:15 p.m. Something must have happened to them, they must have had some kind of trouble. I guess we should go out and check on them.

September 17th. Art and Marie came back into camp today and Isaac went back to Kotzebue. Art wanted to know why I was buckling everything up. He thought it was early 'til it snowed again the next morning. We finished cleanup this evening and not too shabby, looked good. Then we just sat around and really enjoyed the evening.

September 18th. About 3 inches of snow this a.m., looks like winter is upon us. We hauled fuel from Deering, and our D7 sure is a good buy, should make us good money next year. We're getting things ready for winter, we'll be leaving tomorrow about noon. Marie's been real nice and everything's okay.

We're going to buy Taylor Moto a ticket to Lawton, Oklahoma, round trip, and give him $100 to spend. He told us, "You know, I never can get out to see my sister down in Oklahoma. I've been trying for 10 years, but I can only make it as far as the bars in Kotzebue, or maybe one time I did make it to Nome." And he got in the bars there. So, anyway, what we're gonna do is buy him a non-refundable round trip ticket to Lawton, and then just as he gets on the plane in Anchorage we're going to hand him $100.

September 19. We left camp today. Shallabarger sent three 206s over to get us out, groceries, people, etc. It was storming at Utica and I was surprised that Leon got in. We'd sent most all our groceries out to Kotzebue on the first plane, and were setting around with just a little chunk of moose meat and some pancake mix to eat. We heard Leon late in the afternoon, about 3:30 or 4 o'clock. He found a little opening in the clouds and dropped down through the clouds and snow. He took us out and into Kotzebue, so everything was fine, but it sure was cold in the plane, no heater. Shorty teased him, saying he'd build a fire in the back, but he didn't.

Monday, September 22nd. I gave Shorty a check for $219 today. That was his share of the gold that we'd panned down by the old cleanup shack there in Utica in our spare time.

September 23rd. I met Hugh Chatham at the airport this morning and he was real nice, it's good to see him again. He's up for a hunting trip with Art. I'm still cleaning gold, should be finished this weekend.

September 24th. I paid Shorty $1000 today and will pay him the rest of his wages in gold as he wishes. We picked Taylor Moto up at the airport at 1:30 a.m., and took him out to our home on Campbell Lake, a beautiful tri-level. We went downstairs to the bar, and then showed him his bedroom. He kept looking at the bottles and said, "Jimmy, could I have just one drink?" I said, "Yeah, you can have one drink, and then you go to bed." So he poured himself about half a glass and downed it, then said, "Now I'm ready for bed. Where's the bed?" He spent the rest of the night with us and we got him to the airport this morning. He went on to Oklahoma and should be there for about 2 weeks.

Sunday, September 28th. Hugh, his boy, Stan, and Art came out this morning and we weighed out gold. Marcene went out and picked up a bucket of Kentucky Fried Chicken for lunch. I was surprised, there was no problem at all. Hugh took one half of the gold with him and left my half, approximately 9 pounds. We took Hugh and Stan back to the Holiday Inn, in Anchorage, and dropped Art off at the Gaslight Bar. Marcene and I came on home after having a couple of drinks.

September 29th. I took Hugh and Stan to the airport, and picked Art up at 2 p.m. We went to the American Motors dealer and got Art's check back, then went over to Northwest Ford and got him 2 new cars for $4400 each. They're for his cab service in Kotzebue. My shop's doing pretty good today, so everything's fine. Art had talked to the banker in Kotzebue today, and we only got $131 per ounce for the gold that we sold up there. That's gold that we sold for supplies, fuel, and so forth.

September 30th. There were quite a few people around town today. Art, Marcene and I went out tonight and went all over, we made the rounds. Art had some gold in a bank, and they absconded with his coarse stuff. They really did him a job, and did him around. Anyway, Art is not accepting his fine gold until they get something straightened out, and I think he's gonna sue the bank, or something like that. So, I went ahead and gave Art a half pound of gold for his dentist. Art missed his plane and will have to catch Weins in the morning. Note: Art never followed through on his missing gold. The banker was no longer there anyway.

Wednesday, October 15th. Got all settled up with Shorty today. He's happy with everything, so that makes us even for the season.

Taylor Moto got back from Oklahoma, and, boy, was he ever tickled. He called me up, wanted me to come by and pick him up at the airport. He started out telling me all about his trip, and he was excited. His sister was so happy to see him, and he was so glad to see her. He said, "Jimmy, I got back with part of my money. Gee whiz! I've still got $38 left." And I said, "Well, my goodness, that's good for you. You know, you really watched your money down there." He said, "My sister wouldn't let me spend anything, but I spent for a pair of cowboy boots, and she bought me a new hat." So he had his cowboy hat and his cowboy boots on, and he was happy. After congratulating him, and hauling him around town a bit, I took him back out to the airport. He caught the airplane and away he went, on his way back to Deering. I'd told him, "That just goes to show you, Taylor, if you put your mind to something, you can really do it."

1976

Wednesday, June 16th. We're rushing around, getting things in order to take off for the mine today. We caught the plane and went to Kotzebue, and spent the night. The weather was real nice.

June 17th. We went over to Utica this morning, Art, Marie, and her grandson, Chipper, with Shallabarger. Art went back this p.m. with Shallabarger and flew his Piper Cub back over. I got my dozer going and went down by Black's, and fixed the road to Deering from the mine. It was all washed out.

June 18th. Art and Marie went into Deering. I fixed the 6-inch pump we got from Studnik Brothers last year, put on the new mag and leveled up shims. Sure runs good. Art and I started working on the D7 Cat we got from B & R Barge and Tug, looks like about 2 days work, or better. When we got it, it had a picker crane mounted on it, and it had been setting on it for all those years, with no hours on it. They never did use the crane. It was a little awkward, so we just took it off. Sure tired tonight.

Saturday, June 19th. It's cloudy out today. Art and I worked on the D7 Cat just about all day, freed up the track adjusters, got the crane off, and everything. Got it running okay, and boy, it's purring like a little kitten. We should get the sluice box working tomorrow, at least get it set up. My back hasn't accepted the mine yet, lots of bending and stooping, working on equipment. Herbie Karmun brought 3 boxes and a tire for the old army 4-by rig up to camp for us. Sure was nice of him. Ray Snyder came over today, flew Weins to Deering, and then came on up here with Herbie. He's gonna be working for us at the mine. I went to Deering this p.m. and called home. Everything is fine at home, and Wes Hamrick is coming up Tuesday. Taylor Moto came to work this evening, he's good help and a nice guy, we get along fine with Taylor. We got Ray, Taylor, Art and Marie, and myself in camp. Ten p.m. and I'm tired and sleepy, gonna go to bed.

Monday, June 21st. This was our first day of sluicing. We got the sluice box all hooked up and ran about 45 minutes, but not much show, very small color. It rained most of the morning, and Art flew into Kotzebue.

June 22nd. Wes came in with Art today. We ran the sluice box at Mile 16 about 6-1/2 hours. The equipment that we're running here right at the present time is: a D7 Cat with less than 100 hours on it, a Case 450 dozer in good shape, a 6-inch pump, one of those navy high pressure pumps that is a good one, and two D4 Cats. We've also got a pickup.

June 23rd. Everything went pretty good today. The weather was good, we ran the sluice box 7-1/2 hours and had a good showing. Material is getting a little scarce because of permafrost here, we need to open up some more ground. I went to Deering and called Marcene. Shorty's coming up Saturday, I guess.

June 24th. Art flew Ray into Kotzebue this a.m., his stomach was hurting, and he got back about 1:30. The weather was kind of icky today. We ran the box 7 hours and had pretty good showing in the riffles. We're just about out of material at Mile 16, so looks like we're gonna have to go up and do some monitoring at Black's pit, or do some more stripping here. Wes is going back Saturday, I guess, but don't know for sure. He doesn't really care all that much for this camp life, and working out here at the mine is not his cup of tea.

June 25th. The gold looks good in the riffles today. We have close to a pound of nuggets already, just from picking the front riffles. Wes, Taylor Moto and Chipper went to Deering tonight for a movie.

Saturday, June 26th. Shorty got in today, and Wes left for Anchorage, to tend the shop back there. The weather was fine today and we had no problems at all. We stripped at Mile 16. Moto told me tonight that he was going to Deering to work on his boat. That's about right, he's been here a week tomorrow. That's the way it is up here with the Eskimos. They just come up and let you know they're leaving, or they're looking for an airplane. Every time one lands they want to snag a ride and go back.

Monday, June 28th. Shorty and I ran the sluice box 6-1/2 hours today and got good showing. Art's running the D7, stripping at Mile 16, and started stripping by the dredge. With Art, you gotta watch him if he's around the sluice box. He's a nice guy and a heck of a pilot, but boy, when he gets on that D7 if there's something to run into, he bumps it. Or, if there's a mudhole, he'll stick it. But anyway, he tries, and does the best he can with it. Everything's running fine today. The weather was good, but a cold wind was blowing, and at 10 p.m., it's starting to rain.

June 29th. The weather was pretty nice today. Art ran the D7, stripping at the dredge and Mile 16. Then he went to Deering this p.m. and took Marie and the kids with him. Shorty and I washed, and the washing machine worked good. Looks like we'll have a better year this year than last. The D7 really helps. Don't know how we ever did as good as we did before, with what we had to do it with. The sluice box is working real good, got just the right amount of water flow.

June 30th. The weather was icky and cloudy, rained a bit, then it snowed this p.m. We had a good showing in the sluice bx, not as good as when we first started Mile 16, but still good. A State Highway guy came by today from Nome. He needs a rubber-tired loader for a little roadwork, but we don't have a loader. It we did we'd be happy. We do have the backhoe with a loader on it, but it's broke down. We decided that we would get it fixed for him, get the parts and everything, and put it back in shape. That way, they can utilize it.

July 1st. It snowed today. Art flew to Kotzebue this a.m. to get Bob. He's a guy that was an archeologist. He told us someone had shot a hole through the fuel tank in their Coleman stove, and they ran out of fuel and different things, so they had a little pow-wow. He walked out about 29 miles, with a pack on his back, and come in to Jack Hoogadorn's. He's coming to work for us. Leon's 206 came after Marie and the 2 girls this p.m. She was complaining about her neck, and don't know if she'll be back. Everything's running good except Art's plane is acting up a bit. It's been acting up ever since it was new.

July 2nd. The weather is lousy today, snow, cold, and rain. The riffles in the sluice box didn't look as good as they have in the past. We're getting the pit at Mile 16 pretty well worked out for right now. Everything's running pretty good. No word today from Kotzebue or Anchorage. Marcene should be in tomorrow. Jack Hoogadorn came by today in his 1936 Ford stake bed truck with the old crank hanging out of the front, and didn't even stop. He's a real nice guy though. He's been up here in this country for about 60 years.

Saturday, July 3rd. Shorty and I ran the box today about 4 hours, and Shorty stockpiled with the D7 at Mile 16. Everything was running good, but it rained about all day and was cold out. Marcene and Jadene came in with Shallabarger today and I was sure glad to see them. I sent 3 drums back to Kotzebue with Terry, in Leon's plane, the 206. Art's still in Kotzebue with his Super Cub, trying to find out what's wrong with it and get it fixed. It keeps cutting out on one side. Marcene gave Art some money today. Shorty and Bob drove into Deering tonight. Bob, the archeologist, ate 6 eggs for breakfast, 9 pancakes, and about a loaf of bread.

July 4th. We kind of slept in today and took most of the day off. We did run the sluice box about 3 hours. Looks like we don't have much left at Mile 16 right now to run through the box 'til we get more material stockpiled, and overburden pushed. Total sluicing time to date - 70 hours and 45 minutes. The weather today was fair, at least it's not snowing. Bob is leaving Tuesday. He's good help, we call him the "garbage disposal" 'cause he eats so much. Art sent a message he'd be over tomorrow, and Marie's friends sent over groceries. Oh boy, we got plane flights and all kinds of things coming today.

Jack Hoogadorn stopped by and we had a nice visit. Jack told me that he came into this country with his dad, walked in from Nome. His dad first came over in 1900. He pulled a little steam boiler on a sled 179 miles from Nome over to here. He did real good, sinking a shaft and burning wood in his little steam boiler, thawing the ground and bringing the muck up out of the ground in buckets. He had a good deal going, and he built a big barn and a nice log home. He hauled the logs over from the Candle River in the winter, with a team and Russian sled. He was doing real good and decided to invest in a dredge. He bought one of those dredges with a big bucket chain on it, and gave $24,000 for that dredge back then, in the early 1900's. That dredge was the downfall of Mr. Hoogadorn. Jack has been mining ever since, and he's done quite well. He's got several different claims around and so forth.

Tuesday, July 6th. The weather was good today for a change. Shorty and I stripped all day, Shorty on the D7, and I with my Case 450. Art got back this afternoon, and he brought the Kotzebue Chief of Police, his wife and kids, with him. Yessir, the Chief of Police, Auggie Nelson, took his vacation and came over to see us here at the mine. Art said he was going back to Kotzebue for a track wrench, but I don't know what the track wrench is for. He flew back to Kotzebue this p.m.

July 7th. Shorty and I ran Cats until noon, stripping at Black's pit, then moved back to Mile 16 and got ready for sluicing. We stockpiled enough for today and tomorrow. The Kotzebue Chief of Police, and all his clan, came over with Art yesterday, and he's riding around in our pickup. He likes coffee, and he likes to ride around, and he likes to carry his gun on his hip. Got a message on the radio that Art would be over tomorrow.

Later, in the evening, Marcene, Jadene and I went up to the house on the hill that Jack Hoogadorn bought. He's going to move it off, and I offered that Shorty and I would come up and give him a hand. He said, "No, Mr. Simpson, I don't like to hire people, because if someone ever got hurt and they were working for me, I couldn't get over it. That way, if I get hurt, there's no problem." Anyway, that's the way Jack is. He's a nice guy who's worked all alone all his life, and he'd like to continue working that way.

July 8th. The weather today is real nice. We ran the sluice box 8-1/2 hours, but not too good showing in the riffles. Art got back from Kotzebue today. He brought Ray Snyder over, and took Auggie Nelson and his wife back into Kotzebue. How he did it, I don't know, but Art got the new D7 off the track this p.m. He stayed for supper and then flew back to Kotzebue.

July 9th. Today Art got in about 3:30 p.m., brought 2 cans of hydraulic oil with him, worked about an hour and a half at the mine, and left back for Kotzebue about 7. I broke the fan belt on my 450 today and Art is to get one in Kotzebue. Ray is working with us and he's a pretty good hand. Shorty and I went fishing and caught some graylings this evening, Marcene and Jadene are cooking them. The little squirrels around camp are getting tame now that the kids are gone. We feed them and talk to them. We were running big rocks today and I'm tired.

Saturday, July 10th. It's beautiful out today. We ran the sluice box about 4 hours, and we'll clean up tomorrow. Art got in from Kotzebue this afternoon and brought 30 gallons of gas, and the fan belt for my dozer. Shorty got it on and going by 2:30. Art and I went flying and spotted a moose, Marcene and Vicky went to Deering to meet the plane and get mail. Bert and Vicky didn't show today. Shorty and Ray took the pickup into Deering tonight.

July 11th. The weather's beautiful. Shorty made 3 trips into Deering last night hauling fuel up in the old 4-by G.I. truck. He was up all night. He took a rubber glove, punched a hole in it and made a nipple for a beer bottle, and fed his girlfriend's baby milk. What a character! Art was in camp today and stripped most of the day. I broke a hose on my dozer this a.m., but got it going okay. It's sure easier for me to keep the sluice box going with it. We did a bit of panning in the pit and it still looks good, so maybe we'll run the sluice box a bit longer before we clean up. Art flew back to Kotzebue this evening. I don't know what for, but he did. Jadene spent the night with the Karmuns and they brought her up to camp this p.m.

July 12th. The weather's beautiful again today, sunny and hot. We ran the sluice box 6-1/2 hours today. We're still in pretty good ground and the equipment is all working real good. Art's in Kotzebue again. We got a message that he would be over tomorrow with Bert and Vicky, that's Shorty's wife and daughter. The squirrels are getting real tame now, they'll eat out of your hand and crawl up on your shoulder, and so forth. We have a bird that we call Jack, a seagull, and he comes wanting to eat 3 times a day. He'll come in the morning and squawk until we feed him. If we happen to be down at the mine working at noontime, he'll come down there. In the evening he'll come looking for us. He has a mate that never comes up to camp. But old Jack, he'll set right on the pickup hood and squawk until we feed him.

Jadene and Marcene washed today. Shorty had used the washing machine one day that I wasn't with him, and he washed his coveralls. I think Marcene found about 6 or 7 nuggets in the bottom of the washing machine when she got ready to clean it out, so all indications point to Shorty.

July 13th. Ran the sluice box a little bit today. We tested the pit and the gold is kind of spotty, so looks like we'll clean up as soon as Art gets back. Shorty and I stripped by the dredge this afternoon. Marcene and Jadene went to Deering for the mail. The pickup was running a little warm, so I shut it off and was looking for a can to fill up the radiator. I looked under the seat of the pickup for a tobacco can, and unbeknownst to me, Shorty had dumped the tobacco out and put some gold that he had panned out of our riffles in the can. Thinking the can had rocks and sand in it, I dumped it. The gold has got lava coating on it, so the nuggets do actually look like rocks, in fact, until you feel them and look at them real close. So, anyway, as I started to throw the material out, Shorty hollered at me and said, "No, there's gold in there." But I'd already slung it out, and I said to him, "How do you know there's gold in there?" He said, "Well, I checked the riffles last night, and that's what I got out of them." I said, "What are you doing checking our riffles in the sluice box?" But, anyway, I took the dozer and shoved all that material back over into the pit, and shoved it up the ramp. I guess we got a small percentage of the gold back.

Art's still in Kotzebue, guess he's weathered in over there.

July 14th. It rained most of the day and we didn't run the sluice box. Shorty and I built a dam. We did some stripping to get down and get samples, so we'll know if the ground is rich enough to take off 14 feet of permafrost so we can mine the material underneath. We fixed the suction for the big 10-inch International pump. Ray watched the pump at the dredge. We're going to clean up tomorrow if the weather's good, we do need sunlight for a cleanup. Art's still in Kotzebue, no word from him.

July 15th. The weather was beautiful today. We had a cleanup at Mile 16, and got about 6 pounds of gold, with 3 and a half pounds of nuggets. That makes about 9 and a half pounds of gold to date. Total hours on sluice box was 112, for 114 ounces of gold. We're getting ready to run the giants at Black's pit and start washing the 35-foot overburden down that we've got to take off. Art came in this p.m. He said that Shorty's wife, Bert, called him for $100 and he sent it. Leon Shallabarger's plane brought over 20 gallons avgas and fifteen 5-gallon cans of regular gas. Marcene and Jadene left this p.m. with Shallabarger, and Marcene is paying for today's trip.

July 16th. The weather's fair today. Art was here all day, and we went up to Jack Hoogadorn's this a.m., got stuck on the way up. We walked on up and Jack gave us a hand and pulled us out. We were right by the Pinnell River, about 5 miles up. Shorty and Ray worked on the International pump engine and we finally got it going by 6:30 p.m. We may have to buy a battery for the old International pump. Guess we'll start getting set up tomorrow, set up the pipe and giants. Ray is really getting ready for Kotzebue. He keeps looking up at the airplanes as they go over, so he's ready to go. Ray was out of cigarettes and I gave him a carton. Shorty told everyone that he had quit cigarettes, but he bums them off Ray all the time. He laughs and says, "I'll smoke anything that's free." The squirrels are real tame here now, but as soon as kids come around, guess they'll get scared off again. Art is trying to get Shorty to go into Deering tonight and order a batch of groceries, etc., and have Shallabarger bring Bert and Vicky and Marie over. Charter after charter after charter, just keeps on being chartered. $$$

Saturday, July 17th. We set up the giants at Black's pit and got started running one giant about 5:30. I ran it until 9:30 and the bearing went out of the pump. We'll tear it down tomorrow. I guess we can't complain about the old pump and so forth, as it sure did good last year. Shorty went to Deering today to pick up Marie, Bert and Vicky. No message from Marcene today, probably tomorrow. It's 10 minutes to 11, and I'm tired.

July 18th. The 10-inch pump blew an impeller today, I mean, it's what they call "junkyard totaled".

It was real nice in Anchorage, after I flew down from Kotzebue, looking for parts. Art flew me into Kotzebue to catch the plane on into Anchorage. We spotted a large tusk, about 9 feet long, near the beach between Deering and Kotzebue. Sure a big one, so Art's gonna go back and pick it up.

July 19th. We've been running all over, chasing parts. The weather's sure nice, and it's good to be home for a change. Wes went with me most of the day. Rush, rush, all day, looking for the parts, called all over, just couldn't find them. We went to a movie tonight and, son of a gun! a guy walked by down the aisle and saw us setting there. His name's Fred Wilkes, and he asked me how I'm doing. I told him I was doing fine, except I had a broken down Jaeger pump. He said, "Is it the engine, or is it the impeller?" I said, "It's the impeller gone." He said, "I've got a good pump, but the engine's blown up. If you'll go down with me tomorrow to Mills Creek, on the way to Seward, I'll help you pull the impeller and you can take it back with you." So, that was a stroke of luck. We went down to Mills Creek, near Summit Lake, to tear the pump apart, and got back to Anchorage about 8:30 p.m., July 20th. So I'm on my way back to Kotzebue and Deering.

Wednesday, July 21st. Marcene and I went back to Kotzebue and caught Shallabarger's plane to Utica, $144. The total paid out on the pump parts and some welding I had to have done was $290. Shorty and Art have been stripping at the dredge, and at Mile 16. Ray took Auggie and Diane Nelson, and 5 kids, and groceries, and a D4 Cat and trailer, up to Old Glory Creek today. What a deal!

Old Glory is our other mining claim up that way, and Old Glory is a real good creek for mining.

July 22nd. The weather was real nice today. I built the dam back on the river. We got the pump all back together, started running the giant about 5:30 p.m., and ran 'til about 11 p.m. Shorty, Bert and Vicky went to Deering tonight to pick up her bags. Art flew up to Old Glory this p.m. to check on his friends. Art and I are going to Nome tomorrow to take care of getting paperwork for patenting our claims.

July 23rd. We flew into Nome, got the certified claim papers, and will send them to Oswald, of Dickenson-Oswald, in Anchorage. Ossie is one of a very few people in the state of Alaska (I think there's only 3 people) that's authorized to fill out the paperwork and file it, and certify it for patenting mining claims. I paid $72 for certification of claims and copies. Shorty was running giants today at Black's pit. Art went up to Old Glory this p.m. to check on Auggie, and he came back with Ray. They didn't have any oil for the Cats or backhoe.

Saturday, July 24th. Shorty went up to Old Glory this morning and took oil for Auggie. We moved the giants and set them up, got them going by 1 p.m. Black's pit is melting good. Art is stripping this afternoon at Mile 16. Marcene and I went to Deering this evening and no mail. We sent a check for $1000 to Oswald today to start trying to file papers to patent Utica, Black's claims, and Miles 16 and 15. He has to wait 'til Division of Lands, or BLM, lets him know if he can survey and go ahead.

July 25th. The weather was fair today and we're running the giants at Black's pit. Art and I stripped at Mile 16 by the dredge. Ray is going to Kotzebue tomorrow with Art. Art flew over Old Glory Creek to check on the crew up there, on all his friends, the Chief of Police and crew. Marie and Bert chased the ducks in the river.

Tuesday, July 27th. The old International pump was hard to start this a.m., when it gets cool it starts hesitating and balking. Shorty slept in, he's gotta go one of these days. Marcene and Marie went to Deering and took 9 drums, but the mail plane didn't get in. Art went up to Old Glory, got Auggie and his clan, and moved them down to camp, 7 of them. That's the price of being a miner with an Eskimo partner. We ran the giants at Black's pit until 9:30 p.m.

July 28th. Shorty didn't get up 'til about 5 to 8 this morning. Art woke him 2 times and I woke him once, honking the horn and etc. We're in real good paydirt at the pit, about 50 feet long, and don't know yet how wide. Auggie and I drove into Deering tonight and picked up mail and about 7 boxes of fish. Mr. Karmun had the mail boxes in his pickup, ready to bring up to us. He sure is nice people. Marcene got her red satin sheets in the mail today, sure is nice for out here in the bush. Taylor Moto told me, in Deering tonight, that their old truck broke down and the boss sent him into

Deering to get some 5-gallon buckets to haul gravel in the back of an old pickup. He drove all the way to the pit and forgot the buckets. I just can't hardly believe that in 1976, they're working on a state road with 5-gallon buckets. This is supposedly a maintained state road that comes up to the mine here, but it leaves a lot to be desired.

July 29th. The weather is icky. We're running the giants at Black's pit and the paydirt is fair. Art flew into Kotzebue today and brought Ray Snyder back. Just what we need, more people. We have 17 people eating, and 5 workers. Auggie is chasing around in our pickup, just going from camp down to the mine, back to the camp, drinking coffee and putting miles on the pickup, and burning gas. I asked him, "How come you're driving the pickup so much?" He said, "I always like to keep moving. When I'm in Kotzebue, Chief of Police, I have to keep moving." One day, he put 78 miles on the pickup, and it's only 4-1/2 miles down to the site where we're sluicing. I told Shorty today that it would be best for him to go back to Anchorage because of the way things have been turning out with him.

July 30th. The weather's good today. Art and I moved the sluice box at Mile 16. Ray ran the giants all day. He's a good hand when he's here. These mining camps just aren't made for too many families. Marie's on her high horse. Auggie's arrogant, should be a taxi driver. I can't believe 87 miles again today on the pickup, when it's only 4 miles down to the mine, and a mile and a half to the other pit. But our friendly Chief of Police is doing a lot of riding. Filled up the pickup yesterday and again today. Shorty's getting ready to go home. I'm paying Shorty tomorrow, and that makes us even. We're gonna bring him up in full.

Saturday, July 31st. We paid Shorty in full today, paid him $1875, plus all the other advances, and things that we brought in, like cigaregttes, and all kinds of goodies, etc. Anyway, Shorty, Bert and Vicky took off to Deering to catch the plane today. Art and I set up the sluice box and repaired the D7. Auggie's bird watching and just goofing around, and Marie's on her high horse again today.

I'm going to Deering with my dozer tomorrow. That's it, I simply cannot cope with this type of operation. We hauled in a 206 planeload of groceries and stored them in the storeroom, night before last. Last night, Auggie used the pickup, backed it up to the kitchen, and took about half a pickup load of groceries down to his cabin for his clan, and he's got about 7 of them down there now. None of them working. It's just a little bit more than I need to be coping with. Not that I don't get along with Art, he's great, and we've never had a cross word, but there's just too many obstacles in camp, so I think I'm gonna move along from this part of the country.

Sunday, August 1st. I talked to my partner, and friend, Art Fields, last night and I told him that I would work it either way he would like. If he wants to keep the camp and cabins and buildings, the claims and equipment, all except my Case 450, I will take it and all gold on hand, and $2000, or vice versa, or however he wants to do it. We'll work out something any way he will feel comfortable with it. So he suggested that would be fine, I take the gold on hand, $2000, and my dozer, and leave everything else there. I left everything except my dozer and battery charger. Why I took the battery charger, I don't know, but there was just a little sentimental value with it.

I walked the dozer to Deering and graded the road as I went down. I always wanted to level that road up anyway. It's about 18 miles of road down to Deering from our camp, and I smoothed it up as I went. Art flew over me on the way to Deering and he saw I was grading the road. I stopped and cleaned up and changed clothes just before I got into town. Marcene had all my stuff in the pickup. Art met me when I got into town. He walked over and said, "Partner, you come on back. You can keep all the gold, you can keep the $2000, just be my partner and come back." And I said, "No, I'm going, I'm all through. So, no hard feelings, but I'm leaving."

Marcene and I chartered Shallabarger to Kotzebue, then Weins to Anchorage. Herbie Karmun is to ship my dozer out by B & R Barge as soon as they come in, send it to Nome and then on down to Anchorage. I'd like to mention, too, that Art flew on over to Kotzebue and asked me again to come back from Kotzebue, but I think, deep down, I just couldn't be comfortable over there around Marie, his wife, and also, Auggie Nelson, the Chief of Police. I just couldn't put up with having to pay so much money for the upkeep of those people over there on what they called a "vacation", "holiday", or whatever. I know it's nice to be nice to people, but there comes a time when there's a limit.

August 2nd. It's sure a pleasure to be back in Anchorage. I guess the Chief's still walking around with his gun on his hip, he was when I left. B & R confirmed that they would get my dozer and bring it on over to Kotzebue. That way, if I don't get it barged into Anchorage, I can fly it out on a Herc (C-130), so there's no big deal. I talked to Bobby Sholton today, with Northern Air Cargo. He said he'd fly my dozer back from Kotzebue for $1700 in a flying boxcar, so everything will be pretty well taken care of.

Thursday, August 5th. Boy, the weather was real nice out today. I picked Art up at the airport and took him home, and gave him all of the paperwork regarding the mine and claims. Then I took him back to the airport and he caught a plane for Fairbanks. Everything's pretty good around Anchorage.

1977

Sunday, May 29th, 1977. I talked to Mr. Gilbert Smith, from Pensacola, Florida, regarding mining, and he has a lot to learn about mining in Alaska. I can't move my loader up to Brandt's at mile 125 Glenn Highway 'til the weight restrictions go off, about 3 more weeks. The snow is still hanging around.

May 30th. Bill DeFrang and I went up to Brandt's Lodge today. It rained last night and is raining again this morning. Bill and I took off with the loader, 6x6, and trailer. It's sure a mess, we made about 3 miles, but it's just too mucky during the breakup here. We goofed, it's too late, should have been in on the trail at least 3 weeks ago. We walked all over trying to find a decent way to go, but just couldn't get around the muck, so we had to turn around and come back. I had to "go potty" this morning and couldn't find anything to "wipe with", it was all snow up there on the mountain, so all I had to use was my glove, and I used it. We went by L.E. Wyrrick's and looked at the trail by his house up to the pass. It looked good, but I'd have had to plow a whole batch of snow through the pass. Bill and I ate supper with L.E., and I flew over and looked at the trail with Eldon Brandt. It sure looks rough, too much water between here and Gold Creek. Smith's group got in this p.m. They're throwing good money after bad, I feel.

May 31st. Bill and I went up to the Nelchina River, it was up and really rolling. I was thinking about going up the river with my 6x6. It has aircraft

DC-3 tires on it, a waterproof engine, and the intake is on the dashboard. I figured I could make the river, but it's a little bit too high, even for the old 6-by. It was really rolling, so we came on back to Anchorage to think and regroup.

Friday, June 3rd. We checked out leads about working gold claims, checking everything we can find. We're looking under all the rocks, and maybe one of these days we'll find a little crawfish under there. I talked with L.E. today to see if we can work out something with him on Alfred Creek. I'd like to do it, but I don't know about doing it with Bill. With L.E. I can work fine, but Bill seems like an old granny to me.

June 4th. Bill and I went up to Gunsight Lodge today. We were going to help L.E. fix the road, but got rained out, it's sure a mess. The Smiths were going in to their claims, sure lots of water, hope they made it this time. They had 2 Nodwells, so I'm sure they can make it with wide-track Nodwell machines. There's lots of traffic on the highway. We're not sure yet where we'll work this summer. Got back to town about 1:30 a.m., sure tired.

Monday, June 6th. I talked to Pat Parker today, and he's interested in going up on Mastodon Creek by Millerhouse, north of Fairbanks on Circle Road, to do some testing. A guy named Calvin, that owns those claims up there, asked me if I would take a machine up there and do some testing. If so, I could use one of the claims, of my choice, to mine on. He only had a little bitty Case 350 loader and a wooden sluice box. So Pat and I decided to go up and give it a whirl, see what happens. We'll take his lowbed and backhoe up, and we're gonna go partners on the deal if we find something worthy of working.

Wednesday, June 8th. Bill and I hiked in to Hicks Creek today, not far out of Anchorage on Glenn Highway, and got out about 10 o'clock tonight. I'm sure bushed, got home about 12:45. Gotta go north tomorrow with Pat Parker. I'll tell you something, I've had it in the bush! And today was a sticker.

Bill DeFrang is a lazy person. We walked up the hill, up over the pass there at Hicks Creek, and when we went down the creek, Bill decided that he would cross the creek. He'd go over to the other side and walk down that side to do a little prospecting, and I'd go down the west side. So, I walked down the west side, prospecting all the way, to within about a half mile of the falls down there just before you get to the highway. I looked up on the hill and there's goats standing up there looking at me. I looked around and got to thinking about Bill, couldn't figure out where he went. I hollered for him and didn't hear him, so I walked about 4 miles back up the creek. I saw a backpack with all the gear tied to it in the creek, and it kind of shook me up. There's no one around, and I hollered for Bill, kept hollering for him and walking up and down the creek. I finally waded across Hicks Creek, waist deep, over to the other side, and went south again on the east side looking for him.

I was really worried when I couldn't find him, so I decided to go out and call Air-Sea Rescue to see if they could find him. I'd take about a hundred steps and then I'd set down and rest, I was so give out. I got up just almost to the top of the pass where the trail from the highway goes up Hicks Creek, and there, along side the trail, Bill was sitting. He was laying and setting down, hunched over, laughing. I think if I'd have had a water pistol, I'd have shot him. Anyway, we started walking down the trail, and Bill would say, "Hey, I'm give out, man, I've been setting up here watching for you all afternoon, I wondered where you were." "I'm give out", he would say, but I just kept walking. I knew once I stopped, I'd be there, so I walked all the way to the highway, got in my pickup and checked my watch. I waited 2 hours and 15 minutes for Bill to show up. Then we went down to Glacier Lodge and I called Marcene on the phone. I told her where I was and what time we'd be coming in. I'll tell you, this taught me a lesson with this guy Bill.

June 9th. Bill, Pat and I left Anchorage about 9 a.m., blew a tire at Healy, and made it into Nenana. We got it fixed and made it okay the rest of the way. The tire cost $85 at Coghills in Nenana. The weather was real nice. We stopped and ate supper at Pedro's Dome about 12 p.m. Skeeters sure are friendly up here.

June 10th. We got to the claims at 4:30 this morning, looked around, and went over to Circle Hot Springs. Bill and Pat slept and snored from 5:30 to 9 a.m. I couldn't sleep so I went downstairs and ate early breakfast. We went down to the claims and tested all over. The only good showing that we got was on Calvin's spot. What a deal! We just felt sorry for Calvin and his partner, they were like 2 little kids, and I just didn't have the heart to try talking them into letting us work the one good spot that we found, and it was super good. They couldn't afford to pay us the money for fuel, or anything else. They asked us to dig a drainage ditch down to Mastodon Creek, and I told them, "If you could just put the fuel in for the backhoe, we'll dig the drainage ditch for you." But they said, "We're sorry, we can't because we're broke." I just know how Pat must feel.

We had a flat on the backhoe and took 2 hours to get it fixed, it was a tubeless. We went to Circle Hot Springs, and Pat and I went swimming. "Granny" Bill said that he was too tired to go swimming. Guess we'll just go on back to Anchorage tomorrow.

June 11th. We got breakfast at Circle Hot Springs, went on down and picked up Pat's backhoe, then headed for Anchorage. We got to Nenana and stopped for the night, sure tired. I'm gonna quit this before long, I got just about enough.

Tuesday, June 14th. I'm checking around for claims to work again, so far, nothing definite. My old friend Fred Wilkes called today. He wants me to go to Dawson City and run the backhoe that I had sold him previously, for a percentage of the gold. It's up on Bonanza Creek. Basil Bryant is the guy that he's going up with. I just find too many "ifs, ands, or buts", and I can't see going up there and working with those guys.

I drove up Parks Highway from Anchorage to Cantwell, took Highway 8 to Denali, the old mining town, and checked ground which today is the site of Alaska's largest gold mining operation. My reason for not wanting to mine that ground was 120 to 200 feet of overburden, so I passed it over. I could have bought the claims for $60,000, but I never look back. At that time I just thought of all the headaches I would of had trying to promote such a project.

Wednesday, June 22nd. Boy, it's a nice day today. I saw Junior Thomas this a.m., he's going to haul my wide pad Komatsu dozer up to Brandt's Lodge for me. Bill and I went up to Brandt's and looked things over. We decided we'll go ahead and move our stuff in to Gold Creek. We went back to Anchorage, made the deal with Denny Lynch, and Junior's lowboy will pick up the dozer at the Komatsu place and drop it off at Brandt's. Shorty and Marty Rinke came to Brandt's and we spent the night in the trailer. We'll leave in the morning.

June 23rd. Rain woke us up this morning - we got all the luck. We left Brandt's about 8:30 a.m. and had no trouble 'til we got to Cameron Pass. We ran into some sticky, slicky clay, that crazy yellow, jelly-type stuff, and almost didn't make it over the pass. It rained on us all the way so far, and we almost got into a jam after we dropped over the pass. We lost about 3 hours trying to find a way out of the valley. Finally we got out about 11 p.m., and dropped and slid all the way into Flat Creek. What a relief to be on solid footing! Shorty and Marty are doing fine, but "Granny" is just completely pooped and out of the picture. I'll tell you what, it was nice that we could stop at Flat Creek and let everybody rest up a little bit. There's not enough room in this diary to explain the times that I almost lost my loader back on that stupid pass.

The sun was shining when we went to sleep, and it was shining when we woke up. We left with the 6x6, trailer, 977 Cat loader, wide pad Komatsu, sleeping bags and groceries, a 6-inch pump, hoses, sluice box, 35 feet of sluice run, hopper, welder, batteries, torch, the bottles of acetylene and oxygen, and 10 barrels of fuel.

June 24th. We spent last night about 2 miles upriver from Black Creek on the Nelchina River. I woke up about 6 a.m., sun was shining, nice out. It took Shorty and Marty about an hour to finally get up, but we bedded down about 2:45 this morning, so we made out alright. We made it up the Nelchina to the horse pasture and across to Conglomerate Creek. On the way over through the horse pasture we saw the Mahoney kids up there on horses, and we saw their teepee. They followed us around the horse pasture, about 4 or 5 miles. We noticed they kept their distance from us on the horses, but we'd looked up and see these 2 teepees way up there, and it was just like in the old days in the western movies. There was us, going across that big plateau, and they resembled Indians watching us and traveling with us as we went. We were going along about 4 or 5 miles an hour, and they just kept pace and stayed with us.

We got over to Conglomerate Creek and saw a lot of caribou there, thousands of them. Most herds were on the Little Oshitna and Big Oshitna Rivers. The Little O was real high, at many crossings the water was over the tracks, and lots of flooding. We made it to where the trail leaves the Little O, to go over the hill to the Big O. We made a cut down the hill into the Little O, and the crossing was fine. It saved us from a steep climb on the original trail.

We went to sleep about 1 o'clock in the morning. Rain woke us up about 5:30 and we got up, built a fire, and got underway about 2 hours later. We hit what we called the boulder field, nothing but big round rocks. We ran over them for about 4 hours with the dozers, just had to idle over them. It was the most disgusting thing I had ever driven over. We only had minor trouble today, trunion arm nut came off a dozer and we had to fix it. Lucky we had a 5/8 nut to fit. It snowed, sleeted, and rained on us today. We got to the claims on Gold Creek about 5:30 p.m.

Marty, Shorty, Bill and I all slept late this a.m. When we got up we unloaded the truck and trailer, and Shorty started work on the air strip by Gold Creek. We got ready to go out, and Mr. Smith stopped us, he wanted to have our dozer do some work for him, and he wanted me to build the air strip a little bit longer. So I agreed, went down later, took the Komatsu from Shorty and built the runway longer. Mr. Smith said he would pick up the dozer at Brandt's after we got finished, and lease it for 2 months. We left the strip at 9 p.m. to return to Brandt's Lodge at mile 125 on Glenn Highway. It was cloudy and raining, and the Big O River was coming up. Sure was high before we got to the turn off to Little O. Our first stop to refuel was on the east bank of Little O, just after we crossed the river. We didn't have any problems, sure a nice rig, this Komatsu.

Shorty, Marty, Bill and I got out to Brandt's, made it out in about 20 hours with no real problems, but there was one thing I want to tell you about. We came up to this one creek, it was about 12 feet across and about 10 feet deep. The water was so high I knew we couldn't cross it, so I gathered up a whole bunch of willows and made a big ball out of the willows with the Komatsu wide pad dozer. Marty and Shorty looked at me like they thought I was crazy, that there was no way we could get across this creek. The banks were straight up and down. I shoved that big ball of willows into the creek and poured the coals to the Komatsu wide pad. I was pulling the G.I. trailer behind the Komatsu. When I got to the other side, running uphill, barely out of the creek, up on the bank, I looked back just as the dozer broke over, to see the trailer just about under water, but coming up out of the water at the time. Everything we had on there got wet, but that's no big deal, we still made it out just fine to Brandt's Lodge.

Tuesday, June 28th. Bill and I paid Equipment Services today for rental on a dozer, $1147 each. Mr. Storm gave me full and clear title to the Atco Bush Trailer, called a wanigan. I traded Les Storm gold for the trailer, gave him 12 ounces overlay and 2 ounces of fines for it, valued at today's prices at about $2500. The wanigan is to be towed behind the 6x6 truck.

I talked to Wilson Air Service in Glennallen today, and he'll fly fuel in to the mine and land on the strip that we built over there. It'll cost $90 an hour for a 206 Cessna, and run about $30 a barrel, to get the fuel in, that's the freight on it.

Thursday, June 30th. Bill and I went up to Brandt's and Wilson Air Service hauled us in. We hauled 2 barrels of fuel and all our gear. We brought some stuff for the Smith crew, down on lower Gold Creek, and they didn't even say "thank you". We got into camp about 10:30. We'll get set up and start sluicing, probably tomorrow.

July 1st. Bill and I are working on the sluice box, getting the hopper and grizzly set up here on Gold Creek. Looks like we'll get things rolling by noon tomorrow. We had nice weather today until about 6 p.m., then it got cloudy and cold. Mr. Smith's crew came up this p.m. and said that rocks were hanging up in their grizzly. A Cessna 206 is coming in on Sunday for Smith's crew, and to haul fuel.

Saturday, July 2nd. We're still rigging up the sluice box, almost ready to sluice. Mr. Smith and crew are goofing around, good thing that they're rich. Bill and I repaired the torsion bar and power steering on the big 6x6 truck with the DC-3 tires on it today. We went down this morning with the big 6x6 and drove over the runway, packed it down real good. We waited for the airplane 'til noon, Smith and company all just taking it easy. It's all chiefs and no indians down there. We got our sluice box going and ran about 2 hours. Grizzly not quite right yet, but we'll get'er.

Monday, July 4th. We ran the box about 6 hours today, ran about 70 yards through. It's going pretty good, moving enough material to make us happy, no breakdowns, and the Cat 977 loader is working just fine. Wilson Air flew in this morning in his 206, made 2 trips and brought over 4 barrels of diesel, so I guess Smith will pay for today's flight one way. Bill and I got the 6x6 running with new parts, sure nice not to have to tow it up the hills. We had crazy weather, rain, sun, hail, cold, windy, and all of it.

Wednesday, July 6th. The weather was good today, didn't rain. We spent an hour welding and 2 hours panning, checking the pit. We panned the first riffles and it looks pretty good, but not as good as it should, lots of big rocks. I couldn't find my toothbrush so I made me a brush out of a willow limb.

Saturday, July 9th. Marcene came in yesterday with Eldon Brandt, brought goodies, etc. She paid Eldon $75 for bringing her over in his Super Cub. Marcene and I slept in Smith's Nodwell track rig with a bunk last night. This morning the sun come up and it was nice and warm in there. All of a sudden a great big hornet stung me on the leg. It got my attention. We had a pretty good showing today, but boy, the rocks are big, and lots of them. Lots of black sand, too.

July 10th. This morning we went fishing and caught 7 graylings in about 15 minutes. Sure good fishing over here on Gold Creek. We met a Mr. Brown and his sons at Hartmans today, sure nice people. That's on the Big O River. Two hikers from Washington came over to see us this p.m. We had fish for supper.

July 11th. Marcene and I waited 6 hours for the plane today. She hung one of her red blouses up for a wind sock down at the air strip and left it there. We were setting there, and man, was it ever hot! We flew over the trail and the Smith kids were stuck good on the way over. Mr. Glen Heatherley had his Nodwell by them so they won't have to walk out. Bill stayed in camp and I really don't know what he'll do. We got into Anchorage at 10:15 this evening. Our camper park should be full, but it isn't. Mr. Smith said that we didn't owe him anything for coming in on the 206, real nice of him.

July 12th. I went out to see Shorty at the Teamsters' Hospital. He'd had a wreck on a motocycle and really messed up his face and back. Looks like he'll be laid up for a week or more. Ann Vandola called and she thinks we can work things out at Collinsville, Alaska, regarding some gold claims she owns. That's over in the foothills of Mt. McKinley. I picked up a screen today for the grizzly at RCJ's pit, will take it back to Mr. Smith.

Thursday, July 14th. I met with Attorney Tallman and Ann Vandola, everything seems good for Collinsville. Marcene, Jadene and I drove up to Brandt's today, and I had Eldon fly me over to Gold Creek. It's raining cats and dogs today and the creek sure is high. We had to move the pump tonight because the water was high and rising. We'll try and run some material through the box tomorrow.

July 15th. It's raining again today, sure miserable out. We ran 4 loads through the box before Andy, Mr. Smith's son-in-law, came up. We helped him check out 2 claims below on Gold Creek. We got some pretty good color. By the way, Andy lost the little backhoe out of the back of the Nodwell on the way back. He poured the coals to it and went in and out of the creeks like a wild indian, so he lost the motor, the hydraulic tank, and the whole tool box and all. The backhoe was just hanging out the back of the Nodwell (that's a big track rig) as he pulled into our camp on Gold Creek.

Saturday, July 16th. I've talked to Bill about Gold Creek. I really don't think there's enough gold here to warrant staying, and I feel that I'm spending more on fuel than we're getting in the box, so I talked to Bill. He wants to stay, so maybe I'll sell him the sluice box, grizzly, and maybe the pump, I don't know, we'll see. Some other stuff I'll keep, but I'll find out what he's thinking tonight.

July 17th. We got up at 5:30. Bill wanted to pan the first 2 riffles and take it in to show his wife. I did a little more work on the runway today, made a turnaround on the south end so the Twin Otter can turn around when hauling in fuel for Mr. Smith. I paid Brandt $115.90 for the flight over to the mine, and service on my pickup truck. I got home about 3:30 p.m., sure nice out. Marcene and I went out and looked at a new Taylorcraft airplane. It looks nice. We also went to The Max for supper.

Tuesday, July 19th. I talked to Dick Dickerson at Brandt's Lodge today and he'll be down tomorrow. He's gonna go with me to Collinsville and check out Ann Vandola's ground over there on Twin and Mills Creeks.

July 20th. Dick and I took off for Collinsville today. We took a battery with us so we could jump start the little John Deere loader which has an automatic transmission. We got over there and the dad-gummed D7 Cat was buried. Someone took it out last fall during the moose hunting season, I guess, got it stuck in a creek and just left it. It had gravel all around it, over the blade, clear up to the floorboards, up to the seats. We got it all dug out and was gonna start it up, but when we put water in it, it ran out the pony engine and different places. We couldn't figure out what in the world we were gonna use for Stop-leak, and of all things, we found some Bondo over there. Dick suggested that we use that, so we tried it and it actually worked. We got the old D7 running, and out, and up to camp. We've got the D7, the John Deere, and a crew cab Dodge truck running. There's about 40 gallons of gas left and about 5 barrels of diesel.

Friday, July 22nd. We came in from Collinsville with Neilson's Air today in a 206. Bill DeFrang told me that he wants to buy the 977 Cat loader, so I think it's a deal whereas Mr. Smith wants to buy it for him.

July 23rd. Dick was telling me that Mr. Smith and crew had pulled out. One of the boys was bringing the 977 loader out across L.E. Wyrrick's field up there, well, actually it was a swamp. They had a cleanup in the bucket, that's the concentrated gold, etc., probably about 70 to 80 ounces in there, and the guy got stuck. He was so unconcerned about things he just dumped the load he had in the bucket and tried to push himself back out. Mr. Smith gave L.E. the gold if he would go over and try to salvage it, or clean it up, or whatever. So, L.E. took over a loader and scooped it up by the shovel and got what he could. He got 38 ounces out of it.

Monday, July 25th. I met with Ann Vandola today and she will have to talk with Mr. Tallman about us going over to Collinsville and doing her assessment work, etc. I talked to Wyrrick, he and his wife and daughter came down today and spent the night with us. They're sure nice people. I told L.E., "Be careful in that bedroom, because that big mirror on the wall has a tendency to make it look as if you're walking right into another room." So, he got up to use the bathroom about 3 o'clock in the morning and walked into the mirror. I let Smith's crew borrow my pickup to take up to Brandt's to move some of their equipment into Anchorage.

Friday, July 29th. The weather's nice today. Mr. Smith told me that he would bring a check for $20,000 for my 977 Cat loader on Monday. Bill has him conned into something on Gold Creek, don't know yet just what. I'm going up tomorrow and get my big truck and stuff. Dick and Buzz Hoffman, the banker, are going along with me.

July 30th. Buzz, Dick and I went up to Brandt's and had Wilson Air take us over to Gold Creek, $190. We loaded up the 6x6 and started out. We went fishing and caught about 12 nice graylings. We left about 4 p.m., traveled from Gold Creek down Big Oshitna River, with no problems until just before Little O. The hitch broke off the trailer and we had to chain it to the hitch on the truck. We just barely made it to the top of the hill with the truck, it was so mucky. We stopped and cooked the grayling for supper about 5 miles up Little O River. The weather held nice until we started over the horse pasture to Conglomerate Creek, then it started to rain. We saw hundreds of caribou up on the horse pasture. When I say the horse pasture, it's a big, big plateau like the old western movie settings. We saw about 25 or 30 albino (all white) caribou, all segregated by themselves. We got over to the Nelchina River about midnight, it was raining cats and dogs, and we made camp, used our tent for a lean-to. I'm sure tired, and all were ready to turn in.

July 31st. Well, the skeeters sure chewed on me last night. Buzz and I slept under the lean-to, Dick slept in the truck. We broke camp about 7 a.m. We just built a fire and boiled water for coffee and bullion, too much rain to fix breakfast. It's raining, foggy, and the Nelchina River is muddy and rising. We took off right down the middle of the river with that big 6-by truck. We went all the way down the Nelchina, dodging rocks and potholes, went all the way to the highway. We kidded one guy and his family at the bridge, we asked them if we were near Fairbanks. We played lost and they thought we were nuts. They took pictures of us in the river, the water over our big tires.

We ate supper at Brandt's this evening, and Buzz ordered a steak. As soon as they brought it out, he ordered another, so he ate 2 big steaks. He'd asked us this afternoon, "When in the world do you guys stop to eat?" I took the 6x6 and trailer on into Anchorage tonight. We had a flat by Glacier Lodge and had our share of troubles getting the flat fixed, the wheel and studs were broke, so that complicated things.

August 1st. Dick and I finally got into Anchorage about 5 o'clock this morning, sure got sleepy coming in. Mr. Smith is sending over the check for my loader tomorrow, and he's going to buy the little travel trailer we left up at Eldon Brandt's for $2000.

August 2nd. I met with Mr. Tallman this morning. He said to go ahead over to Collinsville and get what equipment going that we can, and try to get the wash plant out of the creek. Also to go ahead and test ground and do the assessment work. He also said that if I didn't get ahold of Ann Vandola, he would, and get a letter to proceed as he instructed. I told him that I would take pictures of things in camp, broken down equipment, etc. Dick and his wife, Leah, flew over to Collinsville this p.m. to start getting stuff ready to do some testing and sluicing.

August 3rd. I went to Collinsville today, flew in with Neilsons. Neilsons flew over 2 barrels of diesel and 1 barrel of gas this p.m. We spent most of the day getting equipment ready to start mining. We started dozing around the dry land dredge, but it sure is wet, lots of water there. We need a good pump, so we'll have to fly one in, I suppose.

August 4th. It rained all day today. We moved the sluice box and pipe, getting ready to sluice. Mining sure isn't for lazy people. We checked the pit, color looks good, nothing big, but we did have quite a few colors in the pans.

August 5th. The weather was nice today, no rain for a change. We have the creek dammed up and have the right amount of water. The old D7 sure is sick, and the John Deere is on its last roll. I just hope they hold together for a week or two. We got started sluicing at 3 o'clock and ran 'til 7. Clint Seyer brought over propane and groceries. He's flying for Neilson out of Anchorage.

Saturday, August 6th. The sluice box ran about 8 hours today. We were able to get about 75 yards of material through the box with the wore out little 350 loader. It has less than 1-yard capacity. The old Cat and loader are still hanging together. We have 4 drums of diesel left, 1 barrel of gas, and a full tank in the old Dodge crew cab truck.

August 7th. It rained today. Marcene came over with Mr. Wyler, our neighbor on Campbell Lake. He's an inspector for the

FAA, and he flew her over in a Citabre plane. We ran the box an hour and a half, and the John Deere broke down. Looks like it's done for, guess we'll have to just run 2 cats and push in the hopper. I sure hate to though, as wet as it is over here. When you push gold bearing material in water, the gold goes down, as gold is 40 times the weight of sand and gravel.

August 8th. We worked all day on the John Deere and finally got it running about 5:30 p.m. The box ran about 30 minutes. Marcene went back to Anchorage this p.m. Neilsons hauled out 2 barrels of diesel and 1 of gasoline by 206 Cessna. The Canadians were here today checking around, and left at 8 p.m. They seem like promoters. They are part of the group that has some kind of lease with Ann Vandola.

August 9th. It rained last night and this a.m. 'til about 8:30. We ran the sluice box about 7-1/2 hours today, approximately 75 yards, and the color looks good. The work on the sluice box is hard, but is good for me, makes me feel better. Total hours to date on the sluice box is 22. If only we had some good equipment we could make quite a bit before freeze-up. The pads are coming off the old D7, and the John Deere just barely makes it from the pit to the sluice box. We have 5 barrels of fuel oil and 2 barrels of gas left. The reason we don't bring good equipment in is we can't build a decent runway for heavy aircraft with wore out equipment. It's about 90 miles of swampy ground between the mine site and the road.

August 10th. The weather was nice today after about 9 a.m. We ran the sluice box 6 hours, but the John Deere just quit, so we parked it and cut a ramp into the sluice box to push material in with the old Cat. It sure is a shame to have good gold in the ground and just don't have the equipment to get it out. By using the Cat to push material, I'd say that we're losing about 40 to 50% of the gold, as we have to push across the creek. The Cat is only pulling on one track and keeps running off the track. You sure have to have patience to put up with this kind of junk. We took the D6 down this afternoon and we'll use it tomorrow. It's a wore out antique from the early 40's, World War II, like a '41 or '42 model.

August 11th. The weather was pretty good to us today, and the sluice box ran 3 hours. We checked the 3 front riffles in the box and took out about 3-1/2 ounces of gold, real nice stuff, three nice nuggets. It sure is a different twist to have such nice gold in the ground, only one hour from town, and no equipment to get it out with. Boy, today took the cake! The D7 hydraulic arm broke off, and 6 pads are gone on the left side. Also, Dick broke an arm on the D6, metal fatigue, and the John Deere only pulls on one track, so we are down temporarily. Tomorrow we're going to work on the John Deere. That's that! I sure wish a plane would come in so we could send word to town. Never one around when you need someone. No one's been in here since Monday when Marcene left. It's like being in a different world over here. What we need is a radio-telephone.

August 12th. The weather is pretty out today, but everything's broke down. We tore into the John Deere, cleaned everything up and it's ready to go back together, just need some parts. A pilot from Palmer stopped in and we sent word in to Marcene for parts and a welder. I know if the guy got through to Marcene, bless her heart, she'll get the parts and take care of us. We need the parts from Craig Taylor in Anchorage, the John Deere dealer. We got word tonight that Mr. Smith and Bill, Mr. Smith's mechanic, are coming over tomorrow. It's sure heck to be in this shape. We could be mining in about 2-1/2 hours if we had parts and a welder.

Saturday, August 13th. Marcene brought over parts for the John Deere and groceries, etc. She'll be here 'til Monday. Mr. Smith and Bill, came over here today to look things over, and liked what they saw. He said he'd go in with me, to go ahead and make any kind of deal with Ann Vandola and Mr. Tallman that I would like, and he'd go along with it. Neilsons took 2 barrels to town, that's $40, a $20 deposit on each barrel.

August 14th. We got the John Deere going and it does pretty good now. We're in some real good ground and the color sure looks good. We got about an ounce from about one-fifth of the front riffle. We welded the arm on the old D7 today and it is just barely hanging together. It's raining cats and dogs.

Tuesday, August 16th. Our dam washed out last night and we lost an hour and a half rebuilding it. It was cloudy all day, but it didn't rain much, just a little light rain. We ran the sluice box 7 hours today. This makes 41 hours. We ran about 70 yards through the box for a total of 415 yards to date. We sure are in good ground, checked the riffles and they look pretty good. Dick's stripping with the D7 today and I ran the John Deere loader. I had the track off it 3 times, and the D7 has 12 pads missing, but it's still hanging in. Marcene flew back to town this p.m. We got the wood stove going in the cook shack, and I hooked up a stove in my cabin. It's sure nice to have a warm cabin.

August 17th. It rained all day, all day long, most miserable day so far. We had to work on the John Deere again. I welded spacers on track tightener arms, and pins and bushings are gone, but I hope to keep it glued together for a few more days. Just wish that Dick would take it a little bit easier on the equipment. He just won't work the sluice box, therefore, I can't run the equipment and be careful with it. So, Dick sets on the equipment and I have to go back to the sluice box. Also, Leah works the sluice box. I think he has a thing with a #2 shovel and handling rocks. I think we should have about 2 pounds of gold (24 ounces) in the box by now. The water is sure high in the creek, just hope the dam holds. That would really fix us if the dam broke and washed out the sluice box and all our gold. I cut wood and started a fire in the cabin this evening. I burned the pair of old boots that I wore today, they both leaked so I got rid of them. Note: Dick is a person that I do not respect. He treats Leah as if she is a servant and he's king. Need not say anymore.

August 18th. I had the D7 off the track 2 times today. Sure is well used. Didn't check the box today, looks like about 2 or 3 more days, don't know yet. Dick sure is wanting to check the box. Clint Seyer flew over us today and landed, but I just couldn't drive down to see him. Got cigs for Dick, clean clothes, pipe and filters. This old junk just seems to hang together. We put bolts in the engine of the John Deere and had to tighten up the starter again, and we're using about 5 gallons of hydraulic fluid a day. Everything is wore out, the equipment is so metal-fatigued, bolts are all stripped and everything. In order to fix it you just have to lay everything out and start all over, and it wouldn't be worth it.

August 19th. We ran the sluice box 2 hours today and the loader broke down again. Dick is entirely too hard on equipment. I tried my best to get him to take it easy and slow down, but it didn't phase him. It doesn't belong to him so he doesn't really care. We went to shut off the water on the box and our intake pipe collapsed. With everything as was, we cleaned up the sluice box. Got through at 10 p.m. The little sluice box, the cleanup box, what we call a Long Tom, worked real good. And Dick just flat refused to drive the truck over to Mills Creek. It drives hard and steers hard, so he doesn't want any part of it. The Coleman lantern is running out of fuel. I pumped it up, so it's good for awhile, I guess. Dick and Leah sure want to stay over here for the winter.

Sunday, August 21st. I flew into Anchorage today and brought the acetylene bottle with me. I agreed to give Dick half of the gold after all bills were paid, and agreed to buy Dick's half of the gold for $150 an ounce. We've got to get a loader, or something, to work with, otherwise we're just fighting a losing battle here.

August 22nd. I'm looking for a loader today, and trying to find someone to haul it over. Bobby Sholton couldn't haul it. I'll have to take the captain of the Hercules over Wednesday to check out the runway and see what needs to be done. We may repair the D7 Cat enough to widen and extend the runway.

August 23rd. I found out today that I couldn't get the Herc captain to make a trip over until next weekend. So I bought parts at Craig Taylor's for the John Deere 350 loader. Marcene took a sample of the black sand to Skyline Lab and we were supposed to get the results back this p.m., but we forgot to call by 5 o'clock.

August 24th. Neilsons hauled me and a radio-telephone to the mine. We started work this a.m., and worked 'til the weather got so bad we had to quit.

August 25th. The weather's good today. Dick and I are working on the D7 Cat. It sure is well used, but I think that we'll get it going and make it string us out the rest of the season. We're just about out of oxygen, but just may be careful and make it.

August 26th. We worked all day long on the D7 Cat, and sure didn't go by the book because we couldn't, but we got it all back together. We "Joe McGee'd it", and it should hold out 'til we shut down this fall. I guess we'll tear into the John Deere tomorrow, hope the weather permits. Clint is to bring his wife and Marcene over, and the clutch for the John Deere, the "johnny popper". The weather was icky here today.

Saturday, August 27th. Marcene and Denny Jones came over today. We spent most of the day panning and checking the ground. We're all going into town tomorrow. Moose hunters are already coming around. A preacher from Palmer, Alaska, came over today and gave Marcene a piece of his mind, gave her a hard time, but I guess she let him know where we stood, and where he stood. The preacher was the guy with suspenders in the 206. He came over and said, "I hunt over here every year and I'm going to move into the kitchen and the cabins." Anyway, it was real funny. We just let him know that he wasn't moving into our kitchen and into our cabins, but he could use the runway. So, he didn't like it, but he accepted the fact that he couldn't just come over and bring all his congregation to do moose hunting out of our camp.

Monday, August 29th. Yesterday we all flew into town from Colinsville, and got all settled up with Dick and Leah. I told them that we aren't going back to the mine, and when I say, "we aren't going back", I meant that they two weren't going back with me. Today I met with Buzz Hoffman, the banker at First National Bank, about my going to Chicago to buy a Cessna 206, and we went over the airplane deal. We got the agreement pretty well figured out. I talked with Clint Seyer, with Neilson, and he's gonna order the 206 with all King instruments and automatic pilot, DME and 2 ADFs, and everything, and Quillian and I are gonna fly out to get it. Quillian flew helicopters in Viet Nam.

The weather was nice out today. My shop was pretty active, nothing big, just lots of interest in the snow machines. I fly out tonight to pick up the 206 in Harvard, Illinois, just out of Chicago.

August 30th. Quillian and I got into Chicago and waited for those nuts 'til about 5 p.m. Four hours and 4 phone calls later, finally we got picked up and got out to where the 206 was, and the people treated us like peons. We finally got the old man that owned the place, Mr. Dacey, and he took us to town for a motel and food. What a day!

When we finally got ahold of Mr. Dacey, he told us we'd have to have the money for the airplane, in order to get the title on it that we needed to fly it back through the border. My banker had told us that we needed a clear title for it, and the old man wasn't gonna let us have it. We called the banker and got him to explain it to the guy, the owner. We left Harvard, Illinois, with that plane and a clear title to it, a $55,000 airplane, going north.

We got back to Anchorage, and Buzz Hoffman looked at me and laughed. He said, "Looks like you've got yourself an airplane." I said, "What do you mean?" He said, "You've got the title for it, you don't owe him anything." I said, "No, we can't do that." He laughed and said, "Well, yeah, I told the man that we'd send him the money, so we'll send it." But it was kind of ironic that Mr. Dacey would even think about letting us take off with that airplane, with absolutely no money, and just the guy's word on the other end of the phone. This guy was from the old school, the guy that started and owned the company that sold the airplanes there in Harvard, Illinois.

August 31st. We walked from the motel to the airport and got the plane. We checked out the instruments first, took the plane up and made 3 or 4 landings, checked everything out. Then we taxied over and filled up with gasoline, and the kid pumping it was going to charge us for the fuel. I laughed at him and told him, "Hey, when you buy a $55,000 airplane, at least you can get is a tank full of fuel." He asked us, "What in the world are you doing with all those instruments in that airplane?" They were King instruments, and I told him, "Well, we got a bunch of rocks sticking up, there in Alaska, that you don't have down here." We took off about 9 a.m. and had quite a bit of lousy weather. We were on instruments just about all the way to Winnipeg.

When we were making the approach coming into Winnipeg, the people there sure treated us nice. We turned the radio on to check in with the Winnipeg station, and they told us that they had us under control and to take no other instructions from anyone else except them, so we went right on in. They walked us right in to the airport, right around the taxiing, took us right over to Customs, and everything was fine. We really enjoyed our stopover there in Winnipeg, everybody was nice. We called an Arctic Cat dealer that I had met last winter in Hawaii, and he came over and picked us up. We had a nice visit, played guitars and sang 'til late.

September 1st. We flew from Winnipeg to Watson Lake, Yukon Territory. We were held up for about 2 hours in Winnipeg until the fog lifted off the runway. The sun was shining beautiful, we could see the sun from our motel. We were actually looking down on the airstrip and there was just a little patch of fog hanging on the strip, but they have a ruling in Canada that you can't take off when there's any fog at all on the strip. I flew right over Edmonton and almost to Grand Prairie, and I flew from Fort St. John to Fort Nelson. We had good weather about half the way. We were kind of tired when we got to Watson Lake. I called Marcene and everything was fine.

September 2nd. It was raining when we woke up this morning. We waited 'til 8 a.m., then we took off in the clouds and rain on instruments, and made it just fine to Whitehorse; then on to Northway, Alaska. My landing there was lousy. We gassed up, checked through Customs, and got to Anchorage at 3:20 p.m., sure nice to be home. The weather was pretty nice all the way in and we didn't have a problem. I sure like the 206 airplane. It had 34.2 hours on it when we got to town. This is the hour reading that we go to work with. We spent a total of 22 hours flying time from Harvard to Anchorage.

Sunday, September 11th. I made my deal with Clint Seyer and Neilson Aviation regarding leasing the 206, and today it's loaded to go to Kenai tomorrow. The hours on the airplane were 39.2 this p.m. We just kind of hung around town today, and took it easy.

Tuesday, September 13th. We went over to the mine today, and the weather was lousy all day. There was a guy by the airstrip that had a bull moose, he flew it out in 2 trips. The weather didn't bother him at all. Marcene and I went over on Twin Creek and ran 5 buckets full of material through the little sluice box, and it's pretty good. We used our plane about 2 hours today at the most.

September 14th. We got up early, went over and got the D7 dozer, brought it over to the airstrip and rigged up an old grader, but it was too wet to grade the strip. We went up Mills Creek, dug a test hole and got into some good ground. So we went back to camp to get shovels, washtubs, and the little sluice box. We loaded the tubs with paydirt, set up the little sluice box and ran a batch of material through. It sure looked good, best I've ever seen.

September 15th. A black bear woke us up about 5'oclock this a.m., scratching on the storehouse door. I banged on the wall and hollered at him, and he ran off. It was raining cats and dogs all day long, only got out to cut wood for the stove. And, yes, we burned all the shoes and boots that we could find in camp. We sure didn't get anything done today, except for reading.

September 16th. The bear woke us up again this morning, so we got up and watched him, took pictures of him in the garbage can. The weather turned nice today and our 206 came over and got us.

Saturday, September 17th. Art Fields, my ex-partner and friend from Kotzebue, came by this evening and wants me to check with Attorney Tunnely on Monday, so we'll check it out and see what's happening.

Monday, September 19th. I talked to Mr. Smith today and he wants me to find out something regarding Collinsville, and get back in touch with him.

Thursday, September 22nd. I went to the BLM and Division of Lands this a.m. and got maps and info for the attorney, and then Art Fields and I went to see Attorney Tunnely. This is pertaining to Black's claim that we were trespassing on their mining claims, which was absolutely wrong. We had all the permits and everything that we needed for that ground at Utica.

I found out today that the claims and the ground in and around Utica, and the mining district of Utica, were left out of the Native Claims Act, so things look pretty good for us. That should rectify the problem of the Blacks claiming that that is their ground. The Black family claims that their grandad at one time worked and owned these claims in question, but assessment work hasn't been kept up on them, so they reverted back to the state long ago. Art and I filed on them legally.

Thursday, September 29th. Mr. Smith called today, and is anxious to get something going regarding Collinsville.

Monday, October 10th. It's cloudy, but no snow yet. Shorty and Marty came into town today. They got my big 6x6 truck and trailer, took them back up to Shorty's house, right by Glacier Lodge, and left his pickup for me to bring up tomorrow. We'll go up and do some assessment work on Glacier Creek. Our claim is just below Matanuska Glacier.

October 11th. I went up to Glacier Creek this p.m. We took the 6x6 and wanigan in across the Matanuska River, over to Glacier Creek, and had no trouble getting in. We crossed just below the Matanuska Glacier, about 8 or 10 different channels that we had to cross there. The water was just coming into the floorboard of the old 6-by, but everything worked out fine. We also took a John Deere dozer in.

October 12th. We did quite a bit of digging with the dozer cutting test holes. There was no permafrost over there, but we didn't find anything, no color at all. Stakes were still in and everything was fine, but we just didn't find any gold. I guess this area is only good for hunting. Shorty stepped on my hat and I made him apologize for it. Shorty cooked on this trip, such as it was.

October 13th. It's raining. We made it out to Shorty's and I came on into town. It snowed on my way back. A State Trooper stopped me and said to get my lights and etc., fixed up, but he let me go, he was real nice. That was back in the days when you could talk to them and they could talk to you. I talked to Mr. Smith today. He seems to be a pretty nice person, but I just don't quite think I could get along with his help for long. The boys just abuse things so much, I don't believe I could cope with that.

Tuesday, October 18th. I got paid for my airplane lease today - $1054. Covers for the plane's wings came out of the lease.

Friday, October 21st. L.E. Wyrrick, a miner from Alfred Creek, and a friend for quite a few years, came by this morning. He likes the used, double wide track, Skidoo snow machine, and will take it for $1500 in gold.

Monday, October 24th. Mr. Smith called again today, and he's wanting to get something going. Riney Berg called this afternoon from Candle. Actually, he does mining in the Kougarok country up there on the Seward Peninsula north of Nome. He's coming out to our home for supper tomorrow night. A real nice guy, we've bought gold from him.

Tuesday, November 15th. I met with Mr. Loren Hite this a.m. and bought gold. I paid him $2300 cash, and am going to meet with him tomorrow to finish our deal. He's a miner from Harrison Creek, up north of Fairbanks. Note: I was real busy at the time I bought the gold and didn't ask him the percentage of the gold, and he charged me the going price for it. Two years went by before I sold that gold. If the price of gold hadn't of just about doubled, I'd have lost money on it because the percentage of gold was only 59% purity.

Thursday, November 17th. Art Fields came by today on his way to Frisco to see Hugh Chatham, who is still his silent partner. Too bad things didn't work out up there at the mine with Art.

Wednesday, November 23rd. Art called today and said that Chatham and the guys didn't give him any money, and that Bob Kirsch was down there in Frisco trying to get money from those guys. I can just imagine it. Art took his gold down, and Hugh and those guys took the gold and didn't give him any money for it. Then there's Bob Kirsch, trying to stab him in the back, go behind his back and wind up with money to operate that mine there at Utica. Art should have split the gold before going south to Frisco. The price of gold today is $157 per ounce.

Tuesday, Novermber 29th. I met today with Attorney Tunnely and Art and went over what would happen tomorrow during the deposition. We have to go to Attorney Josephson's office, and the Blacks will be there. I sure would like to see this thing settled. I picked Art up at the Westward Hotel, and he had a burlap bag full of she-fish. Nowhere else but in Alaska could this happen. He brought them down on Wein Airlines, they were frozen. The bag opened up and tourists standing at the baggage carousel watched as the frozen she-fish started coming around, one and two at a time.

November 30th. Attorney Tunnely, Art and I went to Joe Josephson's office, and Joe took a deposition from us. It went pretty good. Mr. Tunnely took me out to my shop when we got through.

He's spent about 2-1/2 to 3 hours with us regarding the Blacks case, and it's just something that's like a rock in your shoe. That's basically what it amounts to, but it's still expensive trying to fight something like that.

    Thursday, December 8th. I got a call from George Grimes in Flint, Michigan, today. He can get a new pickup, the one I want to get for Daddy, for $3775. That sure is different from up here. Mr. Grimes is with General Motors and is a friend of Charlie Walker, the Grand Old Opry star.

1978

Friday, January 13, 1978. We bought gold nuggets today from Sealskin Charlie, an oldtime, colorful Alaskan. He left his office once, with Marcene and me, with about a million dollars worth of gold, and it sure was a weird feeling.

Monday, January 16th. Mr. Alfred Karmun, the Eskimo reindeer herder from Deering, came to see us this evening. I picked him up at the airport and took him to see the boxing matches. He got a big kick out of them. He brought reindeer carcasses for us, and that sure was nice of him. We went over to pick them up at the baggage claim. They were in meat netting bags, going around and around on the luggage carousel. Only in Alaska!

Saturday, January 28th. Mel Pardek, a Canadian from Vancouver, called today. Due to the fact they have that property at Collinsville all tied up with Ann Vandola, they agreed to let us mine there, do the assessment work, etc. So, this sure is some good news for mining this next year.

Wednesday, February 8th. The price of gold today is $175 an ounce.

Tuesday, February 28th. I let Clint Seyer lease the 206 airplane today, and his time starts at 152 hours on the plane. Neilsons haven't paid me and I had to pull it from them. I'm not letting them get any deeper in debt with us. Looks like what Neilsons owes us at this date is $1123.

Sunday, March 12th. We took snow machines cross-country, about 90 miles, to the mine in Collinsville. We rode around Collinsville, went ptarmigan hunting, and cut wood. Also, we packed down the airport runway with our snowmobiles so planes can land on skis. There's about 6 feet of snow up there around camp at 5700 feet. With me were Armond's friends, 2 big Indians from Oregon on their double track snowmobiles, and Dave Kissinger. Dave and I were on Panthers, Arctic Cat snowmobiles.

March 13th. We were up at 5:30 this a.m., and took off at 6:30. It was about 20 degrees outside and the machines were running good. We ran into a real bad snowstorm, a whiteout, about halfway in to Shorty Bradley's Roadhouse over on Peters Creek. We got into Anchorage about 6:15 this p.m.

Saturday, March 18th. I've been talking and meeting with Fred Wilkes regarding mining in Dawson City. Fred is a walking calculator. He's supposed to get a lease on some claims on Upper Bonanza Creek in Dawson Monday, and is gonna get back to me. I tried to call Mel Pardek in Vancouver today, but didn't get ahold of him. Shorty called and he's ready to go over to Collinsville. I gave Shorty $125 today and let him take my welder, cutting torch, oxygen and acetylene bottles, chain saw, and battery charger. He's going over to the mine Monday morning, and he's gonna take Levi, his brother-in-law, with him.

Monday, March 20th. I talked to Mel Pardek today. He told me that he met with his partners, and that I could go ahead and get ready to go to Collinsville to do prospecting and assessment work, and I could keep what gold I got. He said that a letter would follow right away. We're getting ready to go outside tomorrow, and then we'll get back and get with the course. I've decided not to go mining with Fred in Dawson City, and told him so today.

Sunday, May 28th. Bill, Mr. Smith's mechanic, Clint and I flew over to the Collinsville mine today in our 206 and took pads for the D7 Cat and an oxygen bottle. Shorty had things in pretty good shape.

May 29th. Mr. Smith and crew, and I left early today for Circle Hot Springs, trying to help him find something to work. We went to see Mr. McIntosh on Harrison Creek, and then on up to see Larry Hite. It snowed on us about 20 miles this side of Central.

May 30th. We spent last night in the hotel at Circle Hot Springs. I stopped by to talk with Mr. Hite and he'll work out a deal, but I don't think that Mr. Smith wants anything but an absolute guarantee. We met with McIntosh at 2 p.m. in Fairbanks, and he wanted $500,000 for 35 percent of his claims. It makes me appreciate Collinsville. It was a long hard drive for nothing, I guess, and it's good to be home.

May 31st. Clint flew a load over to Collinsville, also took Marty Rinke over and brought Levi back. I'm chasing around for parts, etc. We got burlap bags for the bottom of the sluice box. We use plastic carpet under the riffles to catch gold, and put the burlap bags under the carpet to collect fine powder gold. Today, our friend from Las Vegas, Jim Prochaska, Ernestine's husband, came in and we picked him up at the airport. Ernestine worked at the Frontier in Vegas; she's the lady who got us in touch with Mel Tillis, and we met Radio Red, his bus driver, when Mel was working there. Jim's going to go to Collinsville and work with us this summer. Quillian came out tonight for a visit. Our plane flew to Kodiak today, it's getting pretty busy.

Monday, June 5th. Jim and I went to Collinsville today. Clint flew us over. Things look pretty good at camp, but the weather's kind of lousy.

June 6th. Clint flew a load of fuel over this p.m. Most of the day we spent tightening bolts on the D7, and welding on the John Deere bucket, etc. The water's a little high, but we'll make out okay, should get the sluice box set up and going by tomorrow.

June 7th. We got the sluice box going today. We built a dam and ran about 45 minutes, and the dam broke, had to build it back again. We ran a total of 4-1/2 hours. We started work about 9 a.m. and quit about 8 o'clock this evening. Shorty, Marty, Jim and I working. The weather was good today, and the equipment is running pretty good. Shorty called tonight for canned fruit, batteries, and cigars for Jim.

June 8th. I checked the riffles on the box this a.m. and it didn't look too good, but we only had 4-1/2 hours on the box yesterday. I got one nice little nugget though, and we ran the box 7-1/2 hours today. The ram broke on the D7 this a.m. and Jim welded it, he's a good welder. The old D7 tracks sure are getting worn, and it's getting hard to keep the left track on. We put new tracks and undercarriage on the John Deere. We got a message from Marcene tonight. It rained, but we had a good supper, moose steak, gravy and corn bread.

June 9th. The weather was pretty today. We got started and ran the sluice box about an hour. Shorty was running the John Deere and lost a pad, so I had him pull it out of the pit and tighten all the bolts, they were all loose. I noticed oil coming out of the bottom. It was coming out of the reverser, so we pulled the engine and called for parts. The D7 Cat track is loose, and almost lost it off about 3 times, so we pulled it out, pulled the idler ahead and welded a block behind the yoke. It should be good for another day or two. I'll quit fiddling around with junkie equipment one of these days and buy all new stuff, I hope. Al tried to start the old rubber tired loader, but something's wrong with the engine.

June 10th. Clint brought gas over to the mine this a.m., and Marcene came over with him. He's supposed to split this load with Cal Keatner. I flew back to Anchorage with them, picked up a load of parts, and then Clint flew me back to the mine. The boys put our loader back together.

Sunday, June 11th. The sluice box ran about 6 hours today. We found a nice little nugget in the box this morning. It rained and hailed, and our dam broke over this p.m., but it didn't take the whole dam out. So far the D7 is doing okay, and the John Deere is holding up just fine.

June 12th. The John Deere broke down about 5 p.m. We parted tracks and pulled the left steering clutch, the bearing was gone. Just one thing or another! Half the day the weather was nice, and the other half raining and lousy. It looks like we won't be in this pit much longer. We still have 3 barrels of diesel and a barrel of gas. The old Dodge truck is running good and doesn't take much gasoline to run now since we put the new carburetor kit in.

Friday, June 16th. The weather's been lousy all week, raining cats and dogs, and cold. We got some good gold out of the front riffles, but by 5:30 this p.m., it looks like we flat ran out of gold in this pit, so we're either gonna have to move, or strip some more ground. The old D7 is just barely making it, but if I baby it I think I can make it go for awhile yet. Clint came in yesterday and brought 3 barrels of fuel oil, diesel.

June 17th. It's still raining, all day, never saw so much rain. There's either too much, or too little. Boy, she's been raining here this year. We went up to the head of Twin Creek with our equipment and dug test holes. Didn't find anything worth digging for up there. Clint flew the little sluice box over. We're going to use it for clean-ups, even though it's a little large. We came back to the cabins about 2:30 p.m., it's just too miserable for working, almost freezing rain. We'll try to clean up the sluice box tomorrow.

June 18th. We put the backhoe attachment on and dug test holes on Twin Creek, and the tests looked good. It was still raining cats and dogs all day. Clint came in with Marcene, Mr. Smith and Bill. Mr. Smith is still interested in Collinsville.

June 19th. Today is beautiful, it quit raining and the sun came out. We can see Mt. McKinley just as plain as if it was next door, it's absolutely beautiful out. We were sure in good ground today for about 3 or 4 hours. Bill and Marty got the old drag line running, but it needs repairs too, right swing won't engage, only swings left. Well, maybe the only thing you can do is go around in circles with it. We can fix it if we need to, we'll know tomorrow for sure. The old D7's still hanging together, don't know why, it's so used up it should just fall apart.

June 20th. The color was real good in the riffles this day, and we got some nice nuggets. We were in good ground most of the day. The sun shined all day and it sure was a pleasure to work in sun instead of rain. Bill and Marty are working on the drag line, looks like they'll get it running and Marty is going to run it.

June 21st. We got the drag line running, with Marty running it. We dug test holes, ran the sluice box 8 hours today, got real good color in the box, and Mr. Smith really liked what he saw. He caught a plane to Anchorage at 5p.m. Marcene came over with Clint, and it was sure nice to see her. She brought groceries. It sure takes a lot when you're feeding a crew. The weather was pretty good, no rain. Skeeters were out in force for the first time this season.

Friday, June 23rd. We brought the loader with the backhoe attachment up to camp and tested the ground up Mills Creek. We found gold right in front of the cabins, and at Marcene's and my glory hole where we did the testing before. We broke the boom on the backhoe, and there we go again, had to weld it up. Jim cut it out and put a nice weld on it, and I think it'll hold up okay. I think we'll just run the pit where the box is, maybe 2 or 3 more days, then we'll move from Twin Creek over here by camp.

Monday, June 26th. We ran the box 7 hours today. It finally stopped raining and the weather was pretty good today. The old D7 sure is getting sick on the tracks and undercarriage. We finally just ran out of good ground in our pit on Twin Creek. Someone flew 7 barrels of fuel in to our strip today. They landed and took off while we were working, we don't know who it belongs to. This morning we got diesel in the pickup out of the gas barrel. No one knows how diesel fuel got into the gas drum. Man alive! We keep having miracles! Maybe Clint emptied the diesel into a wrong barrel, or something, so he could carry empty barrels back to town.

Tuesday, June 27th. We cleaned up today and got quite a bit of gold, but haven't got it all panned out yet. I had 2 pans of gold, and set them on an old oil stove there inside the cabin, and was gonna dry it out. I told the guys, "Be sure and don't bump into those pans, because that gold will spill down into the oil and fuzz and stuff behind the old oil heater." I turned around about 3 times and zap! I knocked them both off on the floor. It scattered all over the floor, into cracks, and that oil and fuzz. I tried to clean it all up, took the mop boards off and, gold from behind them, and got it out of the cracks with an old case knife. When I got it back into the pans, I put liquid soap in the pans to get rid of the oil and fuzz. The soap did the trick and everything came out alright.

Some outfit hauled in 7 more barrels of fuel today, jet fuel for a chopper on the strip. So that's where the fuel came from.

June 28th. I finished panning from our cleanup and then moved the box and hopper up to camp. We tightened the tracks on the old D7 Cat, hooked up to the tow grader, and graded the runway. We got through about 2 o'clock this morning. We should get set up and running tomorrow in the new location in front of the cookhouse. It'll save on gas for the truck. Everything's going just fine today. I got Marcene's message tonight and we're all going in on the 3rd.

June 29th. We made another pass on the runway this a.m. and it's in good shape. We set up our sluice box, built 2 dams, and will start working it tomorrow. We'll know in about 2 or 3 days how much longer we'll be over here. We have 3 barrels of diesel left. We'd like to get a message to Clint to bring fuel in on the 3rd, when he comes to get us out. I hope the environmentalists don't come by, or Fish & Wildlife, as we have no permits, unless the Canadians have them. I'm tired tonight.

June 30th. I sure would like to get just 1 week of sun, it rained hard all day and all last night. We spent most of the day repairing the dam and finally got it to hold. We're getting the drainage ready to run the box. The D7 broke down, and we had to spend about 2-1/2 hours welding on it, also had to adjust the clutch on the John Deere. It's been a booger. I guess the poor old D7 will just keep on plodding along, and hopefully, we can make the season with it.

Saturday, July 1st. More rain today. Quillian and Marcene came over today, brought groceries, etc. Sure nice to see her. Clint Seyer flew in this morning and had some friend's plane, didn't bring our 206 for some reason, but he brought us a pump. We're in some real good ground, getting a lot of ruby sands and black sands, ironite. We've got 14 ounces of coarse gold and over 15 ounces of fines, plus what we've got in the box since last cleanup.

Friday, July 7th. Clint flew us over to the mine today with groceries and so forth, in our 206. The weather was nice at camp. Water was a little low, but I think we'll have enough. The D7 broke down again, sheared gears on the shaft that powers the hydraulic system. We welded it up, but it only lasted for 1 pass, so we'll have to pull it out and get a new one.

July 8th. The weather was nice today. Jim and I worked on the D7 dozer all day, rebuilding the hydraulic pump. We found enough parts, used and new, to make repairs. Hope we can hold it together somehow for another 3 or 4 weeks. Shorty ran the loader and Marty worked the box. We're running a little 2-inch pump around the clock to keep the pit dried up and drained out. The ground is fair to good today.

I went down to check the pump tonight and I had 2 glass vials of gold with me, each one had 7-1/2 ounces in it. I stooped over to fill the pump and they slid out of my shirt pocket, hit in the rocks, and broke. I had to be real careful picking it up, and I assumed I got all the gold.

Sunday, July 9th. Cliff Hudson's pilot and a guy from the Department of Interior came by today, checking on the miners. Can you imagine, or understand, why our government hires people to work on Sunday, also hiring bush pilots, to check on us? We ran the sluice box about 7 hours today, having to push tailings with the little loader, the D7 is broke again. Hope to have it working again tomorrow.

July 10th. The John Deere broke down this evening, a bearing in the final drive. And the old D7's still sick, we need all kinds of things for it, seems you have to work on it more than you can run it. Sometimes I wonder if the Good Lord really meant for man to take out the gold. Seems there's always so many problems getting it out. It's 1 a.m., we just got finished working on the John Deere loader.

July 11th. It rained again today. Clint flew fuel into the mine with our 206, and Marcene sent over groceries. We're working on the John Deere and the D7 again today. So, what's new!. Everything is cool, and wet, and moving along pretty good.

Jimmy Simpson   1978   A VANISHING BREED

July 12th. The ground looked real good today and we have cut our hauling time in half, so we should do good from now on. We built a new ramp into the pit. My foot's hurting because I stepped on a couple nails yesterday evening. They went through my foot and came right out the top of my shoe. The swelling is mostly on top, and I should go in to get it checked, but what the heck, I think it'll be alright. Marcene's gonna check with the doctor and see if maybe I need some antibiotics, or something. I soaked it in hot water this p.m. It rained about half the day.

July 13th. Mel Pardek, the guy from Vancouver, B.C., came up today. He came over in a helicopter and took me for a ride in it. I got a real good look at the area around here. We were in some good ground today, and everything held together. Whoopee! If we aren't making much money, we're getting a lot of good experience. And we're eating good, we have lots of grub. Think we'll need water bad in a few days if it doesn't rain. It's either too much or too little. I'm all tired out tonight.

July 14th. We went to work at 8:30 a.m., took about an hour and a half off at noon, and quit about 8 tonight. The weather was good today, no rain, no sun, no skeeters. We checked the riffles at noon and they looked okay, but no big stuff. Quite a bit of fines gold. The old D7 is sure sick, keeps coming off the track. Guess we'll have to "afro-engineer" it some way and see what we can do to make it last a few more days. We're gonna have to lose a day to work on the D7 pretty soon, just take off a whole day and see if we can patch it enough to keep it going. The pit is going good, got good color, the gold is still with us. Our water is starting to get low and I hope it doesn't drop any lower. I heard Marcene's message tonight. 'Tis 11:30 p.m., I'm tired and my foot's still sore.

Saturday, July 15th. We're in good ground today, good color. Sure hope we have a good cleanup this time. The water sure is getting low. We may have to go to another pump, or narrow the box down somewhat with timbers. By placing timbers inside the box, it will take less water to run it. The D7 is so sick that we can't build another dam with it right now, so we're gonna have to kind of limp along with it and baby it. It's like a duck with both wings broken, watching its pond dry out. We had about 30 minutes downtime flushing the radiator on the John Deere. I cooked supper tonight, fried chicken, biscuits, corn, and fruit cocktail. Wish it would rain a little bit tonight. It's 12:40 right now, while I'm writing this.

July 16th. The sluice box ran 6 hours today, good ground, lots of good color. Clint flew 1 barrel of diesel, 1 of gas, oxygen and propane, Marcene and groceries over today. Nice to see Marene and everything is alright at home. It rained most of the day, but we need all the water we can get right now. Everything is still hanging together, just hope we can get another 60 days running. Jim shot a squirrel and another squirrel came up and started eating it. I didn't know that they were cannibalistic, but they are, these Parker squirrels are. I learn something every day.

July 17th. We ran the sluice box about 8 hours today. The weather was good and we had no breakdowns, and we're in real good ground. Gold mining's like the weather, you never can tell what tomorrow may bring. I got a letter from Marcene, always nice to get little letters from her. We went hunting tonight, but didn't see anything. Seven planes flew over today, guess lots of people just don't have anything to do.

July 18th. The sluice box ran 8 hours today, and we had no breakdowns. The weather was lousy, rain and cold, but we need the water. Clint brought Marcene over. She sold our house on Campbell Lake to Dr. David McGuire, and I had to sign the paperwork, then she took it back to Anchorage.

Thursday, July 20th. Our sluice box ran 8-1/2 hours today. It rained all day long, so we have plenty of water now. We were in bigger gold today. Everything's running okay, the old D7's still hanging in there. I got a message from Marcene tonight, it was good to hear that the 5 acres at our homestead by Matanuska Borough that Buzz Hoffman wants was approved. He can pay us off, or we'll take a motorhome, either way. Evidently we're going to take a new motorhome.

Saturday, July 22nd. The D7's working okay, but the right track idler is flat worn so bad it just seems each day may be the last. Seals for the finals are leaking so bad that when I push tailings, water gets in the finals and it floats the oil, and, oh, my goodness! Anyway, I don't want to go into it. It's just on its last leg and we're trying to make the thing hang together. If we fixed it right it would cost as much as it would to buy a new one, so we're gonna try to make it a few more days with this thing, then park it and get us another one. We've got to! Shorty went to the outhouse tonight and a porcupine was in there. He walked right in on it before he saw it, and had a heck of a time getting the porcupine out. He and the porky went 'round and 'round. He was hollering, and making all this racket. We went out to see what he was hollering about.

Monday July 24th. 'Bout the time that we think we've got one machine fixed, there's another one breaks. We had to shut down at 4:30 today and work on the John Deere, also worked on the hydraulic pump on the D7 Cat. Jim and I think we have all the leaks fixed on the D7, but the John Deere had a blown head gasket. The riffles looked fair for the short time that we ran today. We should get this pit cleaned up and material run by Thursday. The weather was nice most of today.

July 25th. The sluice box ran 5 hours today. We worked on the John Deere 'til one p.m., "Joe McGee'd" a starter. I just wonder what a starter shop would say if they saw it, but it works just fine, so no problem. We're in fair gold today, and the weather's nice. Marcene sure is doing fine in camp, the food is good, and the kitchen's clean. Marcene and I went moose hunting this evening.

July 26th. I shot a grizzly bear this morning with a trooper's shotgun, 12-gauge. I shot him on our front porch. It did make my hair stand up when I walked out that door. I heard him trying to break into the storeroom about 12:30 last night, so I rapped on the wall. I thought maybe it was a little black bear and he'd go away, but he didn't. He kept tearing away, and I hollered a little louder and rapped on the wall some more. Then I decided I'd get up and get my gun, go scare him. I started to walk out the front door, and he just stepped up on the front porch. He was about 10 feet away from me when I had to go ahead and do him a job. I had double-ought buckshot and slugs alternating in my gun, so I blew him off the porch with the double-ought, then I hit him in the shoulder with the slug and knocked him down again. He dragged himself about 40 or 50 feet before he finally gave up. Clint came over this p.m. and brought a barrel of diesel, and two 5-gallon cans of hydraulic oil. He had his son and 2 women with him, and Marcene went back with them. The equipment hung together pretty good today.

I wanted to mention on that grizzly bear, we skinned it out and Marcene took the hide into Anchorage. It's out of season, so we reported it to Fish & Wildlife, and so help me, I'll never do that again. She called me on the phone and told me I'd have to dig up the carcass, get the head and bring it in to Fish & Wildlife. When I got into town they really raked me over the coals. It's like I told the guy, I said, "Well, you don't ever have to worry about me reporting another one that I kill out of season." He said, "What do you mean by that?" Ha! Leave it between the lines. We could have put it in our deep freeze, it was only a week 'til the season opened. We even had a neighbor who was a taxidermist, Lonnie Temple. Just didn't think.

July 27th. We cleaned up the box this p.m. and the gold looks good. The weather was nice out today, sunshine most of the day. The old D7 just about didn't make the cleanup, so I guess we'll have to do some more "afro-engineering" before we move the box. A plane landed at midnight last night. He flew all over, don't know what he was looking for, or who he was, but anyway, it was probably some moose hunting scout, or one of the guides, or something.

July 28th. Our 206 Cessna came over with 2 barrels of diesel and groceries, and picked up Shorty and me. We had the D7 track broke apart and Marty and Jim were working on it. It sure was nice out today. Shorty and I weighed the coarse gold, and we had over 32 ounces of the coarse. I'll take it as repayment of bills and etc. I loaned Shorty $1000 to apply to getting his pickup out of hock. I checked on the price of gold with Jack Leakander, and fair price seemed to be $210 to $215 an ounce for jewelry gold, so at $210 an ounce it would be this many dollars, and so forth.

Saturday, July 29th. It's a nice day in Anchorage. I talked to Clint regarding the damage on our 206 airplane, and he agreed that it wasn't normal wear and tear, and he would take care of it. Shorty used our Mustang chasing parts in Anchorage. We're going to Tennessee on Monday. Lavelle and Ruth, Marcene's brother and sister-in-law, are going to meet us in Knoxville Tuesday morning. Marcene sent Ernestine Prochaska, in Las Vegas, $500 today.

Sunday, August 6th. Clint flew me over to the mine in the 206, and we carried 2 barrels of diesel. The weather was kind of foggy, but we made it in okay. The creek sure is low. We spent most of the day testing ground. We're going to move the sluice box right down in front of camp, we've got pretty good color here. The D7 is in pretty good shape now, after the guys have been working on it for a week, and the John Deere seems to be working pretty good.

A bear got into the washhouse last night. That sucker went through everything and got into a big box of Tide laundry detergent. The box stands about 2 feet high, is about 8 inches across and about 18 inches wide. He ate it all. I could just imagine what happened to that bear when he got to the creek and got him a drink of water.

August 7th. I ran the D7 Cat all day, stripping, and built a dam. The John Deere broke down about 9:45, and we had to pull the engine. Shorty got through on the radio about 6 p.m. for parts. I got the pit just about stripped. We should get the sluice box all set up and going tomorrow if the parts get here in the morning. No message on the Muckluck Telegram tonight. I quit at 8:45, it was getting too dark to watch the track, having trouble with it coming off.

August 8th. Hal, the owner of a boot store in Anchorage, flew over today and brought me a pair of boots. Sure nice. He says they're waterproof, to go ahead and wear them, and if I don't like them I don't have to pay anything. Hal wants me to buy into the shoe store business with him. We got the sluice box moved and another dam almost finished. Parts didn't get in, but we'll get them tomorrow, per a message from Marcene tonight. The weather was nice out, but we do need some rain for water.

August 9th. Clint flew parts and groceries over today. Marcene came with him, and it was nice to see her. We got the dam finished and the John Deere back together. Shorty spent most of the afternoon digging a drain. I ran the D7 Cat pushing muck. I'm getting tired. It started raining about 8:15 p.m. and I got soaked before I got to camp.

Mr. Orcutt, at Manley Hot Springs, wants me to come up and mine with him next spring. I'd like that, I think, just he and I.

He seems to be an honest person, and I wouldn't have to worry about anything.

August 10th. We got started sluicing this a.m. The ground is very rocky, but good. Lots of fine gold. We had sunshine most of the day. It's moose season and people are on the move. Four planes came over today, everyone wants to go hunting over here. I cooked supper, steaks, the ones with strings tied around them, biscuits, and baked potatoes. I got Marcene's message, and also Roberta's for Al. The boots that Hal brought me sure are nice. It's been a long day, but I'm happy and everything's fine.

August 11th. It's nice out today, but the water sure is getting low. With 2 hours buildup, the sluice box works good for about an hour. We sure need some of the rain that we were plagued with earlier this summer. Oh, well, everything is going to work out okay. The riffles sure look good. The John Deere broke again this p.m., hydraulic pipe sprung a leak and we had to pull the belly pad and all kinds of "spaghetti" to get it off so Jim could braze it. The old D7 is doing okay, it's sure a tough one. Sure glad Marcene and Jadene are coming over on Sunday.

Saturday, August 12th. The color was real good in the box today. Our water is low, so we put 8-inch timbers in one side of the sluice box to narrow the box down and compensate for the low water. I hope it rains pretty soon. Shorty's looking at the riffles with stars in his eyes. We got about 2 ounces out of the front riffles today. We had to go rob oil out of the old dredge motor for the D7. I hope Clint brings some over tomorrow. The weather was icky, but no rain. It's funny how we hope for rain now that we need water. I cooked supper tonight, fried potatoes, hamburgers, all kinds of buns, also corn bread, we had a nice meal. I got a message from Marcene tonight on the Bush Pipeline.

August 13th. Clint flew Marcene, Mr. Orcutt, and Eddie McNabb over today. Eddie is kind of our adopted son. Clint's wife, Marybeth, came along too. Hal and his wife came over, flew his Taylorcraft. Everyone panned, and it rained on them. It's sure nice to have enough water. We got real good color, about 3 ounces, or more, of gold in the front riffle. Eddie had a nice pan with gold in it, and he just rolled the gold right out of his pan. He showed me the nuggets first. I swirled the pan and then he went back over to pan it on down, and lost them.

August 14th. We had a little rain today, and got good color in the sluice box. Marcene's a good cook, T-bones for supper. I marked the runway tonight with crosses at 3 spots, put white lines on them. This way, no one is supposed to land unless it's an emergency. We found our biggest nugget to date this p.m. We got a message from Jadene; today is our 29th anniversary, and it sure was sweet of her. We also got a message from Clint that he is bringing Mr. Smith over tomorrow.

August 15th. The pit panned out real good today, and the riffles look real good too. Clint flew Mr. Smith and 2 barrels of fuel over today, then took Mr. Smith and Marcene back to Anchorage. Sure was nice having her in camp. Smith really wants to get me to mine with him, but I just can't see it because of his sons-in-law. Clint said he could see the crosses on the runway real good from the air. We need rain bad for water for the sluice box, but we had sunshine most of the day.

August 16th. It rained for us today, sure helped us. We added the 2-inch pump, and it helped a great deal. That's the 2-inch pump plus the water we already had going into the sluice box. I got a message from Marcene that Mel Pardek would be in Monday. We left our watermelon outside by the creek, and the squirrels got into it and ate quite a bit of it. It had been cut and we threw out the rinds last night, so I guess they got a taste and started looking round for the source. The equipment's running good. It gets dark about 9:45 now, and it's a little cooler. It won't be long before the frost because we're at the 5700 foot level here in the foothills of Mr. McKinley.

August 17th. We had plenty of water this a.m., but ran out about 4:30 p.m. It's sure a shame when the sun is shining and so nice out, to be so short on water, so we're going to try leaving the water plugged off and get up early, at 3:45 a.m., and run straight through until the water runs out. It builds up better at night as the sun dries it up during the day. Color is still good in the riffles. I had a guy fly in to the strip this a.m. He landed and came over to the pit, and asked about hunting. I told him no. I asked him if he knew what the white crosses on the strip meant, and he said, yes, it meant it was an emergency. White crosses mean you don't land.

August 18th. We got started this a.m. at 4:45 and worked until the water ran out. Jim hardfaced the teeth on the loader bucket, that's welding hardface rod onto the teeth. Marcene and Hal came over this p.m. and brought groceries. It was sure nice of Hal to come over. Marcene's been busy getting things loaded into a van, etc., to move them to Tennessee from the house we sold to Dr. McGuire.

Sunday, August 20th. Boy, did it rain last night! I got up at 5 a.m. and went down to check on the dam, and it just had started spilling over. So I got a shovel, dug another spillover and plugged a hole, just caught it in time. The sluice box was almost washed away, all the gravel under it washed out. Today the weather turned nice, and we had lots of water. We ran the box approximately 11 hours and the riffles looked good. We took about 2 ounces of gold out of the front riffle. Clint flew over with 2 barrels of diesel, 1 barrel of gas, and groceries. We have lots of meat, a case of beer, and candy. Marcene sure takes care of us.

Tuesday, August 22nd. Mel Pardek cooked supper tonight and it was good. He burnt the potatoes, burnt them on purpose. He said, "I love burned potatoes!" We got a dam full of water, running out at the overflow pipe.

August 23rd. Two planes came over this a.m., but didn't land because of the white crosses on the runway. Mel cooked dinner and supper. He's sure a nice guy. I'm tired and going to bed, it's 10:15.

August 24th. We've got a lot of man hours working on equipment. Clint flew over this a.m. in a small plane and got Mel Pardek. Fall is definitely in the air, gets nippy when the sun goes down.

August 25th. Hal flew a bottle of propane over to us, and brought Mel Pardek back. Sure nice of Hal. We ran low on water at noon, and we went over to Twin Creek and dug test holes.

Saturday, August 26th. A guy by the name of Moore, and his wife and 2 kids, came in this a.m. They asked permission to pick blueberries, and they got about 5 gallons of them. We tried building a reserve dam upcreek to save water, but the water ran right under the danged old tailings piles. I'm beginning to wonder if this ground is rich enough to move as much muck as we're having to move. Marty sprained his back, or pulled a muscle, sure hate to see anyone get hurt. I offered to work the box for him, but he's still trying to work it.

August 27th. Marty went into town this p.m. I hope the Doc can help his back problem, he's a fine kid. We still need water, and how! Marcene will be over about next Thursday.

August 28th. Clint flew over in a 172, and brought hammer handles, my clothes, and a letter for Jim. He let me fly the plane, and I took off and landed. I messed up on the brakes, just need to practice. I told Clint it was those new shoes Hal brought over. I'm setting on the right-hand side instead of the left side, and it kind of bumfuzzled me there a little bit. One of my new shoes slid off of the side of the plane on the right side, and I hit the rudder.

August 29th. No Pipeline messages tonight, no word from Marty. We finished filling a cigar tube full of gold, this makes 3 of them from picking the front riffles. That's 7-1/2 ounces per tube. We only saw 2 airplanes today, and neither landed on our strip. Only 2 more days before Marcene gets here, sure will be nice having her here to talk to, etc. I'm working the sluice box and running the dozer, it's good for my waistline.

August 30th. Hal and his father-in-law came over today for hunting season. They're nice people. Our strip looked like Merrill Field today. One plane with 4 people crashed between this strip and the old one down below. No one was hurt. We're gonna have to do something about so many people flying in to our strip. It rained tonight and, of all things to happen, the John Deere broke down again! Could be the Eskimos are right in their thinking about gold, they are superstitious.

August 31st. Clint flew the 172 over today, the cost is to be split with RCA and Tile Keatner. Marcene came over with Clint, and should be over to stay on Saturday. She gave Shorty $200 today. Hal flew Shorty into town to get a fuel pump for the John Deere and got back about 3:30. I ran the dozer, stripping and sealing leaks in the dam. The planes and hunters are driving me buggy! After putting the white crosses and barrels on the strip, a Super Cub still landed on the side of the strip. Boy, oh boy!

September 1st. We have lots of water and the durned loader's hydraulic pump went out, and the D7 broke a track tension bolt and busted a big chunk out of the housing over the bull gear. So we spent 5-1/2 hours working on equipment today.

September 2nd. Clint flew the 206 over, brought Marcene, Kendall, Artie, and groceries. Kendall Hamilton is my Nephew from Tennessee, and he's up for moose hunting. Three men worked on the loader 4 hours today, working on hydraulic fittings, and welding on same. We had sunshine and it was hot most of the day. Dr. McGuire moved into our house on Campbell Lake today.

Sunday, September 3rd. We just lollygagged around today, first day off all summer. Jim, Kendall and Marty went hunting today. It's sure nice having Marcene here. Kendall and his friend, Cowboy, got a moose each. No planes landed today, guess word got around. The weather was nice.

September 4th. The color in the riffles was pretty good today. The old D7 died today, just gave up. That's the end of it as far as I'm concerned, I'm not gonna fool with it anymore. The only good thing on it is the fuel cap. It quit right in front of the sluice box. Also, we worked on the John Deere for about 4 hours. Hal still hasn't gotten a moose yet. Cowboy and his bunch hauled their moose and all gear out today. We should be cleaning up in about 2 or 3 days. Not having the D7 sure slows the production down, but that's the way it goes.

September 5th. It rained all last night and it's raining cats and dogs today. The water washed out our dam this a.m. Kendall shot a big moose, and Hal and his preacher father-in-law took off and left him, didn't even offer to bring him back over to camp with it on their 4-wheelers. He had to walk about 6 to 10 miles into camp.

It's a nice feeling to be finished for the season. I helped Marcene across the water at the creek. She looked like a little puppy trying to find its way across, just walking and looking up and down the bank. The water was so high, and it was sure funny watching her. We got wet, wet, wet. We cleaned up today. I think we have less gold than we had last cleanup, but no sweat. We did the screening and the panning of the gold in the kitchen on the table.

September 6th. We're just goofing around today, taking it easy. Shorty thought he fixed the stove in his cabin. Shorty likes to sleep with a real hot fire going in the cabin, and Marty likes it cool. So, Shorty would turn the heat up real high, and Marty, in turn, would go outside the cabin and turn it off at the tank. About the time that Shorty would get to sleep, the fire would go out and he'd wake up freezing in the morning. Marty would get up in the morning, go out and turn it back on, and then light the heater. Marty, Jim and Kendall got a good night's sleep last night when they did that. We tore out the beaver dam on Twin Creek this afternoon, so we can drive up the road without going through deep water. Then we tore it out again tonight on the way down with the loader.

September 7th. When we went back up Twin Creek this morning, the beaver dam was built back again, so we had to tear it out again. Those beaver built that dam back in the time during the day that we were working on Twin Creek, and overnight, so that's how fast they kept building it back.

I bought a Honda 3-wheeler today. Boy, we sure ran all over today. We went to Palmer to get the Honda, to the bank, to the storage shed, to our camper park, and picked up Chris's pickup at Campbell Lake. We used Bobby Jo's pickup most all day and took it back full of gas at 4 p.m. We went by to see Jadene this p.m., and spent the night with Denny and Jo Jones. They're nice people. We saw Buzz Hoffman for a few minutes today. I flew the 172 plane back from the mine into Anchorage and did everything but talk on the radio. Shorty and Marty are going to try and get the D6 going. We're gonna run another 2 or 3 weeks this fall, maybe. I gave Clint a $2000 watch today, and he is to teach me to fly the 206.

September 8th. We caught the plane for Seattle at 9 a.m. The projected take of gold is over 200 ounces. I went down to talk to Mel Pardek's partners in Vancouver, B.C., regarding furnishing equipment for Collinsville. We got into Vancouver late in the evening; we rented a car in Seattle and drove on up there to meet with those guys.

September 9th. We had the meeting with the people in Vancouver and they sure seemed nice. It looks like we have a deal for next year. They agreed to buy a late model D7 Cat, a rubber tired 966 Cat loader, and a shaker-washing plant. We drove the rental car back to Seattle and caught a plane back to Anchorage.

Monday, September 11th. We sure were busy today in Anchorage, and we saw our accountant. I flew the 206, took off at Anchorage International Airport, and landed at Collinsville. We took over oil, hydraulic oil, groceries, and etc. Clint flew the 206 back this p.m. and took Kendall into town. We're glad to be back in camp, and Kendall sure was glad to get out and on his way back to Tennessee with his big moose.

September 12th. We spent 11 hours today working on the D6 Cat, the old, old, old D6 up the creek that we found and dug out. We're gonna try to get it going. We should get the sluice box ready to go by tomorrow evening, but have about 5 or 6 hours work before we can start sluicing. We're getting another antique ready to run as long as it will. All we need is about 2 to 3 more weeks. We ran the light plant most of the day.

September 13th. We got the D6 running and got started dozing, building a dam. The boys got the sluice box set up and ready to go. Clint flew our friend, Maxine Smith, over today. She owns ABM Escrow and has power of attorney on us. She's a very nice and intelligent lady. We signed quit-claim deeds over to her regarding the property, etc. Looks like we'll get started with the box tomorrow about noon, or a little after. We're working on the equipment again, the John Deere and the D6 Cat. The old D6 Cat runs pretty good and should last a week, or so, I guess. Can't get away from the work. I went over this p.m. and got rhubarb at the Twin Creek camp.

September 14th. We spent most of the day building a dam, and ran the box awhile. We had to work on the Cat for about an hour, adjust the track, take off the pad and adjust the steering clutch. The weather was kind of icky, cloudy and light rain. Our dam is holding good and we have plenty of water. Clint was supposed to bring in fuel, but I guess it will be tomorrow. We have enough to run another day, but will need fuel the day after tomorrow. We tried to tow the old D7 to the shop, but it's so wore out that it wouldn't even tow. The darned track fell off, so we just parked it on the tailings pile.

September 15th. It was kind of nice out today. We had plenty of water, the dam is holding good. We spent about 2 hours stripping overburden, running more paydirt through the box. We should have about a week's running left in this pit. We ran about 190 yards today. It takes a little more fuel for the D6 because we have to work it harder than the D7.

September 16th. Bobby Jo and her folks and kids came over today to spend the weekend. We spent an hour stripping. The Canadians came in this a.m. and brought an engineer to evaluate the potential and feasibility of them buying new equipment. It looks like a "go". Marcene went into town today, sick with the flu, should be back tomorrow.

Sunday, September 17th. Jim Mitchell and I checked the ground. Mr. Mitchell is about 76 years old, but he can outwalk me, that sucker is a "go-er". We dug 10 test holes on Twin Creek near the camp, and by the old glory hole up there, and all the tests turned out real good. We were glad that the geologist was really happy and got the results he wanted to see. I took Bobby Jo's folks over to pan with their little sluice box, and they did real good. I panned the best 2 pans I've ever panned, anywhere. Must be about $100 per yard material, sure good.

September 18th. The boys went over with Chuck Tanner and Bobby Jo and got their 3 moose. Jim, Marty and Shorty took over the loader and two 3-wheelers. Chuck played sick and left us to skin out and dress the moose. We got started late, and I helped skin the moose, then loaded 'em into the 206 while Chuck watched. Chuck made 2 trips with the moose and came back for the folks. The weather's still holding for us. Chuck was going to bring us 2 barrels of diesel over on the backhaul, but Big Jim wouldn't load it for him. We'll just use up our fuel and then shut down. Note: Chuck later got caught counterfitting money and was put away.

September 19th. It's cloudy and cold out today, but not freezing yet. Jadene, Marcene and I went riding on 3-wheelers today. They sure are fun. We'll be glad to shut down, as always at this time of year.

September 20th. It's time to shut down, the "union" is coming out of Shorty. The guys finally got him going at about 9 a.m., and they stopped at 6:15. You'd think that at this time of year, and the weather still nice like it is, that they'd really try hard to get out all they could. I can just guess what would happen if I wasn't over here to prod them.

Jerry came in to get Jadene. He had left Anchorage earlier, but the engine quit on him down in the swamp and he had to ditch it. He had to walk out and a helicopter came to pick him up. His pants were still wet when he came in to get Jadene. When the helicopter rescued him, he just went on into Anchorage, got another plane and came back after Jadene, wet pants and all. He was lucky not to get hurt. Big Jim came with him, and they took Jadene back to Anchorage, even though it was 5 hours late.

September 21st. We cleaned up today and it was fair, about 20-some ounces, and I think there'll be some more yet to come. The John Deere broke again, so we just went ahead and cleaned up anyway. It was cooler today, winter can't be too far away. The guys are sure glad to shut down.

September 22nd. The water line froze last night, first ice of the season. We spent most of the day cleaning up the camp, jacking the shop roof up and putting timbers under it, and putting away things for the winter. Marty and Jim went hunting this evening, down to the trapper's cabin about 6 miles southeast toward Mt. Yenlo. We had to work on the D6 again today. Marcene and I plan on going to our little glory hole tomorrow.

September 23rd. We set up our little sluice box in Twin Creek and ran it with two 5-gallon buckets, carrying the buckets about 600 feet to run it through. We got some real good color in the little box.

Sunday, September 24th. We went into town today. Boy, the weather just about closed in too quick. Jerry barely made it in, and got Marcene, myself and personal gear.

September 25th. I drew $4000 out of savings to pay Jim for work at the mine, and gave him 4 ounces of nice gold for a bonus. I've been running all day, getting paperwork done. I got a check for the plane rental, $5645 through August 15th. This pays us up to date on the plane. I got settled up with the guys, Marty and Shorty, on our percentage deal.

1979

Thursday, February 1, 1979. I called Shorty today, and I guess he's going to work at Collinsville this year with the Canadians. He's a little shrewdie; he went behind my back and made a deal with them. Evidently they bought a D8 Cat, and a D85 Komatsu, a 988 Cat rubber tired loader, a 125 Michigan rubber tired loader, and a new special sluice box built in Richmond, B.C., named the Ross Box. Shorty, little coniver that he is, got to Nick Zoro, one of the Canadians I met down in Vancouver, that I didn't quite trust, and a local attorney in Anchorage, Henry Camerot, and cut a deal with them. He took the equipment in cross-country, and he's gonna be mining over there this summer. But, you give a guy enough rope and he'll eventually hang himself.

I got a call from the banker today, and Clint has our plane subleased to a guy in Kodiak. I bought tickets for Marcene and me to go to Anchorage. When we got to Clint's house I told him he had 24 hours to get our 206 back in Anchorage. Our 206 got back to Anchorage overnight. It got over to Merrill Field today, and Merrill Field Upholstery is going to fix the seats and interior of the plane, and Clint's gonna pick up the tab for it.

I talked with Pettijohn today regarding mining in Peru. He's a dealer in mining claims, based out of Anchorage. I just may go down to Peru and stake some claims, see what I can do there. I met with Stanfield, our attorney, and gave my deposition regarding the Blacks' claim. I'm just keeping my fingers crossed. I talked to Mel Tillis today. It's cold in Tennessee and he has the flu.

Our 206 has 900 hours on it. If we decide to let Clint continue leasing the plane he'll have to deal with Buzz Hoffman at the First National Bank. I'm giving Buzz power of attorney regarding the 206. I wiped out $3150 that Clint owes us, for the lease on the 206, in hopes that he'll put our plane back in top shape. I have to walk softly as we didn't have a thing in writing on a lease. I just thought a handshake would be good enough, but find out it isn't anymore.

I got a call today from our attorney, Stanfield. The natives and Nanna and all agree to settle for $6000. I asked him to try and get them to settle for $5000, against my will. We should have an answer tomorrow. At least we know that the most the Blacks and Nanna will get will be $6000 plus what we've already paid Stanfield. I talked with Pettijohn again today regarding Peru, and it was fair to good. Didn't get a call from Shorty today.

Wednesday, February 7th. I talked to Stanfield today, and he said to go ahead on vacation and not worry about the case, as he had things under control. We bought tickets today for Marcene, myself, Billy Ray and Nancy Jackson, round trip tickets to Peru. Billy Ray Jackson and I went to school together in Ashland City, Tennessee. In fact, I bought my first pocket watch from him, gave him 10 cents for it. He went on to become an attorney, and was out of West Palm Beach, Florida. He knew a guy with the Consulate down in Peru.

February 8th. We went to Miami this a.m. and got our passports for Peru. We'll be leaving for Lima on Sunday, at 2 a.m.

February 9th. I called Mel Pardek in Vancouver today. He said that they plan on buying equipment and mining at Collinsville, and they would like to have me go over there with them.

Sunday, February 11th. We stopped off in Equador this a.m., and made it into Lima, Peru, about 11:30. It took 'til about 12:30 to get through Customs. We rented rooms at the Caeser's Hotel in Lima. Billy Ray Jackson and his wife came down with us. We paid their fares down and back, first class, and they're so high and mighty . . . I guess us country folks just can't quite cope with their way of thinking. They act as if we're absolutely peons. I guess he's so used to representing dumb people that he assumed we're in the same category. He's meeting with Heinie, a big shot that we don't need to meet, so Billy Ray's gonna meet with him tonight. We'll just bypass that and go on and stake our claims on the creek.

The commode in our hotel room had a bidet hooked up to it and we weren't acquainted with that. Marcene wet her hair pretty good with it, she was down looking at it when she punched the little button on the commode.

February 12th. We went shopping in Lima today and bought a few things. Of course, everyone who goes to Lima buys a llama rug. The weather was cloudy, I guess it just follows us around, seems everywhere we go it's the same. Billy Ray left us a note and said he'd see us later, guess he just doesn't understand that we don't have to be led around like kids. I talked with Pettijohn's geologist last night and he was sure nice. He gave us a bunch of information. We got our tickets exchanged to Brannif today and we're gonna be leaving here before too much longer.

I talked to some guys with Flying Tiger Airlines, one was a pilot. He and 2 more guys put in $50,000 apiece, and set up mining operations down there in the head waters of the Amazon River. To get set up and going, what they did was paint all their equipment and put new decals on it, and then tip the guy in charge of the dock where they shipped the equipment in. They tipped him gently, but firmly, gave him a $20 bill, and he okayed their equipment to come on in. Otherwise, they'd have had to pay about 100% duty on it. Because it had new paint and decals, it was classified as new equipment, and you could ship new equipment into Peru without duty in those days.

Once they got set up and going, the "banditos" came through and shook them down, made them clean their box. The first time, that was not too bad, they went along with it. But one guy was telling me that after the third time, and each time it was a different band coming through with their automatic rifles, that he was pulling out and leaving.

And, not only that, when you sell your gold, you have to sell it to the Peruvian Government, and the Government wouldn't let you carry out over $5000 of Peruvian money per year. Also, the most you could carry out in American money was less than $10,000. So what you had to do was to take your gold, sell it to the Peruvian Government, get the Peruvian money, go on the streets and swap the Peruvian money for U.S. funds, and hope you could get out of the country with some of it. We figured it's just not worth it to be mining in Peru. Billy Ray thought that we could work a deal through the "bigwigs", but I just didn't quite see it. I couldn't see getting tangled up paying kickbacks and payoffs, and stuff like that. I figured the sooner we got out of Peru, the better.

The one thing that kind of intrigued me was the Peruvian help. You could get real good workers for $3 a day, and they furnished their own bedrolls and food. They had special panning bowls, they were kind of like bowls, they weren't like our gold pans in the States. The ground was just about equivalent to what you'd find in parts of Alaska, so there's no reason to go through all of the hassle down there, when we can work in Alaska without all the hassle.

On our way back from Lima, we stopped off again at Quito, Equador, and in Bogata, Colombia. I had on a western hat, and the stewardesses on the plane wouldn't serve us anything, and we had first class tickets. When we got to Bogata, we got some stewards on there, and boy, they treated us real nice.

In Bogata, the Army came out to the plane. They had their automatic weapons and everything, and I thought they were going to commandeer the airplane, but they were looking for someone on the airplane, and took the person off. We were held up there for about an hour, but made it back to Miami okay. We'd left Billy Ray and his wife, Nancy, down there because we couldn't see getting tangled up with all those "bigwigs" in the Peruvian Government.

We got into Miami on time and everything was fine. Our motorhome was still at Billy Ray's where we left it. We had to jump the battery, we'd left something on, but no big deal. On our way back to Tennessee, we went by to see old Brad Garris over at Okeechobee, but he wasn't there, he was in Anchorage. Son of a gun! He owns a barbeque place in Okeechobee, and is a roofer in Anchorage.

Wednesday, April 4th. I called Jim Prochaska tonight, and he said he would like to mine with us this summer, wherever we will be mining. I called Clint Seyer this a.m., and he promised me that our 206 would be in A-1 shape and ready to fly this next Monday. He said that the automatic pilot was back in, the upholstery replaced, the tail section repaired and the plastic on the tail replaced.

Friday, May 4th. It stormed all night. We left Ashland City at 6 a.m. and drove the motorhome to Salina, Kansas, about 750 miles. Kendall's along with us and it's sure nice to have him help drive. I tried to call Jim today, but no luck. No problems today.

May 5th. We got to Denver, picked Jim up, and headed for Alaska. We didn't have any real problems and the motorhome was just fine. We took the ferry from Prince Rupert, B.C. to Haines, Alaska.

Wednesday, May 16th. I met with Clint this morning; he said he would bring over a log book, but he didn't do it. Mr. Heatherly came by today and said that he'd haul a dozer and trailer up to Manley Hot Springs. Kendall and Jim are still with us.

May 17th. We went over to Collinsville today and picked up my welder, etc. I still have the pump and hoses, cutting torch, hoses and gauges, and chain hoist over there. Mr. Nick Zoro told me he would send them in with Clint. There was lots of snow still over there. Clint flew us over in Bobby Jo and Chuck's 206. I found the seat from our 206 today, it was in Chuck's 206, so we saved that much.

May 18th. I took Kendall and Jim out to catch Clint's flight to Drift River today. He was gonna take them bear hunting. King Air is still working on our 206. The weather was nice today.

We went to Buzz Hoffman's this p.m. and ate supper. Mr. Heatherly told me tonight that he wants $1400 to haul my dozer and the wanigan, up to Manley Hot Springs. I'll be working with a Mr. Don Orcutt, an ex-Federal Fish & Wildlilfe official, on Eureka Creek, out of Manley Hot Springs. I kind of feel sorry for Mr. Heatherly. The people at Collinsville are just using him, period. He went in with them cross-country, used his Nodwell, and they never reimbursed him anything.

Tuesday, May 22nd. I went by Equipment Services and talked to Bob about getting a dozer. He'll let me know the details tomorrow. Marcene and I had dinner with Don Orcutt and his wife, Nadine. Don is going to check on a lowboy to haul the dozer and wanigan up to Manley Hot Springs. He seems to know a guy who'll haul it cheaper than Mr. Heatherly. We went by and checked on our airplane, the cost is going to be about $2100, not counting the ADF at $900. Clint took Kendall and Jim bear hunting over near Hope this p.m. Our camper park is slow for this time of year.

May 23rd. I bought a Komatsu dozer at Equipment Services today for $27,500, paid a little over $4000 down. The weather was nice. I got my welder, chain saw, and battery charger all fixed and ready to go. I met with Don Orcutt and it looks like we'll leave about next Thursday for Manley Hot Springs. Nick Zoro agreed today to send my things back from the mine that Shorty took over there. I took the 6x6 with the DC-3 tires on it down to Don Bragg's yard, and he is to sell it for me for $5000. The 206 was completed and finished today, the total price on it was $3400, no end to it, guess I'll just have to sue Clint Seyer and try to recoup something on the 206.

I talked to Mr. Heatherly and he'll haul the dozer and rest of my stuff up to Manley Hot Springs on Thursday, or Friday. We stopped by Jadene's tonight and got paperwork from our accountant, and all kinds of goodies. Don Cole, the accountant, told us that we'd have to pay $41,000 in taxes. You just can't hardly win. I'm gonna go see if we can get it reduced somehow.

Thursday, May 31st. Shorty sent me the wrong hoses, rotten ones, and the wrong torch. He's a bad one. I got my pump and oxygen bottle though. After getting the welder from Collinsville, I had to take it to A & P to get it fixed. I got Clint to go and fly our 206, and he admitted that some instruments were missing, and some were messing up. I found my transponder in Chuck Tanner's plane. Looks like we may have our plane sold. There's a guy from Bethel interested in the 206, he's a State Trooper. I hope he takes it, we'll know tomorrow. The lowboy came in last night from Fairbanks and picked up the dozer from Equipment Services. He tried to carry the trailer, but it wouldn't fit on his lowboy. I guess we'll just pull the trailer up with my pickup. We'll have to rig lights and mud flaps, and install a hitch on the pickup.

Sunday, June 3rd. We left Anchorage at 3:30 a.m. and made it into Fairbanks at 2 p.m., and it was hot in Fairbanks today. Marcene and I were driving our motorhome, and Jim was in the pickup pulling the trailer. We got stopped in Fairbanks by State Troopers, but they let us go. We had a snow machine trailer license on our trailer, and no registration on it, but the Trooper just happened to be a nice guy. The pickup had no trouble at all pulling the trailer, it trailed just fine.

June 4th. We picked up 2 barrels of gas at the Texaco distributor, and left Fairbanks this morning for the mine. We got to the mine about 3:30 p.m. The weather was nice, but the road was rough, and even without any trouble it took us 5-1/2 hours. When we got in to the mine, the road bridge was out, so I built a road around the washed out bridge with the dozer. It was kind of scary coming across in the motorhome, and it got full of dust, even in the drawers. Don said, "How come you got all that dust in your motorhome?" So Marcene said she didn't know. We opened the windows and the air ducts, thinking the air would blow the dust out. He said, "No, you close all your ducts and all your windows, and turn your air conditioner on. That way it creates a vacuum and doesn't let dust come in." So, that's the name of that tune.

June 5th. Don and I went into Manley Hot Springs today and got some steel at Bobby Miller's yard. They said to estimate the weight and pay them when we came into town again. That sure was nice of them. Jim, Don and I worked on the box. The welder worked fine. I got boosters from Don for my radio and it works better now. The weather was nice today, but I'm afraid that we'll run short of water up here in Manley.

June 6th. We're working on the sluice box, getting ready to go. We got a message from Don Cole to contact him, so we drove into Manley and called. Our poor little Jadene had to go to the hospital and have an emergency operation. She had a blocked intestine, and they also took her appendix out, an hour and a half operation. Dr. R. Gower from Nashville did the operation. We talked to "Peanut" and she was groggy, but real nice. Marcene will go to Fairbanks, and on to Anchorage tomorrow.

June 7th. I took Marcene into Manley Hot Springs and she caught a plane to Fairbanks. I sure feel sorry for Peanut, bless her heart. It was good that Marcene could go down. Don and Nadine rode in with us and we got some more materials at Bobby Miller's yard. I paid by check for the iron, $75. We ran the sluice box from 10 a.m. until 11:10 p.m. I'm sure tired today. We cleaned out the water ditch, about 3-1/2 miles of it, and cut the creek into it. We dug and shoveled, and cleaned, but beats a pump and pipe. I found an old shovel that the old-timers worked with around 1897. They sure had to be a hardy breed. The water ditch was originally hand-dug by the old-timers in the late 1800s. I guess the birds here don't sleep, they're singing outside and it's midnight. Jim and I ate with Don and Nadine, at noon and supper. They're sure nice.

June 8th. The sluice box ran 7 hours today. We got started at 8 o'clock this morning and ran out of water at noon, so we ate lunch. Jim and I dug test holes 'til 4 p.m., then we ran the sluice box 'til 7 p.m. The color was good. I got a message from Marcene that Jadene is doing good and I'm sure glad. The weather was nice today. Jim and I are eating with Don and Nadine.

Saturday, June 9th. It sure is weird material that we're working in, I just can't figure it out. We ran the box 3-1/2 hours this a.m. before we ran out of water. We let it build up and then ran 2-1/2 hours this p.m. I think that by cutting the water valve off while I'm pushing tailings, we can gain about 1-1/2 to 2 hours a day on the box. We'll try it tomorrow. There are some strange people parked up on the road, just up from our sluice box. I guess we'll take turns watching tonight, you never can tell what people are up to. They're a bunch of hippies, I think.

June 10th. It rained most of the day, cold and miserable out. I'm sure glad that I'm running the new dozer. It didn't seem like Sunday today, I miss Marcene, too. I hope little Jadene is over most of the soreness, sure a shame for that to happen to her.

June 11th. Don and Nadine went over to Archie Pringle's this a.m. for awhile. We dug test holes for about an hour and panned for about an hour and a half, trying to find a good pay streak. I ran the heater last night just long enough to take the chill out of the motorhome. It was raining again this morning, cold and miserable.

June 12th. It rained and the wind blew most of the day, it's sure miserable. Our water ditch broke today and we had to repair it. We had plenty of water though. Sure is hard trying to find gold; the Good Lord sure hid it good. I'm pushing too much muck through the box and I don't think that we're getting as much gold as I've gotten in the past. I went down and fixed the road across Boston Creek so I can take the motorhome out to Manley for propane, as we're getting low. I took Don and Nadine over to see some friends in my pickup. No news from Marcene today. I hope the Trooper from Bethel comes through on the airplane tomorrow. We'll wait and see.

June 13th. We're just about out of paydirt in this pit we're in, looks like we're gonna have to move a little bit. We've got some test holes dug, and it looks like we can move the holding pond. That is where the paystreak runs, right underneath the settling pond. I talked to an old-timer today, and he told me about a spot that might be some real good ground, but there's lots of boulders. It's up over the hill from here.

Friday, June 15th. Tonight I heard that Art Fields lost everything, including his planes and his store in Kotzebue, to Fish & Wildlife, for hunting and flying in the same day, as a big game guide. It's real sad to hear that. I hope things work out for him, and maybe he'll be able to recoup some of his stuff. An IRS agent told me one time he wanted to see Art's paperwork, and "Art ran me off with a gun!" We had a black bear in camp tonight.

June 16th. I drove into Manley today because Don and Nadine told me that I was to call home right away, but they got the message goofed up. The message was that Loren Hite was to call me. We ran the box this morning and got good color before we ran out of water. Then, about 5 p.m., I uncovered a real rich paystreak about 10 feet wide. I don't quite know yet how far it goes.

I kind of hope that Mr. Hite calls, I have another "granny" here. Don said yesterday that he was concerned about muddy water getting out of our settling pond, and that we should flatten out the tailings piles. Anyway, Don keeps reminding me of all the gold that's been taken out of here, but I'm concerned about what we can find. I don't think that he cares to get too much gold. He and Nadine act like little kids with the gold. The best partner I ever had, have, or will have, is Marcene!

June 17th. The weather was nice out today. The color in the box was good today. I can't tell much about this here box, it's a weird one. It's one that Don had when we came up this spring. We cut the good old country ham this evening. Nadine has never tasted country ham, so we'll have some for breakfast. Shorty and the guys got shut down over at Collinsville by Fish & "Wildfeathers". Guess I'll hang on here for a few more days.

A pilot from Manley Hot Springs flew over today and dropped a note that Marcene would be 3 hours late. I drove to town and called her, guess she'll be up Tuesday on the mail plane. Joe King charged $900 for the ADF for our 206. He lied to me, because he told me it would cost $800. I guess the extra $100 is because insurance is involved. Boy, when you have a plane it's like pouring money into a big, ol' hole, you just can't hardly get it filled up.

July 18th. The color is fair in the box, but not what it should be. Mr. Hite sent word for us to come on up to Harrison Creek, by Circle Hot Springs, and we're gonna go up and see him one of these days. Marcene came up with Clint this p.m. She flew the 172 up, and Clint told her to get down to where she could keep the ground in sight. They had fog and it must have been a little tricky. She said she likes the 172 better than the 206, because the 206 is too complicated.

Wednesday, June 20th. The gold looked good in the box today, guess it's coming from about 2 to 3 feet in the bedrock, or from 6 inches above to 3 feet below. Our water sure is low, guess we'll have to muddy up the ditch tomorrow, as we're losing water through the gravel in the ditch. Mud will seal the leaks. I worked on the dozer about an hour this morning, straightening out the rock guard and tightening bolts. Marcene and I went bear hunting tonight, but didn't see anything.

Friday, June 22nd. Marcene and I went to Circle Hot Springs today to see the Hites, Loren and his wife, about gold and gold claims. I have never seen so many rocks in my life, rocks and boulders, and about 12 to 15 feet of overburden. It took us about 8 hours to drive to Central, and over an hour to drive back in to their claims. We spent the night in the Hot Springs Hotel, $32 for the room.

We found an older guy and his wife stuck in the creek, and I drove up beside him in our 4-wheel drive. They were from Washington. He asked me, "Would you pull me out?" I said, "No.", and his face dropped. Then I said, "Oh, well, guess I'll give you a pull. How come the Hites didn't pull you out?" He said he didn't know what was wrong with them. They wouldn't talk to him because they were mining up there, but told him that they'd pull him out after they quit mining. He was a little perturbed about it. I told him, "No, you don't mess with miners when they're mining and using the water like they're doing. You have to wait until they get all finished, and then they'll come and pull you out, or help you, whatever." So, I pulled them out and everything was okay.

Loren was telling us about Pop Speaker up at the head of Harrison Creek. He had a big, big dam up there, and used monitors for everything in his mining operation. He was kind of a stubborn cuss, and he figured that because he built the big dam and furnished all the water for the guys down below, that he'd mess them up, and whatever. So, the guys took turns watching the creek; they'd set up and have their sluice boxes and equipment, and their stockpiled material, all ready to go. They'd use binoculars, looking up the creek, and whenever a head of water started rolling down the creek they'd wake everybody up, and out they'd go to start moving their material through their sluice boxes.

June 23rd. We left Circle Hot Springs this a.m. and filled up with gas at Central. Gas was $1.15 a gallon. We drove on 5 miles of rough road to see Richard McIntosh. He was busy sluicing and we didn't visit long. Then we drove into Fairbanks, got the pickup serviced, and ate supper with Mr. Smith. He's a character. We stopped by to see Allen about hauling my dozer, and he's ready at the call.

Sunday, June 24th. Jim, Don and Nadine cleaned up yesterday. The gold on this cleanup was around 35 ounces. We spent all day today, about 12 hours, digging test holes. The weather was lousy, cold and windy.

June 25th. It rained most of last night and today. We got the dam fixed and ready to go tomorrow. We went into Manley Hot Springs today, made phone calls and picked up 2 and a half inch angle iron for the riffles at Bobby Miller's yard. We talked to Don Cole, Jadene, and Bob at Equipment Services. Bob is going to send a dozer up right away, to replace the one I've got right now. They didn't have the dozer I wanted on their lot at the time, but let me have this one until the one that I had agreed to purchase came in. This one had 36 hours on it when it left Anchorage, and has 171.5 hours now. The difference is building the road and digging test holes.

Wednesday, June 27th. Our dam broke last night due to heavy rains. After I got the dam rebuilt, our water ditch broke about half a mile upstream. We got it fixed and ran the box about 2-1/2 hours. We stopped for dinner at 2 p.m., and when we went back to work the dam had broke again. I plugged a hole, but in the process, I plugged the 10-inch pipe. We got it cleaned and the dam back by 8 p.m. I think we've had enough rain for one day, but that's gold mining. The weather was pretty most of the day.

June 28th. The riffles look good today. We had plenty of water. I'm moving about 18 to 20 yards of material per hour, which isn't too good, but with one piece of equipment it's all I can expect, I guess. I push material into the hopper and I push tailings. I haven't heard from Allen, or Equipment Services regarding my dozer yet, don't know what's happening. That's the way it goes when you're 25 miles from a phone. Don, Jim and I went fishing tonight and caught 13 graylings.

June 29th. Don and Nadine went into Manley Hot Springs today and visited around all their friends. They left about 8, or 8:15 a.m., and got back about 2 p.m. Don worked, or was at, the sluice box about 80 minutes today. We're in pretty good ground and have plenty of water, but it could dry up anytime if the sun comes out. Jim and I panned the 2 front riffles twice today, but I guess Don didn't like it. We panned the riffles, then put all the nuggets back in the right-hand side of the riffles up front, and Don got excited about all the nuggets being on that one side. He thought we'd really hit something good, but when we told him what happened, he didn't like that at all.

June 30th. Don sets on the pipe coming into the hopper, smoking his little pipe. He either sets on the pipe, or the rockpile. The weather's hot and dry, and the water's slowing down. I guess we'll have to go up the water ditch line tomorrow and muddy it up some more to seal the leaks. We went rabbit hunting this evening.

Sunday, July 1st. I cut the water ditch out of the dam and into the creek today. We'll move the dam, for the gold goes right underneath the holding pond and the dam, so we'll have to rebuild that tomorrow.

We went into Manley Hot Springs tonight and were setting in the hotel bar there. An ex-State Trooper owns most of Manley Hot Springs. He bought the old Northern Commercial Company, the grocery store, the service station, the hotel, bar and the post office.

Jack Newbauer is a big miner, and has been around Manley for years and years. Something was said about all the hippies coming in there and taking over miners' cabins, just moving in, and hogging around the bath facilities at Manley. The ex-State Trooper, who was about 6-foot-4 and weighed about 260 pounds, was bartending that evening, and there was a bunch of hippies in there. He looked over at Jack and said, "Is it true what I've been hearing, what the miners feel about the hippies?" Jack said, "Yes, it is." The Trooper asked 2 or 3 more miners what they felt, and looked all around, and said, "I can take care of that." He jumped over the bar, went over and got a piece of cardboard, and wrote a big sign. He put on the sign, "As of today, this establishment takes no more food stamps." Then he walked across the street, and tacked it up on the front of his store. He came back in, walked back behind the bar, and said, "Well, I'll tell you one thing, the government may force me to give them the food stamps through the post office, but I don't have to take them back at the store."

You should have seen the hippies clear out of Manley Hot Springs, because it's 179 miles into Fairbanks, and just about all gravel road. You could just imagine a hippie driving all the way to Fairbanks to get food with his food stamps. Anyway, it cleared them out, and they had no more trouble with the hippies around Manley.

July 2nd. I tore out the dam today, pushed out paydirt underneath the dam, and rebuilt the dam. We ran an hour and a half, and the riffles really looked good, so we are on a good paystreak now. Don worked about an hour today. He spent most of the day visiting, and greasing and changing oil in his motorhome and light plant. He's getting ready to go somewhere. Marcene and Nadine went to Manley today, and Marcene made phone calls. We had some of our gold at Hoover & Strong in Virginia. They're going to send it to us, and Don Cole is going to send it to Blaine, Washington.

We met the Pringles, a very nice elderly couple. They told us about when they cut their road in to their cabin. It rained that night, and the next day, when they were looking at their road, they found a half cup of gold nuggets. Their road was about a foot below where the old-timers' water ditch was, so this was gold they'd missed. Mr. Pringle had a long water ditch and holding pond with a valve. He only had a 1941 TD24 International dozer to work with.

July 3rd. The riffles looked good today. Don was packing his motorhome and didn't even come up to help us on the run. Ed Nelson came by from Fairbanks, looking for claims, and was telling me about some claims of his in, or near, Fairbanks.

This old-timer, back in 1918, dug a shaft in permafrost, ice, and etc., 187 feet in the ground. He finally hit bedrock and took one cubic foot of paydirt out, and got over 14 ounces of gold. The banker was going to let him borrow money to work it with a steam winch and steam pumps, but when he got back to the shaft it was flooded with water. The water had broke in and the guy was so disgusted he abandoned it. We drove into Manley tonight and tried to call Allen McQuaid. He's the guy that's supposed to haul the dozer. No good. I left a note for him at the Turtle Bar, called Kyak Radio and left a message for Allen to pick up my dozer and take it to Anchorage.

July 4th. It rained today most of the day. We cleaned up the box and got quite a bit of gold. Jim woke us up this a.m. firing his pistol. He said, "We have to have fireworks on the Fourth of July." You should have seen those hippies take off down the road in their little hippie van. They'd been parked up by the road for quite some time.

Last night, Don insisted that Jim, Marcene and I go with Nadine and other people over to Les Cobb's homestead. We didn't want to go, as it was 2-1/2 miles from the end of the road, and Nadine was going to ride in on a track rig. At 10 p.m. Nadine wasn't back yet, so Jim and Don took my pickup and went looking for them. It looks like we'll be able to settle up with Don okay, no problems.

Les Cobb is a real nice guy. He homesteaded over the mountain from here. He built him a fishing lodge, just by piecemeal. He's a mechanic that works on the power plants out in the villages. He befriended a couple of hippies that came into the area early this spring. He showed them where to build their cabin about 7 miles from his place, gave them a hand, furnished a chain saw, and so forth. He was real nice to them, helped them build their cabin.

Les had to leave his pickup parked at the end of his road, and either use a little track rig, or a 3-wheeler to go back to his lodge. He started missing gasoline out of his pickup; he always carried a barrel of gasoline in the bed of the truck, but the gas was always missing out of his tank, and he knew that his tank wasn't leaking. He couldn't figure it out. One day he was coming out from his camp on the little Honda 3-wheeler, which was real quiet, and when he came around the corner, those guys were in their old pickup, parked right next to his. They took off down the road toward their cabin right away when they saw him, and left a 5-gallon can with the syphon hose going into it next to his pickup. He took a look at that, and looked at the guys going down the road, and he thought, "Well, I'll fix them".

He let the can go ahead and fill up, pulled the hose out, plugged the can, and took it down to their cabin. He walked up to the front door and said, "Okay, you guys, if you got anything in there that you want, you'd better get it out, 'cause I'm fixing to burn my part of this cabin." Then he sloshed gasoline all the way around the cabin, backed off and threw a match to it. One hippie ran out and said, "Hey man, you better get out of there, this guy's serious, he set our cabin afire." They got some of their stuff out.

Les stood there and watched it burn down, then went on into town and called the State Troopers in Livengood, and told them what had happened. The State Trooper said, "Well, did anybody get hurt?" Les said, "No, no one got hurt." So the Trooper said, "Well, there's no reason for me to make a special trip to come over there and make a report unless I get some complaints from those guys."

Thursday, July 5th. We got the gold weighed and settled up this morning. We were going to do it in Don Orcutt's motorhome, and when I started to walk in, he had a 44 magnum laying on the table. I said, "What in the world's that for?" He said, "Well, you never can tell about these crazies out here, the hippies and stuff."

And I said, "Aw, nobody's gonna be in here ripping us off. You put the gun away and we'll go ahead and weigh the gold." I finally convinced him to put the gun away, and we got our gold split up. Jim was supposed to get a percentage, which he did, but Don was gonna cut him out of the coarse gold and just give him a percentage of the fine gold. Don had his figures all rolling around in his head, and he was making it so complicated, but it was so simple to split and do. I said, "No, that's not the way we agreed to do it." So, anyway, we finally got the gold split up, and got squared away.

One thing I want to mention, when Don was cleaning up, he did all the panning, and he'd turn his back on everybody when he was panning the concentrates into the tubs. I kind of wanted to have him split the concentrates with us, but we're just glad to get on out of the way. I didn't want to rock the boat and get him upset any more than we had to.

Friday, July 6th. We left Orcutt's place at Eureka Creek this a.m. The road was pretty good until after we left Livengood and the road turned to soup for about 5 miles. It was that volcanic ash, about 6 inches of it, and it was just like snot. On our way out we met Allen McQuaid on his way in to pick up our dozer. He had chains on his rig. We just barely made it over the hills, got into Fairbanks about 3:30 p.m. The motorhome kept dying on us and we couldn't figure out what in the world it was. Turned out it was low on oil, and that 440 Dodge motor had an electrical thing on it that cut the engine off when the oil got low. Going up and down the hills made the electrical sensor think the oil was too low. We had some oil with us, and when we finally figured it out, we put some oil in and everything was fine. We drove on to Houston, Alaska, and spent the night there after eating and listening to a live band.

July 7th. We left Houston about 9 a.m. and drove on to Anchorage. We parked the motorhome in our Greenbelt Camper Park, and took the trailer to Glen Heatherly's yard. Tony Zuber has sold the camper park, but I think it's best, he's been so hard to get money from anyway.

Sunday, July 8th. Clint flew Marcene, Jim and me over to check on some gold claims that a dentist, Dr. Yuknis, has on Pass Creek, over the hill from Collinsville. The ground looks good, and there's a good little airstrip there.

July 10th. We went to see Dr. Yuknis regarding his claims at Camp Creek and it looks like we'll be able to work his claims. We're going over Monday to do some testing.

July 11th. My dozer got into town this a.m. and I had to pay Allen $1200 for bringing it down from Manley. We got a letter from Don Orcutt saying we're even regarding the mining claims in Manley and Eureka Creek area.

Sunday, July 15th. We got woke up this a.m. with a knock on the door. One guy was walking across the top of our motorhome, that got me going. Marcene had just mentioned to the guy that our antenna wire was messed up. Some people are funny.

July 16th. The dentist, Dr. Yuknis, backed out on the gold claims. He's gonna save it for his kids, I guess.

July 17th. I talked with Tamara Carr today regarding some claims out from Copper Center. She wants us to pay for a helicopter, and go in and do some testing. I could see right through it when I talked to her, she wanted us to do the assessment work for her. So much for that one.

July 18th. I signed lease papers today with George Jones, owner of Gordon Air Service, to lease our 206, at $50 an hour, I pay insurance and maintenance. Holy whiskers! Boy, I never learn! Total hours on the 206 when leased to Gordon Air, 901.7 hours.

July 19th. Jim and I went to check out claims below Bertha Creek, near Johnson. Not much gold and it's in a federal park, so we're gonna write that one off. We drove on over to Hope, Alaska, and saw Fred Wilkes and the boys. They are losing their butts over there. They got only a little over 5 ounces this summer, even with all the equipment they have. We also checked out claims on Canyon Creek and they're no good.

Sunday, July 22nd. Mr. Smith is still looking for claims. He came down from Fairbanks and I picked him up at the airport.

July 23rd. Jim, Mr. Smith and I left at 6:30 this a.m. for Bird Creek to check out some claims. We got stuck twice, I mean really stuck, we had to jack the pickup up out of 2 big holes. The claims were no good as far as I could see, and it rained on us most of the day. I saw some different gold mining today, for sure. We had to walk in 3 miles to the claims that we were looking at.

July 24th. Gold is $306 an ounce today. Mr. Smith, from Fairbanks, is visiting us. By the way, this is a different Mr. Smith than the one I previously met from Florida.

July 25th. It's still raining, and we're still checking out leads regarding mining. I went to Palmer to check out the claims of the dentist, Dr. Yuknis. He's legal regarding the paperwork in the Recording Office in Palmer. I talked to Mr. Heatherly, and he wants Jim and me to go over with him to Collinsville and do some testing, but I can't hardly see it. It would only benefit the Canadians. Mr. Smith left for Fairbanks this p.m. and is going to check out some ground up on Steese Highway. I checked with Maxine Smith, she gave me the name, and has paperwork, regarding some claims in Copper Creek, near McCarthy. We'll meet and check these out tomorrow.

July 26th. I met with Jo King and she is nice, but the price is too high for undeveloped claims.

July 27th. Ralph Peterson called tonight and might have some ground that I could test, or maybe work.

Thursday, July 31st. I met with Nick Zoro today. He wants me to come over to Collinsville. I agreed to go over with Jim and Marty. We get 30 percent of the gold, and it's to be weighed up and separated after each cleanup, except for black sands, or concentrates, and that goes to the refinery to be split later. He said they were working on getting Shorty out, but they had a contract with him, so they are gonna do away with Shorty at the mine. It's like I said before, you give a guy enough rope, he'll eventually hang himself. So Shorty is in the noose right now with Zoro and the Canadians.

August 1st. I'm working on building a sluice box with Ralph Peterson. We built a big trommel out of Alaska Pipeline pipe, one section 40 feet, and an extension of half, which makes it 60 feet long. We built sluice runs, two of them, that he'll feed with a backhoe and supply the water with a 10 to 12-inch pump. We cut holes in the trommel for the fines to go through. I forget now how many holes we cut with the torch, but we kept cutting, and cutting, until we got the water regulated right. Also, we used the gear reduction off a road boring machine, and we had a Ford diesel motor to power it. We set the trommel on D9 Cat rollers. The trommel rolled on those rollers and they supported it. We finished the sluice box riffles, the runs, and checked out the pump today, and everything's fine. It turned out to be a real good unit and washing plant. Ralph and Dave took it up north of Fairbanks, on the Chena River.

Friday, August 3rd. We left at 7 a.m. going to check out claims on Willow Creek, 75 miles north of Anchorage. We loaded out a sluice box and 6-inch pump, and took off for Hatcher Pass. We got to Willow Creek about noon, unloaded our equipment, and were ready to go into the claims by 12:30. The trail was horrible, we had to build the trail in lots of rock and mud. We finally got the box and pump in for the test on the claims, and got started about 6:45 p.m. Dave, who is Ralph Peterson's son, got the backhoe stuck and he just walked off and left it, took off for Anchorage in the big truck that hauled us up here.

We found lots of color, but sure was fine gold. We found a big nugget that we gave to Ralph. Ralph rode in with us tonight. He stopped at B & J's in Wasilla to get a pair of boots. Here's a multi-millionaire, and he goes in the store in his sock feet. He was so tired that he left his change on the counter. People in the store came to the door to tell him that he'd forgotten his change.
By the way, Nick Zoro called today and I guess I'll return his call tomorrow a.m.

August 4th. We went back up to Willow Creek, pulled the backhoe in, moved the sluice box, set up, and ran the box 3 hours and 45 minutes. The weather was nice. Ralph was working with us, but Dave didn't come out today. He flew over in his plane. We checked the riffles and had some color, but again, it was real fine gold. Ralph took in Coca Cola and some ice, in an old rubber boot. He's a funny guy. We found a big sluice box that Emmet Roteman, the guy who owns Automatic Welding, was telling us about. He told us that it's up there, and if we could find it, we could have at it. We may make a deal for it.

August 5th. We cleaned up the gold in the box, somewhere around 3/4 to an ounce, and left the claims today. We left about 7 p.m. with the dozer towing the pump, and the backhoe, and the sluice box, all chained together, and made it out to the airstrip at Herman Brothers' claims. We stopped by to see a guy named Sam in Willow, about claims on Valdez Creek. We can go up there if we wish. Jim and I got in to Ralph's yard about 12:15 tonight. We had to work on lights on the truck, as they kept going out on the way in. Typical of Ralph Peterson equipment. Lots of black sand and real fine gold, and a lot of big rocks out there on Willow Creek.

Monday, August 6th. I checked on our 206 today and it looks like it's flying quite a bit. I called Don Orcutt today, he wants $90,000 down on the claims on Eureka Creek. That's a little bit steep. It's a long way from staking ground to $90,000, and that's just the down payment. He's trying to make a big profit on them, but so be it. I guess that's the way the ball bounces.

August 7th. The weather was icky out, raining. I checked with Glen Heatherly, and he can't go get the Komatsu up at Willow Creek, so I called Bob McDaniels. He's gonna haul the Komatsu back to Equipment Services' yard tomorrow. Marty came by and we went out for dinner. He, Jim and I are good buddies, so it may be that Marty will wind up helping us at Collinsville when we go back mining there. And for sure he's gonna go mining with us next year.

Friday, August 10th. I talked to Nick today and he said that we'd be going to Collinsville Monday morning, or Tuesday, for sure.

Monday, August 13th. I talked to Zoro today. He wants Jim and me to go over to Collinsville tomorrow. He's taking a State Trooper over to make sure that there'll be no problems with Shorty and his crew. Jerry Green came by this a.m., he's supposed to go to Collinsville with Jim and me. He seems to talk a little bit too much, we'll find out pretty soon. He's hooked up with Zoro some way. I found out today that Mrs. Gross didn't make her payment this month on the camper park. I think that she's a phony.

August 14th. We flew with Clint and Zoro to Talkeetna to pick up a State Trooper, then on to Collinsville. The Trooper presented Shorty with his paperwork, and Clint hauled him out, 2 loads, 4 guys. It was raining cats and dogs. As we were flying into Collinsville, the weather was so bad and soupy that we could just see splotches of ground, hillsides, lakes, and beaver dams, etc., as we went in. The State Trooper asked me, "What do you think? Do you think this guy knows what he's doing?" I said, "Oh yeah, he knows."

We cleaned the kitchen and storeroom, and the bedroom was filthy. Cat boxes were sitting around in the dining room. They had 2 dogs and a cat, sure smelled like it too. Clint brought in a drive shaft for the old pickup and we put it in this afternoon. The big light plant had a blown head gasket, the D6 had a broken sprocket, the pickup was broke down, don't know for sure what all yet. I'm tired, so gonna go to bed.

August 15th. Jim and I pulled the starter off the old Dodge pickup, it was burned out, so we got to get a new one. The tires on the 125 Michigan loader are rock cut, and they're pretty bad. The top U-joints on the loader were dry, and no brakes on the rig. The Komatsu tracks are worn real bad. No fuel today, we sure need it bad. I think we'll go ahead and work some tomorrow in hopes we'll get fuel. The weather is about right for this time of the year, seems to always rain at the wrong time.

August 16th. It rained most of the day. Jim and I went over to Twin Creek this a.m. and put the sluice box back together. We built the dam back and put in an extra 12-inch pipe for overflow. We ran 2 hours and 15 minutes, and ran 125 yards through the box. Everything's working okay, but the Komatsu track adjustment is used up, the pins and bushings need turning. The Michigan loader doesn't have brakes, but runs good. Clint flew in fuel today. Jim Mitchell came in this p.m., he's the geologist from Victoria. Mr. Heatherly ate with us last night and again tonight. He spent last night in camp. Marty and Jerry are supposed to be over tomorrow.

August 17th. We're in good ground today. Mr. Jim Mitchell, from Victoria, B.C., is visiting in camp and doing a feasibility study on the gold here. Marty came over today for a visit, nice seeing him again. Marty said that he was in a hock shop in Anchorage, and the owner told him that Shorty was in and sold gold from Collinsville. There is a definite difference in the gold taken out of the various creeks, and anyone knowing gold would know what area or creek it came from.

Saturday, August 18th. It rained all day. The riffles looked fair today. Jim, Jerry and I are working. I dug through an old garbage dump and it sure looked funny, old tires, bottles, batteries, tables, and even an aircraft engine came out of that dump. It had real good gold under it, and they dumped the garbage right on top of some good paydirt. So we went ahead and ran it all through. It looked like a nest of worms when we got through stacking the stuff out of the hopper. Clint brought 3 barrels of fuel in and everything else is fine.

August 19th. I got tickled today, Jim Mitchell was hunting his glasses and he had them on. He can't hear real good either, he looks like Marcene's Grandpa Best. He mentioned that he didn't know what he was doing out here, he only brought 2 pairs of socks, so Marcene loaned him a pair of mine. He was hunting regular gas to put in his Coleman stove and I told him that he'd have to use white gas. Mel Pardek may come in today, and Clint brought the 3-wheel Honda over.

August 20th. We spent most of the day stripping overburden. The riffles looked fair today for the short time that we ran. We are just about out of fuel, and we also need hydraulic oil.

August 21st. We ran out of fuel this a.m., looked around and found enough to run about 2-1/2 hours. Too bad, as we're in good ground here and we surely could use some fuel. The deal that we made with Zoro and Henry Camerot, was that we're to work the ground, we get 30 percent, we do all the maintenance, repair, mechanic work and welding, and they furnish the fuel and equipment and the ground. Anyway, we'll see what happens. I heard today that Shorty is suing the group for $100,000. Good luck, Shorty. Of course, he always had "diarrhea of the mouth and constipation of thoughts". He's got "rectal-cranial-phobia", got his head up his butt and doesn't have sense enough to pull it out. Mr. Mitchell lost his glasses, again, down the sluice box today. Boy, he's had it with his glasses. Nick flew in a load of lumber while we were out of fuel. Now that makes sense. I got out a big boulder today, about the size of the pickup, from the hopper. Jerry went to town tonight, I don't think Jerry's long for over here, he's not the type.

August 22nd. Bobby Woods, out of Palmer, flew in 1000 gallons of fuel this evening. We were totally out of fuel right up until Bobby got in with the fuel. Jerry and Marty came in this p.m. Marty is going to work for Nick, digging test holes. The weather was hot and dry today. Mr. Mitchell rode the Honda, and he got a kick out of that, he's 74 years old. He also worked the sluice box with Marcene and did a good job. I'll tell you, he can outwalk a billy goat. I tried walking with him, and I'm in pretty good shape, I think, but he just walked circles around me.

August 23rd. We had to pump the pit today, took about an hour and a half. I was dozing overburden 'til 12 o'clock, and we ran the box 6-1/2 hours. We're in big boulders, and lots of them. We should have a good cleanup though, and lots of gold. The weather is clear, but we still got plenty of water. Marty's digging test holes with the John Deere for Jim Mitchell. Clint flew in Mel and another guy from Vancouver. It's nice to have good equipment to work with for a change. Jim Mitchell and the guys were digging test holes and panning, but couldn't find the gold. I'd pan it, get real nice colors, and he couldn't see where I was getting the material. So, I'd show him, he'd get one pan, and pan the material, and then go back to get another panful and miss it. He'd miss it by 6 or 8 inches. He wouldn't be in the paystreak. Anyway, so much for that. He was a nice guy and we enjoyed working with him very much.

August 24th. We ran the sluice box about 4 hours today, ran about 200 yards through the box. We're finished in this pit until we do more stripping. The tracks are getting pretty bad on the Komatsu, the pins and bushings sure need turning. We're not gonna be able to turn them, as we don't have the facilities here and we can't get the tracks into town, so we're just gonna have to pull a pad. That way it will take up some slack, but it won't alleviate the problem. The John Deere backhoe broke down again today with Marty running it digging test holes. Hal Cook came in to see us today. He doesn't have his shoe stores anymore and it's real sad, because he was a nice, energetic boy that should have made it go, but for some reason didn't.

August 25th. The cleanup today was 69.5 ounces of fines and 9 ounces of coarse gold. We separated out Ann Vandola's 10 percent, as owner of the claims, and it was 6.19 ounces of fines and 18 pennyweight of coarse gold. (A pennyweight is a unit of troy weight equal to 24 grains, 1/20th of a troy ounce.) There's lots of people around camp today. We started stripping overburden. The Cat ran all day and most of the night.

Sunday, August 26th. The crowd of "wheels" left today, and that's nice, we should be back to normal tomorrow. Boy, we sure went through groceries while they were here. The weather was hot and sunny today. Glen Heatherly came in this a.m., and I loaded 3 barrels of his gas on his rig. We worked on the 175 Michigan loader today, motor mount bolts were loose, teeth loose, water hose leaking, brake pads wore out. We put a new kit in the air brakes on the loader. The Komatsu oil line had a hole in it, so we worked on it. It was sure a booger to get off, we had to make a wrench for the fitting. We're stripping the pit by the sluice box on Twin Creek. Marty relieved Jim about 4 a.m., and Jerry relieved Marty at 9. Then Jim relieved Jerry at 6:30 p.m., and Marty is going down to relieve him at midnight. I ran the loader about 5 hours moving overburden. It's 10 p.m. and I'm tired, got to get up and relieve Marty tomorrow about 5 a.m.

Tuesday, August 28th. Bud Woods brought in another 1000 gallons of fuel today. Jerry got the dozer stuck this a.m., and that's his last time on it, or the loader. He's not an operator and we don't have time to teach him. I dozed up a black bear today. Someone had killed it recently and buried it. Boy, what a stink! I smelled it before I saw it. When the dozer blade run over that arm, it peeled all the hide and everything down to the muscle and bone. I thought it was a person when I saw it. It really upset me there for just a second. Nick told me tonight that he was going to Vancouver tomorrow, and Mel will be coming up. Clint was over today and tried running the dozer. He flies a plane better than he runs a dozer. I ran the dozer most of the day, it took 3 hours to get it unstuck after Clint stuck it.

August 30th. We had ice on the windshield this morning, first frost of the season. We caught the pickup on fire today trying to start it, but put it out. Kendall Hamilton came in this p.m. and Marcene went into town.

August 31st. The 175 Michigan broke down today, but it looks like we won't have to pull the transmission, it had a broken retainer ring, and I hope that's all. We're running the John Deere, put 150 to 175 yards through the box. The John Deere hydraulic pump is acting up, so we'll look at the filter tomorrow. This morning the weather was a little cool, and we had frost. The riffles in the box looked pretty good today. We lack about a day on the lower pit, if everything holds, including the weather. I talked to Marcene tonight, guess she will be out this Sunday. Jadene is getting ready to go outside to Tennessee.

Sunday, September 2nd. Jim went hunting with Kendall today. Marty pulled the hydraulic pump on the John Deere, and it's gone, kaput! The loader's working pretty good. We finished up the pit east of the sluice box today. Marcene came back to camp after Jadene took off on her first journey to Tennessee driving, her and Cindy. They should enjoy themselves.

September 3rd. We took pads out of the Komatsu dozer today, one on each side, and it sure made a difference. The loader's working good and we're in good ground. The weather's good and we still have enough water to operate. Neither Nick nor Mel came in today, we still have camp basically to ourselves.

September 4th. The box ran 8 hours today. Jerry's working on the sluice box, but I'm afraid he's gonna get himself killed. He's so clumsy on that box, tying onto the rocks and stuff, he doesn't know how to hook things up. Jim was stripping most of the day and Marty's working in camp. I used the loader for pushing tailings and feeding the hopper today. Kendall went bear hunting, sure hope he gets one. Marcene and I called my sister, Louetha, this a.m., and she sure sounded good on the phone, just like next door. The weather was clear and cool, wind blowing.

Thursday, September 6th. Marcene and I flew into town today with Clint. I had to call Mel Pardek regarding the equipment and claims. Clint said that Nick would be back tomorrow. I went by Craig Taylor's and picked up a hydraulic pump for the John Deere, and by Equipment Services and paid for the retainer ring and transmission oil. It was nice to go to town for a visit. I found out when I got back into camp that the 175 loader broke down, so we went over and pulled the cover off the transmission. We figured that 2 gears were broken and we called and ordered same. It may be running by tomorrow if we get our parts. Kendall didn't get a bear yet, but he killed a moose and gave the whole thing to Cowboy and his bunch in Anchorage. Mr. Heatherly went into town this evening, and so did Kendall. I made him wash the blood off the little 3-wheel Honda, otherwise, bears would smell the blood and tear up the seat. It kind of upset him, but that's alright, he'll grow back.

September 7th. I went into town today, I needed some transmission parts. I went over and talked with Art at Equipment Services, and he was so snotty I finally just told him, "Art, I should buy this company, and the first guy that would go would be you. I'd fire you."

Sunday, September 9th. We cleaned up today and got a total of 188 pennyweight of nuggets, and a total of 1526 pennyweight of fines. The weather was pretty nice. We put the loader back together and had no pressure on 4th and reverse, so we had to tear it back apart. It was odd, we got it all together, poured the oil in, cranked it up, and nothing happened. This was about midnight. Jerry said, "You guys are crazy, I'm going to bed." I said, "You go ahead, just go ahead to bed, that's alright."

So, Jim, Marty and I tore the loader back apart, drained the oil, and laid all the parts out on the workbench in the shop. When we got it all out there, Jim didn't say anything, but he looked at one of the new parts that we put in. Anyway, when we got the transmission all back together again, I looked at him and said, "Do you think it will work?" He said, "It'll work." When we put the fluid back in, it worked fine, no problems, and my curiosity got the best of me. I said, "Jim, what happened, what did you do to it, or what did you find?" He said, "Well, there was a little seal missing on that new part, and it was supposed to be on there." It wasn't listed in the book as separate, but it worked fine and everything worked out.

Marcene cooked today, for Nick, Camerot and his wife Carolyn, Nick's nephew Bill, Clint, Jim, Marty, Jerry and me; there were 9 people.

September 10th. We started the box today, the loader was feeding the box and pushing tailings most of the day. It's getting pretty rough to haul in with just the loader, but things are running fine. I sent Jerry in today, he just isn't cut out to do this type of work. The color is not all that good in the box today, but it'll be there later.

September 11th. Bud Woods brought in another 1000 gallons of fuel today. The loader and Cat are running just fine, and everything's looking good in the pit, and box.

September 12th. I ran the Cat 6 hours today, stripping and building a road for the loader to walk on. Everything's holding good, everything's running fine. It rained just a little today and the water is still holding good for us. The ground is a little spotty, but if you launder enough rocks, you got to get a little gold, specially when you're in good ground. Marcene cooked beans today in a great big old pot that she found here. Nick's not back yet. We saw bear signs on the road this a.m.

Friday, September 14th. We spent quite a bit of the day stripping and moving overburden, and it seems as if preparing the ground and getting everything ready is a big part of gold mining. In fact, it is the biggest part. You've got to have the ground prepared and ready to go when you have the water. If you get things going, and then have to shut down to prepare, it's bad. Better to stay like housebuilders, about 4 or 5 steps ahead of yourself all the time. We're hauling material a little bit too far, but that's okay, I just want to finish up the pit before we move the box.

September 15th. It rained cats and dogs yesterday evening, and all last night, and still this morning it was pouring down. The dam broke last night, that's the reason for not running more hours on the sluice box today. We spent 2-1/2 hours rebuilding the dam, and about an hour pushing overburden. Nick came back to camp today. I think we're running too much water, plus the rocks are hanging on the riffles and cleaning some of the riffle. That's the bigger rocks. We really need a good shaker screen over here. Beavers plugged some of our settling ponds today, plugged the overflow pipes, and caused muddy water to spill over into the creek. We have about 3 or 4 more days in the pit that we're in, then we have to move, probably upstream a ways.

September 16th. Clint brought Henry and his son over today. We found a nice large nugget and drew numbers to see who got it. I lucked out and got it.

September 17th. We cleaned up today. Our cleanup included: nuggets, 84 pennyweight; overlay, 254 pennyweight; fines, 561 pennyweight; fine fine fines (black-sand powder gold), 56 pennyweight. I guess we'll move the box tomorrow. Jim and Marty put a head gasket on the Waukesha light plant, but the rods seemed to knock a bit. I discovered that the teeth on the loader bucket were worn pretty bad, so I told Nick. He called Clint and said that he'd be over with them tomorrow.

September 18th. It rained cats and dogs all day. We dug test holes most of the day, and we'll move tomorrow, I guess. I looked at an area on Mills Creek, and it won't be too much trouble to put in a settling pond and get ready to mine by the camp. I got settled up with Jim and Marty on the cleanup, except for the groceries.

September 19th. We moved the sluice box upstream from camp on Twin Creek, got the box set up and built the dam. We broke the dam where the box was set up and it flooded out the settlement ponds, washed one out and raised havoc with the road. It was dark this evening when we finally got through. We didn't have lights on the equipment so we rigged a spotlight and hooked it to the battery. We should be sluicing by Friday, for sure, that is if we get teeth for the loader. This material here that we're working is hard stuff, so you just about have to have teeth on the loader to work it.

September 20th. It rained all day. We replaced 2 dams for holding ponds and put pipe back in both. We had to dig out the pipe and wash gravel and dirt out of them. We all got so wet, we went over to the cabin on Twin Creek camp and built a fire about 2 p.m., ate, then took a little nap. We didn't get started sluicing yet. We found the oxygen and acetylene bottles and gauges on the road where it was washed out last night. It washed them down the creek. It sure was miserable today.

September 21st. The dams that we replaced yesterday were out again this a.m. It sure has been raining, just too much water for the pipes that were installed earlier this summer. The "wheels", the attorney and his friends, flew over today. They used the Hondas to ride down to meet us. We got the sluice box started this evening, but the box needs some working on, the hopper needs to be changed. We didn't run much through today.

Saturday, September 22nd. Nick told me today to go ahead and run the loader the rest of the season without brakes, if it wouldn't hurt it. I run it myself and I don't speed-shift, I'm real careful with it. It's been running all summer without brakes, so I'll just take it easy, don't get too excited. He doesn't want to put out money for the brake job until next spring. We only have 3 more days of fuel left and Nick's aware of it, so we'll see what happens.

September 24th. All the fuel we have left is in the loader and dozer, except what we may get out of the tank right at the bottom. We saw the first snow of the year this morning, on the high hills northwest of camp. It rained all last night and most of today. Marcene came in tonight with Nick, his son, and Clint. The riffles looked good this p.m.

September 25th. We had snow this a.m., and it rained and swowed most of the day. We've got the last of the fuel in our equipment. We jacked up one end of the tank and got an extra 40 gallons of fuel. Jim hard-faced the teeth on the loader this a.m., took about 3 hours. We ordered the teeth a week and 1 day ago, and got them last night. I stripped during this time with the Komatsu dozer. Nick and his son were pulling nails and cleaning up around the old shack by the sluice box. We shut down for this season tonight. We'll clean the box when the weather permits. The riffles look pretty good for such a short time that we ran. My guess is that we probably have 35 ounces in the box. Nick was in agreement to shut down, he said that it wouldn't hurt his feelings a bit, it's so lousy out. Clint flew fuel and a barrel of 10-weight oil in this p.m.

September 26th. We cleaned up the box today and picked up most of the stuff and brought it into camp. Nick changed his mind and wanted to run the box some more, but the guys and I are going in. I don't have the heart to ask them to go back and work for this character, as he doesn't appreciate anything that we've done for him. I told Nick today that I'd like to talk to Jim and Marty regarding all the equipment, as I don't know about us working here next year. If we do happen to work here next year, I'd like to make sure that all the equipment is in first class shape, and that we strip ground ahead, get it all stripped for next season. If we could count on it, then we could prepare and be ready for all these boogers that jump up and bite us. Of course, Nick, with all of his b.s., told me today that they're going to have a minimum of 2 crews up here next season, and they're gonna get the old washing plant going, and I'd have to talk to Ralph about working the claims at Twin Creek and Mills Creek. I can't get anything definite from Mr. Zoro, so we'll see what happens.

September 27th. I took the Komatsu this a.m. and built settling ponds, and moved the creek over next to the berm pile, next to the beaver dam to the west side of the runway. Jim and Marty went hunting this a.m. and got a bull moose. George flew over in the 206 this p.m. and got things that Marcene, and all of us, forgot to load. Clint has loaded the last straw on my back, the dirty little s.o.b.! He was using my pickup and bent the bed, messed it all up. Unbeknownst to me, he just went ahead and used it, hauling fuel barrels, dumping them in it, and so forth. He skinned the bed up and bent it, the fender wells and all. Glen Heatherly came over this p.m. He said that Clint was going over to run things at Collinsville. Whoop-de-doo! I can see the handwriting on the wall. Cute!

September 28th. It rained and snowed in camp. We moved all our things out of Collinsville today. Gordon Air, George Jones, made 2 trips, and Clint Seyer 1 trip. Marty and Jim came in on the last 2 trips. This makes 4 trips for George. We brought in Marty's moose, and he gave me a quarter of it. That was nice of him. Nick Zoro didn't pay the $500 plus bill that he owes me for parts, and I think he just isn't a decent man. He said to get it from the attorney, Henry Camerot. So much for that one, I guess. Clint is going over there tomorrow morning to get the sluice box started, and I guess they're going to run it some more. The weather's pretty nice in Anchorage.

September 29th. All along I thought, earlier back through the years, that Clint was my friend, and there he is working behind my back, trying to make a deal with Zoro. He figures that we got lots of gold over there in Collinsville, and he's gonna come along and get rich, take out lots of gold. Gold does certain things to different people; that's what you call "gold fever" when you get that attitude. Marty and I got settled up and I bought some of Jim's gold today, 7 ounces at $350 per ounce. I didn't charge Jim or Marty for use of the plane. Dick Dickerson picked me up, but I didn't tell him anything, period. He's a sneaky one too. Remember, he's the little sneaky rat that was with us when we first went into Collinsville to do a little assessment work over there. Marcene and I went to dinner with Bill and Marlene McNabb tonight. It's good to be back in town.

Sunday, September 30th. There's lots of snow on the hills around Anchorage today. Jim left for Denver this p.m. Marty spent the night with us.

October 1st. The sluice box ran a total of 170 hours while we were over in Collinsville helping Henry and those guys out, and the gold, less the fines sent to the refinery, was 233 ounces, that was our part. I got a check today from Henry for parts, paid by himself. We also got a check for the ADF on our 206 from Clint's insurance company. We took Maxine to dinner tonight at The Woodshed.

October 2nd. I gotta mention this. We got settled up with Don Cole today, we exchanged checks for $2000. He bought gold and we paid him, he wouldn't accept it under the table, so that's Don Cole. We paid Dr. Gower in full. He was Jadine's doctor who took care of her when she had her operation.

October 3rd. We shipped approximately 75 ounces of gold to Delta Refinery today, and should have money to pay the rest of our taxes in 2 or 3 weeks.

Thursday, December 20th. We called Mr. Heatherly in Anchorage, and he told us Clint and crew worked 20 days at Collinsville and got 10 ounces of gold. Mr. Heatherly said that when Clint first set the sluice box up, he had the riffles in backwards and couldn't get the rock to go through, and couldn't figure out what to do. He kept steepening the grade of the box and everything. Finally, a guy flew in over there that was a miner, after they'd fought it for about a week, and the guy asked him, "Well, why are you trying to run your riffles backwards?" So, then Clint turned them back around. Clint didn't know a thing about mining, or moving dirt. Airplanes was his game, but he sure got out of his league when he latched onto Nick Zoro and Collinsville. All along, Clint had been working on me, even from the time he leased the airplane, had us order the airplane and let him use it. I didn't realize it at the time, but he was using us to get set up for his mining venture at Collinsville.

1980

Wednesday, January 2, 1980. Gold today is $550 an ounce.

Monday, January 7th. We sent 105 ounces of silver, and also some gold, to Delta Refining today. I told Mary Adelkerd to hold the gold for $700 an ounce, and silver to $50 an ounce. She agreed to let us know in advance if they sell the gold and/or silver, or if it looks like it's gonna take a dive.

Thursday, January 24th. Gold today $720 is an ounce.

Sunday, February 24th. We decided today to just go on up to Alaska and try to get our camper park straightened out, also get gold claims lined out for the coming season.

Tuesday, February 26th. I got a letter from Joe Ramstead, the owner of Ramstead Construction, and he wants me to go mining with him. I'll think it over and we'll check it out when we get to Anchorage. We're leaving the 28th.

Friday, February 29th. I went by to see Joe and didn't find out much, gotta see him Sunday at 5:30 p.m. We checked on the 206 airplane and it looks good, looks like George is taking pretty good care of it.

Sunday, March 2nd. We ate supper with Joe and his wife at their house tonight. We didn't learn much except that Joe has quite a few claims up near Manley Hot Springs and wants Jim, Marty and me to work them this summer for him.

Tuesday, March 4th. Mr. I.H. Christy and I went up to Willow today to see Mr. and Mrs. Scarback regarding mining their claims up on White Creek. That's the creek that runs into Valdez Creek. They seemed okay, and I think we can work out something if all goes well.

Thursday, March 6th. Glen Heatherly called tonight, told me of claims on Valdez Creek. I checked it out and will see Strout Realty tomorrow. Joe called again about Jim, Marty and me mining for him this summer. He'll pay us in gold. I checked with George Jones regarding the 206; the engine is out and will cost approximately $11,000 to put it back in the air.

Saturday, March 8th. We flew to Long Beach, California, rented a car and stopped by Encinitas to see Russ Williams, and we may work out something with his claims at Fox, Alaska. He has some good claims and some old equipment. It may work out, I don't know for sure, I've just gotta turn over all the rocks.

Monday, March 10th. Dennis Miller is the guy who has 8 claims on Valdez Creek. He wants $60,000 for them, $6000 down.

And George Cornelius with Strout Realty has some claims listed for a guy in Missouri, so we'll have to check them out.

March 11th. George called today. It came to $12,931.44 to replace our 206 plane engine, that's parts, labor, etc. Seems there's always something. We talked to Alton Denny at the bank this morning and borrowed $11,000 on a signature note. It's sure nice, but costs 16 percent, so we'll send the money up to George tomorrow. Here's some of the things to go on the 206: the engine was $7900, prop governor was $324.50, engine mounts $190, alternator, if installed, was $360, muffler $295, nose port kit $432, installed something there for $70, new tires and tubes $270.22, mixture in prop control $189, reassemble, box and ship engine $120, freight $350. It just goes on and on, doesn't it?

Saturday, March 29th. I called Jack Newbauer in Manley Hot Springs today. He's gonna meet the guy out of Fairbanks and get back with me. He'll let me know what happens to the claims there that we're looking at.

Thursday, April 3rd. "An Anchorage man died Wednesday afternoon when his light plane crashed near Mt. Yenlo, 75 miles northwest of Anchorage." This was the article in the Alaska newspaper, and I'll give you the facts here. It was Clint Seyer, and it was regarding the mining over at Collinsville. "Alaska State Troopers said that Clint Seyer Sr., 46, was killed after leaving the Collinsville mine area, 90 miles northwest of Anchorage, on a supply flight to Lake Creek. Seyer's body burned beyond recognition in the crash and was recovered Thursday afternoon by Troopers taken to the site by helicopter dispatched from Elmendorf Air Force Base Rescue Coordinating Center. Cause of the crash has not been determined."

What he was doing, he'd been flying the guys, supplies, and stuff back into Collinsville, and he was on the way in with some equipment. He'd worked out a deal with Nick Zoro. It comes full circle. When you do somebody wrong, it seems to have a way of coming back to you.

Saturday, April 5th. Denny Jones called me tonight and told me that Clint Seyer had gotten killed in a plane crash. Henry Camerot, the attorney, wanted me to call him, so I'll get in touch with him.

April 6th. Henry wanted me to fly up and help him get the equipment on in to the mine. I told him if it were just him I would gladly do it, but as long as Nick is involved with him I won't go. When you do people, like Nick did us last year, it sure has a way of coming back to you.

Tuesday, April 8th. George called today and our 206 is back flying again.

Friday, April 11th. Henry called again, wanting me to come up and run the mine at Collinsville this summer. He says he's buying Nick out. He wants me to give him an answer by next Friday on whether or not I'll do it. He made his bed, so now he can just go ahead and sleep in it.

Friday, April 25th. Ernestine Prochaska called today and said she and Jim are leaving for Alaska this evening. She said that they would look after the camper park until we get up there if Mrs. Gross doesn't keep it.

Tuesday, May 27th. We drove to Fairbanks last night, spent the night in a motel, and drove out to see Russ Williams this a.m. He made us feel like we were imposing on him, and then got kind of nice after about a half hour. I guess if you have plenty of money, and feel like it, you can be that way. We drove out to Fox and looked at one claim, but it was too deep, and too close to the satellite site out there. We really weren't interested in them after we saw what we'd have to go through to get permits and so forth. We drove on back, stopped off at Valdez Creek and checked on some claims, and got into Anchorage about 12:45 tonight.

Monday, June 2nd. I met with Joe today, and it wasn't any good. He's wanting me to go up to Wales, up above Nome, and tin-mine with him up there. I don't think I much want to go tin-mining. Jim and I went by Archie Step's yard this a.m. They're getting ready to move to Dawson City, Yukon Territory, to mine gold. He has about a half million in equipment and mining gear. Seems everyone has the "fever" nowadays.

Wednesday, June 4th. I didn't hear from Louis Wyman in Central regarding the claims on Porcupine Creek, but I did hear from George in Nome. He has 2 good claims, has a D6 dozer and a sluice box, and he wants $40,000. I'll have to check it out. We got a check today on our plane from Gordon Air, $539.43. It earned $1035. Repairs $400, tie-down $45, and on, and on, and on, and on.

Saturday, June 7th. I checked with George Jones regarding flying our plane up to Nome, and he said it would cost us $438 for him to take us up. That's our own plane! The cost would be just him and the fuel, so I told him I couldn't go for that much.

Tuesday, June 10th. I flew up to Nome this a.m. and it was raining. I saw lots of old friends, Roscoe Wilkie, Stan Sobozinski, and others. Jim West took me all over looking at mining ground, etc. I met George this morning, and we rode out to his claims, but couldn't cross the Nome River, as the front wheels of his 4-wheel drive wasn't working. He took his pickup into the shop to get it fixed this p.m. Jim West showed me some other ground. It's pretty deep, but he said it's some real good ground. I'll have to think on that one.

June 11th. I spent last night at Jim West's house, and June, his wife, sure fixed a good supper. I went up with George today and panned his ground. He had about 3 months' worth of ground already stripped and stockpiled, $40 - 50,000 worth, so we can't afford to move up for that, and that's all he had. I flew back to Anchorage this p.m. by Alaska Airlines.

June 12th. We went to see Bertha, a realtor, today regarding mining claims near Chicken, Alaska. She's Louie Knudsen's mother. I thought that we might consider a couple of the ones she was referring to, and we're to meet Saturday a.m. with a Mr. Hammond. It looks okay, he's got some good pictures. Marcene called the post office in Dawson City and asked the postmaster to put a note in Sam Bowman's mailbox to call me regarding mining there.

Friday, June 13th. I went by and talked to Buzz Hoffman today regarding state mining loans, up to a million dollars. I thought I'd check him out and see what his thinking was. Well, it's okay, but if you do apply for that loan it's just like a Small Business Loan, you have to put up everything you own, all your marbles and your toys, and your cars and motorhome, equipment, the whole nine yards, farm and all. So, I didn't want to get involved, I don't have to do it. Jim is working on a 977 loader at Heatherly's, just about to have it all fixed up.

June 14th. We met with Mr. Russ Hammond today regarding gold claims and camp near Chicken. The total asking price was $800,000. He sure had some nice buildings, but boy, $800,000 ! You know what you could do with $800,000 ? Buy yourself a half million dollars worth of gold, then take $300,000 and just play around, start piddling around in the creeks and laundering rocks, and you'll still wind up with a half million dollars worth of gold.

June 15th. Jim and I, and I.H. Christy and his friend, went up Valdez Creek and checked on Scarback's ground on White Creek. It didn't look too good. I spent over $75 on the trip, and it sure was a long haul for nothing but experience. You know I've had lots of that.

June 16th. Not much today, just waiting to latch onto something. Sam Bowman called from Dawson City and Jim took the call. Sam asked that I write him a letter, so, in turn, I'll do that.

June 17th. Henry called and still wants us to come over to Collinsville and mine for him this summer. I am to meet him tomorrow morning at the Captain Cook Hotel. We'll see what he's got up his sleeve.

June 18th. I met Henry this morning, and we agreed that Jim, Marty and I will go over to Collinsville to work the mine, and I could let go whoever I chose to let go over there. We went by Gordon Air office and waited for about 2 hours for the weather to clear, but it never did, so we'll try again tomorrow.

June 19th. Here we are, back in Collinsville. I could write 2 or 3 books on this place. Jim and I, and Henry went to Collinsville this p.m. George told me that it wouldn't cost us anything, as he was getting paid for the pilot to make the trip over. It looks like the D85 Komatsu and the 988 loader are okay, but the Michigan 125 and the 46A Cat are not jam up. The Michigan doesn't have brakes, and the transmission pump is out of the 46A. Looks like we'll be going back over to work tomorrow, weather permitting.

June 20th. The weather was bad today, so we didn't go back to Collinsville. We're getting parts and things together. I couldn't get a transmission for the old Dodge pickup at camp, or the rest of the parts for it. They have a pump for the 46A at Northern Commercial, and we can get it tomorrow.

June 21st. George flew us out to Collinsville in our 206. The weather's fair today. We met a little pot-bellied guy with suspenders. He was part of the group out of Seattle that, along with Henry, put up the money. Henry asked me, "What do you think, Jim, when do you think we can get started, and going?" These guys had been in there since February and didn't even have the box set up yet, no ground stripped, nothing. They had a 6-man crew over there, and had been over there most of the summer, well, since February. I looked around, and said, "If you can get us some carpet for the sluice box, and get it over for us by tomorrow noon, we'll be ready to roll."

They had a Ross Box, a sluice box with 2 side runs and the main run in the middle. When they took it in over there, they had spilled oil in the box and got it all over the carpeting. We had to do welding on the box, they messed it up bringing it in, and lots of little things. Then we had to set up the box and everything, scrub it out, and strip about 1000 feet of ground up the creek. So, I told him tomorrow noon. That little pot-bellied guy said, "There's no way in the world that you're gonna get no sluice box running by tomorrow noon." I just kind of wrote him off right there.

Anyway, I told Marty to go scrub down the sluice box real good and get all the old oil and stuff out of there, and Jim to do the welding on the sluice box first. Then we had to do some welding on the Cat blade. While they did that, I went stripping with the D85 Komatsu, built some settling ponds. The Komatsu was in pretty good shape, except for the leaking winch, and the cable is tore up. The 988 loader front transmission seal is gone, and it has a great big plug out of the right front tire, and the tube is showing. There's a big cut in a tire on the Michigan loader, the John Deere steering clutch is gone, and the 46A Cat has troubles with a leaky tramsmission pump. Boy, I'll tell you! But I had told Henry we'd be ready to roll at noon tomorrow with the sluice box. I still don't believe that he believed what I was talking about, and the little pot-bellied guy with suspenders, was just setting there shaking his head.

Denny Jones is thinking about coming over and working some up the creek from us. He hasn't got into his claims yet.

Sunday, June 22nd. The weather was pretty today. We stripped all last night and fixed the dam up. We got the ramp for the sluice box, pulled it in place, and got it all fixed up. It sure had some rough treatment on the way in, when they pulled it in cross-country. We put overflow pipe in 2 holding ponds, and got the sluice box all set and ready to go. All I hear from these guys that have been here all summer is Jeep, old machine drag line, and washing plant. And boy scouting. They like to go out and look around and take their picnic lunches with them.

Gordon Air brought Henry and the Dodge transmission for the pickup in today. We started sluicing this afternoon shortly after Henry got here, running the 988 loader and the Michigan 175. I spent most of the morning stripping.

Tuesday, June 24th. The sluice box ran 10-1/2 hours today. We're running roughly about 100 yards an hour, or a little more, in a Ross sluice box, feeding it with the 988 and 175 Michigan loaders. George flew Jim's wife over today.

I think we'll just finish this cut and hook'em, from the way things look around here. Marcene's having to cook special meals for them, and at different times, because they don't understand us getting up early in the morning and working late at night. The agreement is that we do all the repairs on the equipment, run it, do the mining and everything, and Camerot and his associates put up the money, furnish the equipment and fuel.

Glenn, the little pot-bellied guy, was setting out on the front porch this afternoon using a stopwatch counting the loads and figuring the time it took me to haul each load. This evening at the dinner table he said, "It's kind of funny, your production slowed down this evening." Of course, I never did tell him anything, I just said, "If you can't figure that out, then I feel sorry for you." The reason the production slowed down somewhat was that I was traveling farther and farther as the day went on, going up the creek, getting my loads and coming back. This dude couldn't figure that out. But anyway, so much for that.

I talked it over with the guys today, and they are in agreement with me all the way, so we'll go after this cleanup if things don't change. The weather was nice today, the equipment running pretty good. There's a mechanic from Palmer, by the name of Kelly, hanging out over here, and "pretty boy" Kevin, and Mr. Glenn, that's the guy with the pot-belly, Hugo the "flying miner", the Swede, and "greasy" George. Marcene had to stop George from washing his greasy hands over her skillet today. Oh, I'll tell you, this is a crew to draw to.

Friday, June 27th. We finished the pit here at camp today, will clean up tomorrow, and we'll play it by ear and take it from there. George came out in a Super Cub this afternoon for Marcene.

The reason that Marcene was going to Tennessee was that Jadene got married. She married Scotty Magill.

June 28th. We made a cleanup today. Jim, Marty and I got a little over 34.9 ounces of gold for our 30 percent. The weather's okay today. I called Marcene tonight and she's gonna call George to tell him not to come over tomorrow. Camerot was over today with 5 of his friends. A beaver got in our pipe this a.m., and we had to shut down and get him out. Henry is in real good spirits, he's making money now, or at least pulling out of the hole, since we got here and got started. So, we'll see what happens, play it by ear.

I stripped all day with the D85 Komatsu. Denny Jones came down this p.m. He's a nice guy, guess he's got some good ground up the creek above us here. I'm having a hard time getting the guys to wash their dishes, clean up the kitchen and carry out the garbage. That's these "dingers" over here that's hanging on. Marty and Jim made up 2 barrel culverts for holding pond overflows, and put them in. Fish & Wildlife were over this a.m., flying around, and I guess they liked what they saw because they didn't stop in to visit.

Tuesday, July 1st. Fish & Wildlife came over today, chewed me out real good, and there was nothing I could say. He finally didn't cite me, just a warning. Our discharge water seemed to be a little too muddy for him, so needless to say, we built more holding ponds. We worked 'til midnight. He said he'd be back tomorrow to check us out. I thought the dam was going out at 1:45, and got on the Komatsu, woke everyone up. Marty ran down and came back laughing. He said, "It was holding good, everything's fine." What had happened was the dam had filled up and was overflowing. Jim got the 988 stuck, and I got the Cat stuck, trying to please "Fish & Feathers" people. I got a message Marcene would be in Saturday, so that wrapped up the day.

Thursday, July 3rd. Boy, what a day! A holding dam broke this a.m., down at the end of the system. Good thing it wasn't one up above, it would've been like dominoes, all gone out. EPA, "Fish & Feathers", and no telling who else would be on us. We got wrote up in the paper today. Boy, the papers and EPA are after Collinsville. I talked to Marcene today and she'll be up Saturday if the weather is right. Fish & Wildlife told me that if a test on the water didn't prove okay, I'd have to build ponds 'til it did, or shut down. Their plane flew over after the dam broke. I just knew we'd be shut down, but it didn't land.

July 4th. We worked on the settling ponds 'til 11 a.m. Denny and Chuck came down to camp today, but we're not ready to sluice yet, as "Fish & Feathers" hasn't given us the go-ahead.

July 5th. Henry and family were in camp today, and they left this p.m. He and his family sure were nice to us.

Sunday, July 6th. We started the sluice box at 4 p.m. Chuck and Denny started work this p.m. Kelly, the mechanic, came in this p.m. We're supposed to work 2 shifts, Denny and one of my guys, and Chuck and my other guy, and I'm supposed to work most of both shifts. But, it looks like it just can't work out this way, so we'll have to do the best we can. Fish & Wildlife is going to shut us down if we don't get a pump and recycle water. As it's not my ground, I can't make the decision.

July 7th. We worked all last night and today until 8 p.m. Henry said a Fish & Wildlife biologist, and others, are coming out tomorrow afternoon at 5. Our plane flew over to camp this p.m. for Henry, and carried propane bottles to town. I got the loader stuck and Marty got the Komatsu stuck right beside me. Denny and Chuck worked 20-1/2 hours, with 3-1/2 hours for meals.

July 8th. Fish & Wildlife came over and approved our system 'til they check it next week. Camerot agreed to furnish groceries if Marcene cooks. I've got to talk to Jim and Marty about paying her a little something in gold. They just don't think, I guess, I don't quite understand that, but they're nice guys. It rained most of the day.

July 9th. Denny and his partner Chuck are working on the box. The 988 broke down this p.m., it was a U-joint broken. We are in good ground, hope the cleanup is good this time. The last cleanup we did was 80-some ounces, we're looking forward to the next one.

July 10th. It's sure funny. Marcene has her little rope tied on to the doorknob in the bedroom, in there back of the kitchen, to hold the door to while she uses the bathroom. She went into town this afternoon to get gold scales and stuff, and will be back tomorrow, weather permitting. It rained all day today, so what's new. It got so dark tonight that we quit and came in about 12:15. Denny and Chuck are still with us. Our 206 came over today and brought Camerot's kids, and they, along with George, went over to Twin Creek. We got the 988 going today, got the U-joint in, and I'm tired. Fish & Wildlife flew over this a.m., but guess everything's okay, they didn't stop and bug us.

July 11th. Boy, Mills Creek is up and wild today! I just wish Fish & Wildlife could see it now. We're like kids in a candy store without the owner, because we know that Fish & Wildlife can't get over here. I sent Denny upstream to divert the creek against the hill to cut the berm pile down. It will get the overburden off and we can get underneath it and get the gold. Mill Creek is as muddy as our discharge ditch. The 988 broke the other front U-joint about 7 p.m., just can't win for losing. A black bear was in camp this p.m. I went for Jim's rifle, but couldn't find the bullets in time to get him.

We're in pretty good ground today. Our fuel is low, about enough for one more day.

July 12th. Our dam broke today because I took Denny's word that the overflow ditch was right, and I didn't doublecheck it. So we lost 4 hours fixing things. I just can't be everywhere at once. We worked 'til 2 a.m. replacing dams below camp and rerouting the creek, but "Fish & Feathers" will never know the difference. Boy, it sure was lousy weather all day, glad for us, but sorry for Marcene, she couldn't make it in. We're in pretty good ground. Chuck didn't work the box today, his hands were hurting, so I let him stay in the kitchen and cook.

Sunday, July 13th. We ran the box 2 hours and got word that Camerot was on his way over. He wanted to clean up the box, so we did. We got 80-plus ounces of gold in the cleanup. The weather was pretty nice out today. Denny went into town today and Glenn came back over, darn it. I asked him if he brought any meat with him, and he said, "Oh, son of a gun, I left the meat in the Jeep over at Talkeetna at the airstrip." So all the meat that he bought and was supposed to bring over he left in the Jeep, and it ruined because it was so hot, about 80 degrees out. He'd brought some Jeep parts for the World War II Jeeps that he was interested in over here, but he wasn't too concerned about us eating, the Jeeps had to come first. Oh, Henry is smiling from ear to ear seeing that gold, and seeing his big debt of about $200,000 start dwindling and going the other way.

July 14th. The box didn't run today. We were stripping and cleaning up the pit. We sure need parts bad for the 988 Cat loader, and the Michigan 175.

Wednesday, July 16th. The sluice box ran 10 hours today and we got 200 gallons of fuel in. Glen Heatherly came over, just goofing around, I guess. He and his partner said our discharge water looked good all the way down to Lake Creek. Denny and Chuck spent the night in camp. We got some parts in today for the old 988, so that's good news. We stripped 'til 12 o'clock tonight, and moved a bunch of boulders today.

July 17th. Marty, Jim and I ran material through the Denver panner and gold wheel today, representing 12 hours running. From the first 4 feet of each side of the box, we got 9 ounces 11 pennyweight of gold, about 2-1/2 ounces overlay gold, and about 2 to 2-1/2 ounces of nuggets. Looks like we'll do real good on this one. Glen Heatherly left this a.m., took off up the creek with Denny. The 988 is working, but the 46A dozer is still down with a transmission problem. They haven't bought parts for it yet, so we can't do anything with it. The Komatsu needs cutting edges on the blade. The Michigan loader 175 needs a seal, the brakes are bad, and it also needs a tire.

July 18th. Cliff Hudson's plane with wheels/skis cracked up on the runway today. We tried to lift it and set it over to the side out of the ditch, but the picker broke. 'Nuff said. A Skyvan plane is going to come over tomorrow, bring us a tire and pick up Cliff's airplane. Denny came by this a.m. in his little track rig. Gordon Air picked Marcene up and she went into town for parts, and I paid for the parts and etc. I got tired of begging for parts, so I went ahead and paid for them. Marcene can get more done in town than this whole outfit together, including Henry and his superintendent, or whatever this little fat guy out here calls himself. Dana came out this p.m. with the parts and a barrel of gas. This is on Camerot. I got the Komatsu dozer going about 2 p.m. Marty stripped until 8:30, and I ran until midnight. We should have a good cleanup this time.

Sunday, July 20th. We got the 988 going about 9:30, and started the sluice box at 10:00 a.m. We ran good yardage today, and pretty good material. George and Neldina Jones came over and panned for gold about an hour and a half. I called Marcene. She's coming over tomorrow with George and Neldina. We helped Cliff's mechanic set the plane on barrels, ready to load onto the Skyvan tomorrow. That damn "pretty boy" Kevin came back to camp today, I just don't like the guy at all. And Kelly is a piddly old lady, I can see why he never made it in his own business.

July 21st. Gifford's Skyvan plane came in today and picked up Cliff's wrecked plane. It brought in the tire for the Michigan loader and other parts that we needed. Marcene came in this p.m., she sure did a good job getting the parts, etc. We cleaned the front hemp in the box. Kelly is still piddling. The little fat guy with the suspenders was trying to tell me that he could fly that big loader tire out under a float plane, put a bow knot in it and unleash it when he got over the camp, just drop it off. I looked at him and said, "Well, how in the world would the float plane ever get off the lake with the big loader tire swinging underneath it?"

July 22nd. Boy, oh boy! I got the shock of my life this a.m. Henry Camerot came in and told me that Glenn, the little pot-bellied guy with the suspenders, was accusing me of cleaning up and stealing gold. Boy, oh boy! So we're through and the boys are happy. Glenn ordered an armed guard, Karate, and a mercenary-type, over to look over us and make sure we don't take anything that isn't ours, including gold. I sure hate to leave such good ground and the area here, but such is life. And, you know, we got to talking about it, trying to figure out what went wrong, and I finally got it out of the guy. He said that we were making entirely too much money, that our 30 percent of the gold is just too much. He said, "You're making too much." So I said, "Well, gee whiz, you weren't making anything from February until we got here this month." But anyway, he said, "Why, we can get hands for a dime a dozen down in Seattle." And I said, "You better get you about a dollar's worth of them then."

The funny part about it was the guard, the mercenary, that they brought over here was a good friend of ours, and he was real nice to us. He couldn't stand the other crew that was here, and he said, "I don't know who I'm looking after and why, but I could care less about these other guys." We could have ripped them off good if we'd wanted to, but we didn't. We cleaned up and got a total of 87 ounces, with the mercenary watching. It took 2 trips in our 206 to get our gear back to town. The dingbats were still dinging around the camp. Everything went smooth with the cleanup.

It's sure nice to be out and away from those phonies over there. Marcene rode into Anchorage with Fish & Wildlife. And, oh yes, they shut Collinsville down today until they get a pump for recirculating water, per Bruce Barrett.

Friday, July 25th. We met with Henry today and got reimbursed on our paid-outs, and got a letter from him why we were let go. He stated in that letter that the investors were complaining about the deal they had made with us. They thought that our 30 percent was too much. Henry treated us real nice all the way. We went by Equipment Services and left a copy of the letter for their records. We took a check from Henry to Gifford Aviation, that was for hauling the tire over. We got it straight with George regarding the trip to Collinsville June 15th.

Marty came into town this p.m. He and his girl friend Gayla are going to the movies tonight. Jim cut the grass today and June bought him a case of beer. I gave June a big locket full of gold, sure made her feel good. Marcene bought me a new pipe today. Boy, I'm starting to win, it sure was sweet of her.

Well, it's July 26th, Saturday, and here we go, looking again for gold claims. We're heading out for Dawson City. We left this p.m., took off in our motorhome, and stopped off at Eldon Brandt's lodge for the night. That's at mile 125 on the highway, on the way to Tok. Jim and Marty went with us. Marty took his pickup.

July 27th. We left Eldon's early this a.m. after having breakfast, heading for Dawson. It sure was a long miserable drive. We had one hill that I just almost didn't make it up because the road was washed out. They had an old wagon road that wound around up the hill, and was it ever hairy trying to make it up the hill with that 33-foot motorhome without a transmission oil cooler. I didn't have a cooler on it, but I sure did need one, because that old transmission heated up bad. We got into Dawson about 7 p.m. Alaska time. Marcene and I took a ride around for awhile and saw some of the mines. We bought hamburgers, and they were the size of biscuits, for $4.50 each. We crossed the ferry at Dawson, that was a different twist in the motorhome.

July 28th. We went out looking for claims today, drove about 120 miles of rough road, and checked lots of ground. We didn't get to see Sam Bowman today, our contact from Alaska, but we hope to see him tomorrow. We did see Archie Step and the Fowler boys this a.m., as nice as always. They were up Bonanza Creek working on Don and Sue Murphy's ground. Marcene exchanged American money for Canadian and got 14 percent exchange rate.

Wednesday, July 30th. We spent most of the day waiting for a guy from Whitehorse to come in regarding claims on Dominion Creek. It rained most of the day. Marcene and I went out this p.m. to Basil Bryant's spread. He had two 980 loaders, one D4 with a backhoe, one new D8 Cat, one 966 new Cat, and had an enormous pit opened. Sam Bowman is supposed to come over tomorrow regarding his claims on Hunker Creek.

July 31st. Rich, the guy from Whitehorse, came in around noon and we went out to his claims and they don't look too bad. We picked up some old bottles and just could imagine how many people were on the hills around Dawson City during the gold rush days. We got back to town and Sam came in about 6 p.m. Marcene and I took Sam and his wife to dinner. It came to $54 plus a $5 tip. Jim, Marty and I went to Sam's claims and looked around a bit. There were lots of old workings, lots of old wheelbarrows and shovels, all that stuff, old slip scrapers, etc., left behind up there. It's sure odd where he's mining, about 240 to 250 feet above a little creek where he pumps his water, and the gold is in the top 2 feet of dirt up there. Darndest thing I've ever seen. He had a little pond down at the foot of the hill there and he had 2 pumps, one down at the pond. He'd start that pump and run up that hill, and it's almost straight up. He'd get up there and get that other pump started by the time the water got up there, and that pushed the water on over the top where he had another little pond and a little 2-inch pump setting up there. He pumped that water into his little wooden sluice box. His wife was shaking the grass roots out, getting nuggets and small pieces of gold out of even the grass roots. This was where the old-timers had run their sluice boxes with a heavy flow of water, and washed a lot of gold out the end of the box.

The ground up there on Whiskey Hill was so rich that the guy that owned the claims back in 1897 had given a dance hall girl in Dawson her weight in gold if she would live with him during the winter. The claims were rich and they got lots of gold off that hill, but there's still quite a bit left there.

August 1st. We spent most of the day at the camper park. Marty, Jim and I went up and checked on Sam Bowman's claims. I just don't see how we could feasibly work them. We made arrangements for a guy to take his backhoe over and dig test holes tomorrow on Dominion Creek. That was Keirin Daunt at Skookum Gulch on Bonanza Creek. I don't really care whether we find anything or not, I'm tired of looking, of checking out ground.

We had gotten a letter from a preacher on Quartz Creek regarding selling his 18 claims. Jim, Marty and I drove around for about 3 hours before we found his ground. He had quoted in his letter, "$500 per claim." When I talked to him, he said, "Oh, no, they are $5000 per claim." I saw an old D8 Cat that I had owned in 1966, and I asked him about cranking it up and digging test holes. His answer was, 'If you want to do a test on the ground, go down to the creek." I asked him how much he had to have up front and he said, "Enough for a ranch in Oklahoma." So I told him, "Bye!" Just a note, these claims would be some of the richest ground in the Yukon in 1991 after Vern Esterbrook leased the ground.

Saturday, August 2nd. We went out to Rich Hartmeyer's claims on Dominion Creek, paid $240 cash for a backhoe to dig test holes that turned out to be no good, and didn't even get a color. When we got back to Dawson we were so disgusted that we just packed up and took off for Alaska. We couldn't cross the border, they had the road blockaded, so we had to stop for the night. Just one more thorn.

Monday, August 4th. The weather was good today. We left Brandt's this a.m. and drove into Anchorage. While we were at Brandt's, I flew with Whitey in his Super Cub out to Alfred Creek. He wouldn't charge me for it as he said he was going anyway. I talked to Ed Neuser and he's not doing any good at all mining back over on Alfred Creek. I looked over some ground, but I didn't care for what I saw. When we got back to Anchorage we parked at June's place for a couple days.

August 5th. The weather was nice today. I went by and checked on our airplane, had coffee with George and Neldina. I called Eldon Brandt and asked him to tell Whitey about our 206 being for sale. Total time on it is 1131.2 hours, and I would like to get about $36 - 38,000 for it. The low book on it is $42,000. I went by to see Ed Eckles, nothing new, just a nice visit. Collinsville hasn't done a thing since we left over there.

I called Helen in Fairbanks regarding claims on Porcupine Creek and she doesn't have any to lease. I also talked to John Murphy regarding the insurance claim on our 206 airplane. This was Clint's insurance company. He told me that the check had been mailed to our address in Tennessee. His exact words were for me to check with someone on the other end, that our check should be there.

Thursday, August 7th. Jim, Marty and I went silver salmon fishing at Rabbit Slough today, over near Palmer, and got our limit. It's sure nice to just get out and relax, go fishing and get away from all the rat-race. We got a big check today on our 206 plane. After all the deducts for repairs, this, that, and the other, $122.23.

Sunday, August 10th. Jim, Marty and I went fishing again at Rabbit Slough, and got our limit again. From the looks of all the vehicles off the roads around Anchorage this morning, it must have been a weird sign of the moon, or something, 'cause they were scattered all over in the ditches.

August 11th. Marcene finished paying for Maxine Smith's coat. She's the owner of ABM Escrow, and she's done so much for us we thought that she deserved at least a fur coat. It was white mink with leather too, by the way, pretty neat, special design.

Wednesday, August 13th. We read in the paper today where Fish & Wildlife has Camerot and the Twin Creek mine shut down, and that they won't let him start up again until they get a recirculating system. That's one thing I'd been telling Henry all along that they should have had over there, to eliminate all the settling ponds and everything. Glen Heatherly left for the North Slope today. He left in his Kenworth truck, and he's about 78 years old, or young, whichever way you want to put it.

Friday, August 15th. Today we sold the 206 airplane. The 2 happiest days in your life are the day when you get your first new airplane, and the day you get rid of it. That airplane was a beautiful airplane and it would pack a load, but it was just a little bit more than we needed to have setting around in the yard. Plus you deal with these guys that lease them and they take you every way in the world to the cleaners. That's where you finally wind up. So George is gonna go ahead and buy it. Now I did catch George, when we got ready to sign the papers, and told him, "Okay, I'll sell you the airplane, there's no problem there, everything's fine, but there is one thing we have got to have, and that is the rental on the airplane for these last 2 weeks. Bring us up to date, bring your paperwork out and show us how many hours you flew the plane." So, we wound up with $1195 for rental, for just part of the month. And that's the end of the story on the 206 airplane.

August 16th. We left Anchorage this noon and drove up to Talkeetna. We saw Ollie, Cliff Hudson's wife, and wanted to see Cliff, but he was busy flying on McKinley. I wanted to give Cliff some gold because of damaging his plane, the 185 Cessna while getting it out of the ditch along the airstrip over at Collinsville. The drill stem we were using to pick the plane up, broke and did some additional damage on top of the airplane. I was real sorry about that and wanted to leave Cliff some gold for compensation.

August 17th. We spent last night in Talkeetna and left for Fairbanks about 7:30 a.m. We drove on to Fairbanks, found Eddie McNabb, and rented a 4x4 pickup at Hertz Rental for our drive to Manley Hot Springs tomorrow.

August 18th. We left Fairbanks at 6:30 a.m., drove up the Haul Road to Livengood, and over to Manley Hot Springs. We went to Eureka Creek to see Archie Pringle regarding his claims, but didn't get to see him, so we left a note on his door regarding the claims, also a record and a note for Rose. We went up to Don Orcutt's spread and boy, they tore that place up like an old settin' hen. The guy that went in there really tied him up with a contract, and he's going "huckledybuck", using scrapers, dozers, and a loader. He's evidently doing quite well from what we hear. We got back to Fairbanks about 4:30 p.m.

August 19th. We left Fairbanks this a.m. and drove up to Mammoth Creek near Central. We stopped by to see Keith Allen on Porcupine Creek regarding claims and took a bottle of "R&R" for him. As we were going up the creek, Keith was looking and saw us coming. Marcene was waving that bottle out the window of the pickup. We could see a grin from at least a half mile away, a toothless grin, he didn't have any teeth. He was like a kid on Christmas morning. He is flat broke, his equipment is broke down and he's waiting on parts. His partner's wife died and the partner had to take her body outside for burial. This just hasn't been his year. Keith was telling me that he was real happy with the deal that I gave him on the old what he called "Big Foot". It was the three-quarter ton, stake bed, 4-wheel drive pickup with big tires on it. I sold it to him about 3 years ago for $500.

Keith built a helicopter about 2 years ago, and he was asked about its hovering time. What he did, how he got his hovering time in, was he tied a nylon rope to the helicopter so he wouldn't get up and get too carried away. He could only raise up about 25 feet, he said so that way if he fell it wouldn't be very far to the ground. But he got his hovering time with his helicopter tied off with a rope out at his place right below the Matanuska Glacier.

We also went over to see Mr. Alexander on Independence Creek. He was nice, had 7 claims on Mammoth Creek, and wanted $400,000 with $200,000 down. I looked them over, but there was too much overburden, and on the wrong side of the creek. The road sure was rough where they were too. It rained about all the way. We saw an airplane that had landed on the road on top of the pass. He was waiting out the clouds and bad weather right on top of Mammoth Dome. He said he was okay, had plenty of food and everything was fine. He had his airplane tied down so he was okay.

Thursday, August 21st. Henry called this evening about 6 p.m. and wants me to meet him tomorrow at 8 a.m. at the Westward Hotel Coffee Shop. I stopped by to see Ed Eckles over at the radiator shop and he doesn't know anything yet regarding the claims that he was checking on.

August 22nd. I met with Henry and Dick Carey, this morning regarding mining at Collinsville. Henry sure was nice and talked for us 100 percent, but I really don't care much anymore. Dick is as dingy as Glenn and it's so hard to reason with anyone so uninformed on the actual facts of mining. Henry is unhappy with the way things are going and says there just isn't any production at Collinsville, and he has to do something about it. They are to contact me before Wednesday of next week. The weather was nice today. Everything else seemed to go pretty good. I called Mel in Vancouver, B.C. today and he was nice, we're gonna see him on the way south.

August 23rd. This morning, Jim and I went with Glen Heatherly up to Peters Creek to help him fix a 977 Cat loader. We got up to camp about 2:45 p.m. and worked on the loader 'til about 9 p.m. We slept in the guy's cabin; they were nice and gave us sleeping bags, cooked supper for us and everything. I had one problem though, I had to get up during the night to use the outhouse, but they had been doing a cleanup out in the yard this evening before we went to bed. So I had to "hold it" because I didn't have the heart to go out where they had all their pans of gold and stuff setting around. I just felt that they might think I was out looking at their gold so I waited 'til morning. It seems a little cooler up here on Peters Creek than in Anchorage and, of course, it's getting that time of year, a little frosty at night.

Sunday, August 24th. We were up early and had eggs and bacon for breakfast, then went to work and finished pulling the clutch out of the 977 loader. We had to take it into town to get the bearing pressed off and a few other things. We rode on the Cat and trailer for 2-1/2 miles, then a 4x4 for about 2 miles, then we transferred parts, etc. to Glen's pickup. We got back to Anchorage about 3:30 p.m. The weather was beautiful today. I saw an old friend, Lee Teague, up at Bird Creek mine. He had his problems too, one D9 Cat broke down, also a D8 Cat broke, but he had high spirits.

August 25th. The weather was nice today. I went by and saw Henry and got a check for $756 for some concentrates. I split it 3 ways, Jim, Marty and myself. Henry told me that there's been no production since we left Collinsville.

Thursday, August 28th. It was raining this a.m. Jim left with Glen about 6 a.m. to work on the 977 loader on Bird Creek. We saw Larry South this a.m. and he's trying to mine about 95 miles south of Kodiak. I'm getting ready for a change, been setting around too long.

Saturday, August 30th. I went by and talked to Dean Briski this a.m. He and Roger Nordelon, out of Kotzebue, have some claims on Glacier Creek out of Candle. He wants $70,000 for 14 claims, 40-acre claims, but I'm a little leery of them because of the natives up there. They have gone a little overboard since the Native Lands

Claims Settlement Act came into effect, so gotta be careful and walk softly around those people. Still no word from Archie Pringle at Manley Hot Springs, and Freddie Winard's claims at Candle. I hope to hear from them before we leave for Tennessee.

Tuesday, September 2nd. I left Jack Leakander 5 ounces of nice gold today. He's gonna pick out some, send me $650 an ounce for it, then send the rest on to us in Tennessee. He's one of the last of the breed that you can trust. It was a little cold out last night. I found frost on the windshield of our pickup, and it's supposed to get a little colder tonight. I talked with Henry tonight, and he thinks we still might work out something if he can get those guys out of the picture at Collinsville, but we're gonna hook'em to Tennessee tomorrow.

Friday, September 5th. We got into Haines and went out to look around a little bit tonight. We enjoyed the night out at the hotel bar, but as usual there always seems to be a "dipstick". There was an archeologist in the bar bragging about getting some miner shut down around Dietrick, Alaska, on the Hall Road up north of Fairbanks. We also picked up some real good smoked salmon there, best we've ever eaten. The bartender opened up a can and said, "Go ahead and eat it. If you don't like it you don't have to pay for it. And if you do like it, buy the whole case of it." So we bought the whole case of it, it was delicious. We just kind of waited around today and loaded onto the ferry tonight. The sea was calm and everything going real good. We got acquainted with part of the crew and they sure were nice people.

Tuesday, September 9th. We got into Vancouver, B.C. and called our good friend Mel Pardek. He came over for awhile and it was nice to see him.

Thursday, September 11th. Mel and I went by to see the owner of the Rock Box, Norm Pearson, and also the Ross Box, Norm Ross, the Ross brothers. These are manufacturers of sluice boxes. We may get something put together for next year yet. Mel and his wife took us out to dinner. We went across the Bay Bridge and rode the trolley to the top of Grouse Mountain. Sure good food and a nice view from up there.

Mel is a guy that's been around a lot, been into mining. He had a silver mine at Golden, B.C. a few years back when the price of silver was up. When the bottom fell out he walked into the bank and told them, "Okay, guys, we're temporarily out of business, but if you can hang on until silver goes back to about $7 an ounce we'll be back in business." This is the kind of guy Mel is, he's just one swell person to deal with.

September 12th. Marcene and I went over to Delta Refining this a.m. and had a tour of the refinery. The people were nice, Betty showed us around. We left gold to be processed and we also left some concentrates for them to process. Delta still hasn't paid Henry for fines sent in that we have a percentage coming from.

Sunday, September 14th. We stopped to see our old friend Sam Scardi this morning. He's got Alcan Realty in Sutherlin, Oregon, and he had Alcan Realty in Alaska. In fact, we bought our home on Campbell Lake in Alaska from Sam. It's always nice to see him, he's a super nice guy.

September 15th. Gold today was $557 an ounce. We stopped in Bakersfield tonight to see the Willetts, Dee and Rosie, and they're okay. Then we went over and spent the night at Red Simpson's, had a nice visit with him and Bobby Adkins.

Thursday, November 4th. Ronald Reagan was elected president today. Hopefully things will be a little different now.

Friday, December 12th. Henry called tonight. He said to call him January 15th for confirmation regarding work next year at Collinsville.

Monday, December 15th. We wrote Delta Refining today and explained that we didn't like the way they were handling our gold, and also asked them to send back our silver.

1981

Tuesday, January 13, 1981. I helped Mel Pardek take samples on his gold claims just out of Quartzsite, Arizona, on Nugget Road. We hung around there for a couple of days. Also, we went over to see Sid Ragsdale at Desert Center regarding his gold mine, but he wasn't in, he'd gone to Blythe, Claifornia. We'll probably check with him later. Everything is nice and warm out here and it's nice to be visiting good friends. Oh, by the way, Denny Jones was supposed to be in today, but we missed him in Quartzsite.

Thursday, Juanary 15th. Denny got in today and we did see him. It was nice talking with him. He's making gold nugget jewelry, etc., and he had his jewelry display for sale in the camper park here.

Saturday, January 17th. We walked around Mesa today, went to the Gold Prospectors' Show, enjoyed looking around, talking to the different miners.

Monday, March 30th. President Reagan got shot today in Washington, D.C., but is going to survive okay.

Friday, June 5th. I called Billy Hoogadorn in Nome and he still has the hardrock claims there. He has a partner in Anchorage by the name of Andy.

Thursday, July 2nd. We talked with Eldon Brandt today and he said there was a guy mining over on Carribou Creek who needs help bad. Eldon checked with the guy, Bob McKirvey, and said that he wanted me to come on up and help him. So I guess we'll leave after the Fourth of July, go up and check it out.

Friday, July 3rd. We checked on a plane ticket to Anchorage, round trip, and it was $865. I remember when we could fly round trip, Nashville to Anchorage, for less than $400.

Sunday, July 5th. I flew out of Nashville this a.m. and got into Anchorage at 2:45 p.m. The weather was nice and sunny, in the 60's. Jim Prochaska picked me up at the airport and I spent the night with him. We drove around and looked the town over, new mining stuff, etc.

Monday, July 6th. We were up early this a.m. When we cranked up the pickup and started out Jim said, "I think there's something wrong with the back end of this thing." I had let I.H. Christy take the 2 snow tires and wheels off of my pickup last winter and put 2 old rags on. He didn't even bother to tighten the wheels back up when he put them on, he just stuck them on and hand tightened the lug nuts. He's a squirrel. So I had to buy 2 new ones, $198. Seems it's always something, but I finally got started down the road.

I went on up the Glenn Highway and stopped to visit with Marty. He was getting the site ready for his house, that is, he's going to move a house onto it. I went on to Brandt's Lodge and met Bob McKirvey, and he seems like a nice guy. He's out of southern California, a contractor down there at Irvine.

July 7th. The weather was good today and we flew into his mine over on Carribou Creek. The sluice box ran 5 hours, then Bob and I did a cleanup. We got almost an ounce of gold out of 70 yards. I don't think that the ground will be feasible to work though, too many boulders for the gold here. Bob has a new D8 Cat, a 980 loader, a John Deere 350, and a 10 x 12" pump, Cat powered. He just has too much rented for the gold we're getting. It's sad that I'm just here to advise Bob. I don't have any interest in this at all.

He told me, "Do whatever you need to do, if you need to let someone go, let him go." We were sluicing today and Bob's partner's son was all wired up. He had earphones on and was dancing around at the sluice box while rocks were hanging up in there. The gold was whipping out, and so forth. I walked up behind him, slapped him on the back and asked him if he knew his way home. He didn't understand what I was trying to say, couldn't hear me at first. Finally, he got the message. I told him, "You're no longer needed." I took his rake and started raking rocks. Bob said, "That's alright, no problem."

We finally got the sluice box working good this afternoon, one person can work it okay, the right person, that is. We're gonna do the final cleanup here and run it through the gold wheel this evening to determine just how much we've got.

Thursday, July 9th. The weather wasn't bad today here on Carribou Creek. We ran approximately 700 to 800 yards through the box. Our cleanup for 12 hours was 3-1/2 ounces, plus some fines and some black sands. Bob and I worked the cleanup at the cabin. It seems as if I always get stuck with doing most of the cleanup. We pushed through quite a bit of bedrock today, got a few nuggets in the front riffles, small ones. The John Deere needs a grease gun to tighten the track, seems as if the D8 is okay, the 980 needs an injector, that's about it. I borrowed a magnet and 3 screens from my old friend Walt Klewine today. I don't think that Walt is going to stay in here much longer. He's been mining down the creek.

July 10th. Jack, Bob's partner, came in this a.m. and seems like a nice guy. It was his son that I sent home the other day and he didn't have one complaint. We put 3-inch riffles back in the center of the box and they sure work okay. We ran the box about 2-1/2 to 3 hours today, then shut down to move the pump out from the creek as the creek was rising fast, and we got it out just in time. Carribou Creek looked like a river this p.m. and is still rising, about lost our road. I ordered a cocoa mat today. The cook went in and is supposed to bring it back. The dozer sucked a rock into the fan and messed up the radiator. The "dinger" operator on the loader is kind of goofy. Mary Brandt sent me a note that Marcene called; she said Jerry Brutton paid, and Marty is ready for work.

July 11th. We reset the pump today and got the box running about 1:30 p.m. We run about 100 yards of material an hour through the box. Things are running good. The dozer didn't do much work, Bob and Gordon were working on the D8 all day. It rained all last night and this a.m. We had to dam and divert the creek today. The riffles didn't look too bad this afternoon, but didn't look all that good either.

Sunday, July 12th. I'm just kind of marking my time here on Carribou Creek with Bob and the boys. They seem like nice people, but just not getting enough gold for the amount of equipment they have. Bob's connected some way with Queenstake.

July 13th. Steve went in to Brandt's today, and all the guys were off, except Bob, Jack and myself. We're checking ground up and down Carribou Creek, on the benches and so forth, and running material through. This cleanup was 6 ounces, 1 pennyweight, plus some fines and black sands.

July 14th. We let Jeff, Jack's boy, go and of course, he's going back to California today, he and his dad. I flew in to Brandt's today, got my pickup and drove into Anchorage. I picked up a kid just east of Palmer. He acted funny, and just outside of Palmer he pulled a gun, a 44 magnum, and wanted my money. I told him I only had $20 and some change. Just before we got into Palmer I told him that this was as far as I was going because I had to stop and get fuel for the guy I've been working for. I said, "I haven't been paid all summer." I had about $400 in my billfold, but I had the $20 in my Levy shirt pocket and I just pulled it out and handed it to him. I pulled into the gas station there on the edge of Palmer and told him that the gun route was not the way to go, so he got out at the station. I took off and called the State Troopers, and told them what had happened. It started raining this p.m. on the way in.

July 15th. This morning I called the State Troopers again and they wanted to know if I wanted to file charges on this guy that I picked up yesterday, they had caught him. I said, "What is he charged with?" They said he was charged with armed robbery, attempted murder, rape, and all kinds of things. I told them, "If you can't make those charges stick, the little one that I've got doesn't mean anything." So I didn't even bother to go by and file charges against the guy.

I checked around town and got some new materials for catching gold in a sluice box that are supposed to be better than the cocoa mat. I talked to several people and don't think I'll have much trouble getting lined out for next year.

July 16th. I went back up to the mine on Carribou Creek today and brought groceries, some burlap bags, and some matting for the sluice box. I flew in to the mine with Don Deering and everything was kind of at a standstill when I got back.

Saturday, July 18th. We're still digging test holes, even went up on Alfred Creek and dug a couple.

July 19th. I flew into Brandt's with Don Deering today and drove into Anchorage. I spent the night with Jim Prochaska, Ernestine is still gone. Before I left Carribou Creek I panned out one of the tests and it looks as if they could just about break even with this one. But that doesn't include equipment rental, just labor and fuel.

July 20th. I spent 'til noon chasing and getting figures regarding the sluice box. I bought material to revamp the sluice box, got some more material for carpet. I think we can up the production some with this expanded metal, enough to see what the ground is really worth. Walt Klewine flew the material in with his helicopter. It's sure a lot better than cutting it up to fit in the Super Cub, then rewelding when we get it over, or sending a Cat all the way in to Brandt's Lodge for it. That's about 40 miles of tundra to cross. I learned quite a bit this trip. I called Marcene again today. She doesn't know yet if Kendall can drive our motorhome up. Lavelle and Ruth called her and just maybe they'll come up with her and drive. Don Deering flew me back into camp about 4:15 this p.m.

July 21st. We ran about 800 yards of material through the box even though we didn't get to run any until about 9:30 or 10:00 a.m. The weather was nice out today, and clear. Bob did clean up the front riffles on the side runs and it wasn't really too good. The boys rode 3-wheelers in to Brandt's tonight. I sent a note in for Mary Brandt to call Marcene and have her make reservations for me this weekend. I'm going to fly to Nashville. I'll go down and drive the motorhome back up here myself.

July 22nd. Bob paid me $1000 tonight. I could have held him up for more, but just didn't see the reasoning for it because they're not getting much gold, and so forth. We cleaned the box this p.m. and it didn't look too good. This Carribou Creek is just another teaser, you get just enough gold to keep you hanging on.

July 23rd. We got started sluicing about 11:30 a.m. and had to make some riffles, but first we had to unload the concentrates into tubs. Gordon took the John Deere wide pad and went in to Brandt's for fuel, and he made it back okay. Whoop-de-doo! We didn't have to go after him this time. We moved the fuel tank down to the jobsite. I worked the box today and Ernie signaled. Steve,

Bob McKirvey's boy, operated the 980 Cat loader. He's sure a good operator and a nice kid.

July 24th. I caught Don Deering and his Super Cub in to Brandt's today and drove on into Anchorage. Gordon took the rollagon wheels, that's the fuel wheels that he pulls behind the wide pad John Deere, back to Brandt's today. I caught the plane tonight and headed for Tennessee. I left my pickup in the airport parking lot, $15 a week.

Sunday, July 26th. We're getting ready to leave tomorrow. I pulled some corn, tomatoes, cucumbers, cantelopes, all kinds of goodies to take back up to Alaska in the motorhome.

Tuesday, July 28th. This is the second day out from Tennessee. We got away about 6 a.m. this morning. It was raining last night and we sure slept good. No problems today, made it to about 80 miles west of Winnipeg and stopped in a camper park. We filled up with good water.

Thursday, July 30th. We stopped in Regina last night for money exchange, groceries and gas. We parked for the night about 50 miles east of Edmonton and it was a 3-ring circus this a.m. getting through Edmonton in the rain. There are no signs, just guess and be danged. We finally made it to the right highway, north to Dawson Creek, B.C. We had problems with water in the gas, but finally made it into Fort Nelson. You just have to go through a trip like this to understand; I'd have to drive 70 miles an hour downhill on muddy gravel in order to make it up the next hill.

July 31st. We spent the night in Fort Nelson and slept in this morning, didn't get up 'til about 7 a.m. We ate at the Chinese place, filled up at the Texaco and found the electrical adaptor that we have been looking for. We just barely made it up Steamboat Mountain. I didn't think that we'd make it because it was cutting out on both tanks, we just creeped over in the lowest gear. We stopped at the German's place at Muncho Lake and bought fresh bread, and filled up. We stopped in Watson Lake, filled the main tank, and I just happened to check the lug nuts on the wheels. It was a good thing, too, I had to get them all tightened. We would have never made it to Whitehorse without doing that. Boy, this drive is for sure full of surprises. We stopped at a camper park about 20 miles south of Whitehorse, Yukon Territory, tonight.

Saturday, August 1st. We got started pretty early this a.m., stopped in Whitehorse to fill up and drove on to Brandt's Lodge. The road was so rough between the border and Brandt's it just made me sick to drive the motorhome over it. We stopped at Sourdough Camper Park in Tok and visited the guy that's the manager. He said that they aren't doing any good there these days. That Sourdough Camper Park is one that we used to own a few years back.

August 2nd. We're at Brandt's lodge waiting for Mac to get back and we'll go into the mine. It's raining and nasty out. I checked under the motorhome, the fuel filters, etc., and found that I have 2 bad tires in the rear, so we'll replace both of them. We'll do it when we go into Anchorage.

August 3rd. I helped Eldon Brandt drag in an old track loader that fell off of a guy's truck up on the hill a ways east of Brandt's Lodge. We went up with the big Kenworth wrecker and hooked onto it, and drug it right down the highway. I'm going over to camp tomorrow. The weather is still miserable out. We saw lots of old friends today. Mac went on over to camp this p.m., so I'll see him over there tomorrow.

August 4th. I waited for Northern Commercial's mechanic to show until 3 p.m. I just didn't want to call Don Deering twice and make 2 trips over to the mine. We got into the mine about 5 p.m., got the pump tore apart and the mechanic's tool wouldn't pull the injector on the 980, so he had to go back into town to get more tools. That's the way it usually is. I helped Bob pan out some gold this p.m. after I got to camp. One test on a bench across from the cabin was $3.50 per cubic yard, at $350 per ounce for gold, and one test about $1 per yard. In other words, you'd have to move approximately 100 yards of material to get 1 ounce of gold on the first test, and over 300 yards on the second test. These were the 2 best tests, but not enough yardage to pay for a big operation.

August 5th. We got the mechanic's tools, pump parts, etc., loaded on the plane and gone about 7:30 a.m., and then went down and set up the big sluice box. Our big pump broke down, so we cannot sluice. Walt Klewine said that he'd loan us his pump, but he isn't back from town yet, so we can't get it. Ernie used the welder this a.m., working on his Mack, a little rubber tired rig. I took the John Deere up to make a cut down the hill into Alfred Creek this p.m., and ran into permafrost. I had a heck of a job getting started, but finally got down about half way and the ground slid down, came down on the dozer. I had to walk out to camp, get a shovel, walk back in and dig it out. There was only one guy in camp who would even think about going back up there to give me a hand. He was a guy out of Oregon who had been a logger and had a crippled leg, but he went up and gave me a hand. It was real nice of him and I'm sorry I don't have his name to put onto this. But this guy had driven a log skidder in to Brandt's Lodge all the way from Anchorage, 125 miles. He had a backhoe on the back of the skidder, he was doing some testing for another guy. We got it out about 11 p.m. and finally got in camp about midnight. You sure find people out when you're in trouble. We looked for a way off the hill, but had to go around the head of Jim Crow Creek.

August 6th. We got started first thing this morning and punched a road up at the head of Jim Crow Creek to get the skidders, sluice box and pump over to Alfred Creek. I finished cutting the road off the hill into Alfred Creek about 3:30 p.m. It took 8 hours total to make the cut and switchback, about 500 feet. The skidder went after the pump, but kept turning the trailer over, so I had to take a Cat, go get the trailer and bring it over to Alfred Creek. I went on downhill to where we were going to dig the first test. The guys didn't come on down to unload me, so I waited about 15 minutes, unhooked from the trailer and went back up the hill. They were gone as if they were punching a timeclock. I'd sure hate to go into cambat with these characters, any one of them. I just wonder what people think, I suppose they just think of themselves.

Brandt called me on the radio-phone and looks like Collinsville is up for grabs, again. Mel Pardek called, and will call back Sunday, so just maybe . . . .

August 7th. I went up Jim Crow Creek and cut about a quarter mile of road up to the head of the creek and out on top. We went into Alfred Creek, dug test holes and checked ground, it was no good. We went on back to camp, took the sluice box, pump and etc. Boy, did it rain tonight!

August 8th. It rained all last night, and hard. This morning Mac and I went down to Walt's, but he wasn't home so we couldn't get his pump. He's supposed to be in this p.m. We need to borrow his pump to run our box, as our pump is broke down and we're waiting for parts from Northern Commercial. I went in to Brandt's, it's good to be back and see Marcene again. Marty and his wife came by to see us. Also, Bill and Marlene and the boys were up, they were on their way to go moose hunting. Lonnie fixed the dash lights and running lights on the motorhome. Lonnie was a real nice guy, who later on got run over and killed. I got a quote from Eldon today on tires for the motorhome, $175 each. Bob brought the John Deere in to Brandt's with the trailer and 4-inch pump, just one trip today, what a waste.

Sunday, August 9th. Mel called this evening. He's meeting with the Canadians tomorrow to see if he can't work out something regarding Collinsville. The weather was nice out today. We ate breakfast at the Lodge, also supper, country ham for breakfast and burgers for supper. Mike and Gordon rode their 3-wheelers out today, just goofing around on their day off. I guess we'll spend another day here, as Mel is to call us here tomorrow night. I haven't checked on Mrs. Gross yet, but I guess she's made her payments.

August 10th. I talked to Mel this evening and he gave me Jack Wilson's number in Vancouver. He's one of the people I met with last year regarding Collinsville.

August 11th. We drove into Anchorage today, got the pickup at the airport parking and it cost $40. We ordered 4 Goodyear steel belted radial tires for the motorhome, $170 each, and we should get them in about 2 weeks. We drove out to Jim Prochaska's and saw June. She's still the same. Ernie came by and she's still talking a mile a minute. Jim is welding for Parker Drilling on the North Slope. I called Jack in Vancouver and he's almost sure that the guys from Washington are pulling out of Collinsville. He'll know for sure next Tuesday and he'll call me then. Mac called from Brandt's Lodge and wants me to look for ground for next year's work. Marcene checked with Don Cole today and I'm not even gonna go into what we owe the IRS.

August 12th. I called Charles Tulin, an attorney, today regarding claims on Harrison Creek north of Fairbanks. He was supposed to return the call, but he didn't.

Saturday, August 15th. It was clear and cool this morning. I talked to a guy regarding claims on Forty Mile River, about 120 miles north and east of Tok. Then I called Mary Brandt and she'll have Mac call if he's interested. We'll drive up with the guy next Wednesday.

Tuesday, August 18th. I waited all afternoon for the phone call from Jack Wilson or Mel Pardek. I finally called Mel, and he in turn called Jack, and Jack called me. He doesn't have any information regarding Collinsville as of yet. I'm going up tomorrow to Forty Mile River to check out claims that a guy from Kenai has and Bob McKirvey is going along with me. He would like to check out all the details also. It rained most of the day.

August 19th. Perry, the guy that was supposed to go up to Forty Mile River with us, didn't show up at the airport this a.m., so I decided the heck with him. I think he's a phony. I called Mary Brandt and told her to tell Bob McKirvey that I wouldn't be up because the guy didn't show. I talked to Bob later this evening and explained everything.

Friday, August 21st. I talked to George Jones this morning regarding flying us to Homer next Tuesday. He said that he'd do us a big favor and just charge us $300 for the trip. For a guy that's looking for work flying into Collinsville, or wherever I'll be mining, he is sure a greedy person. We gave him a deal on our airplane, let him have it at about $10,000 under what it should have gone for. It was a super deal and here he is, wanting to gouge us on a little measly trip to Homer.

Friday, August 22nd. Nothing much is happening today, I'm just hanging around waiting for a telephone call from the guys in Vancouver. I'll hold tight a few more days. I can't help wondering what's happening on the Collinsville property. For some strange reason we keep going back to Collinsville.

August 23rd. We went by to see our old friend, Jack Leakander, the friendly jeweler. Jack buys gold and you can trust him 100 percent, he's from the old school. You can leave your gold with him and he'll pick out what he wants, then send you the money for it and all your remaining gold that he doesn't buy. Jack has emphysema real bad, also cancer, so he's in pretty sad shape, but he's still got high spirits and we enjoy going by and visiting with him. He's a super nice guy. Mac called this p.m. He and Eldon, Steve and his boy, are coming down Tuesday, and we're going to Homer halibut and silver salmon fishing. We made arrangements with Bud and Audie Berryman at Homer to take them fishing.

Friday, August 28th. I loaned Frank Talley $2000 this a.m. and he gave me $3000 worth of gold nuggets for collateral.

Sunday, August 30th. Glen Heatherly called today and gave us a report on Collinsville. There's been another change of operators, same old same old. If you ever want to know anything about Collinsville, even to this date, he's still right in there and knows all about it.

Wednesday, September 2nd. I talked to George today and he tells me that everything in Collinsville right now is broken down. I'm still waiting for word from the Canadians, but I don't really care one way or the other whether I hear from them or not. We put an ad in the paper today regarding trading property, our 40 acres in Anchorage, for mining ground, and we'll see what happens.

September 3rd. I talked to George Bishop regarding claims on Kowukuk River up north of Fairbanks, 235 miles along the Haul Road. We might work out something, it's hard to say.

September 4th. My old buddy, Glen Heatherly, popping up here again. I talked to Glen today and he said that all 3 loaders were broke down at the Collinsville mine. I went by this a.m. and told the Goodyear people to go ahead and put the tires on our motorhome. Our old and dear friend, Bob Tuttle, passed away last night. He had cancer, and he's to be buried tomorrow. We used to see him at all the snow machine races throughout the state of Alaska, he was an avid sports supporter. He made his living as a masonry contractor.

Sunday, September 6th. I talked to Mel today and he was the same as ever, always nice, but there's nothing for sure regarding Collinsville except one thing, O'Lorrey is broke and can't do anything. I think I'll check out Nome area next week. I talked to Eldon and the California group got off okay. Also, Walt got moved over on Alfred Creek and is going to mine on Whipple Lucas's claims. Big deal! I talked to a guy today by the name of Jim Morgan and he has some gold claims up about 50 miles from Glennallen. I don't think that they're any good, so I'll kind of pass on them. He's a little shifty anyway I think.

September 7th. Frank Talley called this a.m. and wants now to borrow $5000. I think he's nuts. The only way that we'd possibly do it is if he'd put up $10,000 in gold, and I don't think he's gonna do that. No mail today, no word from anyone regarding mining claims. I sure got lots of feelers out and maybe by tomorrow we'll get some answers.

September 8th. The weather was nice out today. We saw, and had coffee with, Rudy Malone and Dick Marks this a.m. Both are old timers up here. I met with Henry this p.m. and he's gonna talk to Dick Carey regarding Collinsville. Henry's gonna call me tomorrow, but I'm leery of Dick because he's a "dipstick" and couldn't pick his nose with both hands when it comes to common horse sense. So much for that. I had to turn down the $5000 loan to Frank because he didn't have enough gold to back it up. Marcene called the Nome newspaper regarding an ad for gold claims today, and also the Fairbanks paper. We'll just keep looking 'til something gives.

September 9th. Henry called and wants me to meet with him and Dick tomorrow morning. Mr. Heatherly went to Collinsville today.

September 10th. I went to meet Camerot and Carey this a.m., didn't see them, so I came on back home. I got a call, so went back to Camerot's office and met with Dick. He's the same old character, looks down on everybody that isn't on his level, he's an attorney. I met this p.m. with Dave Simpson, with the FAA on O'Malley Road, and we just may make a deal regarding claims at Dawson City, on Gay Gulch, off Eldorado Creek. He has a couple of partners. We have 40 acres north of Klatt Road and we just might make a deal with him. I should know a little more tomorrow. I just hope we can make this deal and put Collinsville out of our minds and forget it. The weather was real nice today.

September 11th. I talked to Henry and Dick today. They want me to go over to Collinsville, look the equipment over and see what all it will take to get it repaired and in working condition. Also, they said that they'd have to get permission from "scroungy" George, the computer expert turned hippie, for me to go into camp. This thing at Collinsville is so ridiculous it's funny. I talked to Joe Ramstead and he's to call me back regarding swapping his gold mine and equipment for our 40 acres. We're going to turn up something yet.

September 12th. I flew over to Collinsville this a.m. with George Jones, and checked out the equipment. The Michigan loader had a wheel bearing out. A wheel was off the 988 loader and it has problems of transmission oil getting into the rear end. The Lorraine loader has the rear end tore up and one tire and wheel missing. The Komatsu dozer needs a complete undercarriage, $38 - 40,000. The D8, 46A needs the same, another $40,000. Two pumps were broke down, the 12-inch pump with the D7 Cat motor has a clutch out, and the new AC pump with Deutz engine has problems, sounds like the bearings are siezed in it. I think the bearings are gone. I don't think we could get things going in time to do much mining this year, and I would only be getting the equipment fixed up for them so Henry could bring in another outfit this winter. Either that, or he might decide to bring the equipment out and sell it in Anchorage.

Sunday, September 13th. I talked to Henry again today and explained to him that I can't go over to Collinsville and guarantee anything as just about all the equipment is broke down. Also, Jim Prochaska left today to go up moose hunting with Marty. They wanted me to go, but I have to see Mr. Simpson regarding claims in Dawson City. Dave Simpson called tonight and we are to meet tomorrow at 1 p.m.

September 14th. I met with Mr. Simpson today, he's the gentleman that's retired from the FAA. We drove out and looked over my 40 acres, then went on to meet his partner. We talked for quite some time and we're going to Dawson City tomorrow morning, myself and his partner. We're going to check the ground, etc. I just want to make sure that what they're telling me is true.

September 15th. Don Keach, Dave Simpson's partner, and I went to Dawson City. We left at 5 o'clock this morning and arrived there about 5:30 p.m. We had an okay trip, but Don's got diarrhea of the mouth. Man, he'd talk the horns off of a billy goat! And I think every other word is misrepresenting the truth. I'm not saying he's a liar, but he misrepresents the truth.

September 16th. David Simpson has 2 partners, Don Keach and Jim Vail. We spent last night at their camp over on Gay Gulch. We did some panning this a.m., the pit and gold looked good. It will be hard to mine, but it will pay good.

We left Dawson City about 1 p.m. and drove on to Anchorage. I'm sure I'm gonna swap Don and the group my 40 acres for their 8 claims. I got home about 1:30 and talked to Marcene 'til 4 a.m. Whew! I'm tired.

This swap occurred because we ran an ad in the newspapers which said, "Experienced placer miner has large acreage in Anchorage area. Trade for proven gold claims, preferably with equipment." We put that in the paper September 6, 1981.

Don Keach kept wondering what I thought on the way back and he kept asking me. He said, "Everything over here goes." Well, the little Case 350 dozer was scattered all over the location, tore all apart, pieces laying every which way. The Komatsu loader was one season old, but one of the brake bands was gone out of it, so I could see how Don took care of things. But we liked the area, it looked good. I think that we'll get our trade and go ahead and deal with them.

Monday, September 21st. We went down to Maxine Smith's ABM Escrow this p.m. and signed an ernest money agreement. This is for trading our 40 acres for the property on Gay Gulch. We went by CIT and I think it will be okay to assume the note on the Komatsu with "skip payments" through the winter.

September 22nd. Dave Simpson made the September payment on the Komatsu loader and I have "skip payments" until April 25th next year. We picked up our gold and silver from the bank, put it in our safety box in the motorhome, and left our pickup at Glen Heatherly's for the winter. We saw our old friend Jack Hansmire today. He used to be our banker with First National Bank, and he's still the same as ever.

We left for Dawson City and should get there sometime tomorrow. We're supposed to meet Jim Vail and Don Keach over there and go over a few things. I want to check the records and make sure there's no liens against the property, that the assessment work's all up like they say, and everything is copacetic.

September 23rd. I saw Davis Fowler at his camp on Bonanza Creek and he told me that I could use his 966 loader next spring and to pay him in gold. We're going on up to the mine tomorrow morning. Jim and Don are coming down to get us in a pickup.

September 24th. We spent the night on Eldorado Creek, got up this morning and met Don. He took Marcene and me up to the mine on Gay Gulch. I met the Johnson brothers and they seem okay. They seemed like nice guys to work with, we'll wait and see, I have this feeling. Don took home a truckload of goodies, groceries, tools, etc., but that's okay, we'll start from scratch next season. The Case 350 needs all kinds of things, rollers, hydraulic hoses, and a few odds and ends. The Komatsu loader only needs a brake band, I think. It looked pretty good. We got the paperwork started at the Claim Recorder's Office and got money exchanged at the bank. We got on the road going south about 4 p.m. We made it to Whitehorse about 11 p.m. It's kind of cool.

Our 40 acres in Anchorage that we traded for the claims on Gay Gulch, we traded mineral rights for mineral rights, so no IRS was involved.

Sunday, September 27th. We drove down to Williams Lake today, no problems. The roads sure are better than when we drove our '52 Buick up in 1957. We don't have to worry when we travel now like we did back then.

Tuesday, October 20th. Today I went out to Lisa Harris's class at East Cheatham School. Lisa is my niece, Charlene's daughter. I told the kids about gold mining, I had pictures and gold nuggets with me. It was nice. One little boy was thinking though, and he asked me, "Why would you prefer gold to money?" I told him, "Well, if I gave you a dollar's worth of gold and a $1 bill in 1974, today in 1981 that gold would be worth about $35, and the $1 bill would be worth less than a dollar, with inflation." Those little kids really seemed to enjoy that.

My nephew, Derek Simpson, invited me to his class in grade school at Charlotte, Tennessee, to do a similar presentation. I knew I was in the wrong crowd when I opened up my nuggets and the kids started pitching them around the classroom. They were all talking at once, totally out of control, I couldn't even talk to explain to them how we got the nuggets out of the ground, the mining techniques. Then I asked the teacher if there was any way she could control the kids, or if they acted like that all the time. Her answer was, "I can't do a thing with them." So I picked up my pictures and gold, told her I was sorry that I'd bothered her and left.

Monday, November 30th. I called Don Keach in Anchorage today, he'd left a message for me to call. I told him that I can't take 1 claim off the Gay Gulch claims to sell to him, I'm not really interested.

Sunday, December 5th. Lavelle and Ruth, Marcene's stepbrother and his wife, called today. They want to go up to Canada and come over to the mine next summer and visit with us. They'd like to do some panning and maybe run a little material through a sluice box.

Monday, December 21st. Glen Heatherly called us and he's just fine, same as always. Ann Vandola, the lady that owned the Collinsville Twin Creek mine, died last week, so I guess Collinsville will be in turmoil as usual. I found out later that she never got her 10 percent of the gold I let the Canadians have to give her. Her niece told me.

Wednesday, December 23rd. I got a nice call from Gilbert Smith today. He's the multi-millionaire out of Pensacola, Florida. He's just fine and into mining in Arizona, he's silver mining now. I figured somewhere down the line he would latch onto someone, put his money up, and he would be mining. It was something that was just in his blood and he couldn't quite get it out.

1982

Saturday, January 20, 1982. I called Jimmy Patton in Dawson City and worked out a deal for him to lease the fuel truck this summer. That's the stake bed truck I got in the deal at Gay Gulch, with the fuel tank on the back.

Wednesday, February 24th. We called Whitehorse regarding water rights today. It looks like we won't have too much trouble.

Saturday, March 6th. Mel Pardek called this p.m. regarding Collinsville, and also Jack Wilson and his lawyer partner called. They rambled on for about 30 minutes, about the same old stuff.

Tuesday, March 23rd. Today the gold price was $326 an ounce, silver was $7.17. We called a Norcan Leasing Company in Whitehorse and talked to Mike Ensley about vehicle rentals. They're as follows: for a 4x4, $288 per week, $1400 per month, and $7000 for 5 months. Or they have 4x4s for sale, around $5500 to $6500.

Thursday, March 25th. I called Marty Rinke this evening and he and his wife, Gayla, are planning on going over to the mine on Gay Gulch with us.

We left Ashland City in our motorhome this morning and it was raining. Just out of Louisville, Kentucky, on the way to Chicago, we hit a blizzard. Boy, I'm telling you, it was slick out, and just out of Chicago a big old girl driving a Mayflower Van with Florida license plates was going right down the middle of the freeway. We didn't know it until we were passing her. She was just setting there, looked like she was all tensed up, gripping the steering wheel with both hands. I finally got around her and we went on in to Chicago and spent the night in a truck stop. We pulled in between 2 big trucks, had one on each side. There was also one in front and one in the back of us. No one was going anywhere so we just cranked up the little light plant, had our TV, cooked supper, and everything was lovely the next morning when the sun came up about 8:30. We gave it a couple hours and the traffic kind of died down, then we took off for Alaska and the Yukon.

Saturday, April 10th. We stopped off at Northwest Equipment in Fort St. John and got acquainted with Dale the parts girl. We bought a set of rollers, 4 hoses, a battery, and oil for the 350 Case dozer at the mine. They're going to ship the parts up to Whitehorse via White Pass Trucking.

April 11th. This doesn't pertain to mining, but I thought it was worth notation. We took our time today and got into Watson Lake, Yukon Territory, at 7 p.m. Earlier, a guy towing a trailer with a large sailboat spun out on Steamboat Mountain and the road was closed for awhile. We were in a restaurant in Fort Nelson, waiting for the road to open, and we talked to a guy from Phoenix, Arizona. He was going to Anchorage, he said, but when he left he took off in the wrong direction and went back south. I can understand that with it storming like it was, the bad weather and all. We sat there in the restaurant watching for him. We knew he had to go a long way before he could turn around and in about an hour, here he came back and took off up the Alaska Highway heading for Alaska, and we didn't see him anymore. We figured that he was quite a trooper when he told us about tying the master cylinder on his brake system up with a clothes hanger. He wired it up and it was working. He was in a motorhome pulling a little car behind him, so we figured he'd make it in Alaska if he could get this far north.

It was just about as slick as snot going over Steamboat. We saw an Indian woman hitchhiking at Lower Post just south of Watson Lake. She was going either way, I don't think she knew which way she really was going.

Tuesday, April 13th. It was snowing this a.m. We went to the Recorder's Office in Dawson City and put Marty Rinke on the claims as 25 percent owner so he can get his work permit here in the Yukon. We saw Mr. McAlpine at the Yukon Water Division and he seemed nice. He doesn't think we'll have much trouble with mining on Gay Gulch.

Friday, April 16th. We took Don and Sandy Keach out to the Sea Galley in Anchorage for supper tonight. He has no teeth, so he gummed his steak. Ernie Prochaska is the hostess there. We were running around today chasing parts, etc., and getting ready to go back to Dawson.

April 17th. Marty came to Anchorage today and brought the 3-wheeler. It needs a chain and 2 sprockets. That's the way it is when you loan something, I suppose, it always comes back needing something. We went over to Heatherly's and they sure are nice to us. They told us that we could stay in their trailer, or in their bedroom there at the house.

April 18th. It snowed last night, about 2 inches. We went over to Dave McClure's and bought some material, Astroturf, to go in the sluice box at the mine. I talked to Glen today about the little Denver panner, the one Mr. Smith gave him about 3 years ago. Even though it's new in the crate, Glen wants somewhere between $4000 to $5000 for the little shaker-panner and I think that's a little too high. They only cost $3500 new.

Saturday, April 24th. We had to stop at the border at Beaver Creek on our way to Whitehorse and eventually Dawson. We left last night, drove all night and most of the day and had no real problems. We did have to put up a $60 bond at Beaver Creek.

April 25th. Mr. Heatherly hauled our things over on his Kenworth. We had to pay a total of $194.70 for the permit to unload in Canada. We spent last night at Destruction Bay and had no problems today. We unloaded the pickup at Avis in Whitehorse, which is Norcan Leasing, and will load a 4x4 tomorrow as we used a 2-wheel drive pickup to go to Anchorage to pick up our parts, etc. We brought it back over on Heatherly's lowboy, along with the wanigan, loaded with different things, welder, parts, etc., that we'll be using at the mine.

April 26th. We got news today that our barn back in Tennessee on the Cumberland River got wrecked by a tornado. It got totally wiped out. Just this spring we had cancelled all the insurance on our barns. We insured the cattle for $500 a head and one of the cows got picked up in the tornado and dropped at one of our neighbors about a mile downriver. We checked with Jimmy Allen, the guy who was insuring the cattle, thought we'd wind up at least with a consolation prize of $500. He said, "Oh no, it's a $500 deductible policy." So, that's that.

April 27th. Last night we made it up from Whitehorse to Pelly Crossing, stopped for the night and cranked up the generator. We picked up TV right from the Natives' satellite dish there and Glen came and had supper with us in the motorhome. We drove on to Dawson City, got in about 10:30 a.m., got unloaded, and Glen got off about 3:30 p.m. for Whitehorse and back to Anchorage. We called Jadene.

We found a place to park our wanigan and 3-wheeler at Keirin Daunt's place. He's a friend of Jimmy Patton. I think we'll be able to get Keirin to take his dozer up and clear our road for us. There's just quite a bit of snow up Gay Gulch way, up Eldorado Creek. It was pretty nice today. Dave Fowler left word that we could use the fifth-wheel at their camp, sure was nice of him.

April 28th. Jimmy came by this a.m. and we went up to Keirin's. We helped get his dozer going and he went up and cleared the road into our camp. Everything looked pretty good, the dam was okay. Keirin got up this a.m. and took a ride on our Honda 3-wheeler in his shorts and T-shirt. "It was warm out", he said. None of the keys that Don Keach gave us fit the Komatsu, but we got a key out of Davis Fowler's big Komatsu and will try it tomorrow. The hill up to our claim was a bit raunchy, but we made it okay. We got into camp and Jimmy walked over to the pickup. It was a flatbed half-ton pickup with a little stakebed, and it had a fuel tank on it. The keys were in it, he cranked it and it started. It had been setting there all winter and it started up like a top. He then drove it on into Dawson.

It was kind of weird about the pickup, because after he took it in to Dawson, he later told me that the monitor up at our camp was his, but he would trade us the monitor for the pickup. We had to have the monitor to wash the banks down, that's the giant.

April 29th. It was snowing this a.m. We picked up parts at the bus lines in Dawson, battery cables, etc., and deposited $2000 American money in the bank here, and it was $2404.04 Canadian. We got papers filled out at the Recorder's Office regarding the mine, then drove up to the mine and I picked ice in the overflow with my pick. I got the water running, flowing in the overflow below the dam. We had about 5 inches of new snow today at the mine. I saw Keirin, he said to wait 'til he got his Cat moved, then he'd give me the bill for plowing the road into the mine. Jimmy took my battery into town to get it charged. I paid Keirin $250 for the Cat work clearing the road into the mine, paid by check. We got permission to park in the camper park in town until it opens. We went into the mine this p.m. and chopped more ice in the overflow.

Saturday, May 1st. We went up to our mine today and I worked on the Case 350 dozer. It's thawing a little out today. I called Marty and he's coming over next week. I told him to check on the sluice box that Bob McKirvey had left at Brandt's Lodge. We gave a $50 donation to a couple whose house burned, friends of Jimmy. We ate at the Eldorado Hotel this morning.

May 2nd. We went to a benefit dance last night and I sang with the band, and enjoyed it. Lots of people want to go to work for us here around Dawson. There are lots of people in town because the price of gold is up. I phoned Jim Prochaska to get us 2 RV batteries, the heavy duty ones, 6-volt, and he's going to send them over with Marty.

May 3rd. We bought a barrel of diesel this a.m. It was $95.20! We went up to the mine and I got the dozer running and hydraulic lines hooked up. We still have some nuts and bolts to put in, about an hour's work, I guess. It's sure melting out this p.m., but it was snowing most of the way into camp. I gave John, the welder, some loader teeth and dozer cutting bits to hardface. Marcene drove the pickup out from the mine today and she did real well. We're living in Dawson City in the camper park. Gas for the motorhome was $130 when we filled up at the Standard station.

May 4th. It was real nice out this a.m., sun was shining. We went up to the mine and I got the 350 dozer together, brought it down below the hill at Dave Johnson's ground and parked it with the loader. We paid the welder $280 for hardfacing the loader teeth and cutting bits for the dozer.

May 5th. It's sure nice out today, the snow's melting fast at the mine. It seems every day we get just a little more done, it just takes time. We looked at a wood cook stove at Bear Creek today, but it was too high, it was $300, and used at that. In the camper park there was a girl hanging out in an old bus, and about 9 a.m. she just walked out of the bus and squatted. She had no panties on and used no paper, no nothing, just shook her rear end! Another guy, a hippie sleeping in his pickup, keeps starting the pickup all night to keep warm. The sun's still shining at 10 p.m. tonight.

May 6th. We got gas for the pickup this morning, $60. Marty got in today and we went up to the mine. We tried the propane fridge in camp and it works okay. Everything is melting and we should be mining in about a week if we get our water permit. I put the 4 built-up teeth on the loader and have another set to get hardfaced. The Klondike River's running, but the Yukon hasn't broken yet (ice broken up and flowing).

May 7th. Marty and I got to work on the Komatsu. We pulled the steering clutch and it needed a complete brake band. It's just a year old so that would have come under warranty had Don Keach looked into it a little bit. I guess he didn't want to mess with it. Don knew what he was doing last year, he just didn't want to tear into it. He told me about how much he'd been tightening the brake, that he went right by the specs in the book and all. We found the shop manual underneath the seat still in the celophane wrapped packet that it came in from the factory.

Saturday, May 8th. It's sunny and warm today. I called Fort St. John regarding the brake band for the Komatsu. They're going to have to send it up from Vancouver. They'll put it on White Pass Trucking and we should get it, along with filters, about Thursday. Marty and I got to working on the dozer putting on the draw bar, cutting blade, and rock cutting edges. We found a draw bar for the Case and that saves us close to $500. We found parts scattered all over camp for different pieces of equipment. We also put the rest of the teeth on the Komatsu loader. We're just doing chores and taking it a number at a time.

May 9th. It rained, snowed, and was cloudy today. Marcene called Mama and Jadene today and everything's okay. Marty and I went up to the mine, worked on the dozer and brought it down to Grand Forks. It needs some welding on the frame. I talked to John and he'll let me know tomorrow evening when he can get to it. We ran a bit of material through the small sluice box today, but it's still too early to start mining. Marcene called Davis today. He may be over next week.

May 10th. Marty and I got the pipe under the dam thawed. We used a steam thaw rig to do it, and the pipe and valve and everything was fine, so now we've got water coming through the pipe system. We now are ready for other things in camp. We helped Keirin with his dozer, let him use my big, heavy duty electric drill. I saw Dave Johnson today and he was nice. It was cloudy and drizzly today.

May 11th. John took his welder up to Grand Forks and welded the frame underneath the 350 Case dozer. Marty and I changed oil and filters in the Case and then drove it back up to the mine on Gay Gulch. The weather was rainy and we had lots of water at the mine. We've got to hook up the monitor tomorrow and get some use out of the water. I hope we get the parts for the Komatsu loader soon. We called Billy, and Bobby, and Lavelle and Ruth. Lavelle and Ruth are leaving to come up to see us next week.

May 12th. We changed fuel filters in the Komatsu, then went up to the mine and hooked pipe to the monitor. It sure works good for washing the banks down, but I need to get it closer to the work. We need a 6-inch hose about 100 foot long, but that will come later. We got the pit cleaned up and everything looks good. Marcene went up to the mine with us today. We've gotta get the battery serviced and the power plant going, hopefully tomorrow.

May 13th. The Yukon River went out at noon today, the ice broke up and started moving downstream. It's a sight to see. Marty and I went up to the mine, repaired a leak in the pipe and ran the monitor about 5 hours. It was nice out. We paid John, the welder, for work on the dozer. We're still waiting on parts for the Komatsu.

Friday, May 14th. We watched the Yukon River for awhile this morning. It was filled with big chunks of ice, some of them as big as houses, as far as we could see both up and downstream. Marty and I worked at the mine and I ran the dozer a bit, built a road up out of the pit. We're going to drop the monitor down into the pit with the pipe and fittings so we can reach all the paydirt. We're in some real good ground, we'll just be glad to get started mining. Marcene called to check on parts for the loader, we should have them tomorrow. The weather's mixed today, cloudy, sunny, and windy. Marty washed our work clothes.

May 15th. We got the parts for the loader. Marty and I got it running and took it up to the mine. We had John, the welder, make us a 45 degree bend to get pipe down into the pit so we could move the monitor down into the pit with us. The reason that we had to set the monitor down in the pit was that it was setting high up on the bank and the water wouldn't reach all the way across to the other side. If the wind blew it just blew the water up or downstream and wouldn't reach over and get across. It rained a bit today. We got into town tonight about 11:45.

Sunday, May 16th. This is May 16th and we've got snow! We got the giant set up in the pit and working. Then we changed the oil and filters in the old light plant and got it set and running. Everything works okay except we have to adjust the electric motor on the shaker, put carpet and riffles in the box and start mining. We should start mining tomorrow. We've gotta get fuel tomorrow morning. At $95 a barrel, the ground had better be good! I noticed when we started the old International light plant that there's about a case of empty starting fluid cans laying around. I knew something was going to happen and it wasn't going to be good. I just knew what that meant. Don Keach had told me earlier that he could start that light plant in just a split second and nobody else could start it. Now I saw what he'd been doing. We pulled a guy from Fairbanks out of Eldorado Creek crossing today, he was in a 2-wheel drive pickup. What a place for a guy, supposedly from the north country, to get stuck with a 2-wheel drive pickup.

May 17th. Rain, rain, and more rain. We got started sluicing today, ran about a half hour and the water just got too high. It rained cats and dogs all day, so we finally gave it up about 7:30 p.m. We cut the Astroturf, got the box leveled, and tailings hauled. The tailings are our biggest problem here because we can't push them downstream. There's guys downstream from us, the Johnson brothers, and they don't want anything on their property. So we have to haul all tailings up on the hillside. We dump in 10 loads of material and haul 10 loads up the hill, that's basically what we're doing. When the Johnson brothers finish down below we'll have it made. We saw some gold in the riffles this p.m., so that gave us a little renewed interest here.

May 18th. Marty and I tried to get back into Dawson City this p.m. and ran off into Eldorado Creek just down by Jim and Robbin Archibald's place. The water came over the hood of the pickup, didn't look good at all. We thought the pickup was going downstream even though it was a big, heavy duty, three-quarter ton Ford crew cab. The front end bounced up and the bumper got hung on the far bank before it died, so the engine was up out of the water. We finally dried out the engine and got it running, and the pickup was just setting there teetering. We worried with it and packed rocks in the pickup to keep it from rolling downstream, made the bed heavy on the upside. We finally got out of there after jacking and worrying with it, took about 3 to 4 hours to get it out. It made believers out of us though, really did. We got back across, but couldn't come on toward town, so we went back up to camp and spent the night.

May 19th. We made it into Dawson tonight.

May 20th. David Seed, Terry Mulligan, and Betty Moody, of Delta Refining in Richmond, and Alex and Mary Sealy and one more girl, stopped by the motorhome. The Miners Meeting is tomorrow night. Davis came by and said he'll let us use his 966 loader. We moved our motorhome to Andy's and Maria's claims on Klondike Highway. We can't get any TV there. John intends to fix his yard for us to park our motorhome there, that sure would be nice.

May 21st. It's sure warm out today. We let Davis use our pickup. We didn't get started 'til about noon as we had to clean up the pit and haul tailings. I talked to Ron Johnson today and he seemed okay. We're going to have to work things different than we ordinarily would with the box for just awhile here. We didn't have any troubles today, how 'bout that! We have Dave Fowler's 966 Cat loader, but it's still a bit too wet and soft for using it. We just barely made it up the road. Marty was coming up the road with it and boy, he was really having to fight it to keep the loader going and keep it from sinking out of sight. We're gonna have to haul a bunch of tailings to get our road rectified. If it stays dry as today we should be able to use the loader in a couple more days.

Saturday, May 22nd. We ran the box approximately 2 hours and the riffles looked good. We spent most of the time hauling tailings. We're still not able to use Dave's 966 loader. It was pretty nice out today. We're spending tonight at the mine. We went to a party last night put on by Finning Catapillar Company and Delta Refining Smelting.

May 23rd. The riffled look good today. Davis came up, his friend got stuck and we pulled him out. It was sunny most of the day.

May 24th. We're spending most of the time hauling tailings. It rained, hailed, sleeted, and snowed today, and it was just miserable. The danged old wood stove in the plastic shack is just not cutting it. We're going to have to do something different. It smokes, the lids are all warped, and it just won't draw, so we have to keep pouring diesel in it to keep the wood burning.

May 25th. It rained, was sunny, then hailed today. We have leaks all over the kitchen. It's pretty good that we traded property worth over a half million dollars for these claims, but after all it's the gold that we traded for and not the buildings. The buildings will come later. We sure have some good ground up ahead of where we're working. Marcene washed clothes today and I think that brought the rain out, again.

May 26th. It was raining this a.m., but it finally cleared up and was real nice later in the day. We cleaned up the sluice box and it didn't look bad. Marty left for Anchorage this evening. He left to go get Gayla, the sluice box, and pump spares. We're going to make some changes in the pit regarding the giant and the box and we'll be in the money then.

May 27th. It was sure nice out today. We ate breakfast at the Eldorado, then Marcene and I went up to the claims. I worked on the road and started the giant. It's sure thawing good today. Ruth and Lavelle got in and it's sure nice to see them. I took my gold wheel in to Dawson to clean up gold for Lou Provonovich. We ate some good ham at the Chinese place this evening. That's where Marcene found a billfold and turned it in. The girl that got it back was really happy.

May 28th. Lavelle and I went up to the mine. I hauled rocks and ran the giant.

Saturday, May 29th. Ruth and Lavelle, Marcene and I went up to the mine. I hauled tailings and ran the monitor. There was on old black raven in the pit in camp this morning and I figured I'd fix him, so I turned the water hose on him. I never could quite hit him though, he'd just jump out of my way and kept squawking at me. The weather was nice out today. Ruth found some nice gold.

May 30th. Ruth and Lavelle went up to the mine with us again. I'm gonna go over and help Lou clean up his fine gold this evening.

May 31st. We went by the RCMP today to see the Customs people, and they'll be in Tuesday a.m. We moved our motorhome to Grand Forks where the Eldorado joins Bonanza Creek. A rock shattered one of the holding tanks, I think it was the grey water tank. That's the way it goes. We were parked in Andy's yard and there were lots of rocks. I didn't think to check to see if any were hanging up in the duals when I took off.

Wednesday, June 2nd. We got 500 gallons of fuel today. Our riffles look pretty good. I had to go to town and get a fuse for the conveyor and I'm gonna get rid of that conveyor as soon as we can get a road out of the pit. I don't like conveyors hooked up to hoppers, specially if you're in wet material and sticky stuff. You lose too much fine gold.

June 3rd. I picked up 2 barrels of fuel from our 500 gallon tank at Dave Johnson's this a.m. Marcene and I spent the night in the motorhome at Grand Forks. Ruth and Lavelle were up, panning and running the little sluice box when we got to camp. They did pretty good for the material they ran. Davis came by and I went down to test some ground for him on Oro Grande Creek, it looked good. We had a breakdown about 4:30, had to do welding on the shaker and hopper. We had nice weather today.

Sunday, June 6th. Marty's back. We went over to see Lou and tested his ground by Paradise Hill. He has good claims over there. It was a nice hot day out. Lavelle and Ruth told Marcene that they're leaving tomorrow. Marty and I hooked up the giant to the 100 foot hose today, mounted the giant on a little trailer and boy, it works slick. We're running the monitor, washing down the hill on the other side of the creek from camp. Don and Sandy Keach came up this evening for a visit.

June 7th. We got the road finished for the 966 to come out of the pit with tailings and it started raining, so we don't know just what will happen. We went down and got the motorhome. Marty took the Komatsu loader down to the foot of the hill and towed the motorhome up the steep part of the hill coming into the mine. Jerry, a guy from Florida who has claims above me and to the north, came up today in an old school bus. I don't really like him and I think he's bad news. He couldn't make it up the hill coming forward, so he turned around and backed that bus up the hill. They didn't have any food with them, or anything, didn't even bring a beer, so they were drinking our beer and eating our food. They wanted to stay in camp, but we just didn't have room for them. The color looked good in the riffles today.

    June 8th. I dug test holes for Jerry. He's a little bit screwy, but at least I got his assessment work done for him and he agreed to do some welding for me hardfacing the loader bucket teeth, so we did a swapout there. It sure was nice out today. We got about an ounce out of the front riffles. Marcene went to town for parts and propane.

    June 9th. Marty's uncles from Montana came by today to see him and they're sure nice people. They're gonna stay with us for a couple of days. We ran the 966 hauling tailings for about an hour. It's hot out today. We got just over 2 ounces in the front riffles.

    June 10th. We cleaned up the front carpet in the box. All told, we have a total of 21-plus ounces of gold, plus what's in the rest of the box. Our light plant broke down today, a push rod bent and one broke. Some more of "shifty" Don's work, so it looks like we're gonna have to open it up and get all new push rods for it.

    June 11th. Marcene ordered the parts for the light plant, so we should get them tomorrow p.m. We ran the giant and Marty steam cleaned the loader and the light plant. No time was put on Davis's loader today.

    Saturday, June 12th. We had no time on the box today, the parts didn't get in this p.m. I had the airline call Whitehorse and they're in Whitehorse, so they should surely be in tomorrow afternoon. We started cleaning what we're hoping will be a good payday for us. Old Don sure left us a mess. I won't go into it, but he left us a mess. There are lots of old shafts just up ahead of us. I had to get on "Cat Skinner" today. That's Uncle Stevie, Dave Johnson's uncle. He cut right across the road and left about a 4-foot drop-off at both ends of the pit. I got on him pretty good. Anyway, he came over and straightened it up, then he turned the D8 Cat around right in the middle of the road and screwed it all up again. I just went ahead and crawled my 4-wheel drive pickup right over it and then I proceeded to tell him which way the cookie crumbled.

    June 13th. We ran the box 3 hours today, had lots of dirt. The parts got in for the light plant and we got it going. It's going, but we don't think too much of the International engine. We'll have to wait and see if it holds up, it's an oldie. We cleared about 2 acres this a.m., cut and burned willows. We should have a good day tomorrow.

June 14th. The riffles look fair. Everything ran okay today. Marty put little spruce boughs in the cook stove and smoked up the kitchen a bit. It looked like it was afire. We got 2 more barrels of fuel this p.m., looks like we'll have to get more fuel by the end of the week. Uncle Stevie showed Marcene and me the nuggets he's getting. He had a jar of big nuggets. He's running the old dredge tailings down on Eldorado Creek and he's getting the ones that the dredges missed. They only got half-inch minus gold, which means that any piece of gold larger than half an inch went right through the trommel and out to the tailing pile. The old-timers figured there wasn't enough gold larger than half an inch to warrant the wear and tear on the sluice runs.

June 15th. It's raining and we had a big wash today. Of course, that usually goes with washday, rain. We met "Bingo Bill" for the first time today and he's a nice feller. He's Dave Johnson's operator. Bingo Bill, I won't ever forget him.

June 16th. Butch Fowler came up this a.m. and brought a button fitting for the grease gun, but it was too small. That's the gun that greases the rollers on the conveyor belt. We got about 3-1/2 ounces of gold from the front riffles this p.m., looks good. We'll probably clean up tomorrow. Marty and I went down and put the fuel filter on our fuel tank and got 2 barrels of fuel, then went on down to Keirin's and got our wanigan. We couldn't make it up the big hill, so we'll go down and get it with the Cat tomorrow. Uncle Stevie is getting big nuggets, but no fine gold, he's blowing it right through his box. He's got the box setting way too steep, too much water going through, and he's complaining about not getting fine gold. Of course, the dredge got a lot of the fine gold.

June 17th. We moved the giant to a space that will carry us all the way to the dam this set. We spent most of the day clearing the hill above the old shaft. Marty was hauling tailings. I took the Cat and went down and pulled the wanigan up the hill to camp. Davis came by to see us today.

June 18th. It was cloudy and raining today. Marcene went to town, got propane, groceries, etc. We cleaned the sluice box, but didn't have time to clean it all up, run it through the gold wheel. We spent all day getting ready to move the washing plant upstream to get grade, so we'll have room to put our tailings.

Saturday, June 19th. We spent most of the day moving the shaker plant, getting it and the sluice box set up, miscellaneous welding and cutting. Davis came by this a.m. for a nice visit. Mr. Stevenson came up and brought his fine gold from the cleanup to run through our gold wheel. We ran out of water before we finished, but we'll get it for him tomorrow for sure. He's sure a nice guy.

A black bear came to our kitchen door and looked in while we were eating breakfast this morning. I looked at Marty and said,

"Don't look now, don't talk loud, but there's a black bear watching you." He turned around and hollered at the bear and startled him. There was a loose board sticking out from under the water barrels, it was a 2 x 12, and it was just kind of laying there. That bear stepped off the barrels, hit that loose board and the other end of the board came up and plopped him in the butt. Did he ever take off up the hill !

June 20th. Our cleanup looked pretty good, we got a total of 30 ounces, 6-1/2 pennyweight. We're just about ready to go with our plant, we only need plyboard for the back of the ramp, a guard. We have to move the light plant while Marcene gets the plyboard. She's going into town to pick it up at the sawmill. We should get started sluicing about 1 p.m. A kid from Whitehorse came walking up the road this p.m. looking for a job.

June 21st. Marcene's raking rocks today. The riffles looked real good. We have to re-engineer the hopper tomorrow a.m., it'll take about 30 minutes. We're just now getting into ground that Don and Jim hadn't been working and piddling with, so we should be in some good gold. Marcene and I went in under a big spruce tree to get out of the rain and built a fire. That spruce tree is still standing today. Marty was welding under another spruce tree, out of the rain.

June 22nd. The box ran 6 hours today, and it looks like we'll have to buy a new shaker screen pretty soon. Marcene found a pair of rain pants for me. I put them on and worked about an hour, and they split every which way, kind of looked silly but they kept my pants dry. Marcene helped on the box raking rocks. It was nice out today, no rain. We started the monitor this p.m. I like it because it doesn't cost anything to run gravity flow water.

June 23rd. We picked about 3 ounces of gold from the front 3 riffles. We finally are mining on our own terms. They sure left us a mess though, but oh well, that's the way it goes. The willows and muck and dirt are all tangled up and frozen together. That's what happens when you bring a big Cat in a narrow gulch and start stirring the dirt up. Davis came up and he would like to have his loader Sunday. He's sure been nice about it. Also, Dave saw me this p.m. as I was getting fuel and he needs my pickup for a few days, so I let him use it, no problem. We got the last of the 500 gallons of fuel tonight, but we've got more coming tomorrow. The 1-1/2-inch shaker screen is worn out. I called to order one and we're gonna have another one here in a few days.

June 24th. We got into good ground today, lots of gold. We picked out about 2 ounces from the front riffles. I ran the monitor tonight.

June 25th. Marcene went into town and ordered groceries from Whitehorse. We took 25 ounces of gold into Delta today, to pay bills. This leaves 27 ounces. We got paid $305.50 an ounce for gold. We ran the box ran 5 hours, but there was too much muck and dirt. The weather was good today. I had to tell a couple of young boys visiting our camp to get away from the sluice box, they were spooning the front riffles. So anyway, I made a few people mad, but that's the way it goes. Butch and Danny, Davis's boys, came by to check on us today and that was nice of them.

June 26th. We picked 10 ounces out of the first 5 front riffles today. Davis picked up his 966 loader. It was nice and hot out today.

Sunday, June 27th. We cleaned up the first 4 feet of the box and got better than 22 ounces out of the riffles. It was hot today. I monitored for 4 hours and we ran the box 3 hours.

I just want to add a note here regarding Gay Gulch. Mr. Emil Gay was the guy who discovered gold on our gulch. In one 28-day period in 1897 he took out 70 pounds of gold by himself by burning wood to thaw a shaft and the drifts. So, it sure must have been rich back in those days. At one time there were 1500 people living and working on Gay Gulch, and this gulch is less than 2 miles long. Emil Gay didn't have any help as he was broke and couldn't afford to pay help, so he packed everything in on his back out of Dawson City and worked all by himself, and got that 70 pounds of gold. Actually, what he took out was gold worth $10,000. In those days the equivalent of that amount of money would have come to approximately 70 pounds of gold. At today's gold prices that 70 pounds would amount to about $294,000.

June 28th. We didn't run the box today, spent all day monitoring and picking rocks and wood, the old shaft logs, and hauling them out. We had plenty of water for monitoring. Marcene went to town with Danny Fowler and called regarding a new Case dozer, or Komatsu dozer, she called both. We had to re-fix the road. Some people wear the road out staying in the same ruts all the time. Marcene bought 2 large propane bottles today and had them filled.

June 29th. The box ran 6-1/2 hours, but ran a lot of dirt through, a lot of muck other than paydirt. We got over 3 ounces of gold just spooning the front riffles. It's hard work, but worth it. We found our first big nugget today, it was a nice one, over 2 ounces.

June 30th. We ran the box 3-1/2 hours today and spooned about 3 ounces of gold from the front riffles. We ran out of water about 1:30. The sluice box will run until all water is gone out of the dam because of the steep grade of the 8-inch pipe. The Fowler boys brought my pickup back tonight. They're going in to Anchorage and will bring back our shaker screen and other items. They're also gonna bring back some heavy duty rakes for us and take our electric motor to Hayden Electric to get new bearings and bushings put in.

We traded 16.2 ounces of gold for a fifth wheel from Butch Fowler. He's to bring it up when he gets back from Anchorage.

July 2nd. Our total gold on hand is 66.14 ounces. We ran the monitor about 3 hours this a.m., then went into town and did some bull cookin' (shopping, picking up parts, and etc.) and got groceries. Marcene and I went by the dump and got some timbers. Marcene and Gayla went bull cookin', got their hair fixed, and I got my hair cut. We came back to camp, ate, then started sluicing.

Saturday, July 3rd. Bud Saylers, his wife, 2 boys, mother and father-in-law came in to camp. The boys were throwing candy wrappers, pop cans and stuff out in the yard, just throwing them down on the ground. I asked the one boy, "Well, do you do that at home?" He said, "Oh, this isn't home, this is just out in the bush, this just a camp out in the bush. We don't do this at home, we're not worried about it." Bud Saylers has been a friend of ours for a long time. He works on Governor Jay Hammond's staff in Juneau, the Capitol of Alaska. We've been friends and go back a long way, back when he worked for the Greater Anchorage Area Borough. It's always good to see him, plus he brought me over some good cigars.

I'd like to tell a little tale here. Once, Bud and his wife, and Marcene and I were going to Hawaii. We got on the plane in Anchorage, and after we got airborne I pulled out a cigar. The stewardess said, "Oh, mister, you can't light that cigar." I said, "You know, I have epileptic fits and the only thing that will stave that off is a cigar." So she said, "I'll be right back." She went up to talk to the captain, and the captain sent word back that I could use the cigar if I didn't puff on it too heavy. After about 30 minutes Bud couldn't take it any longer 'cause he smokes cigars too. He got a cigar out and lit it, and when the stewardess came by and told him he shouldn't be smoking it, he said, "Oh, I have epileptic fits too." But I'll assure you, when we hit the airport in Honolulu, that lady on the ground with Security got Bud and me both lined out.

We didn't pick riffles today. I went up above the dam and fixed a place for Bud to mine with a little sluice box, and Marty dug for them with the loader so they'd have plenty of loose material to run through.

Monday, July 5th. We got 2.17 ounces today in the front riffles, some nice stuff, too. This makes 70.19 ounces of gold on hand, not including gold in the box. It's hot and dry today and our water is very short, but we're still getting about 1-1/2 to 2 ounces of gold per hour that we run. Uncle Stevie came up tonight and borrowed my oxygen bottle and straight edge cutter. We gave Kay and Harry, Bud's mother-in-law and father-in-law, some nuggets, 7 all told, worth about $400. We gave the nuggets to them because they didn't get any gold in their little sluice box. I think they raked it all out when they ran it through. We drove out to Grand Forks with

Bud and his friends, and found his hubcap that he lost on the way in, so that was nice.

July 6th. We found a 9 pennyweight nugget today. Total gold we have on hand is 72 ounces, 14 pennyweight. It was hot this p.m. We spent 4 hours running the monitor. Everything is working fine, but we do need a better dozer. Marcene and I went down to Stevenson's and got 2 barrels of fuel this evening.

July 7th. I ran the monitor about 2 hours today and then I had an awakening. We ran flat out of water. I told Marty, "Let's go up the creek and find some springs." He said, "What do you mean by that?" I said, "We're gonna find some springs to mine with." And we did. We went up the creek, found a wet spot on the side of the hill and opened up about a 90-foot slot along that hillside. We found one of the nicest springs that you'd ever want to find. It supplied about 3 inches of water and runs year round, it's a beautiful spring. Marcene did paperwork and got straight with Marty and Gayla and then went into town. Whoop-de-doo! While I was running the monitor I put my pipe in my pocket and caught my shirt afire. I was afraid that the motorhome was on fire when I smelled it, but sure was relieved when I found out what it really was. We got a quote from the Case company today regarding the dozer.

Sunday, July 11th. We stopped by Archibald's today and got tickets for the Miner's Dance and Barbeque the 30th of July.

July 12th. We ran our monitor about 4 hours. It's a bit cooler today than usual, but will probably be hot again tomorrow. Marcene went to town to check on the dozer and they're sending it up from Fort St. John. It's to be here at Grand Forks Thursday around noontime. The dozer I'm getting is a Case 450B and I'm trading the little 350 in, getting $18,000 trade-in on it.

Wednesday, July 14th. We went over to Davis's today and he's going to use my pickup 'til he gets the insurance for his truck. It's hot and dry today.

July 15th. I took the Case 350 down to Grand Forks and picked up the new 450. I had a heck of a time trying to figure out how to start the little sucker, it had a new gimmick on it. I finally had to ask the driver of the truck that brought it and he came over and showed me how to start it. I felt about an inch high.

July 16th. The riffles looked pretty good. We ran the box about 4 hours. I ran the 450 dozer this p.m., stripping. Marcene went into Dawson and called the Case dealer to bring up rock guards, they forgot the rock guards on the 450. Eldon and Mary Brandt will be over tomorrow.

July 17th. Eldon and Mary came in today and it's always good to see them. We've known the Brandts for quite some time. We're glad to have them in camp. I went down the hill and got their stuff because Eldon only had a 2-wheel drive pickup, so I brought it up to camp for them.

Sunday, July 18th. It rained last night and the water was high this a.m. We ran the box about 3 hours, but it was raining so bad we just shut'er down and visited with the Brandts.

Tuesday, July 18th. We ran the monitor all day. Marcene and I took the Brandts into Dawson this evening and picked up 2 barrels of fuel at our tank on the way back out. It was hot today.

July 21st. Marty told us today that he had to go to Anchorage and take Gayla. He's supposed to get parts too. I don't know for sure just when he'll be back. I spent about 5 hours running the monitor. We went down to see the Johnson brothers and took them a cold beer, they really enjoyed that. It was hot again today.

July 22nd. The box ran 3 hours and the riffles looked okay. Marcene and I worked the box, she tended the box and I ran the loader. I ran the monitor 5 hours and picked 6 loader buckets of rocks and hauled them out. When I say "picked the rocks" I mean that I picked them out while monitoring, because the rocks were too big to go over our shaker plant. I just hauled them out and dumped them up on the bank way up on the hill. I got 2 barrels of fuel. We don't use much fuel for our small operation here and it's a good thing because the fuel is so expensive. Our garden looks good, the cucumbers are loaded with little ones, the tomato plants are loaded, and the potatoes are about knee-high.

July 23rd. Rich Sewell, with the Case Company in Fort St. John, came up today with John Brown. This was the first time that we met John. He's a miner over the hill on Dominion Creek right now, and he's an awful nice guy. It was funny how he handled gold and weighed it up and everything. It was as if it was just some more dust, or whatever, he was unconcerned. But anyway, John Brown's a nice guy and I'm sure we'll see more of him in the future.

Saturday, July 24th. We ran the box about 2-1/2 hours and picked about three-quarters of an ounce in the front riffles. That's not too good, but still we got some gold. Marcene went into town this a.m. and got the rock guards for our Case 450, also oil to change the generator and the Komatsu. We ran the monitor about 3 hours this morning. We had nice weather, but our water is sure low. I tore up the belt on the shaker plant so I guess we're going to have to get a new pulley, or do something with it. Marty's still in Anchorage. Davis came up, brought shovels and rakes back in his pickup.

July 25th. I put the rock guards on the Case 450 today and stopped leaks in the radiator hose. Also, I changed the oil and filters in the light plant and the Komatsu. Marty's still in Anchorage so I guess I've got to get on the shaker plant tomorrow.

July 26th. I worked on the shaker plant today and Marcene paid some bills. She sent Jimmy Allen $698 on the house insurance in Tennessee and Stenhouse Insurance $750 for a year on the Case 450 dozer.

July 27th. It was hot again today. We ran the monitor 5 hours and I picked rocks about an hour. We took a break this p.m. and went into Dawson. We took the deep freeze to Andy's and we're gonna leave it there, but we can use it. We gave it to him and he says we can share it. That way we've got electricity down there full time. We have about enough material to run 4 to 5 hours. Dave Fowler was up this a.m., needing a drill bit which I didn't have. He's out of water on Nugget Gulch. Marty's not back with the bearings for the shaker yet so we can't run the box.

Friday, July 30th. Marty and Billy helped me change the bearings on the shaker today, it's quite a chore to change them. We got the belts, but they were the wrong ones. Marcene went into town and ordered the right ones. We went to the Miners' Barbeque tonight and really enjoyed it. The steaks were just great. We saw all of the miners and some of them were from over in Alaska.

Saturday, July 31st. Davis brought the 966 loader up for me to use this p.m. It's sure nice of him. Marty and I got settled up today and everything is just fine. While he was in Anchorage he got a very good offer from a drilling company on the north slope to run a fork lift, so this was a better opportunity for him and there were no hard feelings. We paid John for welding the guides on the pulleys for the shaker. We ate supper at Sheffield House in Dawson tonight. I hauled tailings from 9 until midnight with Davis's loader.

Monday, August 2nd. I took Davis's loader back this morning and helped them dismantle the 1066 Koering backhoe. We worked 'til 7:30 p.m. getting it all loaded out.

August 3rd. We went into Dawson and got the belts for the shaker plant. They were the wrong ones, but we went back up to the mine and made them work anyway. I filed on the pulley for the shaker plant all the way into town and back. Red and Colette Leveque came up to see us this p.m.

August 4th. It was a nice day. Marcene's watching the hopper and the box. She sure is a trooper. We took the Johnson boys a drink this afternoon and they enjoyed it. The riffles looked fair today, I think we're getting into some pretty good ground again.

August 5th. Ralph and Ina Peterson, from Anchorage, came up to see us today. It sure was nice to see them. They ate a little snack with us and we enjoyed the visit. I ran the monitor about 4 hours this morning and had plenty of water for work today. I guess the spring we put on the shaker plant is doing the trick, haven't had any trouble since we put it on. We got into some pretty good ground, the riffles looked good tonight. We got some nice little nuggets.

August 6th. Gold is $346.75 an ounce. The monitor ran 3 hours and we ran the sluice box 2 hours. The riffles looked good.

We got a big nugget today, a real nice one. We almost ran out of water, but shut down before we totally ran out. We went to town and got a flat fixed, got timbers for claim posts, and we also got us an ice cream cone. I gave Davis 2 ounces of real nice gold for the use of his loader. Also, I gave the guy who fixed the flat on the truck a $5 tip.

August 7th. We got nice gold today. I didn't get Davis's loader this weekend as Gunther had to use it over on Nugget Gulch, so I guess I'll have to move tailings tomorrow with the Komatsu. Ron and his girl friend Jackie came up to see us tonight. They sure are nice people.

Sunday, August 8th. We didn't get to run the box today. I hauled tailings most of the day when we didn't have company.

August 9th. We panned out of the front riffles this afternoon and got an ounce and a half. We ran the monitor 3-1/2 hours. We found a new shaft and we'll get pictures of it tomorrow. It was nice out today. I dug fresh potatoes out of the garden this a.m.

August 10th. It's hot today and the garden's looking good. I hauled tailings this a.m. Marcene and Colette went to town. The box didn't run today. Red and I moved the overflow pipe at the dam and monitored about 4 hours this evening. Red cut some trees this p.m. He's going to do work for the old pump and International engine, I gave them to Red. He lucked out because it was a high pressure Gardner Denver 10-12 inch pump, and it had a brand new impeller in it. That's fine, I'm glad to see Red get it.

August 11th. We ran the monitor about 2 hours and picked out about 3 ounces of gold from the first 4 riffles in the box. It's looking good. I got 2 barrels of fuel off Steve today, it's just a loan and I'll repay it tomorrow. I gave Red a little Long Tom sluice box and he's sure proud of it. Ron and Jackie came up again this evening. They want to have Red dig some test holes for them with his backhoe.

August 12th. We got 2 ounces of gold from the front riffles today. Since Marty left we have picked 10 ounces of gold from the front riffles. We ran the monitor about an hour this a.m. washing down the slough off. Our water supply is still coming in, but kind of slow. I went down with Dave Fowler this p.m. and found bedrock for him on Nugget Gulch and we found some nice gold. It seems as if fall is in the air, cool nights and warm days, like on the desert. I put a unit in our heater today, it's sure nice to have it working.

Friday, August 13th. We didn't run the box today, ran out of water. Total hours on the box since we cleaned up, 21-1/4 hours. We went into Dawson and ate at the Sheffield House. Dave brought the 966 loader up for me to use tomorrow to haul tailings. And that's nice of him. It was hot and dry today. Yesterday I went down and showed Davis where the gold was on Nugget Gulch, and today they pushed through the material and got quite a few nuggets. I'm happy for them. I'm gonna help them clean up tomorrow a.m. I ran the loader hauling tailings 3-1/2 hours today. The pin came out of the loader bucket and Marcene helped put it back in. I ran the loader and maneuvered it around while she put the pin in.

August 14th. I helped Davis and Gunther do their cleanup. We used our Denver panner and the gold wheel. They sure didn't do all that good really, for the equipment that they're using, but had a lot of nice nuggets. I ran Davis's loader about 6 hours, filled it with fuel and took it back to them. I sure got a lot of tailings hauled with it. We went into Dawson City tonight, ate out, and went to Diamond Tooth Gertie's. We called Mama and Daddy and Jadene, and everything's fine in Tennessee. We spent the night at the Sheffield House Motel, rented one of their little cabins. It's our 33rd anniversary.

Sunday, August 15th. We had breakfast at the Sheffield House and took it easy this a.m., watched the finish of the raft race on the Klondike River. Ron Johnson and Robbin Archibald, our neighbor miner and his partner, won the race. Frank Short brought Marcene a carton of cigarettes to replace the one that he had borrowed earlier. It was hot today, but cooled off this p.m.

Wednesday, August 18th. The weather was nice today, but you can feel fall in the air. Butch came up this a.m. and borrowed my 2-inch pump to prime their big pump down on Nugget Gulch. I had the suction hose hooked up to our hopper in the sluice box, so we'll have to get it back before we can run the sluice box. We took some meat down to the Johnson boys. They've been working on their D6 Cat, the old wore out one, for the past 3 days.

August 19th. We found our first big klunker today, sure is exciting to find a big nugget in the riffles. That's the one that we're going to trade to our accountant to get our little Mustang back. He told us earlier this spring that if we found a big nugget he would swap the car back for that nugget. We ran the box 3 hours this a.m. and then went into Dawson and took our concentrates to the Tech National rep Mr. Berger. We should have our gold refined and back in Dawson in a couple of weeks. When we got back to camp we ran the box another 45 minutes and found another big nugget, this one was 1 ounce, 2 pennyweight.

August 20th. Dave Fowler and company came up today and I helped them clean up. They got 39-plus ounces of gold and some nice nuggets. Dave brought up his 966 loader and let me use it 'til Monday morning. I hauled tailings for 6-1/2 hours, went in to eat, and then Marcene and I ran the monitor about an hour and a half. Then I got tired. It was nice out today, sunshine most all day.

Tuesday, August 24th. I helped Red take the pump apart, the big one that I gave him, and we cleaned it all up. It had a new impeller in it, we put in a new gasket, found the nuts and bolts and put it all back together. So the old engine is bad, but the pump is a good one and on a very good set of skids. I gave Red a Homelite chain saw too. It was one that needs a little work on it. Anyway, Red helped me fix a leak in a water pipe, he's just an all around good old boy and I like to help him any way I can.

August 25th. I went down to our fuel tank and filled Dave's 966 loader this a.m. and he's going to let me use it this weekend. The weather was beautiful, sunny and not too hot. I ran the dozer, clearing the dam site, and Red cut trees above the dam for about 4 hours. The box ran 2-1/2 hours, but we didn't run the monitor. We picked about 5-1/2 ounces of gold from the front riffles today with a spoon, so that tells me that we've got at least 10 ounces in the box for 2-1/2 hours work.

August 26th. We didn't run the box today. I hauled tailings for 2 hours and Red came up and did more clearing above the dam. The weather was nice. Marcene took 25 ounces of gold into the bank to sell, we'll get paid in 10 days. She ordered an alternator for Daves 966 loader, $300, should have it Saturday. I guess we'll mine 'til a week from this Saturday, then clean up Sunday.

August 27th. We had the first ice of the season this morning. The riffles looked real good, we picked 2-1/2 to 3 ounces from the front riffles and didn't run very long. We went over to Gunther's claims this a.m. and gave Butch $300 to get the alternator for the 966. Butch is going to help me tomorrow to do some welding and etc. We're going to leave this good ground for next year. From here on out all we'll be doing will be just cleaning up and everything, here in the pit, and putting things away.

I cleared with the dozer about 4 hours where our next dam's going to be. Butch came up this p.m. to help me put the extension on the top of the Case 450 blade. We didn't quite finish, so he'll be back tomorrow evening.

Tuesday, August 31st. I used Dave's loader last night and this a.m. and took it back at noon. Then we went to town and called regarding the sprockets and pullers for the Komatsu loader. We ran the box about 2-1/2 hours this p.m. and the riffles looked good. Total hours on the box at cleanup was 49-1/2 hours. We cleaned out the box this p.m. and will it run through the cleanup machine tomorrow. Butch came up tonight and welded on the dozer blade. We ran out of oxygen and I went down and borrowed a bottle from Uncle Stevie.

Thursday, September 2nd. Today we cleaned up for last time for this season. It took us most of the day. We brought the motorhome into Dawson and moved into the camper park. We had no problem getting out from the mine because the Johnson boys and Archibald brothers got together and did some work on the road for us. We're real thankful that they did because it was pretty rough before they did that. We went to Gertie's tonight and had a ball.

September 3rd. Gold today was $455 an ounce. We got our motorhome repaired at Andy's and came in from camp early to pick it up before he closed. We got paid on our last shipment of gold to Inglehardt today.

September 4th. It rained most of last night. We left for camp early this a.m. and filled barrels at the tank. Ron came up to talk about the road across Oro Grande Creek. They're gonna change their road around a bit down there and I said to go ahead, it's alright. Davis and company came up and cleaned up, and they brought the 966 loader for me to haul tailings. I helped them clean up and then ran the loader for 4-1/2 hours. I'm getting closer to finishing, only lack 3 or 4 more hours, or less, being ready for next spring as far as cleaning the pit and hauling tailings is concerned.

Sunday, September 5th. We're in town today for the Outhouse Races which are a big get-together. We saw Hank Strom and a couple more friends from Anchorage. We went through the museum while in town. I staked a claim for Marcene and one for myself today on Stampede Creek, on the left fork.

September 6th. Gold was $474 today. Mel Pardek called this a.m. and he said we could get the Collinsville mine back again. I said, "No, thank you." We went up to our mine and I spent most of the day just getting the pit drained and the ramp road coming out of the pit ready for next spring, and putting things away. I got the Komatsu loader cleaned up and ready to start work on it tomorrow, got to put on the new sprockets.

September 7th. Steve helped me take the tracks off the Komatsu and load them on the pickup. We had 10 minutes to catch the ferry and we took off for Anchorage after calling Automatic Welding. We made it into Glennallen. We left our motorhome at Mrs. Close's camper park right there in town and they charged us. We weren't hooked up to anything, just parked there, and they charged us a couple of days for it.

September 8th. We slept in the pickup, what little sleeping we did, at Glennallen. I don't know if you've ever tried to sleep in a pickup with dirty clothes, or not, but I just couldn't quite go it. We had the dirty clothes in a plastic bag. It rained most of the way and we got into Anchorage this a.m. about 9 o'clock. First we took the tracks to Automatic Welding to get the pins and bushings turned. We had lost a U-joint in the pickup at Alpine and I took the drive link loose and drove on in on the front wheel drive. So we had Big O put in 3 U-joints and it drives better now. We went by and saw Eddie, bought 2 Carhart jackets for the Johnson boys, Ron and Bern.

September 9th. We did our running around Anchorage today, picked up the loader tracks and hit the road about 4 p.m. We drove to Tok and spent the night, and stopped by to see Walt Klewine at his lodge up there where Brandt's used to be. Walt was telling me, "You know, I was talking to this feller Don Keach, that's the guy you got the claims from, isn't it?" I said, "Yes." And he said, "You know, Don told me that, 'This guy came up to Gay Gulch there on the Upper Eldorado Creek. He was a musician out of Nashville, and he offered me a million dollars, opened up a briefcase and counted it all out on the hood of his Bronco'." I said, "You've got to be kidding." He said, "Yeah, that's exactly what he told me in here." Walt said, "Knowing you, there's no way in the world if you had a million dollars cash you would have laid it out there on the hood of that Bronco for those claims."

September 10th. Gold today is $440 an ounce. We drove back into Dawson this a.m. and recorded 2 claims. We filled out the paperwork and have our assessment work done up to 1989. It cost us $320 for assessment work and $20 for the 2 new claims. I went by and got Steve and he helped me about 3 hours, working on the Komatsu loader. We had to come in early because Steve wanted to go to the Follies. Paul White, a hardrock miner, had Steve and another boy, Eric, working for him. We befriended him over the summer and he came down to give me a hand. When he gets through I'm gonna give him some nuggets.

Saturday, September 11th. We went up to the mine and finished putting the tracks on the Komatsu and got the brakes fixed. Steve helped me today. We took the cap off the end of our water supply pipe, out from under the dam, and emptied the dam. Old Steve, when he crawled out on the pipe, he slipped and fell about 14 feet. I just knew that he hurt his back, but he got up smiling and said everything was okay. Dave and Gunther came up and did their cleanup today.

September 12th. We went to Diamond Tooth Gertie's last night and had a ball. We kind of slept in this a.m. and ate breakfast at the Eldorado Hotel. We went by to see Big Red and then went on up to the mine. I put the dozer and loader on timbers for the winter. The reason for doing this is because when you park them on timbers, wood, they don't freeze to the ground. If we happen to come up early next year and everything's froze to the ground, it wouldn't be nice. So this way it makes it easier to get the equipment going and moving. We also drained the light plant. Keirin gave us about an ounce and a half of gold to go for payment on the 3-wheeler tonight. We're just about ready to leave Dawson for this season. The leaves are just beautiful now, they're yellow, green and red. I called Mel Pardek this p.m., he sure wants me to go to Collinsville. Ha!

September 13th. We drove down to Whitehorse today. Steve drove the Norcan Avis pickup and we parked in Avis's yard. We'll leave the motorhome here 'til we get back from Juneau. We had no problems today and gave Steve $500 worth of gold nuggets for his labor.

September 14th. We gave Larry at B.C. Bearings 2 nuggets for being so nice and sending the belts and etc. to us this summer. The nuggets were worth about $25 each. We had mailed 40.55 ounces of concentrates to Tech National from Dawson. We went by Tech National and got absolutely nowhere with them. The guy that mailed them, a rep buying for Tech National at that time named Mr. Berger, suggested that we insure the concentrates for a minimum of $10,000 because of all the gold that was in them. We didn't get our money at Tech National for the concentrates and gold. They told us that they would send our check down to Tennessee. Incidentally, we never did receive any money from Tech National. I talked to Avis today regarding purchasing the pickup, and it went on and on. So I figured that I'd wait and do something next year. We took the oxygen and acetylene bottles back to Jacobs Oxygen and Accessories this p.m.

September 15th. We had Canadian Propane and ICG work on the motorhome furnace, this cost us $185. Ed Armstrong was the guy who worked on it and he's a real nice guy. We got acquainted with him and I'm sure that we'll be seeing more of him.

Friday, September 17th. We got to Juneau this evening. Bud Saylers picked us up. Pat and Bud held a party for Tom Fink who was running for Governor of Alaska, and Mike Coletta who was running for Lt. Governor. We've know Fink for a long time, he's from Anchorage. I talked to Tom regarding mining and etc. and we gave him a couple of nuggets for his wife worth $40 each. Bud and Pat took us out for Mexican food after the party.

We left Juneau today and got back into Whitehorse, picked our motorhome up at Avis, Norcan Leasing there in Whitehorse, and drove down to Skagway where we parked for the night.

Tuesday, September 28th. We spent most of the day today with our accountant Don Cole in Springfield, Oregon. We traded that big gold nugget for our '67 Mustang, the one that we sold him in Alaska.

1983

Friday, April 8th, 1983. We started this morning about 8:30. Scotty and I put the Cadillac, Cougar, Mustang, and Pinto in the barn for the summer. We filled up the motorhome at Ashland City, and drove to Indianapolis. We stopped and checked on Beachcraft motorhomes and so forth, on our way up. We're on our way back to another mining season in the Yukon. Jadene and Scotty are going up to work with us at the mine this summer.

We had our normal furnace problems on the motorhome as we're going up the highway. In Grand Prairie we stopped and had it repaired, and we spent the night in Fort Nelson. We went on up to Watson Lake with no problems, drove over Steamboat Mountain and stopped for hamburgers on Steamboat. We stopped by the Liard Hot Springs and rested up a bit.

Monday, April 18th. We were running around Whitehorse today, gathering up groceries and parts, etc. for the mine. We leased a pickup from Norcan for the summer.

April 19th. We parked at Pelly Crossing last night, and when we woke up this morning found that Indian kids had shot a hole in the radiator of our motorhome. I had to put some Bars-leak in it before we could get going, but everything worked out okay. We made it to Dawson today, got the snow plowed out of the road and took our groceries up to camp. The old messhall is just about a wreck, the hothouse is also. It was warm up at camp this p.m. at Gay Gulch.

By the way, we have a microwave we plan on giving to the Johnson brothers, and we also have a color TV for the Archibald brothers. That was for the work that they did on the road last year so we could get our motorhome out from camp. It was our appreciation to them.

April 20th. I called Davis Fowler this morning and told him about the guy who would take the tracks off his Cats and haul them into Whitehorse. He's gonna get back with me. We got a little more done at the mine, took the groceries in. We need spark plugs for the light plant. It was thawing today, and cloudy. Red and Colette came by at the mine for a visit.

April 21st. Scott and I went up to the mine and got the little welder started, also got the overflow pipe opened and water flowing. I called Davis and he told me to go ahead and get Finning to take the tracks off the Cats and to let White Pass haul them into Whitehorse to get the pins and bushings turned. Scott ran the dozer a little bit today.

Saturday, April 23rd. There were 2 D8 Cats broke through the ice in Eldorado Creek this a.m., one at the dredge and one at Poverty Bar. One broke through, and the other was trying to get to the first one when it also went through the ice. It was nice at camp today, sunny and melting. We stopped by to see Vern and he's fine. We saw Bingo Bill McCarty today, he just got back from outside.

April 24th. Red and Colette came up for a visit this p.m. I picked up Davis's 966 Cat loader and took it down to Don Murphy's where his dozers are, and parked it clear of the driveway. I'll help pull the tracks off both Cats for Davis on Wednesday.

April 25th. Jadene and Scott went up to camp with us today. Scott and I hooked up the steam thawing rig. The coil was frozen and cracked in about 5 places, so we took it apart and took it to PJ Welding in Dawson to get it fixed.

April 26th. It was nice today, sunny, in the high 60s to low 70s. Scott and I got the pipe thawed out today and did quite a bit of work on the pipeline. We only have to put in an 8-inch valve and rig up the water by camp and we can start monitoring.

April 27th. We got the valve on and all tightened up, turned the water on and ran the monitor about an hour and a half. Everything looks lovely. Steve came by to see us this evening and it was nice to see him, Sharon and the baby. Steve is the guy we gave the nuggets to last fall. We visited awhile with Dave Johnson on the road this p.m., he always grins and never talks much, but appears to be a nice guy. The road is kind of icky, but not as bad as last year. The rental truck we have has a bad U-joint and possibly a bad rear end.

April 28th. Scotty and I helped the Finning mechanic take the tracks off of the D9 and big Komatsu and load them onto the truck. There were no batteries in either Cat, we had to get gas to start the D9 pony engine. It sure was nice out today, sunny and warm. We went up to the mine this evening and ran the monitor about an hour and a half. We're just about ready to mine, only lack a gasket and pipe and antifreeze in the light plant. It sure is peaceful up here. Dave Johnson worked on the road today.

April 29th. We had lots of ice this morning. The monitor is not doing any good, it looked like Christmas down there in the pit with icicles hanging all over everything. We put antifreeze in the light plant, cranked it up and it ran pretty good. Scott hauled rocks today, he also hooked up the antenna for our radio. The little dozer worked cleaning up the creek, etc. Marcene and Jadene did a big wash today. Tonight Scott and Jadene got a load of wood and it started raining.

April 30th. We ran the box for an hour and a half today and had a little showing in the riffles. Scott worked the shaker and Marcene was on the sluice box. Scott and I picked rocks, fixed a gasket in the pipe, cleaned the pit, and a few other things. I fixed a propane leak in the little blue bippie trailer. We went into town tonight for the Gumboot Dance, and darned if they didn't have it last week. We saw John Brown in town tonight. Jadene and Scott are staying until Monday when we'll get the claims transferred.

Sunday, May 1st. It was cold last night. We're just poking around camp patching a few leaks in the pipe, and we fueled up the Cat and loader. We went down to Don Keach's claim, talked with John Wallace and sold him the conveyor for $500. He gave me $100 Canadian. It sure was cold most of the day.

May 2nd. It sure was cold out last night, 30 degrees when we got up this morning. I fueled up the light plant and tidied up a few things around camp. Seems as if I just can't get everything done. I parked the dozer across our road, as we like to keep out the undesirables when we're not in camp and we drove into town. We transferred part of the claims to Jadene and Scott, then went to the Eldorado Restaurant and ate with Davis. He picked up the tab because Scotty and I took the tracks off the D9 and big Komatsu for him, helped them out. Jadene and Scott came along and enjoyed it very much. The weather was lousy all day, cold and cloudy.

May 3rd. I saw Davis at the Eldorado this a.m. and he gve me a check for McCulley. I'm supposed to write it out for $500, that's for hauling the tracks to Whitehorse and back. We watched the Canadian Parachutists jump before we left Dawson today and Scotty and Jadene enjoyed that. I bought 2 barrels of diesel today at White Pass and 10 gallons of kerosene at the Gulf Station. Dave told me to bring his 966 loader up to camp, so I did, and worked it for about an hour.

May 4th. It sure was cold out last night, it must have gotten down to about 15 degrees. There was ice all over everything this morning. We went into town to pick up the color TV that we brought back for the Archibalds and their gate was locked, so we left the TV on their Cat. We came on back up to camp. Scott changed teeth on the loader and we ran the box 2 hours, the riffles looked pretty good. I ran Davis's loader for about an hour. I'll sure be glad when it warms up.

May 5th. We had snow, sleet, rain, and sunshine today. We burned the brush above the dam, brought the steamer out of the pit, and are going to clean up the 966 loader in a day or two. We ran the monitor most of the day, picking rocks and hauling tailings. Scotty ran the Komatsu loader, he's getting a little better each time he runs it. Ron and Bernie Johnson, and Robbin Archibald came up to see us tonight. Robbin said, "I just wanted to meet the people that left a color TV on my dozer. I couldn't hardly believe that somebody would give me a 21-inch color TV."

May 6th. It snowed about 4 inches last night, but the weather turned out okay, sunny and nice this p.m. The box ran about 2-1/2 hours. We got started about 11 a.m. and started sluicing at one. We got a little gold from the front riffles. Jadene washed clothes today and got her finger caught in the wringer. She called Marcene, snot and tears just running. Marcene was working the shaker, and Scott was below, so Marcene came up and finished the washing.

Sunday, May 8th. We had no heat in our little blue bippie trailer last night. It was 26 degrees when we got up this morning, so I hooked up the propane. It turned out nice today, sunny and in the 50s. We were just bull cookin' around camp today, ate at the Eldorado tonight, the food was good. It was Mother's Day and we enjoyed it. We gave Maria a quart of Georgia moonshine.

May 9th. I took a barrel of fuel up to Oro Grande for Andy and pumped it into his D8 that Dieter was running. We ran our box an hour and a half today. The weather was nice. Jadene's doing good on her diet. The ferry will probably start the 15th of this month. That's the ferry that goes across the Yukon River to the Top of the World Highway and to Alaska.

May 10th. Everything's okay and running. Scott and I went into town and got topsoil. It was nice out today. Dave Johnson and his group camp up tonight, partying.

May 11th. It was cold and miserable today, sleet and rain. The riffles looked okay, we have about 2-1/2 ounces of gold on hand that we picked out of the front riffles. We put a top on the plastic shack that's our kitchen, we call it the "Gay Gulch Hilton". Scott hauled tailings this p.m. with the loader.

May 12th. It was nice out today. Scott and I cut trees this a.m., picked rocks and monitored, getting ready to sluice. We hooked the water up to the fifth-wheel trailer and lit the hot water heater.

May 13th. The riffles looked pretty good today. Scott is doing good on hauling tailings. I took the loader down and filled in some bad spots by Uncle Stevie's place. Jadene washed clothes today, it wasn't quite so cold. I guess we'll go into town tomorrow for the motorhome. It sure will be nice to get it up here.

May 14th. We didn't get the motorhome today because it was raining and the road looked kind of slick and bad. Scotty and I worked on the road. He hauled tailings and I ran the monitor this p.m.

Sunday, May 15th. We went into Dawson to get the motorhome. I took the Cat and worked on the road and Scott took the loader to the bottom of the hill to pull the motorhome up the big hill. The creek was pretty high, so we decided to wait 'til tomorrow to take it in. It was nice out today and the water is slowing down a bit.

May 16th. The weather turned better today and we brought the motorhome into camp. We had to tow it up the hill with the loader. The motorhome quit running on Marcene as she was coming up the hill, so we had to tow it on in with no power steering. Don Murphy came up and he wanted to know why we were towing the motorhome down and up the hill, on level ground and so forth. We told him what had happened, it quit running. When we got it up to camp it cranked right up and ran like a top. Anyway, we got the motorhome into camp and we're glad to have it. It was nice talking to Don again.

May 17th. We got up this morning and it was snowing, there was snow on the ground. The road into Dawson sure was messy with the snow and all. Marcene and I went in to get oil and filters for the 966 loader. Scotty changed the oil and filters in the 966 and added transmission oil. Marcene got her hair done and it looks nice. We got flowers, plants, cucumber plants, and zuccini squash in town today. We saw Lou Provonovich this morning and visited with Sue and Don Murphy. We got a letter from Duey, that's the girl friend of Red, Mel Tillis's bus driver. Mel and the boys and Red are going to be in Anchorage Saturday night, so I guess we'll go into Anchorage Friday if the ferry is running. Don Frizzel, with White Pass, invited us for lunch, and also Finning Tractor invited us for a party Friday. The motor on the shaker broke tonight and we changed it, put a new motor on. The old one burnt the bearings out of it. It's snowing tonight at 11:40 p.m.

Thursday, May 19th. We sure got in some good ground today, beautiful color in the front riffles. We cleaned out the front riffles and put it in a tub in the washhouse and locked it up, as we're going in to parties and so forth. Marcene and Jadene went to Dawson today. Scott changed oil and filters in the Komatsu, also oil and filter in the light plant. It rained, sleeted, and snowed, and the sun shined today. We're going to Anchorage tomorrow morning.

May 20th. We got up at 5 this morning and left for Anchorage. When we left the mine I drove the dozer to the foot of the hill and blocked the road with it. The highway was closed at the border, but we moved the signs and barricades and came on through. Everything was fine and we drove on to Anchorage. Jadene and Scott called Marilyn as we got into Mountain View out there. She came over to meet them and they'll be staying with her while we're in town. We went to see Mel Tillis tonight and visited with Red. We took him out to LaMex and The Pines Club and enjoyed the evening.

We took the pickup to Big O Automotive to get a brake job done on it and roamed around Anchorage taking care of loose ends, picking up parts, etc. We gave a big nugget to Jan, Orville's wife. It was real nice of Jan to loan us a little pickup while our rental pickup was in Big O's shop. It cost $499 to get the brakes and etc. fixed on it.

Tuesday, May 24th. We went up to Eldon Brandt's and picked up a hose, rubber boots, and different items that Bob McKirvey told me to pick up, and I'm gonna send him some gold later. We picked up an electric motor and gold scales from Eldon Brandt.

Thursday, May 26th. We left Anchorage this morning and drove into Dawson this evening. On our way, just out of Tok, we got the back end of the pickup caught on fire, a cigarette flipped out the window. For some reason it got into the clothes bags in the back and caught everything afire. We had to stop and throw everything out. I debated for awhile as to letting everything burn, get away from the pickup and let it blow, because we'd just filled both tanks with gasoline at Tok. But it worked out alright and we made it on into camp this evening. That's just part of life, and mining.

May 27th. The gold looked good in the riffles today. The weather was a duke's mixture. Marcene took strawberry plants to Joan, the lady at Farmers' Market, and she's saving plants for us. It's an even swap, the strawberry plants for other flowering plants.

May 28th. We had nice weather, lousy this morning, but it cleared off and got up to the 70s this p.m. I planted onions and taters today and talked a bit with Ron this a.m. We started work about 9 to 9:30 this morning and stopped tonight about 6 o'clock. We broke bolts in the electric motor bracket and had to exchange motors. It took about 45 minutes.

Sunday, May 29th. We kind of slept in this a.m. Don Keach and clan came up this morning, got the trailer and their trail bikes. The weather was nice, almost hot, in the high 70s. We planted lettuce, radishes, carrots and beets, and Jadene set out flowers. Our strawberries sure look nice. Davis came up for dinner today. We had chicken, gravy and fried potatoes. It sure was good. Scott hauled tailings awhile this p.m. and helped me pick 2 loads of rocks. We went over to see Red tonight. He may bring his backhoe up, dig up some stumps and cut some trees above the dam for me. Marcene found my billfold in a pair of socks and I'm sure glad. Yeah, I lost a billfold and Marcene finally found it.

May 30th. It was hot today, 90 in the shade. "Yukon" Don came up and got his old wood cookstove, and good riddance. The monitor ran 4 hours today, should have enough material for about a 3-hour run tomorrow. The riffles looked good. We now have 15 ounces of gold in a bottle. Red came up this evening and is to bring up his backhoe tomorrow evening.

May 31st. Davis came up and is going to take his 966 loader back to Anchorage. I used it today hauling tailings and took it down to KMA Mines on Nugget Gulch, got there about 12:15. I loaded a pump on Gunther's truck for Don Murphy. Boy, it sure was hot today, 100 in the shade under the spruce tree in camp. We made a pad for a log house that we plan to build this fall. The riffles looked fine today, got about an ounce out of the front riffles, maybe an ounce and a half. Red brought his backhoe up and is going to work for me tomorrow pulling stumps above the dam.

June 1st. The box didn't run today. We spent most of the day clearing above the dam. Red worked his backhoe 7 hours pulling stumps. We ran the monitor this a.m. Marcene and Jadene ran it, cleaning up the pit and getting ready to move down below. It was hot today, but not as hot as yesterday. We went down and visited Ron and Bernie tonight and stopped by Dave Johnson's, talked with Bingo and his wife. We left a quart of moonshine for Dave Johnson.

Friday, June 3rd. My nephew Kendall came to camp today. We ran the monitor all day and Kendall helped pick rocks, etc. The water is coming just a wee bit slower nowadays and the monitor's using it just about as fast as it's coming in. Jim Johnson came to visit us today. He's our ex-banker in Anchorage, and Dave Johnson's brother. Andy Fras and his brother Zalato came up just for a visit. Davis came by and we gave him a big nugget, he was well pleased. He wanted me to help take the Koering backhoe apart tomorrow down at Nugget Gulch, so I'll be down to give him a hand with it. Our lettuce and radishes are coming up, but Marcene couldn't get tomato plants yet.

June 4th. Kendall and I helped Davis tear the big backhoe apart, and Kendall sure was a big help. Scott and Marcene worked the pit today. The Johnson boys got their big plant started about 9 o'clock tonight. I took Kendall up to Stampede Creek this p.m. and showed him the general area where he'll be going to stake a mining claim.

June 5th. It was nice out today. I helped Davis put tracks on the D9 Cat and take off the ripper and blade. Kendall and Scott helped, so did Don Murphy and his partner. We monitored awhile this a.m. until Davis came by. I messed up my back a little bit. When we were taking the ripper off, I tied it off to the 966 loader. Just then Kendall came over to ask me a question about the blade, so I went around to help him get the blade off the D9. When I got back to knock the final pin out of the ripper Davis had changed the hookup on it with a chain, and instead of the chain going all the way around the whole thing he just had it through the top part of it, so it flew apart. Needless to say, the lower part of the metal flopped over and knocked me clear over some other metal and messed up my back there pretty good. I don't think Davis ever really knew what he'd done and I never said anything, but that's the way it happened. He thought I just fell off the ripper.

Tuesday, June 7th. The monitor ran today and we hauled rocks and timbers out of a mine shaft. Kendall helped today and yesterday. Jadene and Scott went into Dawson for their wedding anniversary. Davis came up, brought the 966 loader and borrowed my jumper cables. I cleared out the tailings that Don Keach had stacked up by a claims post on the south side of the creek. Kendall ran the 966 real well, he's good at just about anything you put him on.

June 8th. Davis came by this a.m. on his way back to Anchorage. Jadene and Scott got in at 1 p.m. It was clear today, but a bit cool. We should be ready to sluice in a couple of days now. We've been monitoring and stockpiling material for a week.

June 10th. The riffles looked real good this p.m. We got started and ran quite a bit of dirt through the box today. This morning we cleaned stumps out above the damsite using Davis's loader as much as possible, and got our burning done. We picked up 2 barrels of fuel from our 500-gallon tank by Stevie's, White Pass filled it yesterday.

Saturday, June 11th. The box ran about 5 hours today and we picked over 3 ounces of gold out of the first few riffles this p.m., enough for today. Marcene got some plants today, but no cucumbers.

June 12th. We put tags on claim posts over on Stampede Creek today. Kendall went along and we got everything taken care of over there. We're putting those claims into Kendall's name. We also staked a claim above our 8 here on Gay Gulch, and this makes 9 claims we have on Gay Gulch. We took a beer to the Johnson boys and they just grinned. This evening we monitored from 9 to midnight. I got dirt and set out plants, and Jadene and Scott went off on their picnic.

June 13th. The weather was nice today, it finally got to be summer. I took expanded metal out of the box and put it in the riffles. We used the 966 hauling out of the pit and stockpiling. John Wallace came up today, I guess Don Keach is going to buy him out. I talked to Red regarding his road tonight and I offered him fuel to put in his dozer to pay for my share of the road going in to Stampede Creek. Kendall and Scott went to town tonight. Jadene's little rabbit died.

June 14th. Kendall went to town this morning and came back at noon, and all of a sudden he's changing the oil and filters in his pickup. I asked him what he was planning on doing and he said, "Well, I'm leaving." I asked him, "What's the problem?" And he said, "I've got to go, IRS problems." I sure felt sorry for him, but I just couldn't do anything for him. He was in a big hurry, got all loaded out and away he went. We went into Dawson and tried to catch him in Dawson, as he had to have a tire repaired, but he'd already gone when we got to town. I called the Mounties. They were going to try to catch him on the way to Whitehorse and have him call Maria. We left a message with her to tell him that if he needed money, why, we could let him have money, but they didn't catch him and he did go back to Tennessee.

Thursday, June 16th. It rained pretty good last night and today. I used the 966 stockpiling material. Red, Dennis Brossard, and Darwin Keach started cutting brush this a.m. Scott and I went down and helped load out Dave Fowler's backhoe, boom, dipper and buckets, 2 counterweights, and 2 cylinders. Boy, that truck sure was loaded. Van Avery was the guy driving it for Harry Campbell, Klondike Transport. The brakes heated up on the dozer going down the hill this evening. I found out later that it was a goof-up by the boys at Northwest Farm and Tractor, they didn't check the thing out good before they sent it up.

June 17th. The box ran 1 hour today, total hours on the box to date, 51 hours. The 966 loader broke down this p.m., it was a U-joint.

June 18th. We ran the box 6 hours. The weather today was hot, but we had lots of water. Red came up and took the U-joints out of the 966 loader, 2 were broken and we replaced them. Scott and Jadene went to town tonight and Ron and Jackie came up this evening for a visit, stayed 'til 12:15 a.m. They seem to be nice. Bingo Bill also came up and we looked at our next dam site.

Sunday, June 19th. The box ran 3 hours today for a total of 60 hours on the box now. I spent all day monitoring, sluicing and hauling rocks, also fixed the overflow, and Marcene worked the shaker. The Murphys sent Sean up for the loader, but it's still broke down, we haven't got it fixed yet. Ron and Jackie came up again.

June 20th. I hired Dennis Brossard today, will pay him $1500 (U.S.) a month and room and board. I ran the monitor about 6 hours today. Scott's not doing anything, seems as if he's ready to go home. The total on the box today is 62-1/2 hours.

June 21st. We didn't run the box today, but we have 62-1/2 hours on it and have not done a cleanup yet. We ran the monitor from 8 a.m. to 6 p.m. John Wallace came up, and I went over to Nugget Gulch with him. He had put jets in the shaker and had to get me to show him how to turn the water off on that crazy valve we had on that shaker plant. Red came up and put the U-joints in the 966 loader. I got it going about 3 p.m. and ran it 'til 6 p.m., then we took off to go to the KMA (Kiss My Ass) Picnic.

When we got home about 12:15, someone had broken into our motorhome, took my shotgun, browsed through everything, and robbed our gold out of the front part of the sluice box. The Mounted Police came up and checked everything out. I didn't really want to go to the party tonight, but I went along because Jadene, Scotty, and

Marcene wanted to go. I wanted to run the 966 loader instead, because I knew it was my last day on it and I was gonna have to take it back to Davis.

There had been a hard rain while we were gone and there was only 1 set of tracks coming down the hill. The Mounties kept John Wallace as number 1 suspect overnight twice, for 24 hours. It was John who showed Larry Moore, the investigator for the RCMP, where my shotgun was. It had been dumped underneath a spruce tree just off our claims, not even in sight of the road. The dog they brought up the next morning from Whitehorse followed tracks right down to the cabin where John Wallace and Darwin Keach were staying, so it was almost positive, but they couldn't find the gold. It was circumstantial.

In our motorhome we had some gold coins and also some gold on hand that was missed, so we were fortunate. We had a silver dollar collection that was missed too. We were fortunate that the robbers were in a big hurry. They took my claw hammer and a little pry bar to pry the bottom part of the motorhome door up, and then I'd guess that one of the robbers probably crawled in beneath it. They left the tools laying right there. The way it looks one of them probably got scared and took off and left the other one there, because we saw footprints going down the road and that person was in a hurry, making about 15-foot steps.

June 22nd. I finished with Dave's loader today and took it to the KMA Mine, cleaned it all up and washed it down, and took it down to Don Murphy. He's gonna use it a little bit tomorrow. We cleaned up what was left in our box and it wasn't too good. We figured we lost somewhere around 60 to 80 ounces from the front part of that box. We hauled tailings and stockpiled material, and we'll start sluicing again tomorrow.

June 23rd. We finished cleaning up this a.m. and Marcene took the gold to the bank. It was nice and warm out today, and sunny. Dennis is working out good. We monitored tonight for about 2-1/2 hours and then Dennis and Scotty went to town looking for people that we think might have robbed our sluice box. John Wallace came up this p.m. and he and I looked around a bit, found a few tracks. Ron and Jackie came up this evening about 11 o'clock for a 2 hour visit. It's always nice to see them, but they seem to come at midnight every night.

June 24th. We ran the box 6 hours for a total of 9 hours now. The weather was nice today, hot and sunny, near 100 degrees. Dennis, Scott and I went to Johnson's and got a barrel of used oil, drained out of their equipment, for our road through camp, it's so dusty. I gave Red a key for the fuel tank this p.m. and told him to help himself. He's building the road into Stampede Creek.

Saturday, June 25th. It's hot today, over 100 degrees on the thermometer hanging on a tree out in our yard. Ralph and Nita Johnson came up today. Marcene took Jadene and Scott to town and I don't know what they're up to.

June 26th. Ralph and Nita left this a.m. and it was nice visiting with them. It was funny, Marcene told them which road to take, so when Ralph came to Eldorado Creek he stuck a stick up right at the crossing of Eldorado Creek, and put a note on it. Then when we went down checking on them we saw where the stick had been moved so people could get across, then replaced after they drove on. It had been moved and replaced several times. I built a new road off the hill today and just need to put in the creek crossing. Don Frizzel and his wife came up to visit this afternoon. I was running the Cat, so they visited Marcene and kids and people at camp. A Mountie came up this morning and said that John was going to jail this p.m. Jadene and Scott went to Dawson this p.m. to get Dennis. Jadene told Marcene today that Scott had lost a lot of weight, he'd been working so hard.

June 27th. The Mounties came up this morning at 5 a.m. We ran the box 4 hours for a total of 16-1/2 hours. Dennis and I worked on the road, the Oro Grande crossing this morning, and also dug a test hole on Dennis's claim. We brought a load up to the Denver panner to run through and check it out. Dennis went to town this a.m. and Jadene and Scott went back in this evening. Boy, was it ever hot today! The garden looks real good. Dave Johnson came up this p.m., I think he wants to lease our claims. Jadene and Scott were planning on going in to Anchorage with John, but we decided that wasn't the way for them to go. Dennis said that he would drive them in, so it's best this way.

June 28th. We paid Jadene and Scott $2000 certified check, and $400 cash, and then a post dated check, for July 6th, for $2000. Dennis got a $200 draw. The box ran 3 hours, a total now of 19-1/2 hours. We cleaned the 2 front riffles today. It was hot today, we went up to the spring and opened it up a bit more, stripped some ground, everything looks good.

June 29th. We had nice weather today, but the creek sure is drying up, it's hot. We went down and visited Ron and Jackie at their monitor this p.m. The Mounties came up and talked to me about the robbery some more. I guess Jadene and Scott are all settled in Anchorage now.

June 30th. Dennis got back to camp today. A big black bear was in camp and walked around the fifth-wheel. Marcene smelled him and hollered at him, trying to run him off. He just growled at her and later wobbled on off up into the woods.

July 1st. Dennis and I worked on the new dam site about 4 hours. A guy we met in Arizona, Frank Lynn and his son Robby, brought up one of their metal detectors today. Also, Bill and Marlene McNabb got in this afternoon. Bill and Frank did some panning and running the little sluice box. I hauled a load of material in for them from the creek in the 1-yard Komatsu bucket and it was real good material. They got close to an ounce out of it. Jim Johnson walked up just as they were cleaning up and said, "My gosh, where did you guys get that?" Bill said, "Right here under this rock." There was a big rock laying there. Jim couldn't hardly believe there was that much gold came out from around that rock.

Tuesday, July 5th. The box didn't run today, we're saving water. Bill and Marlene, Marcene and I went to town today. This evening we drove up Eldorado Creek, turned left at Hackinson's drive and went up to the old hardrock mine on top of the hill. When we started down this steep hill, we couldn't make the one turn and couldn't back up because the truck wouldn't go into 4-wheel drive. So we had to hook it and walk off the hill into Gay Gulch. Marlene and Marcene had a bottle of Cracklin' Chabli and it was warm. They were walking behind us and got to laughing. It was a long walk down that hill and I had on my cowboy boots. Anyway, we finally made it in after midnight. Dennis was getting worried and was getting ready to start looking for us.

July 6th. It rained some last night, but not enough. Today was hot and dry. Bill and I took the Cat and went up to get the pickup this morning. We ran the monitor for an hour. Bill and Marlene worked with the Denver panner and got a little gold.

July 7th. It was hot and dry again today. We pushed dirt to the dam site. The riffles looked pretty good. Bill worked on the motorhome today. Robert Trustwell came up this p.m. and visited awhile. Supper was good tonight.

July 8th. Marlene, Bill, Marcene and I rode up to visit Trustwell this evening. He has an old homemade rake, old homemade wheelbarrow and stuff up there, kind of neat. We went up Stampede Creek, but couldn't quite get to the claims up there. Red didn't have the road finished.

Saturday, July 9th. Bill and Marlene are still in camp, still getting gold and enjoying themselves. We pulled out about 3 ounces of gold from the front riffles today.

July 10th. We ran for about an hour this a.m., cleaned the 2 front riffles and it looked real good. We took Bill, Marlene, and Dennis over the hump, over Hunker Summit, and took the "Yukon Lou", piloted by Captain Dick, down the Yukon River. We ate salmon steaks at the island down there and they sure were good. On our way back home we went through an old dredge. Boy, it was hot today too. Pierre, with the nuggeted hat, came by and left a note that Cricket, an old friend of mine, had called looking for some mining ground. It rained quite a shower this evening about 7 p.m.

July 11th. We ran the sluice box last night for about 45 minutes and we all set around the fire. We had us a few cool drinks and decided that we was gonna go down and run the box some more because the ground was so good. We got part of it in the shaker and part of it on the sides, and we finally just quit after running about 45 minutes. We must have got 3 or 4 ounces of gold out of the front riffles. That was some rich ground right there below the shaker plant and right under the ramp. I'm debating whether to go ahead and move that shaker plant and take that ramp out. It rained this p.m., but I don't think it will help the water much. We need about a week's rain.

July 12th. The weather was crazy today, hot, cold, cool and windy, and sun. Clarence and his wife JoAnn, and JoAnn's sister, came up this p.m. for a visit. This is the couple who walked over to Gold Creek in Alaska when we were there. We're getting some gold out of a quartz vein that keeps wanting to float out the end of the box. So we keep having to run it through 2 or 3 times and it still won't stay in the box. We got into good gold this evening. We ran for an hour and got over 2 ounces in the front riffles. Dennis hardfaced the cutting tips on the Case dozer blade this p.m. and put a cute little "smiley" and his initials on it. Our water is still about the same as before it rained, it just didn't rain enough to do any good. I just wish Bill and Marlene could have seen all our nuggets this p.m. They sure would have enjoyed it. Marcene sure made a good supper tonight. Pierre and his sister Lucy came by today for a visit.

July 13th. It looks like it may rain soon, but it's sure dry now. Dennis and I cleared stumps and trees at the future dam site this p.m. We fixed the front wheel drive in the pickup, it was a retainer clip broken. It works okay now, we put a piece of mechanic's wire in there and made a retainer clip out of it. Andy's brother Zalato and Mike Palma, Maria's brother, came up tonight to do a cleanup from Oro Grande and we helped them. They sure are nice guys.

July 14th. We had a good rain last night and early this morning, every bit helps. I spent about 4 hours working on the future dam today, cutting a trough to lay pipe through. I thought I'd have to get a big backhoe, but I think I can make it with this little Cat okay. I talked to Ron and Bernie Johnson this a.m. and Ron says he wants to come up and shoot grade on the new dam that I'm building, just to make sure that I've got grade. I think that I'll have plenty, but he's just gonna come up and check it. The riffles look pretty good after 1 hour of running. We sent gold into town today with Dennis and he thought, "Boy, this is something, me transporting gold to the bank." It was a first for him, that we would trust him to take it in. We gave Dennis an advance to get him some work shoes and etc. He went to town for various things and should be back this evening. We paid White Pass today for a fuel delivery. It sure seems that fall is in the air, but I'm sure we'll have more hot and dry weather. The taters in the garden are about waist high and got little ones on them.

July 15th. Dennis and I went to Irish Gulch today and staked a couple of claims over there.

July 16th. Dennis was out chasing a porcupine in his robe this morning, and he got some quills for souveniers. Ron and Jackie came up this evening and we enjoyed the visit. Ron brought up his level and grade stick and checked out the grade. We've got plenty, lots of grade.

Sunday, July 17th. The riffles looked good today. We took Dennis, Ron and Jackie to supper in Dawson at the Sheffield House.

July 18th. Looks like we finally got our rain. We ran the monitor all night last night, as it was raining and the water was high. Zalota got stuck on our road and we had to pull him out with the Cat. We had tourists here today for awhile.

July 19th. It rained all day yesterday, all last night, and today. It looked like the dam was gonna go out on us once. The supply pipe for the box and monitor got plugged this morning and it sure scared us. We finally got it worked loose and kept the water going around the overflow. I went to town, got pipe to try to unplug it and got a little pump with a nozzle from Big Red, but it didn't get the job done. We found a piece of wood under the dam in the pipe, so we'll try something else. I got a 3-inch pump from Red and will try putting a fitting on and backflushing tomorrow.

July 20th. It rained most of the day and the dam almost went out again. We finally got the trash and all from in front of the 4-foot pipe. I got pipe from Jim Patton to run in and go under the dam, and flush the pipe out. We found out later that the block of wood that was in the pipe was one that Don Keach had put in there last fall when the water was down to a trickle and barely running through. He stuck an 8-inch block of wood in a 12-inch pipe that went from 12 to 8 inches, and it wouldn't make the turn. So anyway, the trash got in there and blocked it up. We backflushed it today, got it all cleared and going, but even so, we still didn't have as much pressure as we should have had. We gave Big Red $200 for replacing the U-joints in the 966 loader.

Friday, July 22nd. We've been running a lot of dirt from the banks and so forth washed down from the flood, but finally hit good ground and should have a good run tomorrow. We're back in the old paystreak. Robert came up today and cut some logs for the drift that he's putting in down by Cheechako Hill, and Marcene gave him some groceries. He's a guy that we all call "2 x 4", mining down on Eldorado Creek. He's got a fraction down there and he stakes claims all around. The reason they call him "2 x 4" is, he was in Diamond

Tooth Gertie's one night, and when he came back from the bathroom some guy had got his seat at the card table. Robert asked the guy to let him have that seat back because he felt that it was a lucky seat for him. The guy laughed at him and wouldn't do it. So Robert walked outside and looked around. Dawson City has boardwalks and there was a piece of a 2 x 4 broken off the sidewalk laying there. He just broke it in two, took it inside Diamond Tooth Gertie's and warped the guy over the head with it, laid him right out. So thereafter they called him "2 x 4" and he didn't get to go back into Gertie's again, they barred him permanently.

July 23rd. Big Red came up tonight and got a barrel of fuel. He's working on the road at Stampede Creek. Jerry and Ed came over to camp today, they brought cigars, cigarettes, and pipe tobacco. I won $10 off of Dennis and $10 off of Big Red tonight on a bet that a fuel barrel wasn't 36 inches tall, 3 feet. They both fell for it. The standard barrels are 35 inches tall, so they measured it and paid me.

Sunday, July 24th. Our riffles looked good, we got one pretty nice nugget today. Don and Sue Murphy came up today for a visit. A guy from Salt Lake City came by and wanted to buy gold. He was buying for the Mormon Church and wanted as many ounces as he could get. He didn't even want names and he'd pay cash out of a paper sack, but I didn't quite trust him.

Wednesday, July 27th. "Bedrock Randy" came by this a.m. and he may be interested in leasing our claims. He got his nickname because he was running up and down the creek asking everybody where the bedrock was, he couldn't figure out what bedrock was. So they named him "Bedrock Randy". We picked up a musk ox from a Mr. J. Harvard, and got papers and all. He's with Fish & Wildlife in town.

July 28th. We picked raspberries this a.m. and Marcene made a nice cobbler this evening. It sure was good.

July 29th. We went to the Miners' Ball tonight, had a good time, and the steak was fine. We got back into camp around midnight and all was well. We gave Dennis gold to pay for the musk ox, he made the deal for us, so everything's squared up now. Ed and Jerry are still in camp. They went to the Miners' Ball with us tonight and are leaving for Anchorage tomorrow. Jerry was wondering if we were going to cut the watermelon. She ate most of the expensive grapes Marcene bought in Dawson. She picked up the watermelon, showed it to Marcene and said, "Only 59 cents a pound, that's cheap."

Sunday, July 31st. Ron and Jackie came up tonight and brought some hot tamales. They were horrible. She called them "tay-malies".

August 1st. Jackie came up today, brought us some greens and onions, and picked some raspberries. We gave a refrigerator to Chuck and Cam, some friends of Jimmy Patton. They ate supper with us and we had a nice visit with them. They had just adopted a little baby and we knew that they needed something to keep the milk cool and so forth, so we gave them the one out of the little trailer that we'd hauled all over, Manley Hot Springs, Collinsville, up to Utica, and finally had a use for it here.

August 2nd. Denis Brossard left the day before yesterday and said that he'd probably come back next spring. Rick Paridey came to work for us this p.m. We went to Clinton Creek to look at buildings for sale over there.

August 3rd. A miner over on Nugget Gulch, by the name of Jerry, and his wife Winnie, came up this p.m. and visited. He's from Kenai, a fisherman down there, and she's originally from the Philippines.

Sunday, August 7th. We changed oil, etc., in the dozer and loader today. I let Rick off early as he was going in to eat supper with his girl friend. We had a barbeque here tonight and all enjoyed it. We invited the Johnson boys, Ron and Bernie, Jackie and Bernie's girl friend, Bingo Bill McCarty and his girl, and Jerry and Winnie.

August 8th. It was kind of cool and cloudy most of the day. Seems like fall is definitely in the air. The monitor ran 4-1/2 hours today and the box ran 2-1/2 hours. We got into a coarser gold. Red borrowed my welder, he needed to do some welding on his dozer blade. Rick went into town tonight on his motorcycle, he's off tomorrow.

August 9th. I shot a bear in camp this a.m., he woke us up getting into the garbage. So we did away with him and we're doing away with garbage cans from here on out. I worked on the dam 5 hours today and we went into Dawson this evening. Rick and Sandy went to Clinton Creek on his bike. He bought a big dormitory building over there for $2500. It's got an enormous amount of lumber, windows, doors, everything in it.

August 10th. We were back in the original creekbed today, the old ancient creekbed. Our riffles looked okay. I had to weld a steel plate on the shaker and I tried for 30 minutes to weld the plate. I found out that the welder was running at half throttle. That doesn't work.

August 11th. The weather was nice out today, just a bit cool, but okay. We only have a few days left to mine, then we have to build another dam and tear out this dam that we're using. Some tourists from Ontario, Canada, gave us a jack salmon and small king salmon they had caught. It was nice of them.

Sunday, August 14th. We went into Dawson today for our wedding anniversary. We watched the raft race, Ron Johnson and Robbin Archibald won again this year. We spent the night in Klondike Kate's Room at the Sheffield House and it sure was nice. Ron and Jackie, and Rick and Sandy came for a visit. We had hors d'oeuvres that weren't good, so we called Hon at the Midnite Sun and he brought over 2 very good trays.

Tuesday, August 16th. We staked a claim up the left pup from Gay Gulch and we staked it in Marcene's name, JDS#10. Gunther came up and told us that that claim was open up there and he did us a favor. He told us about it so no one else could get the claim above us and muddy up the water. That was the only placer claim above us at the time. Marcene took gold into town to the bank today, and tonight Rick went into town on his motorcycle.

Thursday, August 18th. We had frost on the windshield this morning. The weather was nice today, but fall is sure in the air. Ron brought up a load of logs in his loader bucket this morning. They're from an old shaft down there that was built about 83 years ago, and the logs were still solid and in good shape. The squirrels are eating our strawberries and our fresh potatoes, they're even digging the potatoes up. I never heard of squirrels eating potatoes before, leastwise digging them up.

August 19th. Leaves are starting to turn yellow and the fireweed is getting fuzz and blowing, so fall is here. I guess we're getting tired too, it's that time of year. Don and Sue and Sean came up to see us this morning. They left 5 ounces of nice jewelry gold for Davis. That's for the use of his light plant I believe, or the pump, one of the two. It was sure nice of them, I know Davis will like it. Sandy came up with Rick and spent the day. Red and Colette came by for awhile tonight. Rick took our pickup into town tonight and got Keirin's trailer so I can move my dozer to Stampede Creek tomorrow morning.

Sunday, August 21st. Mr. Gunther came to visit with us today. He offered his big rubber tired loader to me, no charge, and I can use it as much as I need it. That was very nice, but the offer was for next month and we'll be gone.

Tuesday, August 23rd. I took the Cat over to Stampede Creek and had to walk it in all the way over because Keirin's trailer wouldn't pack it. Boy, did it ever rain today, all day long. Rick went with me and he got soaking wet. We did assessment work on claims over there and staked another 40-acre claim, Taku #3. We got back to camp about 6 p.m. and cut the dam in the center. It didn't wash out as fast as I thought it would. I guess we're done sluicing as of today, for this season. It was kind of sad to see the dam go.

August 24th. Rick and I are in the process of moving the overflow pipe and supply pipe, etc. to the other dam site. We're getting everything all prepared and will be ready to go and be mining next spring. Bingo Bill came by while I was out picking blueberries late this evening. We'll be around for another week, looks like.

August 25th. Rick and I dug out the end of the pipe above the old dam. It sure had been tampered with, the screen had been broken off and the flapper had been pried off. We spent most of the day shoveling and the rest of the day filling over pipe in the new dam at the new site. Tonight we went over to Frank Short's and Jack said to come back on Saturday, then we can clean our concentrates on their table. Cass has a rubber tired backhoe and loader and I want him to come up to dig out the pipe under the dam on Sunday. In turn, I'll go down and do dozer work for him at the Eldorado Creek crossing, he's got a pit there.

Saturday, August 27th. We met with Davis for dinner at the Eldorado tonight and enjoyed the visit.

August 28th. The weather was nice today. John, the welder, came up and worked all day. We paid him $300 for the welding. We got most of our welding and cutting done and looks like we'll be getting everything all set for next spring. Rick worked long hours today.

August 29th. Our strawberries don't know it's falltime. They're still blooming and bearing, they're ever-bearing strawberries. Ron and Jackie came up to see us tonight, also Bunny and Stan, Ron's parents. Jackie is leaving for Vancouver tomorrow, driving.

August 30th. We finished building our dam and put in the overflow. It started raining just about when we got finished at 7 p.m. Keirin came by for awhile this p.m. We have lots to do, but we'll make it tomorrow. I dug our potatoes tonight and they're nice ones. Rick took our pickup into town tonight.

August 31st. Rick and I took the Cat and loader down and worked on the road at Oro Grande crossing, then I went on down to do some work for Cass and Iris on Eldorado Creek. Cass brought his backhoe up and did some work at the dam, digging out a pipe that was covered. Rick took Red's pump back. We went into Dawson tonight, kind of partied a bit and had a ball.

September 1st. I filed on the claim Taku #3 and filed assessment work on claims Taku #1 and Taku #2 on Stampede Creek, and we now have all our claims grouped and assessment work done. We got away from Dawson at 1 p.m. Rick and Sandy went to Whitehorse and took the rental pickup back to Avis. I sure hated to leave Dawson and the mine this fall, but everything's ready for next year.

I went to Frank Short's and got our concentrates this a.m. and we sure have our problems with concentrates, didn't get them run over the table. We drove to Tok and are spending the night. We met Sandy and Don Keach on the way over to Tok, halfway from Chicken to Tok, they were wound up like parrots, as usual.

Saturday, September 3rd. It snowed a bit last night here in Tok. We kind of slept in and then drove on to Palmer. We went to the State Fair and drove on to Eagle River where we spent the night.

Later, after we got to Anchorage, we were looking for a duplex to buy. We were talking to a realtor and he told us that Don Keach had really hit a glory hole over in the Yukon this summer. I said, "No, he went broke just down the creek from us and I hired one of his help, Dennis." The realtor said, "Well, he came in here and poured a whole slug of gold in a couple of paper plates, one plate he had fines, and coarse gold in another." And I said, "That's really strange because he didn't even have enough money to pay his fuel bill, labor, and/or grocery bill." So I thought that was kind of weird and asked the realtor if he had any idea where Don went trying to sell the gold after he left his place. He said he did, that Don said if he didn't sell it to him, he was going to go to Oxford Refinery. So we went over to Oxford and Marcene asked a guy at Oxford if "Yukon Don" had been in to sell any gold. The guy said, "Oh yes, he came in and sold some gold awhile back." She said, "Did he do pretty good? How much gold did he sell?" He said, "Sixty-some ounces." Then he realized what he was saying and shut up. He wouldn't say anymore. But anyway, so much for that, and Keach has gone south. They probably won't be seeing him anymore for awhile up here.

Looks like that winds up our mining season of 1983.

1984

Wednesday, March 7th, 1984. We drove our motorhome back up the highway, came out through Arizona, California, up through Oregon, Washington, British Columbia, on up to the Yukon. We got into Whitehorse last night and spent most of today running around town, checking on water permits, etc. We met a lot of nice people in the process of getting our water permit papers. One real nice guy helped us fill out the paperwork, took us about 2 hours to get everything squared away.

We also stopped by to see Larry Moore, a captain with the RCMP, regarding our box robbery last year. When we got there the front door was locked, but the back door was open so we just walked on in and right through to where Larry Moore was setting. He said, "How in the world did you guys get in here?" We didn't know it at the time, but when people come to the Mounties' Office, there in the Headquarters in Whitehorse, they have to get permission to come in. That day someone had left that back door open and I can just imagine the tongue lashing the dude that left the door open got.

March 8th. We left our motorhome in Whitehorse at Norcan, picked up our pickup, drove it on to Tok and spent the night. We'll get the motorhome when we head for the mine.

Tuesday, March 13th. Farley Winson, the guy that bought our house and farm in Tennessee, called today. He's interested in buying our mine and is coming up this summer to check it out. We're here in Anchorage at our home on the hill.

Wednesday, April 11th. Marcene called the girl working in the post office in Dawson City this morning. She said that Greg Hackinson had opened the road up Eldorado Creek and it was melting and quite warm in Dawson City.

We got underway and headed up the highway for the mine, stopping at the border to get our work permits, and everything's fine. We stopped at Destruction Bay for gas, and guess what? We remembered that we left $1800 under the mattress on the bed at our house. So Marcene called Tom Price, the guy up on the hill that we bought our house from, and asked him to get the money and put it in our account at the First National Bank at 36th and C.

April 12th. It's the same old thing, we're getting the furnace in our motorhome fixed again. Ed Armstrong's doing it for us at ICG, the propane place in Whitehorse. We rented a pickup from Norcan again this year and I think we're gonna buy one from them this fall when the season's over.

Friday, April 13th. We got things pretty well taken care of in Whitehorse today, picked up groceries, etc., for the mine and drove on up to Dawson City. Just as I drove into the camper park I blew out a tire, so we'll have to replace that one. It was a nice day out though.

April 14th. It was snowing this morning, and we went up to the mine this afternoon. We drove to Dave Johnson's camp, then Marcene and I walked up to our camp. Rick Paridey was up at the dam working on the overflow when we got up there. We got the loader going, but the dozer wouldn't start. I need to take some starter fluid up tomorrow. The overflow at Oro Grande wasn't bad at all this year. Tonight we went by to visit Rick and Sandy in Dawson, they're staying in a nice little place here in town.

April 15th. Rick and I went up to the mine, took the loader and dozer and came on down to clear the road. We chipped ice in the overflow at the dam and water's starting to run out the overflow. We came back to town and I moved our motorhome over to Andy's yard. It's sure nice of him to let us park there and plug into electricity.

April 16th. It was snowing this a.m. Rick and I went up to camp. I ran the dozer and cleared snow. Rick chipped ice at the dam. We changed oil in the welder and got it started, checked out the steamer and it's okay. We went down to our fuel tank and found that someone had broken the lock, chain, and the valve off the tank. The weather was nice out today, kind of cool, but it was like spring and winter combined.

April 17th. Today it's pretty out. I went by to see Keirin Daunt this morning, he's gonna come up and do some welding on the pipe for us. Rick and I cranked up the steamer and thawed ice. There's still lots of snow and ice at Gay Gulch.

April 18th. Rick and I set up plastic hose for the pipeline coming down from the new dam, put banding material on it.

April 19th. It was cold and snowing and just plain miserable out this morning. We went up and visited awhile with Keirin. It was still nasty up at his place, so we came on back to town. I ran into Frank Short and he gave me some banding material that he had, and that was nice of him. We gave a check and card to Chuck and Cam today for their new son that they're adopting.

April 20th. I paid Keirin for welding and use of his oxygen and acetylene. We got the monitor welded and pipe down to the shaker all welded up. It sure is nice and sunny out today. Don Keach is back in Dawson City, guess he's gonna try mining again this year.

Saturday, April 21st. Rick and I went up to camp, hooked up pipe to the shaker plant and banded a couple of joints of hose. We cranked up the chain saw and was gonna cut some trees, etc., but we need to sharpen the chain. I dozed with the Case in the pit, but there's still quite a bit of ice and it will probably be another week before we can start mining, just depending on the weather. Rick and I moved the fuel tank up to camp today, I don't want to leave it down the road with Don Keach running loose. I met Don on the road this a.m. and he's full of b.s. as usual.

April 22nd. Marcene and I picked up Rick and Sandy and drove up to the mine. We checked the dam and everything's thawing and melting pretty good. Then we went over and ate Easter dinner with Andy, Maria, and others. It was a wonderful meal and we sure enjoyed our visit. Maria had our names on Easter eggs. We went out on the town last night and I sang and played at the Downtowner.

Tuesday, April 24th. Marcene checked at the Recorder's Office today and found 10 claims across the highway, about 5 miles east of Dawson City. We will stake 4 claims tomorrow, one each for Sandy, Rick, Marcene and me, and the remainder later. Rick and I are doing maintenance, changing oil filters, etc., on the equipment around camp.

Thursday, April 26th. Spriggs Jigs is going to clean our concentrates tomorrow, run them through his jigs, and hopefully we'll come up with a pretty good chunk of gold.

April 27th. Rick and I cleared brush and hauled wood today. The Mounties came up this p.m. looking for Don Keach, but Don had gone to Anchorage. We found out that Don has his brother and another friend up at the mine with him and they're working without permits, so maybe he'll get enough rope to hang himself here. We got our concentrates back from Spriggs Jigs and boy, I'll tell you, I can't say what I want to in this book, but I'll never take anything back to him again.

Monday, April 30th. Rick and I worked at the mine today and also cut ridge poles for the cabin that we plan on building. We drug them in and I'll peel them a little later on. I did dozer work in the pit and pushed dirt just below the dam. It's sure melting, the temperature's in the 60's and looks like we'll get started here pretty soon.

May 1st. We should be ready to monitor by tomorrow afternoon. Marcene brought me something to peel logs with, a new draw knife. The weather was odd today, ice balls, snow, cloudy, windy, and sun.

Thursday, May 3rd. I brought a spruce tree in this evening for Mike and Pat. They're working on Andy's building, which today is the bank building. I'd like to add that we gave them three spruce trees and one of them lived. The reason the other two died was because they didn't get watered.

Saturday, May 5th. I brought our steamer into town today and Zalato fixed it for me. I borrowed pipe to thaw the pipe underneath the dam and the steam made short order of it. We went into town tonight and I sang at the Downtown with the band.

May 6th. The weather was lousy today. Rick and Marcene and I went up to the mine. We stopped and got cutting torches and worked all day patching leaks. We sure need some good pipe. We have everything about ready to go, just have to take the monitor down in the pit and do a bit of dozer work. Don Frizzel was stuck in the road with White Pass's Kenworth fuel truck, in Dave Johnson's mess down there. We stopped and helped him put the fuel hoses back on his truck, he was just getting out when we stopped to visit with him. Marcene and I ate supper with Rick and Sandy tonight.

Tuesday, May 8th. Gold today was $373 an ounce, silver was $8.65. I peeled 2 logs that I'm going to use for ridge poles on the cabin. Rick and I brought a nice spruce tree in tonight for Andy's building that they're fixing up in town. I got a check today, it's always nice to get checks. We got our tags for the claim posts, for the claims along the highway. The ice went out on the Yukon River this p.m

May 9th. Marcene and I went up to the mine, Rick took the day off. We peeled 2 logs and I ran the dozer, pushing dirt and ground sluicing. The weather was nice today, warm and mostly sunny. We left camp about 6:45 p.m. and got Andy another spruce tree on the way in. We got a letter from Bobby Adkins, he's fine and still playing in Vegas at the Silver Dollar.

May 10th. I pushed dirt and lots of water, doing ground sluicing. It's warm today, we could be sluicing now, but I want to take advantage of the high water for ground sluicing. Rick and Marcene peeled logs. Marcene and I spent the night in camp and Rick took the pickup to town.

May 11th. It was cold this a.m., 29 degrees and light snow. I pushed some dirt and Rick and I measured some claims. Rick and Marcene peeled one log, but it sure was cold and windy today. We came into town early, Marcene needed to get groceries, etc. The road is drying out. If it's warm tomorrow I think we'll be sluicing.

Saturday, May 12th. It was clear, sunny, and kind of cool today, lots of ice on the shaker and in the sluice box this morning. We nailed tags on our claim posts along the Klondike Highway, then Rick and I peeled 3 logs. I moved dirt into the creek above the old dam. Rick and I put 2 logs across Eldorado Creek for a bridge and he's gonna nail some plyboard onto the logs. That's in order for him to ride his motorcycle across the creek and commute between camp and Dawson. We leveled our wanigan and worked on our future garden, Marcene picked roots.

May 13th. Rick and I finished fixing him a bridge across Eldorado Creek for his motorcycle. Then we ran the box 2 hours, but the material that we were running through was just cleaning up the pit, not too good. Big Red came by to see us this afternoon. Tonight we went out to eat and took Rick and Sandy with us. Later we went by Andy's for a few drinks. Andy Fras and his family sure are a nice bunch of people.

May 14th. We ran a little material through the box today. The monitor ran about 3 hours, but was getting nowhere. Even though we've got gravity flow water and don't have to fight the pumps, with cold water and frozen ground it's pretty hard to get it thawed, or do any good.

May 15th. Don Keach came by and said that Red told him that he could use Red's pump. I told Don that Red should come and get the pump to let him use it, or come and let me know if it's okay.

May 16th. A pipe got airlocked this a.m. and we had a heck of a time with it, but we finally got the air worked out of it. We have lots of water and I'm using it for flushing the muck on down the creek, ground sluicing.

May 17th. Today was Rick's day off. I tried to run the plant, but had no water, so I worried with it for most of the day. Finally I decided to go and get a canoe and try to clean the suction. Marcene went down to the Johnson brothers and got theirs. It wasn't the answer though and I took my first swim in our new dam. The "tippy-canoe" tipped over and I got all wet, and cold, right up to my neck. Big Red came up just as I swam to the bank and was crawling up onto the bank with all my heavy clothes on, my Carharts, my heavy work shoes. He asked me, "You taking a bath this early in the spring?" I couldn't wade out because there was ice on the bottom, and it was kind of sloped up. Every time I tried to take a step my feet would slide out from under me, so I just decided to swim out. I finally just took the dozer and cut the dam. I ripped it out to find out what was blocking the pipe, turned out a screen over the end of it was plugged with leaves.

Ron Johnson and Jackie came up tonight and stayed 'til midnight. They're okay. We're going to monitor and sluice tomorrow, I hope. Ron gave me a hint on fixing my suction in the dam.

Friday, May 18th. Rick, Marcene and I worked the box today. We got water at the spring this a.m. and it's nice and clear. Tonight we went into Dawson to the miners' meeting. Afterward we went to Inglehardt Refinery's suite for eats and drinks. We saw lots of nice people and friends. We closed the Sheffield House. The manager told us and the 2 Inglehardt guys, Mr. Blackwell and Mr. Alex Brody, to lock the door to the hotel when we left. It was about 2 or 2:30 a.m.

May 19th. We both had showers this morning and it sure felt good. Our riffles don't look too bad for the junk that we're running through the box. We took weight out of the monitor box so it would be a lot easier for Marcene to work. We ran the monitor until about 9:30 p.m., ate, then took Ron and Bernie's canoe, the "tippy" one, back. It looks like we only have 3 or 4 strawberry plants left from last year, they froze out over the winter. Jackie, Ron's girl friend, said that she didn't want Marcene to see her without her makeup and Marcene told her that it didn't matter, she's pretty anyway. Ron was measuring the ground up to our property today and he came up to let me know what he was doing. We saw Big Red last night and he said Keach is going to come up to pick up his pump tomorrow.

May 20th. The weather was nice today, sunny. I took the loader down to Oro Grande and fixed the road to bring in the motorhome. Everything is going real good and working fine, plenty of water pressure. If no major problems, we should really have a good season this year. We finally got back to where we were last fall when we broke the dam. It's gonna take a few days to start getting the pretty gold and good gold that we've been missing with all the trash we've been running through. Zalota and John came up this p.m. and it was nice to see them out on the gulch. Jackie came up and visited with Marcene. I set out strawberry plants and I'll have to figure some way to beat the squirrels to them, the little stinkers.

May 21st. We had lots of water today so we decided to run the monitor and ground sluice. I went over to Oro Grande this evening and did some work for Dieter and Andy, helped pull their backhoe up the hill to their mining area on Oro Grande.

May 22nd. We're running a lot of garbage through the box, but it has to be done as it's part of the old dam site. It was nice out today. I took the Cat over to Dieter's and fixed things up for him and Andy, graded the road up the hill. We went into town and got our motorhome, got as far as Oro Grande Gulch. Marcene drove the motorhome across Eldorado Creek and up to Oro Grande. The battery cable came off between Archibald's and Keach's going up the hill. Marcene says it seems like every time she tries to drive it in something happens to it, but that's the way it goes. We spent the night in the motorhome and we'll tow it up the hill tomorrow. This morning Ron said they may work our first claim next year.

May 23rd. Rick towed our motorhome up the hill with the Komatsu and I drove on up to camp from the top of the big hill. Rick and I fixed the road across Oro Grande this morning. We had trouble with the dozer, darned brakes heating up again. We ran the monitor 'til about 10 o'clock tonight. The weather was pretty nice today. Marcene went to town to get groceries and fuel.

May 24th. The weather was nice today. First thing this a.m. we picked rocks and then ran the box almost 2 hours. The water got low, so we ate dinner, then went back and ran another hour this p.m. We cleaned the pit up, started the monitor and Marcene and I stayed with it 'til 8 p.m. Rick left early this p.m., not much for him to do and he had to go get his ears flushed out.

May 25th. We spent all day working on the pit, ground sluicing and a little monitoring, and we ran the box some. Rick tells me he's going to Clinton Creek, he doesn't know for sure just when, but no big deal. He'll go over there and do some work on the building that he bought. We'll work something out, no problem. The darned dozer goofed up again today, brakes heated up. I've checked everything and just haven't found the trouble yet.

Sunday, May 27th. We quit sluicing at 7 o'clock and monitored about an hour. I changed the monitor around about 3 or 4 times before retiring. We set by our fire tonight, sure was relaxing.

May 28th. Our hose for the Komatsu didn't get in, so I went down to Andy's and made up a hose, kind of "Joe McGee'd" it, but it works and got us back in business. We started sluicing at 5:15 p.m. and ran 'til 9:15. Rick went home and Marcene and I ran the monitor until 11 p.m.

Wednesday, May 30th. The riffles looked pretty good today, we're back in the old creekbed. Whiskey jacks, the birds called "camp robbers", are eating out of my hand now and I saw rabbits for the first time today. The weather's cold, cloudy and windy. Rick took the pickup in to get fuel and parts. I'm going to tell Rick tomorrow that we'll pay him $10 an hour and he can have plenty of time off to build his house, etc. That's what he wants, to work part time for us and then take care of all his other things he's got going, so that's fine and dandy with us, no problem. Don and Sue Murphy came by to see us this morning, and Red was up. He's gonna work for them this summer, I think.

May 31st. I saw my first black bear of the season tonight, about 50 yards from camp. He stood up, looked around, and took off up the hill. The birds are eating out of Marcene's hands now too. The Johnson boys are busy ground sluicing, they haven't gotten their plant started up yet. They're just down the creek below us.

June 1st. Our riffles look good today, we're working the center of the creek and washing the sides in with the monitor. Marcene went to town today, got lots of nice flowers and plants, cucumbers, tomatoes, squash, and other nice things from Joan at the Farmer's Market.

June 2nd. Ron and Bernie undermined our road with their big monitor and had to build a road around the area down below us. We transplanted the strawberries today at noon, and I set out marigolds. I think I'll plant potatoes tomorrow, and we still have to put in radishes, onions and lettuce. We ran the monitor from 5:30 to midnight.

Sunday, June 3rd. The whiskey jacks are moving in on us, taking over. One of the birds squawked and flopped his wings for something to eat. He also went into the kitchen and sat on the table. Marcene and I cleaned up the front 2 sets of riffles, but didn't run it through the wheel. I'll get that tomorrow.

June 4th. We tried to clean the gold that we got in the cleanup we ran yesterday, and boy, did we get a surprise. Lead! Out of those old Cat batteries that Keach had thrown in the creek up above us. You cannot do anything with gold with lead in it because if you get it hot, or try to melt it, it will all run together and then the refinery charges you a big sum for separating it. So what you got to do is hand pick every little piece of that lead out of the gold concentrates. Also, we ran into an old cobbler's keg of shoe tacks and had those shoe tacks in the cleanup along with lead. We found the keg when we were monitoring, but the tacks had spilled out of the keg somewhere along the line. Anyway, between the lead and the tacks we had something else with this cleanup.

Sue Murphy and Lynn came up this evening to invite us to their picnic the 21st of June. We're just about out of fuel in the Cat and loader, so we gotta get some more. We put all the plants in the hothouse and will leave them in there 'til it warms up a bit.

June 5th. Rick didn't work today. We ran the box 4 hours, Marcene working the shaker. We ran the monitor this a.m. washing down the hill to find a leak in the water line. I found the trouble, it was under a bunch of material piled up in the old dam, a leaky cap, and I fixed the leak. We're still getting that stupid lead out of our riffles, so it's just gonna be a mess until we finally clean it all out. White Pass delivered 500 gallons of diesel this afternoon and that saved our day.

June 6th. The weather was nice and warm and sunny. I built a road and platform to move our light plant, and did work on our road where the Johnson boys are working. We ran the monitor 10 hours, until we ran out of water, or didn't have enough to work with, about 8:30 p.m. Rick was off today.

June 7th. The box ran 5-1/2 hours today. We're in fair ground and we have about 20 ounces of gold to take in to the bank tomorrow. Marcene was cleaning gold all day, she sure is a great help. Our weather was real nice today. I put swinging flower pots on the archway for some of the flowers that Marcene got from Joan.

Friday, June 8th. We took our first shipment of gold to the bank today.

June 9th. We're having some problems with the light plant, it's the 110 side, and I think fuses will probably take care of it. Rick's a good hand, but he doesn't like to work the shaker or box, he likes to run the loader. So that leaves Marcene and me to work the box, but that's alright.

June 10th. We ran the monitor a couple of hours this morning. We had plenty of water today and the weather was beautiful. Rick got fuses in Dawson last night and we fixed the burned wire and got the light plant going. The tracks are getting pretty sloppy on the loader, but I can't do anything about it until the sprockets we bought come in.

June 11th. Don and Spot, a couple of musicians, came up to camp and spent the night. They seemed like nice people, they're playing music at the Downtowner.

June 12th. A guy from the Labor Board came by today and everything's okay. Marcene is learning to run the dozer pushing tailings. I graded our road all the way to Oro Grande. The riffles looked good today.

June 13th. Dieter came by for a short visit while waiting on water in Oro Grande. And Robert Trustwell came by this afternoon. I sure need to get my sprockets for the loader, I got other parts for the undercarriage. We went into Dawson this evening looking for a rubber tired loader, instead of the track loader we're using, because the tracks are so bad. We started the 2 front riffles cleanup this evening.

June 14th. We finished our cleanup today and I worked on our road tonight. Marcene worked the shaker and hopper real good today, the best that anyone has worked it. Too bad that Rick can't think enough to work it better than he does. I'm using the spring below the dam to ground sluice. I stopped by to see John Waite about leasing his 920 Cat loader, but he's gonna use it he says. I sure hope we get the new sprockets for the loader tomorrow. We got sandwiches at the Downtown Restaurant and had drinks with Lou.

June 15th. The riffles look good today, we're back in the pay slot. Marcene went to town today and our sprockets didn't come in. We didn't get another pickkup and no luck on the loader. The only good news is our daughter Jadene was accepted into the nursing program at Austin Peay University in Clarksville, Tennessee. I cleaned out the ramp and built a new one for the shaker, should get it moved tomorrow.

Saturday, June 16th. Rick worked 7 hours today. The box didn't run. We cleaned the box, moved the shaker plant and box, and hooked up the water. I did some ground sluicing. It was sunny and very hot today.

June 17th. The weather was real nice today, in the 70s and sunny. We got the light plant moved and hooked up, also got the bulkhead and ramps in, so we'll start sluicing tomorrow. A 3-inch hose came off the shaker plant this evening as we turned the water on and I got a cold shower without the soap in about 34 degree water. Tonight I took a real shower and it sure felt good. I went up the creek late today and muddied it up above the dam, so it may plug up some of our "little pisser" leaks. We finished a cleanup and it looked okay. Rick just put in time today, he seems to have his mind someplace else. It's sure nice out tonight sitting around the fire.

June 18th. Our water's starting to slow down as it's getting warmer. The riffles looked good this afternoon. We picked about 3 ounces of gold out of the front riffles. The new location of our shaker plant sure makes it easier on the loader. Iris and Cass came up to visit us tonight, they're sure nice people. I welded the rakes up this evening.

June 19th. Marcene is getting better on the dozer. The plant's working okay and the weather is fine. I picked up a roll of Davis Fowler's pipehose, and we'll tell him about it when he comes over. I started pumping water back up from some springs below the dam with a 2-inch pump, saving all the water I can. I know it will probably make some difference in our sluicing. Bud Harrington, with Finning Company, the Caterpillar company, came by. They want us to take a 920 loader and trade in the Komatsu. I'm just waiting 'til Finning's mechanic gets up here and appraises the loader, we'll see what happens. A rubber tired loader in the creek and water would be a lot better.

June 20th. It was hot today. We ran the monitor 3-1/2 hours using the 2-inch pump to return water from the springs back up to the dam. Everything's going fine except for a few leaks in the pipe. I spooned about 2-1/2 ounces from the front riffles this p.m. Frank Short came up for a visit tonight.

June 21st. There's definitely something wrong with Rick. I'm sure he's having problems with his girl friend, but there's something else wrong because he's just not with it. We cleaned up the first 2 sets of riffles and it turned out good. We got about 15 ounces for 11 hours running. Tonight we went to Don and Sue's party and it was a good one. Davis brought us 2 tires for the motorhome, 2 rakes, and liquid steel. He gave me the 6-inch canvas hose down at his shaker, said to go ahead and take it all.

June 22nd. We monitored a little this morning, did a little dozing, and went in to check on buying a pickup from a guy in Williams Lake, B.C. Bud Saylers wrote a letter saying they would be over July 22nd for 4 or 5 days. Marlene and Bill McNabb are coming over next week. The Finning mechanic came out today to check out my loader regarding trading it for the 920. Their salesman should be out tomorrow to let me know how much they'll give me as trade-in for mine.

Saturday, June 23rd. Davis came by for a visit this a.m. and I went over to pick up the canvas hose. The weather was hot and sunny today and the water sure is slowing down. Our riffles looked good, we spooned 3-1/2 ounces from the front 4 riffles.

June 24th. We found some nice nuggets in the front riffles today. Bob Cummings and Raymond Forsythe came up today from

Norcan, in Whitehorse. They're supposed to get our pickup fixed, or lease us the new one that they drove up.

June 25th. I worked on the road between Eldorado Creek and our camp for 5 hours today. We found a large mastodon tusk while we were monitoring in the pit this p.m. I told Andy and Zalato that Keach was going to mine on the property that the two of them had stripped. I don't think Andy believed what I was telling him. He and Zalato came up to see us down in the pit this evening and they were mad. They're going to get Keach off the claim they say. This ground was owned by Dieter and they had some kind of a deal with Dieter, a percentage.

Wednesday, June 27th. We changed the sprockets on the loader today, took us about an hour. It rained this p.m.

June 28th. Bill and Marlene are in camp and we enjoy having them. The riffles look good, we're in the slot for sure, the old ancient creekbed. Marcene handed her rake to Marlene, and she said, "How do you lift this thing?" We had nice steaks for supper tonight.

Sunday, July 1st. Bill and I went down to Ron's to pick up a barrel of oil for the road in front of camp to keep the dust down. Marlene is getting material and running it through the Denver panner, and she's having a ball.

July 2nd. Marlene did good today. She filled her little bottle with gold, so evidently that's one ounce she's gotten already. The 4-wheeler sure is nice.

July 3rd. It was hot and sunny today. We went to Dawson City this afternoon and ordered spare rails, sprockets and rollers, and pad bolts for the Komatsu. Marlene and Bill left today, we sure hated to see them go back to Anchorage.

July 4th. Marcene caught the plane to go to Anchorage today and I miss her already. Larry Moore, with the RCMP, came up tonight for about a 30-minute visit. He said that he was gonna sic Immigration on Don Keach as soon as the holiday is over.

Friday, July 6th. The price of gold is $349, down somewhat. I sure miss Marcene, she's a big help around camp. I think I'm tired and I'll go to bed.

July 7th. The weather was rainy this a.m. and clear this p.m. Don and Sandy Keach came up and brought the panning machine back that I'd loaned him. Raymond Forsythe brought me an '83 Ford pickup and got Norcan's GMC crew cab. I gave him a $1000 check for one month's rent and signed a lease purchase for the '83 Ford. Then Ron and Jackie came up to check on me this p.m., and Clarence and his wife came up and set by the fire 'til 11:45.

A little on the light side: Jackie went to the fifth-wheel to "use the washroom" and fixed herself a stout drink of tequila. She did it 3 or 4 times and each time she brought back a glass that I thought had water in it, but after they left I tasted a little that she left in the glass, and it was very strong, it was tequila. I had given them 2 beers, but Jackie gave hers to Ron.

Earlier, I'd been setting out by the fire, had my old miner's hat on, and a little squirrel crawled up on my hat and looked all around. I had a drink setting on a big block of wood, a cut from a log, and the little squirrel crawled down my right sleeve and tried to get his little nose down into the drink, but he couldn't quite reach it. So I figured, well, I'll give him a chance. I went in and filled the glass, brought it back out and set it down. I sat there about 5 minutes and here he came back. He did the same thing, he climbed around my hat, down my arm, and stuck his nose in that drink and this time got him a good slug of it. Boy, he jumped off and started barking, and bounced over onto a spruce tree about 20 feet away. He no sooner got over on the spruce tree and he came right back and got him another slug of the drink, and he did the same thing. The third time he came over there, boy, he took off down the road running sideways. I've often wondered what happened to that little dude.

Sunday, July 8th. The Customs guys came by today, checked my paperwork and everything's okay. I'm pushing material to the monitor and right down the slot. It's called ground sluicing and it's okay that we do that now, but I can see the handwriting on the wall, it won't be much longer over here.

The Customs Agents asked if I had plenty of water and I said I did. They said it was too bad that Mr. Keach is shut down because of not enough water. I said that Don was working every day on Oro Grande. The agents said they'd better check out Mr. Keach. He's supposed to be working on Eldorado Creek, so they said they were going over to check if he has work permits for Dieter's claims on Oro Grande. So maybe Mr. Keach is short for this country.

I found out after, that Keach was given 30 minutes to get his stuff together and leave the country, and not come back in for 7 years. I don't get mad, I get even.

July 9th. The Mounties came up tonight and gave me a note to call Marcene. I went in and called, and Dr. McGuire had paid off our house there on the lake. I was on my way to town to call Marcene, and when I got down to Archibald brothers' place at French Gulch I happened to think that our phone number is unlisted in Anchorage. Marcene had left me the number, but I had forgot and left it at the cabin, so I had to drive back up and pick it up.

July 10th. We got lots of water and I ran the monitor all day. It's 11:15 right now and I'm gonna stop and eat a bite or two, then go ahead and run the monitor all night. We don't get a chance to use water 24 hours a day very often around here. Marcene is going to bring Jadene back when she comes from Anchorage. The guy with Finning came up and checked my sprockets and tracks on the Komatsu. What I'm doing is I'm ordering a set of Caterpillar tracks for the Komatsu that would normally fit a D3 dozer. That's extended, it's 2 extra pads more than the Caterpillar has to fit the Komatsu.

July 11th. Jimmy Webb from Longview, Texas, and his son came in today. It's good to see them. We saw him down in Texas a few winters back and he said that he'd like to come up to visit with us at the mine, so it's good to have him in camp. Marcene and Jadene got in and brought the 4-wheeler.

July 12th. Jimmy and his son are having fun running the Denver panner and so forth. Dennis Brossard came up with a "dipstick" sergeant in the Air Force. He figured Dawson City was a shortcut from Whitehorse to Fairbanks.

Saturday, July 14th. Gold is $560 an ounce. Marcene, Jadene and I went into town and got our pictures taken, the old style photographs. They turned out real good.

July 15th. It rained most of last night and this a.m., but it was nice this p.m. We had lots of water today. Finning is supposed to be out tomorrow regarding the loader tracks. Jadene and I went riding on the 4-wheeler looking for little spruce trees and found 2 nice ones. We're going to take them down to Tennessee this winter in our motorhome and give them to Scott and Jadene. We went down to Murphy's tonight to eat salmon barbeque.

July 16th. Jim Webb and his son Kim are still in camp today. They gave Rick and me a hand on the loader tracks. I had to take a pad out of each side until our rails and stuff get in. That way, the tracks will stay on and they won't be quite so sloppy. Kim and Jim got enough gold to make 2 lockets, about a quarter of an ounce each, just hauling material up on the little 4-wheeler and running it through the Denver panner.

July 17th. We got lots of water so I ground sluiced and monitored 'til noon. It was awful foggy out this morning, but nice later on in the day. The loader operates much better since we took a pad out of each track. We should have new ones Friday, but I'll run these as long as they hold together. We went into town tonight and looked at old buildings on a lot down there that belong to a guy in Washington. They sure are a mess. We've offered $10,000 for them and we're going to wait and see what happens. Kim and Jim Webb are going to drive into Anchorage and take Jadene along with them, and that's good.

July 19th. We've got plenty of water and everything is going fine sluice-wise and monitoring. We have strawberries on some of the plants. We paid for our cabin logs at Bill Bowie's sawmill. It's a little too wet for him to deliver them, so as soon as it dries out we'll have our logs and be ready to get started on the cabin. They're de-have our logs and be ready to get started on the cabin. They're demolishing the old buildings in Dawson that we were trying to buy. It was 2 lots, and it was an old blacksmith's shop that had a whole bunch of antiques and stuff, and an old cigar store. They dated back to the gold strike era. We sure wanted to get them, but the city condemned the buildings. They're tearing them down and hauling them to the dump. Marcene helped me put the track back on the Komatsu today, I got it off on a rock down in the pit. She's sure helpful that way.

Saturday, July 21st. Rick worked 'til noon, he works for us part time. By the way, he's building a nice home up on a hill overlooking Dawson and the Yukon River. The weather today is just icky, but the riffles looked good.

July 22nd. Bud Saylers and all his clan came to camp today, 2 boys, Bud and his new wife, and his mother-in-law. We worked on the 4-wheeler for 3 hours, thanks to our last guest Jim Webb, but anyway, that's alright. It had water and trash in the tank, so we had to pull the tank off and drain it. Bud gave me a hand.

July 23rd. We had staked 3 claims on Stampede Creek just to protect Big Red, so no one else would get in there above his claims. I did the assessment work on them ahead for 5 years. We gave those claims to Red and he just couldn't get over it. He couldn't understand why someone would give him three 40-acre mining claims. Bud and his crew went into Dawson tonight. They'd been panning and running a little sluice box all day. Bud's mother-in-law said, "I laundered rocks all day and I didn't get a thing." So Marcene took her over to the motorhome and gave her some nuggets, and she was just thrilled to death.

July 24th. Blackie, a friend of Bud's from Juneau, said that he sure would like to have clear water to do panning with. The nerve that some people have! They come over here and got good ground to pan, and then want me to hold up on my mining so he can pan in clear water. We had thunder and lightning this evening and it rained. The riffles looked good today.

July 25th. We had the first potatoes from our garden and we've got lots of lettuce, onions, radishes, and our first strawberry to get ripe today. The weather's real nice out. The riffles didn't look too bad, we picked out about an ounce at noon. Bud and his troop left this a.m. They sure left the motorhome in a mess. They left a water leak in there that I don't know how they could have missed. The floor was all wet and water was dripping out of the motorhome when we went over to check on it, so I knew that they had to know it was leaking. We ran the monitor 3 hours tonight, had lots of water, it sure was nice. Bill Bowie brought our logs up, 3-sided ones, enough to build a 16 x 24 cabin.

Friday, July 27th. We cleaned up the front 2 sets of riffles today and went into Dawson for the Miners' Barbeque tonight. We heard that when the Customs Agents went over to see Don Keach, they checked him out and he didn't have a work permit to work on Oro Grande, Dieter's claim up there. They gave him his walking papers, gave him 30 minutes to get out and head down the road. They put a tag on his pickup, he was driving illegal, and told him he would have to stop in Whitehorse and make arrangements to pay his fine. He even left clothes in the old wringer-washer setting in the yard at the cabin, so Don Keach was definitely in a hurry. He didn't stop to pay the fine, so they've got him in their computer nowadays.

July 28th. John Wallace came over tonight and went up to where Keach's equipment was. He took a 6-inch diesel pump that Jack Hendricks in Anchorage owned and loaded it on a truck. He conned Klondike Transport's loader operator to go up the hill and bring it down to the road. He even took a fuel tank with 1000 gallons of diesel fuel in it, loaded them on his flatbed truck and away he went.

July 29th. Rick helped me tear down the Gay Gulch Hilton and I'm really glad to get it down and out of the way. That's the old plastic kitchen that we've had around here for the last couple of years. Don Keach and Jim Vail built it and I'm glad to get rid of it. Rick and I put rollers underneath the Komatsu, getting ready for the rails and idlers.

July 30th. Finning's truck brought the tracks and sprockets this a.m., we should get the Komatsu all back together and going by noon tomorrow.

July 31st. The weather was hot and sunny today. Rick took off at noon, left me and Marcene to put the tracks back on the loader. He didn't say a word when he left, just hopped on his motorcycle and took off down the road.

August 1st. I talked to Rick today regarding transferring the claims on the Klondike Highway, and he agreed to transfer all of them but 2 claims, he was going to keep those 2 for himself. I wasn't aware of that.

August 2nd. The new Cat tracks are working real good on the Komatsu loader. Marcene and I picked raspberries today and Sue said that she'd make a pie for us if we'd bring the berries down. I hauled tailings to go underneath our log cabin.

Saturday, August 4th. I got strawberries from the garden today. The squirrels aren't getting them this summer after I put chicken wire around them.

August 5th. It rained last night and this morning, and we kind of slept in today. I filled a big bezel with gold for Maria and it sure looked nice. The reason I gave Maria this locket was because they let us park our motorhome on their lot this spring and use their electricity. She's done us a lot of favors.

August 6th. The Case 450 dozer started making a funny noise, sounds like a piston, or a valve, or maybe a valve spring. I took the cowl off, etc., so a mechanic could go right to it when he gets here.

August 7th. I picked rocks off our road this a.m. I go along with a little 4-wheeler and pick up rocks of any size and throw them out of the road. Marcene went to town and tried to get a mechanic, but didn't have any luck. She called the Case people in Fort St. John, but no soap there. I took the hood and valve cover off, the push rods are okay and also the valve springs, so it must be something inside. I used the loader for hauling tailings and also hauling material to the shaker plant as the dozer's down. The riffles looked fair today. We peeled 10 more logs this evening. Our plyboard should be here tomorrow.

August 8th. Big Red came up this evening and we checked out the trouble on the dozer. I was surprised that it was only a valve adjuster had stripped threads. So Red and I "Joe McGee'd" it and the dozer runs fine now. Marcene went in to tell Finning not to come out, that we got it fixed. I pushed tailings and was getting the pit and ramp ready, and I saw Marcene waving. I thought she was just waving at me because it was so hot and I didn't pay her any mind. I was just about through anyway, but on the last pass up the ramp, I saw blood on her arm and I shut down the dozer and ran over. She had gone over a 24-foot embankment with the 4-wheeler, backwards, and the machine rocked over on her. The poor thing was skinned up pretty bad and bruised. I sure felt sorry for her. I thought she'd lost her watch, so I raked with a rake down there for an hour or so, and then I saw her come to the top of the bank swinging the watch, letting me know she had found it. She had taken it off and left it in the fifth-wheel. Anyway, she's gonna be sore for awhile.

August 9th. Marcene's feeling better today, but she's still sore. I ran the box this morning and pushed tailings getting ready for tomorrow. I pushed up about 2 hours worth of ground. This evening I peeled logs.

August 10th. I peeled logs and sawed off floor joists for our cabin today, also set the stringers. Cass and Iris came up tonight, he said that he'd give me a hand working on the shaker until Marcene gets able to work. I think that will be about freeze-up. Maria invited us for supper Sunday night and we'll find out if Mike and Pasquale can help me on the log house.

Saturday, August 11th. Cass is working the shaker plant and does it well, the best I've seen other than Marcene, of course she does good. The gold looked good. Well, Marcene's slowly improving, but darn it, I sprained my good ankle today. We went into Dawson this afternoon and picked up plyboard, paint and brushes at Frontier Trucking. I squared up the cabin base and put down 8 sheets of plyboard flooring tonight.

August 12th. We had the first ice of the season in the sluice box and water at the dam, and most of the day it was cold. The frost got our squash last night, but we'd covered the tomatoes and flowers and stuff, so they're okay. The bank slid into the pit last night, so we're having to clean all that up this morning. Cass worked the shaker 4 hours today. He helped me put siding back on the motorhome that I had to take off in order to repair the water leak from when Bud Saylers and crew were here. We went down and had supper tonight with Maria and Andy, and we're supposed to go to a party tomorrow night for Pasquale and Mike. Mike's her brother.

Wednesday, August 15th. We had our 35th wedding anniversary yesterday, and last night had lots of our friends come by. We went by Diamond Tooth Gertie's and gambled a bit afterwards. Ron Johnson came by last night, he said that they would be interested in working our first claim, the one adjoining the ones that they're working. I goofed up today, I let the Komatsu loader run out of fuel, so that gave me about an hour's downtime. I talked with Mr. Mulatto, at the Case Company in Racine, Wisconsin, this morning and it looks like I'll get some results regarding the brakes and engine on the dozer. I tried to talk with the president of J.I. Case, a Mr. Greene, but he was out and I couldn't talk to him, so we'll wait and see what happens.

August 16th. Cass is still working with us, he's a good hand. Gary is a young lad from town who's up visiting with us in camp. He helped me peel logs and also worked the shaker while Cass was pushing tailings with the Cat. We got 4 good sized nuggets today. We're working in the middle of where the old timers worked and we're still getting good gold. I sure wish we could have gotten in this creek before anyone else.

Saturday, August 18th. Ron, Jackie, Bernie, Stan and Bunny came up tonight, it was quarter to one when Ron, Jackie and Bernie left. We had real nice weather today.

August 19th. Marcene and I ran the monitor today and washed for 3 hours. We got most of the material that slid off in the pit cleaned up and we're almost back to normal there. We worked on the log cabin quite a bit today.

August 20th. The price of gold's like a yo-yo, today it's $344 an ounce. We went to Rock Creek this evening and I got my chain saw fixed. I now have almost 6 rungs of logs up on the cabin, it sure makes it faster with the chain saw working right.

August 21st. Cass is still working with us. We got a little more done on our log cabin today. The weather is nice, not too cold last night, heavy dew but no frost. The riffles looked good today. I'm going to monitor tomorrow and won't run the box 'til Thursday. We have more water this year than last.

August 22nd. I called the Case dealer in Fort St. John tonight and I think he's going to try to do something about my Case 450 dozer yet. We did some more work on the cabin today, got most of the 9 rungs of logs up, got 2 doors cut in.

August 23rd. Don and Spot came up today and brought a little dredge they set up by the big rocks. I had to take the little engine off the 2-inch pump and put a new one back on. I think it's the gas that's doing damage, they carbon up so bad they just quit running. I got a few more logs up today on the cabin. The weather was cloudy and icky, drizzle off and on all day.

August 24th. Clarence Ablegard and his wife, and friends from Minnesota came up to visit today. Abe took us to supper at the Triple J in Dawson, Chinese food, and it was good. We called Jadene this p.m. and they're okay. I called the Case distributor in Fort St. John. They're coming up in 2 weeks to check out the 450 dozer. We visited awhile this evening with Norm Summers, he's still the same grinning Norm. We put up some more logs today on the cabin, only have 2 more rungs before the ridge poles, then decking and the roof.

Sunday, August 26th. Big Red came by and said he's sold the big pump that I'd given him, to Greg Hackinson. There will be some guys up this evening to pick it up. We got some more logs up on the cabin, we lack just one more rung now. We went into Dawson to check with Andy regarding windows for our cabin, but he wasn't at the station. I guess he was over at Clinton Creek. We had the first snowflakes of the fall this evening.

August 27th. We had lots of snow this morning. A little bear came through camp, he just walked on by like nothing was happening here. He just walked right on through camp as if he owned the place, knew where he was going and hooked it right on up the creek. We didn't run the box today. The weather was cold out. I'll bet that little dredge Don and Spot set up freezes up, but it's none of my concern, they should think about those things. I checked on a 980 loader to haul out the tailings and it rents for $85 an hour. It would take about 12 ounces of gold to do what I want to do here at camp and also the assessment work on the Klondike Highway claims. It's still snowing tonight at 7:30, the first real snow of fall. The highway to Alaska is the Taylor Highway, but everyone calls it the Top of the World Highway. It was closed today due to 6 inches of snow and drifts.

August 28th. We didn't run the box again today, it was too miserable, snow and freezing. We ran the monitor about an hour and a half, maybe we'll get to sluice tomorrow. We went to Dawson to pick up our windows and 2 doors from Andy, $65 each. I had to buy a lock for one door and a doorknob. The windows have screens, and I think the total of $399 was a pretty good deal. Zalota and his brother gave me some concentrates to run through the gold wheel. I drained all the lines this p.m., it's still snowing out and 30 degrees. I just hope we have a week or so of nice weather for finishing the cabin, and we'd like to sluice at lease 10 more hours.

August 29th. We didn't run the box today. It was snowing hard this a.m., we had about 6 inches of snow on the ground. We slept in, but finally got off for Dawson to do our wash. We saw Bingo Bill in town and he's gonna give us a hand putting up the ridge poles on the cabin. He's gonna charge us $10 an hour and that's fair. I did a little more work on our cabin this evening and peeled 3 more logs. I think I have almost enough logs peeled to finish the cabin. When we were in Dawson we saw Jackie. She said that they would come up to talk to us about wanting to work the claims next year. Rick and Sandy came up this p.m. for a visit.

August 30th. Bingo Bill is helping us out, working the shaker, etc. and the riffles looked fair today. The weather sure was miserable though, snow, rain, sun, but very little sun. I guess it's about time to shut'er down for the winter. My little pump is still acting up, I guess it's stuck rings. I didn't drain the pipes, etc. this afternoon, I don't think we'll have a hard freeze tonight. Don and Spot came up and got their little dredge today. Bill helped me put up some logs after dinner. We got the last rungs up on the cabin, now we just need to tie them down with big spikes and we'll be ready for our ridge poles.

August 31st. Today it was sunny and warm. I hope to clean up the box tomorrow afternoon and run the material through the Denver panner Monday. I drained the lower end of the pipeline today just in case it freezes hard tonight. Marcene went into town this morning and got me some big spikes for the top logs on the cabin. Most of the logs we have left we'll use to build a greenhouse.

Saturday, September 1st. Bingo Bill helped me set ridge poles on the cabin today first thing when he hit camp. This is our last day of sluicing for this season, we have to finish the cabin and get buckled up. We should get everything wrapped up in a couple weeks. The riffles looked real good, so we'll have good ground to start next year.

September 2nd. The logs have mildew on them. They laid out and got wet in the rain, so now we're having to clean them up with Clorox on a rag. We drove into Dawson for the Outhouse Races. We saw Mike and Connie Hayden from Anchorage, they're looking for some ground over here in the Dawson area.

September 3rd. Bingo Bill and I worked on putting ridge and end poles up on the cabin, and tomorrow I'm gonna go in and get the 1 x 12 decking for under the roof. Marcene and I bleached 2 more of the round logs, those are the ridge poles. We'll get the cabin up, it just takes patience. I spent about 1 hour pushing dirt for next season.

September 4th. We're just bull cookin' around, putting things away for the winter. We'll have a day to move the conex (shipping container) and steel from Davis Fowler's. It looks like 2 or 3 more days to finish the cabin, except the windows and doors.

September 5th. We got along good on the cabin today, got all the roof decking down and we'll put the tin roofing on tomorrow. I cleaned Zalota's gold today and he sure didn't have much. I had rather had him here when I cleaned it, but he said, "I trust you, go ahead and clean it." So I guess it's okay.

September 6th. It was raining all day. I nailed the roof decking this a.m. and hauled some tailings to the cabin. We drove to town and I called Ted Mills at the Case Company in Fort St. John. He's coming up, leaving tomorrow, to work on the Case dozer. Frank Parmitter and his wife came up to see us today, they're sure nice people and we enjoyed their visit. They're from Anchorage originally. It was still raining, misting, this evening, so I just thought I'd wait 'til tomorrow to work on the cabin, to put the rest of the tin on the roof.

Saturday, September 8th. Sewell and Mills, with Northwest Tractor in Fort St. John, came up this a.m. and fixed my Case 450 dozer, fixed the brakes and fixed the valve adjusters. Marcene and I put down insulation and finished the floor in the cabin today.

September 9th. We moved the conex up to camp from down where Davis had it parked, also brought an 8 x 20 foot sheet of steel up here. The weather was nice today. We went to the Miners' Gold Panning Steak Supper. It was nice and there was music. We sat at a table with Maria and Andy, Mike and Pasquale, Ron and Jackie, and Jim Archibald and his girl friend.

September 10th. We're just tightening up loose ends around camp here. Bingo and I hung one door and cleaned out the conex. Sam Bowman and his wife came up to see us this afternoon. Stan and Bunny came by tonight, their last visit of the season. We should get everything done by about Wednesday. It was clear and cold today, but nice this afternoon.

September 11th. We got settled up with Bingo Bill today and we're busy getting ready to go. We took the motorhome into Dawson and parked it at Andy's and Maria's, and ate supper at the Eldorado Restaurant tonight.

September 12th. We went up to the mine this a.m., painted the floor in the cabin and I put on a doorknob. I ground sluiced awhile and then covered the light plant. We came back to Dawson City this p.m. and flew out with Lou Provonovich and Bernie Gagnon in a helicopter to check out claims on Brown Creek. The ground looks good where we panned, so I'll call Mike Hayden and let him know about it. The weather is slowly closing in, it's frosty and clear out. I told Bill Bowie at the lumber company that he could have the old conveyor belt up at our place, so he's gonna go out this evening and check it out. We brought Don Frizzel's loader home today. We made a deal with Don where I gave him a snow machine engine, or a big part of one, and he let me use his loader for our claims on the Klondike Highway. Don was manager of White Pass Services in the Dawson district.

September 13th. I called Mike Hayden this a.m. and he's interested in Bernie's and Louie's claims on Brown Creek. Then we went up to the mine, finished putting a knob and lock on the cabin door, put things away, and Marcene finished painting the floor. We got a bale of straw and covered our strawberries. The camp sure looks good without the old Gay Gulch Hilton plastic shack Don Keach left up there. I greased the pickup and motorhome this evening, and we went out to the homestead of Joan and George. They're our friends who own the Farmer's Market. It sure was nice out there.

September 14th. I took Don's backhoe out and dug a trench on our claims on the Klondike Highway today. We still have some work to do there next spring. We went up to the mine and finally got everything tucked away. I talked to Ron this p.m. and they're gonna ground sluice another 2 or 3 weeks, depending on the weather. We took 6 baskets of strawberries down to Murphys to put in their underground tunnel, the one in back of their place. I put brake fluid in the motorhome this evening and patched up the muffler pipe.

Saturday, September 15th. We went to Diamond Tooth Gertie's last night, as usual our last night in Dawson for the season. We ate breakfast at the Downtown this a.m. with Don and Spot, and a couple from Palmer, Alaska. We got away about 11 a.m., got out to about Rock Creek, and picked up a guy. He drove our pickup to Whitehorse, and it was funny. He'd been prospecting all summer and had buried some of his belongings down on the hill just as you go into Whitehorse. I had told him we were going in to Norcan Leasing up on top of the hill. So just before we got into town, he got around us and went on down the hill, I couldn't figure out where he was going. He turned off to the right and went in a ways and I thought, well, he's just going to the bathroom. He came back out and I asked him what he was doing back in there. He said, "I dug up my winter gear for going south and buried my prospecting gear." What he did was he wrapped everything in plastic and dug a hole in the sandbank. He said that way it's thawed when he comes back up in the spring and in the fall, of course, it's not frozen yet so there's no problem digging in the sand. We parked the motorhome on Norcan's lot and will go on to Anchorage in our pickup tomorrow. We had no problems coming down from Dawson City today.

September 16th. We left Whitehorse this morning and got into Anchorage tonight about 10 o'clock.

September 17th. We spent all day running around, took the 4-wheeler to Arctic Rec, ate breakfast at the Fork and Spoon, saw Davis, Larry, and Gene Fowler, and had supper at La Mex. We went by to see Buzz Hoffman and yes, we checked at First National Bank. We got paid on the property on New Seward Highway, $30,000, so I guess we'll get us a new rubber tired loader. The weather was warm, more like summer than fall. I went by Craig Taylor's and asked about the Briggs & Stratton engine, etc. and checked on the little pump.

September 18th. Gold is $340 an ounce today.

September 19th. I met Danny Thomas at the Fork and Spoon this a.m. and paid Davis the $100 that I'd borrowed from him on Monday morning. Ken Hinchey, ex-Mayor of Anchorage and former owner of Alaska Aggregate, Marcene and I got to talking Sunday night at the Peanut Farm, about mining and all that stuff, and I offered to buy him breakfast the next morning to tell him about some property around Nome. So we met at the Fork and Spoon Restaurant on Old Seward Highway. When we got finished and I got ready to pay up I reached for my billfold, but didn't have it in my pocket. I looked at him and said, "You know something, I don't have my billfold. I'm sorry, but I don't have it." He scratched around and didn't have his either, but I saw Davis in there and borrowed $100 from him to pay the bill 'til I could get back home and get my billfold.

This evening, it thundered and lightninged and rained hard, it's something we used to never have here in the state of Alaska. We tumbled our gold and it looked pretty, but the one batch that we put some green soap in, oh boy, I don't know what we're going to do with that yet. It turned the gold green.

September 20th. We saw a cow and calf moose in our yard this morning and I took pictures, but they didn't turn out all that good. We had lunch with Bob Brinkley, a musician, today at the Barbeque Pit. Tonight we cleaned gold.

September 21st. Gold is $347 an ounce today and silver $7.35. We made reservations to catch the ferry for the 10th of October. Marcene bought a jacket and 2 hats at Brewster's Western Wear Store over in Mountain View and we had a nice visit with the owner, Mr. Brewster. We took Maxine Smith to dinner at the Chef's Inn tonight.

Saturday, September 22nd. Mike Hayden flew us to Dawson City in his plane and we checked out the ground at Brown Creek with Lou and Bernie. Things looked pretty good. Mike is thinking about going on and purchasing their claims. Bernie took me up to our mine to get some concentrates that I'd left there.

September 23rd. We took a rope and worked the ice off the wings of Mike's airplane this morning and left Dawson City about 10 a.m. After a brief rest stop at Crosswind Lake we got into Anchorage about 2 p.m. Tonight Marcene and I ate dinner with Eldon and Mary Brandt. Jim Prochaska came in from commercial fishing and it's so good to see old Jim again.

Monday, October 1st. We went by to see Jack Hendricks this p.m., "Junkie Jack" we call him, he owns a salvage yard in Anchorage. He doesn't seem to care a hoot about the 6-inch diesel pump that John Wallace took from over in Dawson City. That's the one that Don Keach took over there and never paid for it. He said, "Oh, I haven't got time to fool with stuff like that, or be concerned about it." So be it.

Friday, October 5th. Gold is $341 an ounce and silver $7.28. We went to Palmer and filed a Proof of Records at the Recorder's Office regarding claims that we had on Glacier Creek. The lady that waited on us was up from California. She seemed to be a staunch environmentalist and didn't even care if she waited on us miners or not. That's the way this whole state of ours is going now. All the "dippy-doos" come up from California, Chicago, New York, and they're gonna reverse the situation up here, turn everything back into wilderness. Right now there's more property in federal parks and D-2 lands in Alaska than the size of the whole state of California.

We drove on over to Big Lake and looked at property, and saw old friends from snow machine racing days, Jack Helms, Hester and Joe Miller. They were as nice as ever. We stopped by to see Don Cole and he presented us with a bill for over $700. Also, he told us that we couldn't use that money that we got off of the property on New Seward Highway to buy a rubber tired loader for the mine. Later on we found out that was baloney.

Sunday, October 7th. We got back to Whitehorse and drove down to Atlin this p.m. looking at a 920 Caterpillar loader, a rubber tired loader, but the guy had decided not to sell it. He had it leased to the Highway Department.

October 8th. We made a deal for a 1984, 4x4, club cab pickup today, a red and white Ford, for $17,000 Canadian (about $12,000 U.S. funds) and it sure is a nice one.

October 9th. We spent all day waiting to get tires installed on the motorhome. About 4:45 p.m. the "ding-a-ling" mechanic at Norcan told us that he didn't have a socket to take the wheels off. He just didn't want to fool with them and that's that!

October 10th. We left our pickup at Norcan's yard and also left Forsythe's pickup there. We got our tires on the motorhome changed at the Michelin Tire Shop this morning and were on our way to Skagway and outside by 9 o'clock. On the ferry to Prince Rupert we had a nice visit with Oley Lundy from Goldbottom Creek, Dawson mining district.

Monday, October 29th. We stopped in Phoenix to check out a cyanide machine. The manager said if we give him notice of when we'll be back through he'll be glad to run our concentrates and show me how the machine works. They sell for $1500.

Monday, November 12th. We took the little spruce trees over to Scotty today to set out in their yard, the ones that Jadene and I had picked out up at Gay Gulch, put in buckets and hauled all the way back to Ashland City.

1985

Sunday, January 27th, 1985. We stopped by to see Marcene's sister Inez and Lewis, just outside of Austin, between Wimberley and Dripping Springs, Texas, and we gave Inez a bezel of gold. Toni and J.D. Vance have a ranch right across the road from Inez and Lewis. They're going to come up to the mine and see us this coming season and we're looking forward to their visit because they're really nice people.

Saturday, March 2nd. We're in Vancouver, B.C., on our way back up north and Mel Pardek came over to visit us this evening. He offered to take us over to Sears Roebuck Monday morning so we could look for furniture for the cabin on Gay Gulch. We drove all around Vancouver today, talked to Ron and Jackie Johnson, and they're gonna come over tomorrow and take us up on Grouse Mountain for dinner. We presented Ron with his cowboy hat, and both of them a pair of cowboy boots. We gave Jackie a pair of Kenny Rogers boots.

Monday, March 4th. Mel picked us up and took us to Sears Roebuck and we did buy furniture for the cabin. I got the surprise of my life when we were told we'd get it delivered all the way to Dawson City from Vancouver for $35. I couldn't imagine getting anything delivered for $35, even across town. I couldn't figure that out so I talked to the manager. He said, "That's true, every item going north, whether it's a set of tires, a battery, washing machine, or whatever, it's $35 per order." What they do is they wait and get a vanload and then ship it up north to Mayo, Dawson City and Whitehorse. Mel also took us by the Vancouver Stock Exchange today, and that was something to see.

Wednesday, March 6th. We traveled up the highway, left Quesnel this morning and drove to Smithers, B.C. We stopped and ate at Prince George, the food was good. It snowed last night, about 3 inches. The road was okay, but we did find a few ice and frost heaves along the way. We should get in to Prince Rupert tomorrow afternoon.

Friday, March 8th. We caught the ferry and headed for Haines, Alaska.

Sunday, March 10th. We got into Haines about 2 o'clock this afternoon, checked through Canadian Customs and headed up the summit, 8000 feet. It was blowing and snowing, a total whiteout. We drove in the whiteout for about an hour and it sure was nerve wracking. Canadian Customs stopped all small vehicles, only the bigger rigs and 4-wheel drive rigs could go on, and the only way we could see to drive was by the snowplow stakes, the markers. The Mounties were checking along the way, and the Mountie that looked at my driver's license said he could tell by our license numbers, eighty-seven thousand-something, that we'd been in Alaska for a long time. He said, "Well, you've been up in this north country and drove here a lot, so you're probably acquainted with whiteouts. It's okay to go ahead with your big motorhome."

There was a guy behind me from Texas in a 4-wheel drive Ford three-quarter ton. He was being transferred to Alaska. He'd been following me, and the Mountie said to him, "Just follow this gentleman here and I think you'll be alright." So he followed us over the mountain, and when we got down on the other side we stopped at a lodge and the guy pulled in right behind me. I said, "How in the world did you stay so close to me in that whiteout?" He said, "Well, I drove by your running lights up on top." He said that he spun out twice and thought that he'd lose me, but he could see those running lights in the distance, so he kept fighting it and kept coming back, and stayed right on our tail. We got into Whitehorse about 8 p.m. and there was lots of snow.

March 11th. We finished paying for our pickup at Norcan, the '84 Ford three-quarter ton, checked with the Water Board and we're jam-up for this season. We spent the day checking prices for things to go in our cabin. We bought a gas refrigerator and a gas range.

March 12th. We left Whitehorse this morning and drove into Anchorage. The pickup got good gas mileage. We stopped at Glennallen to see an old friend, Saint Amonds, there at the Valdez, Tok, and Anchorage junction. He's the Arctic Cat snow machine dealer at Copper Center.

March 13th. We mailed Bob McKirvey's gold, that's payment for the hose that we picked up last summer and a portion of the sluice box. We're 'bout ready to go mining. Mike Hayden has already shipped his D8 Cat over. The weather was real nice today, sunny and melting.

Friday, March 15th. Andre, a Mountie from Dawson City, called me this morning and wanted to know if I'd given Rick Paridey gold for some payment of work last fall, and I said that I had, it was a bonus. He said, "Well, we just wondered." Rick had sold it to a guy in Timmons, Ontario. The guy was picked up in Timmons on another count and they saw he had gold on him. When they asked him where he got the gold, he said he got it from a guy that had mined in Dawson City. That robbery that we had from our sluice box at Gay Gulch was still in the computer, so they kicked it back to Dawson. Andre called me to check and see if Rick had actually, in fact, gotten that gold from us as a bonus, and sure enough he had.

In fact, they were holding Rick down there in Timmons until they clarified it, but everything worked out alright.

Thursday, March 28th. We went up to Faribanks for the Miners' Meeting and spent the night.

Tuesday, April 2nd. We took 2 nuggets to Peggy Fowler, Davis's daughter. Also, we left a bottle of jewelry gold overlay nuggets to get Sam Scardi's watchband fixed, and 2 diamonds to get set in his watchband. We're gonna take care of that for our old friend Sam, he's helped us so much in the past.

April 3rd. Dave McClure called tonight. He's going to be mining up on Clark Creek out of Kiana along the Kobuk River north of the Arctic Circle. I know the area well and it's good ground.

Monday, April 15th. We left Anchorage this morning and drove to Destruction Bay Lodge where we spent the night. The weather was nice, but the road was full of frost heaves. The native at the border didn't bother us at all, we just didn't talk to her. I think she likes the role of being the boss and important. We got our work permits, no problem.

April 16th. We got back to Whitehorse and picked up items for our cabin. We checked on our furniture from Sears in Vancouver and they got it lost somewhere between Mayo, Faro, and Dawson City, so it'll come up, they'll find it someplace.

Thursday, April 18th. It's good to be back in Dawson. The road up from Whitehorse was mud, snow, sleet, and sun, normal Yukon driving. We saw Pasquale, Mike, and Andy, and found out that Maria'a going to have a baby. How 'bout that! We met some miners from the Sixty Mile country down at Lucerne Lodge and they were real nice. They were telling us about a bear getting into their camp. The bear just tore the windows and doors right out of their cabin. Needless to say, they had to make a trip back to Whitehorse to pick these items up and get ready for the summer mining season.

April 19th. It was very cold last night, but real nice today, thawing a bit and sunny all day. We drove up to see the Johnson brothers and there was lots of snow. I'll have to get snow shoes to walk in. We took George, at Farmer's Market, 2 pairs of overalls that we brought from the States for him. We visited around town, saw Rick's old girl friend, invited Mike and Pasquale to come over tonight. I got a flat fixed at White Pass Service and they didn't even charge, so I tipped Bob $5, he's a nice kid. There were 2 other cabins on the lots we wanted to buy last year in Dawson, and they burned them down. It was such a shame and such a waste of old antiques, there were so many things in them. We had gone into Whitehorse, had our money to purchase the property, but the attorney told us that the owner had gotten in a hurry to sell. This p.m. we went out and visited with Big Red and Colette.

April 20th. There was lots of overflow on Oro Grande Gulch, so we're not going to be able to drive the pickup in for a few days. I walked in on snow shoes and boy, what an experience that was. I fell through the snow and it was up to my armpits. I fell through so many times I lost count and when I got to camp I was just flat give out, so I crawled up on the dozer and sat down on it for awhile, just reared back and relaxed. After resting about 30 minutes I plowed the road to the bottom of the hill with the dozer.

Sunday, April 21st. Our cabin on Gay Gulch sure looked good today when we were up there and we'll be glad to get our furniture into it. Who did we meet on the way to town this afternoon but a little dude we knew from Las Vegas, Steve Laskey. Whoop-de-doo! There was a dude, Tom, that came up with Steve and boy, he's another one. We took them around and down to the Eldorado Hotel, and of all things, they sneaked a great big old dog into the room. Tom had to go to Vegas, so we tried to figure how to get him out. The Top of the World Highway was all drifted in, so he had to take Steve's Bronco and go around by Whitehorse into Fairbanks, and then fly out of Fairbanks to Las Vegas. I had to pay for Steve and Tom at the Eldorado Hotel for another night. Of all things, Steve had a Greenpeace sign on his Bronco.

Tuesday, April 23rd. We went up to the mine today, ripped ice at Oro Grande and got across okay. I started the loader and brought it down to Oro Grande just in case I needed it. Bernie Johnson got back and we talked to him this a.m. He offered to take their D6 up and rip for us. We told him thanks, but we're okay for now. The dam looks okay, I don't think we'll have to mess with much overflow. Tom got off today for Fairbanks driving Steve's Bronco. He's going to leave it at Eddie's, our kind-of-adopted-son in Fairbanks. I gave him $100 just in case he has trouble on the way. Steve and his dog stayed in camp, he says he like it up here. It's sure nice seeing all our friends back in Dawson. Marcene mailed a Milepost magazine to Jadene and Scott today.

April 24th. We picked Bernie Gagnon up this a.m., helped him start his Bobcat and had breakfast with him. We picked up oil and kerosene at White Pass and got water for camp, then we went up to the mine, clearing snow. Steve said he ate only a peanut butter sandwich for breakfast, so I guess he can't cook. He helped me clean snow out of the dam and overflow, and he and I put cutting edges on the dozer. The Oro Grande overflow was okay and we're melting pretty good at the mine, but still have lots of snow. Bernie came by tonight and we helped him write a letter regarding his electricity getting cut off.

Friday, April 26th. When we got up to camp this a.m. Steve told me that he had to go home. It was kind of a shock, but I'm glad, even though we had to take his butt all the way to Fairbanks because his buddy had driven his Bronco up there. I couldn't just put his gear and dog out beside the road. It was nice out here today, but boy, did we hit it after we left Whitehorse going toward Tok. We got to Whitehorse close to midnight and drove on through a blizzard of snow. They'd had about 5 inches of new snow this morning. Steve went to sleep in the back of the pickup with his dog on Marcene's pillow. I asked him 2 or 3 times if he would relieve me driving and he said he couldn't drive a stick shift. The snow was blowing sideways, that was the big reason he didn't want to drive, I think, and he just wanted to sleep. I had never driven in such blizzard conditions for 300 miles. It was snowing so hard that the carburetor filter, etc., froze up on the pickup. I had to stop and chip ice out of the filter of the air breather. We ran out of snow just east of Tok and got to Eddie's in Fairbanks about 11 a.m. Saturday.

We went to Western Union to get Steve some money, but they were closed until Monday. Marcene called the Salvation Army and got Steve a place to spend 2 nights and days. When that character that drove Steve's Bronco to Fairbanks left it at Eddie's the oil was so low it wouldn't even register on the dipstick. Eddie had changed the oil and filter in the Bronco, lubed it, steam cleaned the engine and washed it real nice, had it all cleaned up for him. I'll have to do something nice for Eddie later. That little fart Steve didn't even thank me for going to all that trouble to drive him to Fairbanks, over 1000 miles one way, but that was the only way we could get him there with no plane flights, or buses running.

Sunday, April 28th. We took off this a.m. heading home, and just look at all this old road, all for nothing, it really was a shame. There was no planning, no nothing, Steve just had to pick up and take off. At least you'd think he could have stayed until the ferry went in, but he said he had to go and that was that. This morning, just as we got ready to leave Eddie's, I told little J.D., Eddie's little son, "You should just go back with us to the mine." And the poor little feller ran downstairs, got his boots and his little raincoat and hat and so forth, and came running back up. Eddie told him that he couldn't go with us and big tears come in his eyes. I felt real bad because I had just mentioned that to him and he took it for serious.

April 29th. This morning we got up and went right to Sears' office. They finally found our furniture in Mayo, so Frontier Trucking is going to haul it back to Whitehorse and then on to Dawson City for us at Sears' expense. We talked to a guy at Sears and he offered to send up a duplicate order right directly to Sears in Whitehorse if, for some reason, they didn't find it. He offered to send it out today, but anyway, it was located in Mayo and everything's okay. It was real nice of him.

Wednesday, May 1st. We saw Pierre Monfet this morning and he told us his cabin on Upper Eldorado Creek burned last night.

Saturday, May 4th. We're getting the cabin all finished out. The water is starting to move in the creeks, that's Gay Gulch, Eldorado, and Bonanza.

Monday, May 6th. We got ahold of Marchant, a plumber, today. He and his girl friend went up to our cabin to check out the pipes and fittings, etc., that we need and they're gonna do the plumbing for us. The weather was sunny and warm today, thawing, and about 3 feet of water's on the road above the dredge on Eldorado Creek.

May 7th. We picked up our furniture from Sears today at Frontier Trucking and took it up to camp. Water above dredge #4 was pretty high over the road, but we made it through okay. Dieter wanted us to drive his pickup on up to Oro Grande as he was taking the rubber tired backhoe and loader up to his mine, so we did. He came up this p.m. and helped me unload the hide-a-bed which was a real heavy sucker. I was glad to have him on the other end of it. The weather was pretty good today. Ron and Bern bought a D8K Caterpillar, it's sure nice, it's got a big ripper on the back. Water is starting to work a bit more to thaw the ground. It's nice to be in our new cabin, new bed, couch, hot water heater, cookstove, fridge, cabinets, commode, and the works. It sure beats heck out of the Gay Gulch Hilton, the old plastic shack we started with.

Friday, May 10th. The time is sure slipping by and no sluicing yet. We got 5 inches of new snow out this morning and it sure is pretty. We got our porch deck finished today and it sure looks good.

May 11th. It's snowing again this morning and we slept in. Ron and Jackie came up tonight at 8 and stayed 'til 12:30. They brought Marcene a Mother's Day rose in an old bottle, sure nice of them.

May 12th. It's Mother's Day. A couple we met in Parker, Arizona, last winter came up to see us, but it's entirely too early, they just don't understand. Jim Patton and his wife, Mike and Pasquale, and a few more people came by to see us today. And we met Harry, the poor guy that Keach conned into buying one-half interest in his worthless claim. He came up to meet us. I just don't see how a grown man could be taken in like that, but Keach has got a slick tongue. Someone should skin Keach and hang his hide up on a tree to dry.

Last Tuesday when we were bringing our new furniture up to the cabin, there was a little mini motorhome setting there by dredge #4, and Don Keach was hiding in it. We didn't know that at the time. When the Canadian government kicked Keach out of Canada last summer, he wasn't to come back in for 7 years, but he'd sold the lease on the claim Jimmy Patton owned on Eldorado Creek to this guy for $24,000 and he had to come up from Arizona to show the guy the property. Don really took him, the claim had been all worked out and they just had a little shack on the property. He was hiding from Dieter also, because he owed Dieter gold from working his claims there last summer, and Dieter didn't get his gold. Anyway, after Keach showed the guy the shack and property they went to Dawson City. They went to see Jimmy Patton, Sr. and got him to write up the paperwork. Keach accepted $24,000 from this guy, then immediately went out to the airport and bought a ticket to Fairbanks. Of course there's no problem with that, he's a U.S. citizen and the United States didn't have any squabbles with him, but if he'd of checked through Customs at the border coming into Canada, the Canadians would have nailed him.

He sneaked into Canada in the bathroom of the motorhome. This guy told us that he met Keach in Washington, and when they came across the border he ran into the bathroom and the Customs Agents let the guy go on through. After they got across the border they stopped at a restaurant. Don felt in his pockets and said, "Oh my gosh, I've lost my billfold somewhere." So the guy had to pay his way all the way up to Dawson and then, when they got to Dawson and he gave Don all that money, Don took off. He flew the coop.

May 13th. We stayed in the Eldorado Hotel suite last night and they had a bunch of little bitty bottles in the room, it was stocked with all kinds of goodies and things. We didn't realize it at the time, but this morning when we went to check out, they tallied up all the little bottles, and all the little cans, and all the little things, and boy, it threw us for a loop, it shocked us. We thought those were just compliments of the Eldorado Hotel and Mayor Peter Jenkins.

Wednesday, May 15th. We hooked the little welder up to the thaw cable, the one that Bill McNabb talked us into putting through the pipe under the dam and leaving it there for the winter. We got water through in about 5 minutes. It started moving along pretty good and thawed itself out from there. It took the running water about 2 hours to completely thaw the 8-inch pipe.

May 16th. Looks like we've got the best pit started this summer that we've ever had on Gay Gulch, we're down to the the goodies. Bob Marchant came up today and plumbed propane lights, stove, fridge, and hot water heater. They got here around noon and left around 5, and we fed them lunch. They really got with it. This was the nicest day we've had this year.

May 17th. This morning we discovered that our fuel tank slid off the bank, broke a fitting and lost all our fuel. It's sure thawing at the gulch. We went to the Miners' Meeting tonight, then went to Finning's party, and also Inglehardt's at the Sheffield House. We spent the night in Dawson in our motorhome. We had some folks from California parked by us at Andy's, and they wanted to tie on to our electrical cord, but we refused to let them use it because it was Andy's electric bill and he was doing us a favor.

Saturday, May 18th. This morning we had coffee and toast with John Brown. When we stopped by to see J.C. and Bernie Gagnon we were told that Mike Hayden is having a lot of problems with his D8 over on Brown Creek. I did some ground sluicing on Gay Gulch.

May 19th. We went down and got the Komatsu at Oro Grande and picked 3 loads of rocks. Marcene ran the loader today. Big Red came up and I gave him 2 used sprockets for his John Deere. Bob, a guy who's up here with Harry, the guy that bought one-half interest in Keach's claim, picked up a section of 24-inch sluice box, riffles, and expanded metal that I gave them. Also, some black Astroturf.

May 20th. It rained, sleeted and snowed all last night, and it's sure an icky day. We went down and fixed the shaker bar and fueled the light plant, got antifreeze in it, and we're ready to start tomorrow, except for hooking up electric and the heaters. The Johnson brothers are using their D6 and D8 dozers in the pit right below us.

May 21st. It's our first day of sluicing and we ran 100 yards through. The riffles looked fair, but it's this way cleaning up the pit, etc., each year when you start up. We have lots of water, almost too much. Ron was ripping all day in the ice down there. I graded out our pit last fall and we didn't have ice buildup at all. It's the grade that you leave on the pit that determines the ice buildup.

May 22nd. The riffles looked real good today. It seems as if every time we get in some real good ground something just has to happen to slow us down and boy, the dam went out today. The sandbags that we had for overflow by the pipe gave way. I told Marcene to jump, and about that time the bags all started going. If she hadn't jumped she'd have lost her whole works, her hat, her butt, her everything. Anyway, if Steve Laskey had been here he'd have probably bit the dust because the dam went in about 30 seconds. It's sure nice to be in our nice warm cabin and have propane lights.

May 23rd. We had nice color in the riffles today. We ran 231 yards through the box, but had too much water. The overflow washed out, Don Keach's old pipe underneath the dam just laid down and died, collapsed, broke, sprang a big leak, no more good! We both worked hard today, built the dam back this a.m. and had to go back this evening and build it up higher. We have so much snow melt and runoff I just felt like telling Ron to take the claims tomorrow. You got to be part billy goat to get to where the busted pipe is, let alone take a Cat to it. It will take me about half a day to shovel and pick enough muck to get the old pipe out. The Good Lord didn't mean for man to get gold easy, I guess. Art Fry's grandson came up today looking for a job.

May 24th. Boy, the water was high and muddy crossing Eldorado Creek, water splashed over the top of the pickup hood. We used a piece of carpet, put it under the hood of the pickup and draped it down almost to the ground. We'd drive across the creek and then remove the carpet. I cleared lots of ice out of Oro Grande road crossing this a.m. We rode over to Dieter's camp on Oro Grande and offered Zalota the use of our fifth-wheel while he's mining over there. He thanked us, but said he had a little camper he'd bring up. Dieter is using a $40,000 backhoe and a $25 sluice box. This was the hottest day we've had this season. Boy, it was hot today!

May 25th. We took Bob Marchant and Mia to Dawson and bought them lunch, and Bob came up to camp this afternoon to help me work on the pipeline. They're sure nice people. Red didn't get the fittings fixed yet, so it will probably be another day. The weather was beautiful today. I caled Rob at Norcan in Whitehorse and he's gonna get me 100 feet of 6-inch plastic hose and send it up. Our pit is sure a mess where the overflow has cut down to bedrock. It washed all the good paydirt right on down the creek, right down on the next claims. Our gold went right on down and we just couldn't do a thing about it. Ron is working the D8 in the pit below us. The water in Eldorado Creek is so deep it came up over the hood of our pickup, and it's almost pure mud. The road was a mess by Dave Johnson's place.

Sunday, May 28th. Marcene and I hooked up the pipe, turned the water on and it worked fine. We saw our first bear this morning on the road just below camp on the way to town. The weather's nice today.

May 27th. Marcene and I fixed our fuel tank, got it set up again. We decided to run some material through today. I hauled 16 loads and broke the track on the loader, bolts came loose and broke. I drug the track out of the pit with the Cat, rolled it up and loaded it into the pickup. I'll take it into town and get the broken off bolts taken out. The guys that bought Keach's claim, Harry and Bob, brought our sluice box and riffles and stuff back tonight. They said they wouldn't need them anymore. I'd given the stuff to them, but they wanted to bring it back. They're taking off, going to Alaska and back outside, they didn't find any gold down on the Keach claim. Bernie's pushing tailings in our old pit this p.m.

May 28th. The water's still high in Eldorado Creek, but only up over the running boards today, and muddy. We got the Komatsu loader all blocked up to where we can slip the track back on as soon as I get the bolts tomorrow. The reason for those bolts coming loose was they were Cat tracks and alligator fittings, but we didn't know to burn the paint out. I took a wire brush and wire brushed it off, but you should burn the paint out. Otherwise, it gives just enough slack when it starts moving and working for the bolts to come loose.

May 29th. We got the track on the loader, got new bolts and checked the finals, and everything is jam-up on it now. We saw Don and Sue in town, had coffee with them and borrowed a couple of 6-inch couplings from them. They're nice people to deal with. The Colemans got their D9 stuck in the settling pond. They had 3 D8 Cats, a D9, and a 980 loader, and still couldn't pull the D9 out. I suggested they get Klondike Transport's big backhoe, that would simplify it because it would break the suction. They could just dig around the D9 that's stuck, and that way they could come right on out with it. That's what they did. The reason I knew about that was because we had gone through that in construction in Anchorage, on the pipelines and etc.

May 30th. It rained cats and dogs last night. We got up early this a.m., drove into Dawson and picked up the 100 feet of 6-inch hose. We had coffee at the Eldorado Hotel with Mary and Butch Sealy, who used to be the gold buyer for Delta Refining. It was the first time in 4 years that we'd visited with Butch. We went over to the Downtowner and had toast and coffee with Bob and Mia Marchant, then came on back to the mine and got the monitor hooked up. Marcene had to hold the end of the monitor on top of her head to line up the bolt holes. At first it wouldn't work. I stepped on the hose and figured out it was air locked, so I stuck my pocket knife in the hose and let a little air out and the darn thing started working fine. Then I cut a little willow peg and stopped the leak after the air got out. Bernie came up and visited this morning. We didn't run the box today, but we will tomorrow.

May 31st. We monitored all day and the pit is ready for sluicing. We're in some good ground and we'll sluice tomorrow. The weather today was windy, cloudy and sunny. Marcene and I cut wood this evening.

Saturday, June 1st. We had lots of company. Guy and Glen, geologists from Arizona, came out today and are gonna spend a couple of nights with us here in camp.

June 2nd. We went over to see John Brown this p.m. and took Glen and Guy with us. He showed us around his mine. Don Sandburg came up here today and I gave him some pads out of the old Komatsu track for the inside of his trommel.

June 3rd. Mike Hayden came up and brought us mail, and we had a nice visit. Guy took samples back with them to Arizona. I wonder what will happen.

June 4th. We left for Anchorage this morning and boy, the road was rough. We got all the way to just east of Tok, hit that nice pavement in our new pickup and boy howdy, I was really flying, not paying any attention to the speedometer when a State Trooper met me. He pulled me over, stopped me, and while he was writing out a ticket he was asking me questions about gold mining, all at the same time. When he gave me the ticket, he told me to just go into Anchorage and pay it. I said, "You know something, you're the first guy that's given me a ticket that I didn't mind getting."

June 5th. Gold was $315 today and silver $6.60.

Saturday, June 8th. We picked up our mastodon tusk at Jerry Kingrey's today. He had mounted it for us with a brass chain and bands, etc., to hang on the wall above the fireplace. Peggy called and said that Sam Scardi's watchband would be ready tonight.

Tuesday, June 11th. We're back in Dawson City on Gay Gulch, and the box ran close to 3 hours today. The riffles looked okay. It was a chilly day, light rain. Marcene and I didn't feel too good this morning. We hung curtains in the cabin. This evening Irv Hawkins came up and he's gonna give us a hand tomorrow.

June 12th. The Customs people came by and checked all our paperwork, everything is in order. We picked about 3-1/2 ounces of gold from the front riffles today. Irv worked 10 hours and we're paying him $10 an hour, that's Canadian. Bernie Gagnon and Lou came up to get my wanigan and are gonna take it mining. I'm just loaning it to them. Lou's gonna give Marcene and me 2 claims on Brown Creek for showing Mike the claims he bought from them. Marcene didn't feel good at all last night and still felt bad this morning.

Friday, June 14th. We picked up our strawberry plants at Murphy's, the ones we left in the cave, or tunnel, at their property last fall, and they were okay. The temperature back in the tunnel is a constant 29 degrees.

June 15th. Toni and J.D. Vance got here today and we had a ball talking and visiting. We ran the box 2 hours and cleaned our gold. The weather was good today, the riffles yellow, we're in good ground for sure, and everything's roses. Ron and Jackie came up tonight.

June 16th. I talked to Andy, and J.D.'s motorhome is okay where it is for now. Also, J.D. left his trailer there with the motorhome. We talked with Lou and Bernie at Andy's place. We saw a dog pulling a bicycle with a girl on it in Dawson, that sure is different. We stopped by and saw the Murphy's for awhile on the way out of town.

June 17th. I helped J.D. and Toni run some material through the Denver panner, they are getting gold.

June 18th. Marcene went to town and got a barrel of gas and I helped J.D. get his light plant on the motorhome going. The road in the pit sure is messy because it's rained so much. We ran the box 3 hours today and got good gold out of the bedrock. J.D. and Toni are running the little sluice box, and they've got some gold.

Thursday, June 20th. We picked up plants at Joan's Farmers Market, cucumbers and tomatoes, and the plants are sure nice. J.D. and Toni ran the little sluice box today and got a couple of nice nuggets. We ran our box 3 hours and did good. I found out where to go fishing, so we're going up Saturday and take J.D. and Toni with us.

June 21st. We went to Murphys' party tonight after cleaning up our front riffles, the riffles looked good. J.D. and Toni went with us and took movies of the party. Later they went to Diamond Tooth Gertie's, and then drove up on the dome overlooking Dawson and the Yukon River, and had a ball. I don't know what time they got in this morning and don't really care. They slept in, and they really enjoyed themselves.

Sunday, June 23rd. Ron Johnson came up this a.m. with his D8, spent 2 hours stockpiling a lot of yards of material right out of the bedrock and above, that which the dam didn't wash out earlier. It started raining, and poured so hard the creek came up and washed over half the material he'd stockpiled on down the creek into the bedrock downstream, into the claim that the Johnson boys are gonna work later on. We could hear the rocks rolling down the creek from up in our cabin.

June 24th. I put in a septic system at the cabin and got it all squared away. Toni and J.D. came to visit us a little while this morning, they have their motorhome parked down below us. They do their thing in the evening, build their fire, and we hear the little chain saw going buzz, buzz, and all, and that's Toni cutting wood for their fire. They build up their nice little fire in the evening, and they're just having a ball up here relaxing.

June 25th. Irv worked for us today and we paid him $400, brought him up to date. We cleaned up the front 3 sets of riffles and ran it through the Denver panner and the wheel. Toni and J.D. took pictures of it all, they really enjoyed that. Ron and Jackie came up to camp tonight.

June 26th. The gold looked real good today. We're sure running some sticky material over the shaker plant, but that's where the gold is.

June 27th. We sat around the fire tonight and chatted with J.D. and Toni, and really enjoyed it. The sun is starting to move over, and the days are starting to get a little shorter, it's sad to see that. Toni said tonight that "the mercury is eating our gold", in other words, she was looking at the gold in there and mercury was around some of the gold.

June 28th. J.D. and Toni left today and we were sorry to see them go, they were just real nice people. We had offered to let them take showers in our cabin, and they did one time. We went in to shower this evening and the water was cool, so I checked and I have only had it on pilot all along. I guess that we're the Beverly Hillbillies, we've got hot water, but don't have sense enough to turn it up. I guess that's why J.D. and Toni didn't shower often. They were so nice they wouldn't even tell us that we didn't have hot water. Our riffles looked real good today. The weather was beautiful and we had no problems with the equipment. I'm working the bedrock that Ron shoved and stockpiled, but there isn't much of it left. Some nice people from California, Jerry and Betty, came to visit today.

Sunday, June 30th. We cleaned the front 3 sets of riffles and they looked good. We're having to haul a long way, but it's worth it. Our garden's looking good. We went into Dawson and ate with Bernie, J.C., Andy, Maria, Mike, Pasquale, and others. It was sure nice of them to have us over. We drove out to see Jerry and his wife, but they weren't in their trailer, gone someplace. We stopped by to see Ian and Pig Man Bill tonight, and Pig Man was laughing. They put a 2-inch nozzle on the monitor and kicked in the 12-inch high pressure pump, and Bill said, "Strange and weird things was happening on the hill up there. The pipe started to moving around like sneaky snake, and spaghetti, and the pressure kicked the pump back into the pit down below, and all of a sudden the water was flying every whichway." So Bill was still talking and laughing about it when we drove up on them. That was right down by Little Skookum Gulch on Eldorado Creek.

July 1st. Irv worked 9 hours today and the weather was good. Richard Reese and his family came up this p.m. and are coming back tomorrow. Richard used to drive truck and run the dozer and loader for Simpson Contracting. Our riffles looked real good this p.m. We picked about 8 ounces from the first 4 riffles. Jerry, Betty, and their partners from California came up this p.m., brought food, steaks, and they sure were nice. They brought up a satellite dish that they set up on our front porch and it picked up 3 stations. We went down and talked to Gene this evening, he hasn't gotten his D9 running yet, and that's too bad.

July 2nd. The riffles looked good today. We picked about 3 to 3-1/2 ounces of gold from the front riffles. I'm having to haul material about 300 feel, but I just don't want to move the shaker plant right now.

July 3rd. The weather's good, and the riffles looked real good today. We had a little too much company though. I ran the wheel and we cleaned up our gold this p.m. I took the dozer down and made pull-outs on our road for the traffic tomorrow. Oh, by the way, I want to note that we put up gold for the house that Irv and his wife purchased, we stood good for it. I think everything will work out alright with Irv, he's a good guy. He'll be working with Mike from now on this season, I guess.

July 4th. Gene's starting to monitor on the hill down by Murphy's, he's washing trees, mud, grass, everything off of Murphy's hill there. Oh boy, what a mess. We had a nice party tonight, lots of friends came up, and Bernie even came in his helicopter. We had fireworks and all. Jim Johnson, our banker from Anchorage, and his friends came up this p.m. to pay us a visit.

Saturday, July 6th. Irv picked up my welder and I told him that Mike could use it for the rest of the season, no charge.

July 7th. Raymond Forsythe, of Forsythe Equipment Rental, came up tonight and we talked regarding a rubber tired loader. He wants $70,000 for the 930, 2-1/2 yard rig, and he wants $5500 plus $70 for insurance per month on it for lease or rental.

July 8th. I signed a lease with Raymond Forsythe this morning for a month on the rubber tired loader, $5570. We're gonna pick it up tomorrow, I guess. We have a new boat in Dawson, running to Eagle and back. The owner is Brad Phillips from Anchorage and boy, it's a nice one.

July 9th. I picked up the loader at Klondike Transport's yard and drove it up to the mine. We tried using it and the bucket's too wide for our hopper. Lou came up tonight, worked the hopper a little while and got all muddy and wet. Anyway, we'll stockpile with the rubber tired loader for now. Ron, Bernie, and Jackie came up tonight. I pushed a trail up the south side of our claims for Bernie to get his dozer up on top. They couldn't get the big Cat up there, so I built a little road for them. It rained today, I sure wish it would get dry.

July 10th. "Smokey" Mark went to work for us today. He's staying in the fifth-wheel and is going to help me clear trees above the dam on the next claim. The plants in the garden are looking good. The 930 loader is working good.

Saturday, July 13th. This morning while looking out our cabin window, we saw bees on our artificial flowers. They were going all over, looking very frustrated. I noticed today that the tracks on the Case 450 dozer are ready for pins and bushings to be turned. This is the fourth season on it and it's sure earned its way here at Gay Gulch.

Monday, July 15th. Ron and Bernie have about 4 more days to work on Dave Johnson's claims and then they'll move onto our claims. The deal we made with them was they were to work our 2 first claims, JDS #1 and JDS #2, pay us 10 percent in gold of the gross amount of ounces they took out, and we were to settle up after each cleanup.

July 16th. Marcene took gold to the bank and Mark worked today. He's a hard worker, but he has very little coordination on the dozer or loader.

July 17th. The weather was beautiful today. We had a bear eating the squirrel's food this a.m. and he made me mad when he walked across our strawberries. I took a shot under his belly and he really took off like gangbusters. This afternoon I started Mark on clearing the 500-foot strip above where we're mining right now, the next claim up. Irv and Lou came by this p.m.

July 18th. The riffles looked so good today that after a 45 minute run, they looked better than they had the previous 2 hour run. I think we'll run again tomorrow. We have a puzzle where we've been working. It looks like the old creek bed is changing and I'm just anxious to see where the water is coming from, coming out of the bedrock.

July 19th. We cleaned the box today and ran through the Denver panner. I hated to shut down for the summer, but the Johnson boys are getting ready to move up on our claims, so I guess it's best we get out of their way. The reason I'm letting them lease the ground is to open up the gulch more, widen it out, and go into the fractured bedrock 6 to 8 feet with their big heavy equipment, something I can't do with the equipment I have.

Mark cleaned the 2 loaders with the monitor today. Gene and Kathy came up this p.m. for a visit. Gene said that Don and Sue just weren't doing any good on Indian River, the gold is just too fine. Also, Dave Johnson had a real good cleanup, about 1000 ounces of gold down there on Eldorado Creek. It sure was nice out today, in the 80s.

Saturday, July 20th. We hated to do it, but we moved the shaker plant and sluice box out of the pit today.

July 21st. We finished cleaning our gold today. Lou and Bernie came by the motorhome this a.m. and we had a nice visit. We went out to Mark's place and picked up an old gate that had been used to park bicycles at school in previous years. He'd found it up at the dump, but it will make a nice gate for our mining road.

July 22nd. Mark brought 2 dogs out to camp this a.m. and it's nice to have them in camp to keep the bears away. Mark and I cleared and hauled brush, preparing for the next dam. I used the leased loader about 5 hours. Marcene went to Dawson today and called Automatic Welding in Anchorage regarding our dozer tracks. Boy, it's been hot out today. Our strawberries are starting to turn, but I've got a jump on the squirrels 'cause I've got little rings around them with chicken wire. Dave Johnson lost some of his concentrates last night. He was cleaning up and celebrating a little too much. He had gold in buckets, pans, concentrates all over, and his boys were playing with the gold in the pans. Gene was monitoring down at

Murphy's claim and Dave went over there with a pan full of gold, stumbling all over, and almost fell off a 40-foot embankment, but Gene caught him. Gene called Jim, Dave's brother in Anchorage, so Jim's gonna come and help him get straightened out tomorrow.

July 23rd. Marcene will have to go to Dawson to get more fuel tomorrow, the big loader gobbles up the fuel, that's for sure.

July 24th. We cleared ground up on the next claim above where we just got through working and I found a nice jar, a cream jar of some kind, and an ink bottle, or ink well, in the old miners' dump. They were in perfect shape. The 930 loader's working fine and moving lots of material. I found 2 yellowjackets' nests and boy, I got acquainted with them in a hurry. Ron moved the big shaker plant up to our claim today and plans to start sluicing our ground around Saturday.

July 25th. Marcene found an old English tobacco can today to add to our collection.

July 26th. Mark is learning and getting a little bit better on the equipment, but I'm afraid he's gonna roll that loader over. He doesn't think, and his coordination is kind of out of sync with the rest of his body. Ron came up for a visit this afternoon, and supposedly, Big Dave Johnson got robbed last night, evidently part of his sluice box. We went to the Miners' Ball in Dawson City tonight and had a super good time.

Saturday, July 27th. I paid Mark in full today. Gene and Kathy came up for lunch, and tonight we went into Dawson. We're going to spend the night in the motorhome and then drive to Anchorage tomorrow.

Tuesday, July 30th. I got the thaw wire for Ron that he asked me to pick up while we're in Anchorage. That's to go through his pipe underneath the road down by their camp, to thaw out in the spring. You just plug it into electricity.

July 31st. We're back in camp, and Bill and Marlene came in about 11 p.m., it's sure nice to see them. The weather was good today and they had a nice trip over.

August 1st. Bill and Marlene are hauling concentrates up from the pit in tubs on the 4-wheeler and running the little Denver panner. We had a super nice supper tonight, steaks, etc. Mark ate with us and all is well.

Saturday, August 3rd. It's sure nice to have Marlene and Bill in camp, we sure enjoy them. They got some gold today and everything is good for them. I pushed brush, ripped out stumps and hauled trees with the Komatsu. By the way, bears are bugging Mark's dogs that are tied up out here, so what he's gonna have to do, I guess, is turn one of the dogs loose. Ron and Jackie, and Bunny and Stan came up to visit. Incidentally, Ron decided not to take that thaw wire I got for him, said it was too expensive.

August 4th. Guess what? We had fireworks here in the Yukon last night. It sure was nice.

August 5th. The weather was nice today. Bill and Marlene are still in camp and we went fishing. Marlene caught a nice grayling and I caught one. I picked up an old steamer up the creek and brought it down to camp. It was from the old-timers, long about 1897-98. Lou came up this a.m. and told us that he and Bernie had transferred two 40-acre claims on Brown Creek to Marcene and me, and it sure was nice of them.

August 6th. Mark worked today and he finished up today. We paid him in full. He's a total disaster. He had both chain saws goofed up, busted a guard on the loader, busted up 5 joints of our pipe, almost turned the big wheeled loader over, messed up our washing machine, and messed up our hothouse. I could go on and on, but so be it. Mark was telling me that if it didn't have a blade or bucket on it, he would do just fine. I don't know what he was referring to, but anyway, if you're mining you're dealing with buckets and blades. Bill and Marlene left for Anchorage this morning and we're sure sorry to see them leave.

August 7th. I made a deal with Ron and Bernie: I told them if they provided fuel, I'd use my leased rubber tired loader to haul tailings for them, push and haul rock and tailings, and see if I could keep up with the rig that they had feeding the hopper and shaker. I said I wouldn't charge them anything, only the fuel for the loader, and they agreed. I did that for a reason, I thought I'd find out how much material, for sure, they were putting through, and I found out all I needed to know. I had a load counter in the cab with me and I was counting the loads that Bernie dumped in. I also wanted to check the material that they were getting out of that spiral at the end of the box, approximately how much gold was in the tub, and how long it took to fill the tubs. So I learned all of this in the 2 days that I offered to haul for them. I stopped for a break once, went over and took a pan and dipped a little material out of the tub from the spiral, and panned it. I found out what I wanted to know, though, that they had all kinds of gold in that tub. I can see now that when Jackie came up and showed us pictures of them melting bars, I can understand how much gold they took off Gay Gulch.

August 8th. I pushed for Ron and Bernie for 6 hours today, pushing tailings, hauling tailings and rocks. I took the loader back and tried to wash it in town, but White Pass had water problems, and Guggieville Camper Park washer was out of order. I talked to Harry Campbell and he said not to worry, that his mechanic would clean up the machine and wash it off for me. That was nice of him.

August 9th. Bernie came up to eat supper with us, and then Ron and Jackie came up.

Saturday, August 10th. We went into Dawson for breakfast, then went over to Lousetown, the old red light district across the Klondike River from Dawson City. We found a few old things, like a solid rubber tired bicycle, one that they'd made using steam hose around the wheel. Evidently they couldn't get tires and tubes, so that's how they had to improvise. We also got several old bottles and different things. Ron and Bernie are sure secretive about the gold. They haven't said one word about how good the ground is doing, etc. We went to town tonight, went to the Eldorado and stopped off at Gertie's for awhile. We drove on home and spent the night at the mine.

August 11th. Scott and Jadene got in camp tonight. It was nice out today. We took out pipe coming from where our shaker was setting and put it in the stockyard.

August 12th. Scotty and I hung the gate down at the bottom of our mining road, and cut in a window in the cabin. We drove into Dawson to get 3-sided logs for a greenhouse, but the sawmill had to cut them and we'll have to pick them up tomorrow. We stopped in town to get us some hamburgers.

August 13th. We took Scott and Jadene on a boat ride down to Moose Hide and had the salmon dinner.

August 14th. Scott and I painted windows, and I did some dozer work, test holes up the creek, etc. It's our anniversary today and we went into Dawson City where we had a suite rented at the Eldorado Hotel. It sure was nice to have all our friends up to visit. We went to Gertie's later in the night and won about $35 or $40, and that was kind of nice for a change. Bernie told me tonight that I must be part Chinaman, as I had cleaned the gold out of the gulch pretty good. I asked Bernie, "How come you came to see us, and Ron and Jackie didn't show up?" He said, "Well, I got out of camp before they did, and they knew I was coming to your party, so they didn't show up." Bernie was telling me that Jackie has a case of, well, I don't know what you call it, but she picks up things, takes them and hides them different places. He said one time he came in looking for his shoes and couldn't find them. Another time she hid his bicycle and he found it about 2-1/2 years later.

Friday, August 16th. Scott and I worked on the cabin this a.m., and Jadene and Scott went to Dawson this p.m.

August 17th. Jadene and Scott left this morning. They took off, had their money and everything else, they're all paid up in full, but Scotty forgot his tools. He had done some remodeling on our house in Anchorage, and also at Marlene's and Bill's house.

August 18th. Marcene and I did a little work on the greenhouse this a.m. and then went in to see the finish of the Dawson Raft Race. Ron Johnson and Robbin Archibald won it. The weather was nice and lots of people were in town. We called Ruth and Lavelle,

Mort Saiger at the Frontier Hotel in Vegas, and Bobby Adkins in Las Vegas. We bought peaches, apricots and cherries right at the stand in downtown Dawson. It's nice to be able to buy fresh fruit from the Okinagan country.

August 19th. We're just bull cookin' around camp today. We went over to Ready Bullion to see Andy and Zalota, they have a little operation going and they're getting good gold, quite a few nuggets. I took the 450 dozer down to the KVA Campground. Henry, a guy at Everett's claim down by Eldorado Creek, came running across the creek, old muddy water up to his waist, waving his arms. He wanted me to do some dozer work for him. I told him I'd be back tomorrow and do it for him if the lowboy didn't pick my dozer up in the morning.

August 20th. We went to the Recorder's Office this a.m. and got the 2 claims on Brown Creek straight, also grouped the claims on Klondike Highway by the Klondike River. We went back up to camp to drain and winterize our fifth-wheel. Ron and Bernie are really moving lots of material on our claims. I did dozer work for the kid by Eldorado Creek, about 3 hours worth, but I didn't have the heart to charge him. He's broke and trying hand mining with a little bitty sluice box.

August 21st. Klondike Transport took my dozer to the Brown Creek cutoff this p.m. Mike Hayden's supposed to come over Friday. I guess Lou and I will go into Brown Creek tomorrow and pick out a new road going down the hill to Mike's claims. We went up to camp this evening to get clothes, Marcene is going to do washing while I'm gone. I saw a big grey wolf up at the dam this evening.

August 22nd. Lou and I left for Brown Creek this a.m., me on the Case 450 and Lou on the 4-wheeler going in the road. I graded the road as I went and got stuck about 4 miles in, it was like quicksand and oozing muck. We waited for Bernie Gagnon with his D8 and loader. He was going to pull me out, and he got stuck right away. We worked about 8 hours getting Bernie and myself out. So Lou and I went on in to Brown Creek, took the old caribou trail off the mountain, and Bernie came on back to town to get some parts. I got to the real steep part of the hill and went on down, almost to the bottom, lost a pin in my dozer blade, so I had to come on back up and out. I had been in sight of Mike's camp, it was just a short ways on down to it.

August 23rd. What a night and day! I drove my Cat out to where Bernie had gotten his loader and Cat stuck. I waited for him to show up, figuring he'd fly in this morning. My dozer was just about empty, so I drained some fuel out of Bernie's loader and left him a note that I had to put fuel in my dozer to make it on up to the road. I had to use a water jug to get enough diesel out of the loader, had to syphon it into the water jug, that's all I had. I left his equipment around 8:30 a.m. and went on out to the road. Bernie flew in with his chopper about 2:30 p.m. and landed near his equipment, he didn't see me out by the road. It was raining and I started a fire to dry out. I tried to hitchhike, but people just passed me on the highway, didn't like my looks, I guess. I was all dirty, with a slouch hat, and they would just drive on by, look at me and shake their heads. Marcene was to pick me up at 6 p.m., but, bless her heart, she showed up just after 4. It sure had been raining.

Saturday, August 24th. We went by to see Gene and his crew. Their D9 was stuck up on a hill about ready to go over a 30 to 40 foot embankment, straight down. Butch took the big Koering backhoe up and built a road to drive it down. We piddled around the cabin today and I put in another light over the stove for Marcene, and a few other things. Jackie and Ron came up tonight. Oh yes, Jackie said that she and Ron were concerned about our pickup the past few days, as it was being moved around at the motorhome.

August 25th. We saw wolf and bear tracks up at the dam site today. Ron brought the 4-wheeler back this a.m., he and Jackie took it down to their camp last night after a visit up here. We saw Lou in town this p.m., Bernie got unstuck and went on in to Brown Creek.

August 26th. Irv gave me a hand this morning taking out pipe at the dam and he didn't charge me anything. We went over to see Dave Lorenson near Paradise Hill, but he wasn't around. We drove over to Lousetown and gathered up a bunch of horse manure for our garden, and a few old things that we found laying around.

Wednesday, August 28th. We went to town this morning, saw Mike, and he flew us over to Brown and Bruin Creeks. We looked around and came back to Dawson. Then Mike and I put his bike and our 4-wheeler in the pickup and drove over to Brown Creek Road and in about 4 miles. The chain on his bike broke right away when he hopped on it. He had to ride on in with me on the 4-wheeler. We met Lou walking out, he had been looking for a new trail for the road down into Brown Creek. We got to Mike's camp about 10 o'clock and the road off his hill was just a mess. It was that old black muck, and rutted about 15 to 20 feet down.

August 29th. Mike and I got up early and looked over the ground. We saw fresh bear tracks near his cabin, also saw a big wolf's tracks. We left his camp about 8:30 and got out to the highway about 10:30, so we made good time coming out. Mike fueled the airplane and took off for Anchorage. We took Mike's pickup to Gene's camp and left it, also the motorcycle. Lou came up to see us tonight and he is sure curious as to what Mike and I are up to and why Mike isn't mining.

The Johnson brothers worked late tonight. Jackie was up for awhile 'til Ron came after her. We got 10.3 ounces of gold from the Johnson boys for one month's running with their big outfit. They said they got 100 ounces, and that was only after Marcene asked them if we could get some gold as we were going to Anchorage and needed gold. They reluctantly agreed to give us 10.3 ounces.

August 30th. We drove over to Bear Creek and saw Red Leveque working on Crawford's claims. He's running a 980 loader and working a big trommel all by himself.

Saturday, August 31st. Marcene and I went over to Brown Creek Road and put the pin in the dozer blade, also greased it up and checked things out. Lou had trouble with his pickup. He's a nice guy, but a disaster with a standard shift pickup. We caught him on the road, he had the thing hung in 2 gears, and I crawled underneath and got it out of the 2 gears. I checked the oil in the transfer case and it had no oil in it. I had a quart of oil with me and dumped that in. I told him, "That's better than no oil at all, but I'll just ride with you to Brown Creek turnoff and we'll see what happens." So he went up one hill and down the other in second gear and didn't give a hoot about the rpm's. The engine was knocking, just a-winding up, and he couldn't care less. He just doesn't know how to drive a standard shift. I hope the next one he gets is an automatic.

The weather was nice today and there were lots of people in Dawson. We paid Harry Campbell $225 this afternoon for moving the Case dozer. Dave and Danny Fowler came over for the weekend and we're going in to Gertie's tonight.

September 1st. Zalato came up this p.m. and did his cleanup. Alexander, Zalato's son, came down to camp and said he had to use the bathroom so he could ride with Marcene on the 4-wheeler. Ron and Jackie and Bernie came up tonight. We sat around the fire and enjoyed the evening, but it's not the same with those guys working our claims. As soon as Bernie came up Jackie moved and wanted Ron to leave.

September 2nd. We got all ready to go over and get my dozer. Bill, at the lumber company, was going to haul it over for me on the ferry, but at the last minute the ferry lost an engine. They won't let that ferry run without a standby engine. They told us that it would be about 3 or 4 days before they could get an engine for it. So we decided to drive through Whitehorse and go on in to Anchorage. Bill is to haul my dozer up to camp as soon as the ferry gets going again. We left Dawson about 6 p.m. and drove to Whitehorse where we spent the night in the Gold Nugget Hotel.

Friday, September 6th. We got back into Dawson City today and we're running all over, trying to locate paperwork, receipts, and etc., from Finning, Evans Welding, and Big Red's backhoe, all of these people. Don Cole told us we're going to have to get all these receipts of bills that we've paid and we just haven't been able to locate the paperwork, so we thought maybe they were back at our camp on Gay Gulch. After we didn't find them in camp, we're having to run around to the various people trying to come up with some kind of receipts.

Sunday, September 15th. I told Ron tonight that I wanted to see a cleanup. I asked him if I could see the next one and he said, "Oh yeah, you can see one tomorrow." And I said, "Good." So Ron and Jackie came up later tonight, and Stan and Bunny also came up.

September 16th. Jackie came up this a.m. and said that Ron wanted us to come down to the pit and watch the cleanup. This is the first time that we've been invited to one of their cleanups. The norm is that the owner of the claims always has invitations to all the cleanups. They told me that they only got 20 to 30 ounces in this cleanup. I told Ron and Bernie both, "There's only 3 people on Gay Gulch that know the value of this ground, that's you two and myself."

September 17th. I went down to the pit this a.m. and talked to Ron. I told him to get what they were going to get in the next 2 days. Ron wanted to work 'til Sunday, but as I left the pit, I told him, "Two days left." I told Ron if they're right with the numbers they gave us, that he didn't go to the same school of learning as I did.

We gave Gene a nice gold nugget for Steve, Gene's ex-son-in-law. Steve had come up and done some work for us. This afternoon we're getting things put away for the winter, got the dozer back together and running, got the hothouse ready for the stove, got our washhouse leak fixed, and got the plastic cover on the blue bippie trailer.

September 18th. I checked the hours that we ran this season and it figures out this way: we ran 130 hours on the sluice box, and ran 1950 yards through. I know how much we got per yard. Ron and Bernie, running 10 to 14 hours a day, most days, dumping in a load with the 950 loader, amounts to about 3 yards every 55 seconds. So with the material they're running through, they're telling us that "they're losing their asses".

Marcene had her another wreck on the 4-wheeler this morning, lost control in the deep frozen ruts, her thumb hit the throttle. She hurt her head, face, shoulder and leg. The ground is hard as rocks because it's frozen. Jackie came by to see how she was.

September 19th. Gold today was $317.50. Ron was pushing and ripping with the D8 Cat all day, and Bern was running material through the hopper. We went to town, went by the Recorder's Office and filed our assessment work on JDS #1 through #10 on Gay Gulch. We went by the Water Board to fill out a report and the guys were nice to us. We saw John Brown in town and he said he was coming up to see us this p.m.

September 20th. Gold is $318.50 an ounce and silver is $6.02. Ron and Bernie worked 12 hours sluicing today, approximately a little over 2000 yards through. Total yards since cleanup, well, it's been a bunch. We talked a bit with Bernie this p.m., and he said that they were going to try to finish running material tomorrow and clean up. Marcene is working on the bookwork. It's going pretty good here in camp, we're ready to leave, but we need to get settled up with Ron and Bernie.

Saturday, September 21st. Ron and Bernie are cleaning the riffles each night. We went to Dawson this a.m., stopped by to see Gene and he has his problems too, poor guy. It was cold this a.m., 28 degrees and lots of ice. I guess I got my last big strawberry today, sure was a good one. Ron and Bernie had a bearing go out of their big shaker, or the electric motor, or something with their shaker plant, and it just may be the end of this season for them.

September 22nd. It was cold last night and 24 degrees at 9 a.m. this morning. Ron and Jackie came up last night, but I went to bed before they got here, I wasn't feeling good, kind of had the flu. I think that we're going to leave tomorrow. If the Johnson boys don't give us our gold, I guess they can leave it with Rusty at the bank. Ron and Bernie's shaker motor broke down last night and they took up some of their pipe this p.m. They made cleanup number 8, they say, and so far we've received a little over 10 ounces of gold. They have about 900 to 1500 yards stockpiled, and I guess I'll run part of it through next year. Ron says it's no good, but it's right out of the bottom, and I just don't understand what he's talking about yet. I just hope we get some gold tomorrow from them. It was snowing tonight at 10 p.m.

Monday, September 23rd. We got everything buckled up today and tried to get settled up with Johnson brothers. Ron said today, that for their 2 months on our claims that they only got 220 ounces of gold. It was cold today and it snowed all last night. We're going to see if Andy Fras's mom wants to go to Whitehorse and ride along with us. We're going into town.

September 24th. We didn't get settled up with the Johnson brothers. They agreed to leave the gold for us with our banker Rusty later. We brought Andy's mom down to Whitehorse today and enjoyed her riding down with us. We found a lady in Whitehorse that spoke Yugoslav, so we got them together and went out to get Kentucky Fried Chicken. They were just like little birds chattering and enjoying themselves. Then we took her to the airport and put her on an airplane. Marcene called Rusty, the banker, regarding Ron and Bern leaving our percentage of gold at the bank. Nothing yet.

We're on our way out for another season, like geese when they see cold weather coming, they just hook'em and head south. We'll go back to Tennessee, Texas, Arizona and parts south. But we'll be back on Gay Gulch next spring for another mining season.

1986

Thursday, February 17th, 1986. We left Whitehorse this morning about 11 o'clock and drove on up to Dawson. The road was pretty good all the way up. We stopped by Yukon Pump to check on 6-inch hoses and couplers to hook pipe together for the mine. I think I'll buy about 300 feet of hose and 3 couplers from them. The wind sure was blowing at Dawson, it was 57 below. We checked into the Eldorado Hotel and it was nice to see all the old faces. Everyone seemed glad to see us back in town so early, but we were just in Dawson overnight. We had to sign some paperwork at a realtor's office, then we returned to Anchorage.

Saturday, March 22nd. We got a nice letter from Louetha today, my sister, and she's coming up to the mine this summer for a visit. We'll be glad to see her up here, she'll be up for our Fourth of July party. Gold is $350.90 and silver $5.75.

Tuesday, April 1st. We called Dawson City this a.m. It was 20 below zero there and looks like it's gonna snow some more too.

Thursday, April 17th. We saw Gene Schadle at Forty Mile today and we gave our credit card to him in case he has problems. He's hauling a backhoe over to Dawson City for Gene Fowler. The road's in pretty good shape.

Saturday, April 19th. We got back to Dawson City and a warm wind was blowing when we hit town. We brought up 2 checks to Red Leveque from Gary Crawford in Whitehorse. Marcene picked up 20 ounces of material that the Johnson brothers left with Katie at the bank. We're keeping it as a souvenir.

April 20th. Dave Johnson has a D8 Cat stuck through the ice and it's almost covered with water. I sure feel for him. He has Gene Fowler's D9 up there and they're cutting the ice with a chain saw to try and get the Cat out. It was pretty nice today, but still lots of snow. I'll have to borrow snowshoes to go in to camp tomorrow.

April 21st. I snowshoed into camp and it sure was a killer, uphill all the way. I started the dozer and cleared our road, but the snow was almost too deep for a small Cat. We got the pickup in camp by towing it up the hill, got it unloaded and got back to Dawson by 10 o'clock tonight. Dave didn't get his dozer out of the pit yet. We stopped for a visit with Gene and Kathy, and Don and Sue Murphy on our way back to camp.

April 22nd. Gold is $349 an ounce. We took more supplies into camp today and I guess we'll stay in camp until about Saturday. We ordered flowers and some plants at Joan's Farmers Market. We had no problems getting into the mine. I ran the dozer pushing snow around camp, there's sure lots of it. It sure is good to have a toilet inside the cabin that works. We had sunshine most of the day. Marcene's good at driving the pickup and helping.

April 23rd. We're just bull cookin' around camp, getting a little bit more done each day, we rearranged the furniture in the cabin today. We checked out the pit and I'm sure that the Johnson brothers worked after we left. I know they did because they moved that stockpile of material.

April 24th. I got the 4-wheeler running today and went down to see Dave, he had gotten his D8 Cat out of the ice. Boy, it got cold when the sun went down this evening, 19 degrees before we went to bed.

April 25th. We went into Dawson, got fuel and new tires for the pickup. We took Big Red and Colette Leveque 48 strawberry plants and got a piece of asbestos from Red to go under our little heater.

Saturday, April 26th. It's a miserable day, snow, sleet, and rain all day long, just plain miserable.

April 27th. We had coffee with Frank Short at the Downtown Cafe and went to the Placer Mining Forum. It looks like a few more people are trying to get their 2 cents worth in regarding regulations. We saw Mr. Mahoney in town today. On our way home we stopped by to see Gene and Kathy. Gene was running his D9 Cat, and Dave Johnson was stripping with his D8 Cat up Eldorado Creek. I stripped more snow and some dirt on claim #3, working for about 3 hours this evening. We watched a good movie on our VCR tonight. It's kind of nice to be on Gay Gulch, in the middle of the Yukon, and able to see a good movie.

April 28th. I spent 2 hours stripping on claim #3, and I got the little Cat off the edge of the bank. I didn't have ice cleats on the tracks and it slid over a little sideways with me. I had to get the loader to pull the dozer out. The loader's ripper and bucket teeth were frozen in the ground, so I had to free them with a pick. But we got it going, and Marcene used the loader to pull me and the dozer out okay, and everything's fine.

April 29th. I did some stripping and ground sluicing today.

April 30th. Gene came up today and got the steam cleaner, he's going to use it awhile. We sent 2 dozen strawberry plants with Kathy for the Murphys.

May 1st. We're hauling water in 5-gallon buckets from our spring up the creek until we're able to hook up the water line when it quits freezing at night.

Saturday, May 3rd. I started ground sluicing today, getting serious with it. I started about 9:30 a.m. and I quit about 9:30 or 10 p.m.

Tuesday, May 6th. I leveled the cabin this morning. Ground heaves, frost heaves, and so forth occur during the winter, and then in the spring, sometimes you gotta level the cabin up to get the doors to close and lock properly. We had lots of water today, but it was chilly with a little rain, and cloudy most of the day.

May 7th. Marcene and I put siding on the greenhouse today. I started ground sluicing around 12 noon and ran 'til 11 p.m. I sure moved a lot of dirt downstream. It's cool at night, but starts warming up sometime around noontime, and that way the material is a lot easier to move with the dozer. The water is running faster.

Friday, May 9th. I'm having to rip the ice in the pit. There's about a 10-foot buildup of ice in the pit where the Johnson boys left it pretty rough up at the end there. Anyway, I'm ripping it with the little Komatsu with the ripper teeth. I went to town today and found a welder who's gonna come out and do some work on the shaker, also the ripper teeth, shanks, and the dozer blade.

May 10th. The welder, Hank Berendees, was back today and finished the blade on the dozer and worked on the shaker plant.

Tuesday, May 13th. I've been ground sluicing for the past 3 or 4 days. I worked 'til 1:30 this morning. This was the most water so far this year.

May 14th. Gene still has our steam thaw rig. Frank would like to borrow it and I told Gene that when Frank got ready to pick it up, to let him have it, it would be okay.

Friday, May 16th. We went into Dawson this morning looking for parts for the Cat, but they didn't get in. Marcene and I changed the cutting blade and the corner bits on the dozer today. It was a miserable day, real cold last night and we had a hard freeze. I bet the strawberry plants out in the garden got a test. We have a fire in the greenhouse today.

May 17th. We had snow, sleet, and rain today. Everything's going fine and we had lots of water. I worked 'til 11 p.m. Marcene's busy keeping the fire going in the greenhouse.

Sunday, May 18th. We went to Dawson today and stopped by to visit Gene and Kathy. I sure feel sorry for him and his mess on that big hill down there with the D9 Cats. We got cutting tips and filters from Northwest Farm Equipment, so we'll get on with the program. I ground sluiced this evening.

May 19th. I cut some wood for the fire this morning and spent most of the day pushing dirt and ground sluicing. Marcene helped me move pipe to the new dam site. I hope to get the shaker and box set up and going by the first of June. It was a pretty nice day, but the water slowed down a bit, so I quit kind of early, 8:15 p.m.

May 20th. We went to Dawson this morning, ate breakfast at the Downtown, and then took showers. It sure is nice to get all showered up with nice hot water. I ordered ripper teeth tips for the loader, $180 for 10, and called Northwest Farm and Tractor for sprockets, idlers, rails and skid shoes for the Case 450 dozer. I spent about 11 hours stripping and ground sluicing. I'm sure moving lots of dirt.

Friday, May 23rd. Mike and Connie Hayden came up to see us and brought a fresh salmon and nice halibut. That was sure nice of them. I quit working tonight at 12:30. All week I've been hauling and stockpiling material, ground sluicing and getting the dam and outlet ditch ready to go.

May 24th. We had lots of water and the weather was nice most of today. We were ground sluicing all day and quit about 10 p.m. I broke 2 ripper shanks off of the track loader ripping this morning. You don't see these darned big quartz boulders, the round ones that are just under the ground that you're ripping, and all of a sudden you hit them. Even though you're going slow when you hit them it stops the rig right in its tracks, or breaks something. So, you've got to be awfully careful, your hand on the throttle all the time, and even so you still have things happen like that.

May 25th. I talked to Frank Short about leasing me his 966 loader, and I think we're gonna work out a deal. It's for stockpiling material up at Gay Gulch. Also, I talked to a guy who was cutting wood up on the dome regarding helping me move the shaker plant, stringing pipe, etc. His name's Texas Jim.

Tuesday, May 27th. Marcene went in this morning to get a bearing for the shaker plant and talked with Frank about dropping off the 966 loader at the KVA Campground at Bonanza. It's okay with Frank. Wayne Hawk came up today and is going to bring up his D8 Cat to rip and stockpile material. He's supposed to start Saturday. The weather was not bad today, kind of warm, and we had lots of water.

May 28th. I worked on our road last night, and good thing I did as the fuel truck came up today and delivered fuel to our big tank.

May 29th. Marcene went in to Dawson this a.m., picked up Texas Jim, and he and his dog named "Cat" came up to our camp to work for us. He seems to be a good worker. Jim and Marcene and I put waterline in under the dam. The dozer broke today, idler adjuster seals went out, so we went into town and called Ted Mills in Fort St. John, and he is to send parts in by air tomorrow. We ate at a Chinese restaurant, the Midnight Sun, tonight.

Marcene mentioned something to Tex about a toothbrush, and he said, "Oh no, no, I don't ever brush my teeth. Once you start brushing your teeth you can't ever quit, you have to keep doing it." His dog, "Cat", started catching squirrels immediately. The dog was the bigger part wolf, so he'd lay down in the road, or in the trail, and wait. The little squirrels were pets, of course, we'd been feeding them, and "Cat" would let them get up close enough and then pounce right on them. He'd get them every time. Tex said, "I don't need dog food for my dog, he catches his own food."

May 30th. This morning Texas Jim and I put the pipe into the dam. Then we all went in to the Miners' Meeting, but walked out, there's just too much b.s. We also went to the gold show and spent quite a bit of time with Ed and JoAnn Armstrong, and Stan and his wife, and the guitar pickers. We saw many of our miner friends and had a nice time.

May 31st. Hank, the welder, worked on pipe fittings and welded arms on the shaker plant so we can put a platform on there, and leave it up permanently. Jim and I worked on the dozer, changed oil and filters and parts, etc., greased the track adjusters, fixed a transmission leak which was just a loose fitting, put on skid shoes under the blade and adjusted the control lever on the tilt angle control. We greased the loader and adjusted the steering brakes and clutches. Jim put the 8-inch valve on at the shaker plant location and boy, we're just getting things done left and right around here today. Hank spent most of the day in camp welding and ate supper with us. Bunny Johnson came up tonight and we enjoyed her very much.

Sunday, June 1st. It was a nice day, almost hot. Irv and Jo Ann Hawkins came up for a visit, and it's always good to see them. Irv helped Texas Jim and me with some fittings, no charge. Alex Brody, with Inglehardt Refinery, came by and it was nice to see him. Frank brought the 966 loader up, and we're to use it on the hour meter basis, as agreed. I finished the dam and got water going through the overflow this p.m. Robert Trustwell ("2 x 4") came up this p.m. and ate with us. I wonder about this guy.

June 2nd. It sure was a nice day out. Marcene went to town and got lumber for the ramp to the shaker. I put more dirt on the dam as we raised the dam water level. We moved the light plant, shaker and sluice box today, and lacked just a little bit getting things buckled up to start sluicing. I didn't use the 966 today.

June 3rd. I ran Short's 966 loader 2 hours, stockpiling material. Marcene went to Dawson and got boards for the deck on the shaker and the rack to build around it for protection. We got the ramp in to the shaker and Jim made up the braces. We should get most everything caught up tomorrow or the next day, and get started sluicing. Tex said, "Now I know how Jesus felt" after carrying the heavy timbers and braces for the ramp to the shaker.

June 4th. I was running Frank's loader this morning, going up the hill and had a load in the bucket. I started raising the bucket up, and just out of the clear blue, it died. Of course, the brakes are no good on this loader, and I had to bail out of it because it was going back down the hill, and going over an embankment. I didn't have a seat belt on, I don't know if there even was one on it, but anyway, I had to bail out of the loader. It rolled back down the hill, rolled over on it's side and up on 2 wheels, the bucket kind of caught it in a sense. It messed the steering up a little bit, so we're gonna have to get that fixed and taken care of. We got the steering brace out of it this evening, and Finning is going to have to come out and replace it for us. Wayne Hawk's D8 Cat was broke down, but he thinks he'll be out Monday. We need him for sure now to stockpile this material, we got so much opened up now. Jim worked on the shaker screen and the light plant wiring.

June 5th. Red, Glen, and that little pecker, Andy, came up to see us last night. We still got about a foot of ice in the bottom of the pit. I hauled out of the pit most of the day with the Komatsu. Jim is hard at getting other things ready. Dieter and his friends from Germany came over today for a visit. He mines just over the hill on Oro Grande. Finning's mechanic came up, adjusted the brakes on the loader and checked it out thoroughly. He was to order the bracket that we needed for the steering column. We have to watch the brakes, I guess, and keep adjusting them every so often. I went down and worked on the road by Dave's place.

June 6th. It was hot today. To get the 966 repaired, it looks like it's going to cost around $400, or maybe a little more. Marcene drove Texas Jim back to a native gal's house out past the airport.

Saturday, June 7th. This morning Marcene was looking for her work shoes and couldn't find them. We figure Texas Jim must have taken them. Some of my shorts were missing too, and Marcene's black bra, of all things. Marcene found a little nugget off of a quartz rock close to the top of the ground down in the pit today.

June 8th. I shot a grizzly bear this morning, he came up on our front porch and looked through our window at me. I woke up a little early and was laying on the couch reading a book. I had my head right up to the window and it was opened a bit because it was kind of breezy and warm out. Anyway, the grizzly stepped up on the porch, I heard him and knew right away what it was. I looked over and saw a pillow laying down at the other end of the couch, and I reached and grabbed that pillow and slung it at him hollering, "Get outta here!" That old grizzly just growled at me. His head looked as big as a washtub, but it wasn't quite that big. Anyway, I knew right away when he growled that I had to do something, so I ran over to my 444 rifle by the bed. Then I didn't dare shoot him because I was afraid he'd come inside and tear Marcene and me up, so I kept beating on the wall and hollering at him. I got the window lowered and he growled a couple times, then turned and walked off the porch, walked out by the washhouse.

We had a little ladder going up to the top of the washhouse, and the building itself was heavy gauge aluminum about 12 feet tall. So I took my rifle, went out and climbed up that ladder real quick as soon as he went around the washhouse. He was setting a ways up on the hill and I'm talking to him. I said, "Buddy, you better get outta here because I'm fixing to do you a job." I took real good aim and shot him. Then I just went and got my dozer and buried him, drug him up and planted him right there. That bear had been in camp the day before, and anytime you see a grizzly around camp 2 or 3 days, he isn't just passing through, he's trouble.

I spent most of the day dozing, trying to clean up the pit and find where Ron and Bernie left off. I'm still ripping ice in the bottom of the pit. We went into town this p.m.

June 9th. Marcene ran the Komatsu hauling rocks and practiced hauling muck, and she did real good. It looks like the south side of the gulch where it intersects the pup on the north side will be good.

Wednesday, June 11th. We woke up early this morning, afraid the dam might go out. We have a tin roof, and boy, it sounded like it poured last night, but that roof is deceiving, it didn't rain all that hard. Marcene ran the Komatsu loader this a.m., hauling material below the dam and overflow. We hooked up the monitor hose on the end of the pipeline and hooked up a 3-inch hose to the shaker, repaired the monitor and got it ready just in case. The 966 worked fine today, it just can't load itself though, we have to shove into the bucket with the Case dozer. Marcene ran the dozer loading the bucket. We spent part of the day putting the claim posts back in from the offsets that we had downstream, and I'm glad to get them back setting where they're supposed to be. Cass and Iris came up this evening and we had a nice visit.

June 12th. Bernie Gagnon came up in his helicopter and we had a nice visit with him. Gene got back from Anchorage and brought me a box of cigars. He bought a D9 from Lee Teague in Anchorage and Junior Thomas is gonna haul it over for him on his lowboy. That makes 3 D9s for Gene now. Those D9 Caterpillars gobble up about 200 gallons of fuel a eay, each. I built a settling pond today.

Friday, June 13th. It was hot today. We hauled out of the pit and stockpiled, we'll sure be glad to commence sluicing. Ed Rampone and Dale, 2 Customs guys, came up this afternoon and stayed 'til midnight. We enjoyed them sitting around the fire, having a couple drinks. When the time came for them to get off work they just took their badges off and said, "We're off duty now, we can do whatever we wish." Gene, Kathy, and Dave came up for a visit.

Jimmy Simpson   1986   A VANISHING BREED

June 14th. We invited Ed and Dale to come back to camp today, and they brought us a bottle of wine. They're panning and enjoying themselves. It's their day off, so they're relaxing and happy.

June 15th. I spent most of the day grinding and filing on the pin that I made for the dozer. I had to drill a hole and put a bolt and washer through it. Marcene gave me a hand with the pin, and also, she ran the loader and hauled 4 loads out of the pit when I was monitoring. We'll sure be glad to start sluicing, it's been a long dry spell for us here. It was mighty hot out today.

June 16th. It was another hot day and the water is slowing down in the creek. This has been a really dry spring. Marcene ran the dozer today, loading the big loader bucket. Wayne's helper came up and said that they were on the way up here this a.m. and Wayne's dozer heated up about a mile up the trail. He's sure had bad luck. We got down to bedrock today and I can see the paydirt, sure is good to see it. One more day, I think, and we'll be just about beyond the shaker plant where the rocks come off the end of the shaker into the pit, so we won't have to worry anymore when we can start sluicing. Wayne's dozer started work at about 4 p.m. and quit at 8:30. He had about an hour travel time. I did some dozer work in the pit. Dave came up to tell me that he wasn't finished with the road. He was afraid I might be mad if I had to go out and had to wait on him while he was working there, so I told him we had no problem with that. We saw Dieter and his kinfolks from Germany getting water from the creek down at Oro Grande to bathe in, and I invited them up to all take showers at our place. They're in real good gold and getting quite a few nuggets over there on Oro Grande, but they're running out of water. Ron and Bernie tried to stop Wayne from coming up the creek today and he told them to just "bug off." The reason they couldn't stop him is because they don't own the claims, and even if they did they couldn't keep you from coming up the creek.

Wednesday, June 18th. Wayne showed up this morning and his Cat wouldn't start, electrical problem. It he didn't have bad luck, he wouldn't have any luck at all. We took the switch off of the 966 loader, but that wasn't the problem, and Wayne went in to get some parts, no work for him today. We went to town, but didn't get pins for the dozer. We should have them in a couple of days. I went over to the Recorder's Office with Bernie Gagnon and he did some "switcheroos" on some claims that we had staked for him on Brown Creek. I went down to Dave's this p.m. for a cotter pin and washers for my dozer blade, and got them.

June 19th. Wayne worked 12 hours with his D8 Cat ripping bedrock and pushing paydirt. We piad him $2700 and will pay him the rest tomorrow. We owed him a total of $3040, so we owe him $340.

We drove Wayne's pickup down to KVA Campground, and Wayne called the Johnson brothers "the little weasel and the snake". Gregory and Graham, the Water Board guys came up today. They're real nice guys, and their dog's name was Buster.

June 20th. We have good paydirt stockpiled, but water will only allow us to work about 3 hours a day, and with the grade on the creek and the way we're setting, we just cannot hardly recycle. We could, but it would be a problem. Gene tells us he's finally down to good gold, so we're all glad for him.

June 21st. The riffles look good today. We ran the box 2 hours, then went to town to the Fowlers' and Murphys' party.

Sunday, June 22nd. I killed a snarly bear by the porch this morning. He tore a screen off the window and I didn't know for sure what else he would have done. We don't need "pets" like him around. I raised the dam level today. I took out the 4-foot culvert pipe, put in an overflow, and cut in a ditch around the dam, into the hillside and bedrock. I put big rocks along the overflfow. This p.m. we went looking for springs as we need more water. It's dry, the dryest year we've ever had here at Gay Gulch. I staked tomatoes and planted radishes today in the greenhouse.

June 23rd. It rained quite a bit today, our dam was full of water when we started sluicing. I lost a pin out of the dozer C-frame today and went down to Keirin Daunt's to get a washer, bolt and spare pin. I invited him up to our party on July 13th. Marcene stuck her finger in the hole trying to line up the blade. I had a handyman jack under it trying to jack it up into place, plus a bar on the C-frame. I was holding onto the jack and the bar too, but the bar slipped and mashed her finger, poor thing. I sure felt sorry for her, but lucky she didn't have it sticking in just a bit farther, she would have had it chopped right off.

We have good water pressure for the shaker plant now. We were getting ready to quit tonight at 11:45 and the ladder slipped as Marcene was going off the shaker because Tex didn't nail it down. One leg went behind the step and twisted her sideways. I pulled her leg out and helped her get out of her predicament. It was nothing real serious, but she was pretty sore.

June 24th. We had plenty of water today and our riffles looked great. We picked 3 to 4 ounces from the front riffles when we shut down. We did our washing this afternoon. It's sure hard on Marcene working the shaker and having to cook and clean, etc. With just her and I in camp, she's having to carry quite a load. The hardrock survey crew was up again today, "Boy Scouts", I call them. They go out, pack their picnic lunch, and stop by here and use our table to spread it out on. We went down to see Gene this evening, and it's really sad when he is down about 120 feet in that black muck, gets down to good gold, and it's all souped up. It's about 3 feet deep in the bottom, just pure old soup. He's right into the edge of the gold, and it's all mixing up.

We had a big fire built outside tonight and were sitting around it. There was one big log that had ants in it and we watched the reaction of them. Some of them were real smart, they would run and jump off. The others would turn around and go back in, and they would get burned.

Thursday, June 26th. It was sunny and warm today, no rain. Gerald and Graham from the Water Board were up checking our water and everything's okay. They're really nice guys. Our riffles were fair to good today. We got the Denver panner ready to go. Our equipment ran fine, no problems, and I guess I'll take Frank's loader home Sunday. Our garden's doing okay, but the darn radishes went to leaves, so I pulled them all up and planted some more. We have a new crop of squirrels and they're friendly little guys.

June 27th. It's been a busy day today. Marcene went to Dawson, got propane, and called Jadene. I used Frank's 966 loader for 3 hours hauling out material that we monitored the past 3 days. The box ran 2-1/2 hours, I had to work on the switchbox for the shaker, and I ran the monitor for 2 hours. It was hot today, I was sure glad Frank's loader had a fan in it.

June 28th. It was hot and sunny today. As we were going into town, Vern, who is Frank Short's partner out of Kodiak, flagged us down and gave us some king crab and salmon and boy, that was nice to get. We stopped by to see Gene, he got his plant going this p.m., and he sure has a soupy mess in the pit, but I think if he can get enough material through the box he can kind of stabilize things and get him a payday there. By the way, we saw our old friend, Clarence Abelgard at Gene's camp. Guy Rosey, of Homer, sent us his regards. I slipped off the pickup today while pumping fuel and kind of hurt my back again. That's normal.

Sunday, June 29th. Our riffles looked good today, the box ran 2-1/2 hours this a.m. We cleaned the 3 front sets of riffles this p.m. and ran the material through the Denver panner, it looked good. Ablegard and friends came up and we had a nice long visit. It's good to have company like this. Clarence had a good saying about people who cheat, or screw you around. "They won't sit at your table anymore." Sure makes a lot of sense. Gene told us today that by panning, they would be getting 2 ounces per hour, but things just don't work out that way sometimes. It was hot 'til about 5 p.m., then we had a little rain and yes, we had hail some time a little bit afterward. I wrote Mel Tillis tonight about being in the movie, "The Long Black Veil". He had asked me, earlier last winter in Tennessee, if I would consider it, and I told him, "Yes, I would."

June 30th. I adjusted the tracks on the loader and tightened sprockets, to get rid of the popping and wear. We saw our old buddy, Dick Reese, and his family in town this p.m. and invited him up to camp. He used to drive truck and work for us laying pipeline. He's a great guy, it's always good to see him.

July 1st. It's hot today, in the 80s. I went down and worked on the road this afternoon, and talked with Dave. He told me that he just didn't have enough gold for his operation to be feasible, so he doesn't know for sure what he's gonna do now. Our garden's looking good, we have some strawberries, some green ones, and lots of tomatoes on the plants.

July 2nd. Marcene called Northwest Farm and Tractor and they airmailed a pin for the dozer this a.m. I started to take Frank's loader home today and met him and Vern on the road, so Frank drove it on to Klondike Transport's yard. Gene and his brother Larry, and friends from Tucson came up to visit this p.m. We had some good gold in the riffles today.

July 3rd. It was hot and smokey today as there are lots of forest fires in the area. The bomber planes that drop water bags are flying over constantly. I cleared brush between the cabin and shaker plant today, hoping that in case of a fire it might be a little fire break. I leveled up the cabin again today and the door will close and lock now.

July 4th. I paid Frank and Vern $1300 for the loader rental today.

Saturday, July 5th. Dave and Butch Fowler came up this a.m., and Larry Fowler and his wife came up this p.m., also Gene's friends from Arizona. I sure wish it would rain for about 2 or 3 days so we could get on with our mining.

Monday, July 7th. We left for Anchorage today and stopped in at U.S. Customs at the border and saw Roy, the Customs Agent. He gave us quite an order to bring back for him, all kinds of groceries, vegetables and fruit.

Wednesday, July 9th. Louetha came in tonight and we met her at the airport. We were running around in circles all over town, I guess one of these days we'll be a big wheel if we keep running in circles.

July 10th. I told Carl Black that I'd take the Deutz diesel 3-inch high pressure pump. I'm to give him $3000 and he's to deliver it to the mine in Dawson City. Then we left to go back to the mine.

July 11th. We got into camp about 3 p.m. and I ran the box about an hour this evening. Art Sills and Lonnie came in today in their motorhome, and it's sure nice to see them. We brought snow crab back for Big Red and left it at Gene's.

Saturday, July 12th. We went in to Diamond Tooth Gertie's tonight and Louetha had a ball. We cooked steaks after we got home. Louetha got her some gold today filling buckets and running it through the Denver panner.

July 13th. The loader has a loose nut on the sprocket, it's a stripped one, so I'm gonna have to get another one. This afternoon we had a party at our place on Gay Gulch, and really had a ball. We had lots of company. The 2 owners of the sawmill, Bill Bowie and Ralph Troburg, and their families brought up a big picnic table. It was really nice, painted red, white and blue, and it had maple leafs on one side, red and white stars on the other side. Bernie and J.C. Gagnon came up in their chopper, and gave Louetha and Marlene McNabb a ride in it, so that was a big thrill. Everyone had a good time.

July 14th. Louetha is panning for gold and running material through a little sluice box set up down in the creek and she's in some real good ground. Marcene went into town, ordered parts from Coneco for the loader, and we should have them Thursday.

July 15th. I ran the monitor about 4 hours today. Louetha, Bill and Marlene are running material through the little sluice box. Louetha and Marlene went into Dawson this p.m., and Marcene came down in the pit and helped monitor. Boy, it was hot today!

July 16th. Louetha left this a.m., and Marcene, drove her into Anchorage, 550 miles. Bill and Marlene are running the little sluice box and getting good gold. I pushed material that we monitored yesterday afternoon and worked on the loader for about an hour, then ran the monitor. After supper, I drove the 4-wheeler down to Gene's, talked to Butch regarding the Komatsu, and he said to get a mechanic to press the sprocket on. I talked to Dave this p.m., he figures he's losing lots of gold over the end of his box, about 90 percent of it. The box is too steep and he's using too much water. It was hot today!

July 17th. I was pushing and stockpiling material his morning. We went to town to check on parts from Coneco, but they didn't get in. I talked to a mechanic and will use him to work on the Komatsu. It's hot again today. Cass and Iris came up tonight and borrowed my oxygen and acetylene hoses, gauges and goggles.

July 18th. Marcene and Carl McNabb got in from Anchorage, and I guess they had quite a hairy drive over the Top of the World Highway, couldn't hardly see out as far as the headlights could show on account of the fog. Bill and Marlene are digging around the rocks and getting nice gold. I'm glad for them, they're sure nice people. The parts for the Komatsu got in today. We checked on the parts at noon, and had to go back to the airport at 8 p.m.

Saturday, July 19th. I tried some material on the little crusher this afternoon and it definitely has to be dry. It isn't all that swift, I think we got took on that one, $960. Bill and Marlene and Carl went to Gertie's tonight and enjoyed themselves.

Monday, July 21st. Northern Cat got our loader back together today and it's sure good to be hauling again. We got good gold in the riffles.

July 22nd. Bill, Marlene and Carl left this morning, and we hated to see them go. We paid Finning for parts and labor on the 966 loader. Tina and Dave Johnson and 2 of the guys working for him, came up this evening to visit. He's going to take our little crusher and crush some of his concentrates, and see what happens. Dave's guys, Porky and Andy, trapped squirrels and painted them daglo red, then turned them loose just up from the Johnson brothers camp, and I can imagine what they think when they see them, these red squirrels running loose. The boys were laughing, and they wouldn't quit laughing. I offered them a beer and said, "You guys aren't drunk, are you, what's wrong with you?" Then they told me the story on the squirrels.

July 23rd. The riffles looked good today. Allen Bayless, of *The Wall Street Journal*, came up for a story on miners and was with us about 4 hours. He was a real nice guy. He didn't tell us who he was, or what he was with when he first came up. He visited us quite awhile and even went up and watched us sluice. When we shut down and came back to camp to eat he came with us. Marcene was going to serve ham and he said he was sorry but he couldn't eat it, he was Jewish and couldn't eat pork. Anyway, she fixed him other things and we had a nice visit. He didn't tell us he was with *The Wall Street Journal* until later. We went in to the Miners' Barbeque, fixed up a makeshift table, and he came over and sat at our table. So they introduced him on the microphone as being a writer for *The Wall Street Journal*. He told us the article would be on their front page, and sure enough it was when it came out. Gregory from the Water Board came by today and gave us "A"s on everything, the settling pond, dam, and also the overflow with the rip-rap we had hauled up there.

July 24th. The hardrock guys were up here at camp again. I showed them where the 12-foot quartz vein went across Gay Gulch and the direction it was going. After the Johnson boys ripped that all out, it was pretty hard to detect, but it's rained quite a bit and I could still show them the quartz vein on both sides.

July 25th. We saw Mr. Pete Erickson carrying some gold into the bank, and it was sure cute. He had it in a jar, in his hand, holding it behind him when he went by all the people in line there. Where else in the world could you see something like that but Dawson City, Yukon Territory.

Saturday, July 26th. We had no company today. Marcene found a little rock that looks like a little egg, and a squirrel tried to eat it, and take off with it. The weather was kind of cool this evening and it seems as if fall is in the air. Tuesday, July 29th. Our riffles looked good today, and we had lots of company.

July 30th. We cleaned up the first 3 sets of riffles and they didn't look bad at all. The material sure is sticky and hangs in the hopper. We went fishing this afternoon and caught grayling. We enjoyed ourselves and enjoyed the trip up the Dempster highway. I met a guy from the Netherlands today who had caught a nice big fish. An old duffer tourist came along, saw the fish flopping on the bank and threw the sucker back in the creek. That nut should have been thrown in himself.

July 31st. Wayne came back up with his D8 to stockpile some more material and rip some more bedrock. Wayne's kids, Lucas and April were up, and it's kind of a chore babysitting 10 and 11 year olds. They tried to get the 4-wheeler started by pushing it up and down the road. I wouldn't let them have the keys for it because we have steep banks. We didn't run the box today. Lou came up this p.m. and we crushed some rocks for him that he picked up on Brown Creek. We left concentrates to be cleaned with Stevie at Fowler's and I told him to keep 1 ounce and give Gene 2 ounces of the gold. That's for being nice enough to do our cleanup and run it through their big wheel.

August 1st. It was nice and hot out today. We went into town and found out that our Onan generator had been stolen out of our motorhome. We called the Mounties, and they came out and made out a report, and that's probably about the end of that because we didn't have the serial number. The Mountie we contacted was J. Gettis.

Sunday, August 3rd. We got our jewelry from the motorhome safe and brought it to camp. We sure don't want to take a chance on it getting stolen. We crushed about 3 gallons of rocks and ran it through the wheel. It didn't look too good, but had some fine gold in it. We stopped by and gave Jim Archibald's wife some magazines and a fresh cinnamon roll. She thanked us for being so thoughtful. Marcene got a couple of stings the other day while working on the shaker from hornets. Her hand and arm is all swollen up, muscle sore, and it hurt for quite awhile. We finally found out that the hornets' nest was inside the electrical box. We used Hot Shot Hornet Spray on their nest and got rid of them.

August 4th. The box ran 3 hours today. I caught a camp robber bird, called whiskey jacks, and played with it awhile, petted it and then turned it loose. It came right in the cabin with us. We built a fire in the greenhouse tonight, but the stove was too big for the plants, it gets too hot. It's okay for springtime and thawing the ground, etc., but we need a smaller stove for cool nights in the summer.

August 5th. Wayne finished up with his pushing today, plus one hour travel time. We went to town and called the insurance company regarding our stolen generator. Lynn was the girl Marcene talked to in Anchorage, and we got good favorable results from them. We talked to Brenda Caley regarding us parking the motorhome at Guggieville Camper Park, and it's okay, it'll be $20 a month for dry parking.

August 6th. It's hot and dry out, and we're awful short of water. I went down and fixed up another settling pond today, that makes 4 ponds. We picked raspberries for Sue Murphy, about a gallon, and she's gonna make some pies. Mark Daunt came up to see us this evening.

August 7th. A guy came up here in a motorhome looking to buy gold nuggets, also gold dust. He started getting smart, so I told him, "I'm just trying to be nice to you and explain about gold, how the purity works, and everything. If you don't trust me and don't want to believe what I tell you, go on down to the bank and get Maple Leafs." One guy in a motorhome came up and said Don Sandberg told him we were just a little way up the road. He told me it seemed like about 18 or 20 miles over this rough road. Anyway, he turned around and took off, sailed back down the road.

August 8th. The box ran 2 hours today, we got about 3-1/2 ounces out of the front riffles. We went into town to move our motorhome, but the battery was down and I left it with Don at Northern Metallic to charge it up.

Saturday, August 9th. The riffles were real good today. I went up the creek, muddied it up a bit with the dozer and opened up another spring. It looks like we'll have a little more water now, also the mud will seal up some of the leaks we've got in the dam. We went into town and moved our motorhome to Guggieville Camper Park for the rest of the season. It started up okay after I got the battery charged. I talked to Frank Short regarding the difference on the 966 loader and what I paid him, and he said to just buy him a steak dinner sometime and we'd be even. He's got our steam thaw rig, and we'll just kind of swap out on that.

August 10th. Mike Hayden was over on Brown Creek this weekend and mined a bit. He started back with concentrates in a bucket on his motorcycle. The bucket caught fire on the exhaust and the bottom burned out of the bucket, so he lost all of his concentrates coming up the hill and out to the road. We went to Andy's birthday party, there was so much good food and drinks. They sure are nice people, these Italians and Yugoslavs.

August 11th. We got 6 or 7 ounces from just spooning the front riffles, we're sure in good dirt. It was nice today, seems like we're holding a lot more water in the dam. Jim and Roy Conklin, from Brown Creek, came up to visit. They're the guys that Mike gave a claim to for putting in a road for him. They seem to be nice guys, but not miners.

Wednesday, August 13th. We got about 7 ounces of gold picking the front sets of riffles after the box ran 2 hours and 20 minutes. It's sure good ground. Gene came up to visit, he wants to work our claims and give us 25 percent, but we've worked too hard, and just want to go on up the creek like we're going. It rained today, a slow drizzle which was good, but the creek didn't rise any.

August 14th. We had a nice 37th wedding anniversary at the Eldorado Hotel suite and had lots of friends visit.

August 15th. I got sick tonight, running a fever and kind of hurt a bit, hurts me when I urinate, might be kidney stones. Dick Gillespie and Maryann Holbrook came up this p.m. and we enjoyed visiting with them. It's the first time that Dick has set down and visited or talked with us. It's very seldom that Dick goes out any place and spends any time, but he spent all afternoon with us, and I sure felt bad. When he got ready to leave he said, "You know, after all these years up here, I'm gonna get me a setup like you've got, keep it small." Of course, they went up and looked in the riffles just after we'd shut down and saw all the gold in there. He told us, "I'd see you guys in town, wearing all your gold and everything, and I thought you were a couple of assholes, but you're really nice people."

August 16th. I had to go to a doctor and get some antibiotics. It's sure disgusting to be sick and be in such good gold, and freeze-up's coming on.

Sunday, August 17th. Gene and Kathy came up to see if he could run the loader for me, and Lou came up and wanted to help too. It's nice when everybody wants to pitch in and give me a hand.

August 18th. The riffles looked good today, but I just haven't felt like visiting people. Keirin Daunt came up this p.m. and visited awhile, he offered to clean our concentrates on his wheel. We took them down and came right on back to camp. I had such a fever I didn't feel like visiting, so he's gonna clean the concentrates and bring them up to us.

August 19th. Keirin brought our results from the concentrates and it was okay, hard stuff to work. I told Lou that I'd go in to Brown Creek with him Thursday morning, and we'd have breakfast at the Downtown before we left. This was just to check some ground out for him and do him a favor.

August 21st. We went to Brown Creek for some tests with Lou and it took about all day. Did it rain! And the road got muddy. It seems as if we lost a day of sluicing, but you gotta be nice to nice people. I talked to a lady at the insurance company, Kim, and she told us to go ahead and order a generator for our motorhome, to have Andy get it out of Vancouver at Simpsons. I told Andy to go ahead and order it.

August 22nd. The box ran 2-1/2 hours today and we got 3 ounces out of the front riffles this p.m. Boy, it sure was cold and windy today, and we had a few flakes of snow.

Saturday, August 23rd. It was cold this a.m. We had a hard freeze and it got our garden. Beautiful tomato plants, peppers, cukes and squash, it just got them all. We had to thaw valves at the shaker this morning. The water pipes froze up at the cabin, it was 10 degrees when we got up. When we went to bed last night it was about 50 degrees.

Tonight we went to Dawson and to Gertie's. We also went to the Midnight Sun where we were listening to a musician that we know. Some big old Indian sat down across the table from us at the Midnight Sun Bar and Dancehall, and I had to kind of line him out, he was giving me a hard way to go. He kept snickering and laughing, and making fun of me. He said, "Did you ever shake hands with an Indian?" I said, "Well, no, not really." And he said, "Would you like to shake hands with an Indian?" So, I stuck my hand out, trying to be nice to him, and I had my big gold ring on my right finger. We shook with our right hands, and he was squeezing, and hurting my finger. His grip was pretty good, but I'd been picking rocks all summer, and I felt that my grip was pretty good too.

So we set there and looked at each other, he was snickering and laughing, and I got mad. I told him, "You know something? Your handshake is a little stouter than I kind of like, and I'd like for you to turn my hand loose." He laughed some more and didn't pay any attention to what I said, so I just pulled him right across the top of the table, swept all the glasses and everything off, and shoved him right down underneath the table. I twisted his arm with my other hand and I said, "Whenever you're ready to get up and act like an Indian, why you just say the word. And whenever you do get up, I want you to get my hat that we lost in the scuffle and put it back on my head. And when you agree to do that, I'll let you up." So he agreed. Anyway, we went on and we saw him again at the Downtown Bar, but he walked right by me, didn't say a word or even look at me, just kept walking right on by.

What do you know! It's August 25th, and the weather is good. It warmed up and I hooked the water back up to our cabin. The riffles were real good today and the box ran 4 hours. I've got Henry Walker, the Canadian from down at the Eldorado Creek crossing working for us, he worked 5 hours today. A Mountie, Dave Kingston, came up today checking on our stolen light plant. His sister Teresa was with him. We invited them to eat with us and we had steaks, cooked them outside on the fire, and they sure were good. They panned for gold, got some gold, and were real happy. He's gonna check out a couple of leads that we gave him on the light plant. We let Henry drive our 4-wheeler down to his camp, and told him whatever he did, don't drive it into Dawson.

August 26th. Henry was late for work this a.m. and I met him at Dave's on the way up Eldorado. He was on the 4-wheeler looking like he had a real bad hangover. He finally admitted, when we got in camp, that he rode the 4-wheeler into Dawson and got drunk last night. Marcene went to town today and told the banker to sell some gold. Henry and I put in a 24-inch culvert pipe to handle water out of the left gulch by the dam for next spring breakup.

August 27th. I'm feeling much better, it's sure nice not to have a fever. Marcene works the shaker much better than Henry, who I've had hired for the past 3 days. He went to sleep yesterday morning the first load I brought up out of the pit, so I just shut the loader down. I went back and dumped the load, and I had to walk right up to him and whistle at him. I told him, "Hey man, you're all through, I don't need you up here sleeping on the job." So, I paid him up, sent him home, and that was the end of him.

August 28th. I drove into town today and called Dr. DePalatis in Anchorage, and he said, "If things don't look better for you in a couple days, come on in to Anchorage and I'll check you out." We should have our light plant for the motorhome by Saturday. We had a guy cleaning the inside of it today, he does that as a specialty.

August 29th. I lost my smoking pipe in the tailings today, but found it in the fine tailings.

August 30th. I saw an old boy at the auction this morning that I've known a long time in Alaska, Steve Agababa. He's quite a radio personality over there, and he's gonna be around here 'til Tuesday. Mike and Connie are building a cabin over on Brown Creek for themselves. She's going to interior decorate that cabin, put in carpet and so forth. Can you imagine miners walking on carpet over on Brown Creek?

Tuesday, September 2nd. I built up the dam for the winter, and cut a drain above the dam and around in the bedrock overflow.

September 3rd. We're bull cookin' around camp. We drove over to Brown Creek to see Mike's and Connie's cabin, it looks good. The fog burned off late this morning and it's a beautiful day. We got some good pictures.

September 4th. It sure was nice out today. We had lunch with Lou, Cass and Iris at the Triple J.

September 5th. Zalato Fras finished wiring up the new power plant in our motorhome. I put up a radio antenna this evening and Marcene helped thread the wire into the cabin. We got the dynamite wire from Dave and he explained to me how to make the antenna and put it up. You take a flat board about 8 x 5" and cut out the center part. Wrap the wire around the center of the cut out, run 1 end of the wire outside to a ground rod and the other end about 100' out to a tree. Then set the box just behind the radio and it really makes a difference in the reception.

September 6th. Bernie Gagnon came up about 9 a.m. and picked up the dozer with Bill Bowie's flatbed truck. We went over to Brown Creek to work on the road. I helped Bernie take the wanigan and hopper down the hill to Brown Creek, and we got to bed about 11:30.

Sunday, September 7th. I dressed up the road all the way down to Brown Creek and Bernie and I took the shaker plant down, and Mike's lumber. It sure was nice out last night, northern lights and stars were beautiful. I slept pretty good in the wanigan. We brought the dozer back and got home about 6 o'clock this evening.

September 8th. I did work on the settling ponds this a.m. and pushed tailings before sluicing. We started on the porch this evening and it isn't gonna be a bad project, I don't think. It's sure nice to hear the radio since we made the antenna. We moved the washhouse just enough to put the hangover porch roof on.

September 9th. We picked up 4 pieces of tin for the porch roof. Marcene and I put up more logs on the porch and we have the hardest part done already. We went by to pay Andy for the doors and windows and he wasn't in, he's hard to catch sometimes.

September 10th. It's cold at night, and awful dry for so long that the water is getting low. We finished putting up logs on the porch and will put the decking and tin on tomorrow. It was another nice day, cool this a.m., the water line froze up, but it thawed out around noontime. Russian gold buyers were up to see us this p.m.

September 11th. We finished the porch on our cabin, put the roof on this a.m. It was sure a nice day, warm this p.m., but I drained everything this evening. No one came by to see us today.

Sunday, September 14th. We cleaned the front 5 sets of riffles this p.m. and I had to quit, I was hurting so bad. We were in Dawson last night, made the rounds, went to Gertie's and all the other places. So anyway, we'll see how I come out, we'll get all squared away here pretty soon, I hope.

September 15th. We cleaned the box today and I took the concentrates down to Gene's, Stevie is going to run it through the gold wheel. Jim Conklin and his son came up this p.m. and helped me clean the rest of the box. It sure was cold last night.

September 16th. We spent most of the day just getting ready for winter, winterizing things. Bernie and his partner Vern came up this p.m., they wanted to run their concentrates, but I was all unhooked and water drained, so I let them take the machine down to their place. We went into Dawson tonight, stopped by to see Gene and Kathy, and went on and ate supper at the Downtown Hotel. We picked up the loader sprockets. We should get away around noon tomorrow if everything goes right.

Wednesday, September 17th. We left camp about 8:30 this a.m. I took my Case 450 dozer down to Dave's to park for the winter. We went by the Recorder's Office and took care of paperwork on the claims on Brown Creek. We got a geologist to drive our pickup to Whitehorse. We left Dawson about 1:30 p.m. and got into Whitehorse about 9 o'clock. We had 5 miles of super rough road on the way.

We left Whitehorse, drove on in to Tok, and Anchorage. We did our running around, and we'll be heading down the highway. I have to add this note, one of our bankers in Anchorage, Buzz Hoffman, told me a goodie. He told me that his doctor was examining him, had his finger up his butt checking for prostrate problems, and started laughing. Buzz wanted to know what was so funny, and the doctor said, "I always did want to get a banker by the ass."

We went back through Dawson City on our way to Whitehorse and outside. We went to the Downtown Hotel and saw Lou, had breakfast with him and he took us over to the Eldorado Restaurant. We're to meet with Dick Hughes and Mr. Lang and their people regarding hardrock mining. They're gonna go up to our camp tomorrow, and we'll meet them there.

We saw Gene and Kathy on our way up to camp, they're sluicing and getting good gold, hope they get a bunch.

Friday, October 3rd. We're in Whitehorse, making final adjustments and tuneups to the motorhome, etc. We had to get our furnaces fixed again at ICG, and Ed fixed them. It seems as if every time we get close to Whitehorse he's got to attend to the furnaces. We left our pickup at Norcan Leasing, and Gene and his people will pick it up and take it on in to Anchorage when they shut down their mine.

It all over for this summer, this year at Gay Gulch, in Dawson City, Yukon Territory.

1987

Sunday, March 29th, 1987. We're back in Anchorage. Mel Pardek called tonight and is interested in some gold mining ground on Stikeen River, about 30 miles out of Telegraph Creek in northern British Columbia. He wants to talk to Charlotte Vandola and get me to set up a meeting with her regarding Collinsville, and also Leonard Yukness's ground on Pass Creek.

Friday, May 1st. Mel Pardek and I picked up Glen Heatherly and went to the Bureau of Land Management and U.S. Geological Survey for maps and information regarding mining claims. There sure is more paperwork nowadays, and no one seems to know what the heck is going on. After meeting with Charlotte and Dr. Yukness, Mel went back to Vancouver.

Saturday, May 9th. We left this morning for Dawson City and the mine, drove as far as Kluane Wilderness Lodge and spent the night.

Monday, May 11th. We got the insurance and license for our pickup, and the rest of our running around Whitehorse done, and left for Dawson about 4 p.m., getting in about 10:30 tonight. We drove on up to camp and everything looked good, the snow is all gone.

May 12th. We went to town and checked on some ground on Moose Creek, and it's open.

May 13th. I thawed water pipe under the dam and did a little dozer work in the pit. It was cold last night, 20 degrees this morning, and it never did get very warm today.

May 14th. I got water at the spring and ground sluiced a little today, it was 12 degrees this morning and everything froze pretty hard. We drove into Dawson this a.m. and stopped by to tell Bill it's too cold, too early to start sluicing. That's "Dipstick Willie" I'm talking about.

Saturday, May 16th. We drove into Dawson this morning, checked on a few things, had breakfast at the Eldorado Hotel, and went to the Gulf Bulk plant to get kerosene for the heater. We also checked on diesel prices, 51 cents a liter. On our way back to camp we stopped to see Gene and Kathy Fowler, and Jim and Shirley Conklin came up to see us this p.m. Jim helped me take the big cast iron stove out of the green-house, and I gave it to him. We set up a little one in there that Dave Lorenson had given me last year. We still don't have water into the cabin, we have to haul it from the spring in 5-gallon plastic buckets on the 4-wheeler.

Monday, May 18th. Boy, it sure was nice today, a real summer-like day. Our little martins came back today, and we also saw our first mosquitos. Marcene rode down on the 4-wheeler to Oro Grande Gulch to put rocks in a slot in the glacier over the little creek at the foot of the hill, so she could drive across it tomorrow morning.

May 19th. Gold was $470 and ounce and silver was $9.08. We went into Dawson, ate lunch at the Midnight Sun, got a barrel of diesel at White Pass, and paid for the can of kerosene that we picked up Saturday. It was like summer out today. They were putting the ferry in the Yukon River this p.m. and it should be running in 2 or 3 days. I got some black dirt below Gene's this p.m., to mix with peat and manure, for our garden.

May 20th. It was a nice day, in the 60s and 70s, sunny. We had no problems at all today, everything ran beautiful. Bill worked 4-1/2 hours, starting at noon and quitting at 4:30. I set out strawberries and onions and sowed some wild flowers this afternoon. Lou Provonovich came up to visit us tonight and Marcene fixed him a little bag of fruit, etc., to carry with him to Brown Creek tomorrow.

May 21st. It sure was nice today. Bill works the shaker good, holds back the material if it's too sticky and rakes the rocks along if they're washing good. I set out another row of strawberries this p.m. It sure is peaceful up here, no phones, and no one telling you what you gotta do.

May 22nd. We went to Dawson tonight, went to Gertie's and had supper with Mike and Connie Hayden. We come on back to the mine around midnight and saw a black bear on the way home.

May 23rd. It's that time of year, the weather was icky today, cloudy, rain and small hail, a little snow, and I don't know what all. The big stockpile that Wayne Hawk stockpiled for us last fall is still frozen, but so far we have been able to keep nibbling around it like a little mouse nibbling on a big chunk of cheese. Dave Johnson's girl friend Tina came up to visit Marcene on a 4-wheeler this p.m. I'm going to Moose Creek near the U.S. Border tomorrow with Mike. We're hoping to stake a couple of 5-mile leases.

Sunday, May 24th. We got up early this morning and Marcene fixed breakfast. I got going about 6 a.m., caught the ferry at Dawson and drove over to meet Mike. We went to Moose Creek, and I took strawberry plants to Lynn, Big O's girl friend, on the way over.

I flipped my 4-wheeler over backwards and sure banged my back up. Mike had a 4-wheel drive 4-wheeler and I didn't realize it, mine was 2-wheel drive. He went up the embankment, crawled right on up it, so I got a run at it, then started to slack off, changed my mind right at the last minute and poured the coals on. It just reared right up and flipped over, fell about 5 feet back down on the ice, landing with the machine on top of me. But I went on in with Mike and we got posts in, we staked a 5-mile lease. There sure was lots of water on the overflow, and lots of ice in Moose Creek. We were in and out of the creek so much I felt like a beaver before we were through. We walked at least 3 miles down there and back, and I guess I hit 50,000 niggerheads and rocks coming up the hill, back up to the top where we'd parked our pickup. And I felt every one of them right in my back. I sure was glad to get back in the pickup and get set down on a comfortable seat.

Down on the creek, we saw cabins from the old days, 1897, old bottles, bake pans, pots, washtubs and pans. We saw an old steam boiler, old water wheel, that's where the old-timers had worked. Jennifer and Tia, when you grow up and read this, just remember that your granddad helped make history mining, just like those old-timers did.

May 25th. We went into town to record the lease on Moose Creek. The girl in the Recorder's Office showed me paperwork where another guy had filed on 1 mile of the lease, the best mile, so we'll have to do something different. There was no post there that we could find, any place, but we don't want to contest it. So Mike and I flew over Moose and Brown Creeks again.

Wednesday, May 27th. Yesterday I planted taters, and today I set out another row of strawberries. My back is sure sore, and Marcene's foot is not well yet from her bunion operation, but she set out onions.

May 28th. It rained and was kind of icky today. My back bothers me a lot, I think I have a broken rib or something. Bill worked 5 hours today.

May 29th. We cleaned up the 3 front sets of riffles and put them in the washhouse. Mike came up and I went into Dawson with him to the Recorder's Office. He went on to Brown Creek after hearing that a bear had broken into his cabin. I'll pick him up tomorrow in a Trans North helicopter and we'll go do some more staking on Moose Creek. I checked on the helicopter, and I can't leave until 2 p.m. tomorrow. I hope Mike will wait 'til we get there. I picked up my Denver panner cleanup machine from Bernie Gagnon and took it home. Most of today was nice, but my back was sure sore.

We went to the Gold Show this p.m. and saw quite a few old friends, Oley Lundy from Goldbottom Creek, Raymond Forsythe from Vancouver, also Bingo Bill McCarty who used to run Cat for Dave. We saw Dave and Tina at the Finning Tractor party, good food and nice people, also the old gang from ICG in Whitehorse, Ed and Stan and their wives.

Saturday, May 30th. Jim Johnson came up this morning for a nice long visit, had coffee with us, and it's nice to visit with friends who don't want anything. I rented a helicopter, went over to Brown

Creek and got Mike, then went on over to Moose Creek and staked 2 leases, 3 miles and 4 miles, starting at the U.S. Border and going south. Mike came back to camp with me tonight, took a shower and ate supper with us. He's a nice guy.

May 31st. The riffles looked real good today. Mike spent last night with us and left about 8:30 this morning. It's clear out now, the sun's shining, it's 9:30 p.m.

June 1st. Everything's going good. It's a nice day out. We ran a mini cleanup through the Denver panner and gold wheel, and it looks real good. We have one pet squirrel and he chases all the others away. He's king of the roost.

June 2nd. It was cloudy and kind of cool. We went to Dawson and checked at the Recorder's Office, then called Mike in Anchorage regarding the leases on Moose Creek. We ate at the Downtown Restaurant, and saw Butch Fowler, Gene's mechanic. He had to go to the border to meet a lowboy load coming in from Anchorage.

June 3rd. It rained last night and started again this p.m. about 4. The riffles looked good today. We picked about 7 ounces of gold out of the front riffles this afternoon and had a nice nugget, about a half ounce. Zalato and his friend, who mine on Ready Bullion Creek, came by for a nice visit this evening, it's always good to see them. They wanted to do their cleanup through our Denver panner, so everything was cool and we did. Boy, it's really coming down outside now, 9:55 p.m. It's so nice and cozy in our log cabin with the tin roof. We don't have to worry about the dam washing out the overflow anymore as I've got the overflow cut in the bedrock on the hillside now.

June 4th. Boy, did it ever rain last night and some more today. The box didn't run, I spent the day ground sluicing. Bill hooked up the monitor valve, and we put in a pipe and ran the 6-inch monitor hose through it so we won't have to keep unhooking the hose after we use the monitor.

June 5th. Marcene went to Dawson and picked up pepper plants, cabbage, hanging baskets and flowers for the arbor. The hardrock bunch, who work for the Hughes-Lang group up at the Lone Star Mine, waded across Eldorado Creek, and have a 4-wheel drive vehicle on each side of the creek. I don't understand it. The old creek channel is changing and we'll just simply follow it. There's a layer of clay and black muck just above it, it sure is weird. I guess someday they'll streamline gold mining and it'll make our type of operation obsolete, like us in comparison with the late 1800s and early 1900s. Back then it was pick and shovel and mostly hand work, cutting wood to thaw the permafrost and ground, eventually graduating to steam. The men who worked it back then sure had to be some tough dudes. Frank Short said today that the safety guys were out and told him to get backup alarms on his equipment. He told them when they make the alarms bilingual he'll do that. He said that they asked him about his sprinkler system and he told them Jimmy Simpson told him how to rig it up as he'd used something kind of like that when he was mining above Nome, in Utica, on the Inmachuk River, in 1974.

Sunday, June 7th. We did our cleanup today and the new wheel works good, that's the Little Camel gold wheel. It's slow, but gets the gold clean. We ate supper at the Midnight Sun, Chinese food. It was nice out so we went for a ride over to Dieter's on Oro Grande, and down to see Dave and Tina on Eldorado. Dave just got started sluicing and it didn't look too good. He's going to run through his tailings from last fall, as it was a lot of frozen stuff that went through then. He thinks he'll do pretty good with it this spring.

June 8th. It was nice today and the water is slowing down quite a bit because it's getting warm and dry. We're in the old ancient stream bed and boy, the riffles are looking good. I had to go to the outhouse at the shaker this morning and I had cigars in the pocket of my overalls. One of my nice big cigars fell out and down the hole. I fished it out, it had cellophane wrapping still on it, so it was okay. Raymond Forsythe was up to see us this p.m., he wants to see me get a rubber tired loader, but we'll have to wait and see. He asked me how Ron and Bernie made out mining our first 2 claims, and my answer was, "I don't know." He laughed and said, "Oh, one of those deals, huh?"

June 9th. Dipstick Willie is still with us. It rained pretty hard this p.m. Gene and Kathy brought over a whole week of newspapers, the Anchorage Daily News, and that was thoughtful of them.

June 10th. We went down to see Gene this evening. The Water Board is giving him a hard way to go, while the Johnson brothers, Crawford, Art Fry, and many other Canadians don't seem to have to worry much about settling ponds. Art Fry's discharge from the sluice box is running right straight onto the road on Cheechako Hill. Gene and Kathy brought the keys for my Case dozer today.

June 12th. Bill worked today. Dieter and his wife, or girl friend, whichever, came up to see us this p.m. They were impressed with our gold. Everybody tells us how lucky we are, but somewhere along the way you have to make your luck. The four-letter word for lucky is W-O-R-K!

Saturday, June 13th. We went into Dawson tonight, ate supper at the Eldorado, and went to Diamond Tooth Gertie's to do a little gambling. It rained hard this p.m. and we got lots of water. Bill and I set up the monitor and started running it late this evening.

Tuesday, June 16th. The weather was cold 'til about 2:30 p.m., then it got real nice. We drove over to Ready Bullion this evening to see our friends Zalato and Robert. They're getting good gold there. The road was rough as a cob, I don't guess we'll go back over there for awhile.

Friday, June 19th. It looks like we'll just have a wet summer this year, but no rain today, the weather was okay. I worked on the road this p.m. and we ran the monitor for 2 hours this evening. Our riffles looked "yeller", and we found a nice big nugget. Bill was surprised at the gold in the box as we just cleaned up yesterday evening. My rib is still sore and every rock that I run over with the dozer or track loader has a name on it. I'll sure be glad when it does what it's gonna do, I'm getting tired of the hurt.

June 20th. Gene and Kathy, and Joe Andres and his wife came up to visit us today. We drove into Dawson this p.m., but didn't stay for Gertie's as we had to come back and run the monitor. We had lots of water.

Monday, June 22nd. We had lots of company in camp today. The weather was hot and the water has slowed down quite a bit. We either have too much or too little. The riffles looked good. We ran some material through the Denver panner and through the gold wheel. Bill had to take off at noon to go to Dawson and we'll see him tomorrow.

June 23rd. Today wasn't as hot as yesterday, just warm, and we had a nice breeze coming up the gulch. I talked to Andy Fras today regarding claims on Ready Bullion. Joe Andres and I may go over tomorrow, if everything goes alright, and I'll show him around, do some panning and etc. It strated raining real hard about 10:30 p.m., so I may work more hours tomorrow than I had planned.

Saturday, June 27th. Bill helped me take the tracks off the loader last night, and load them into the pickup. We left for Anchorage this morning, and I ran out of gas. But that was no problem as I had some with us in a barrel with a pump. I took a couple of pills that some dude from Fairbanks gave me the night before last. He said, "Take these for your back, that's what I have to take for my back when it pains me, and you'll get a good night's sleep." I hadn't had a good night's sleep in a long time, so I took one of those pills last night. I felt so good this morning I figured that for riding to Anchorage I'd just take two. But I'll tell you, those pills just made me do all kinds of weird, sleepy, funny kinds of things. We didn't have any problem going through the border, Marcene just explained to the guy what was wrong with me. We stopped to eat in Tok and stopped for coffee at Gunsight Lodge. When we got to Anchorage we found out that those pills were Demerol. I don't want any more Demerol.

We heard from Gail and Robert Vanderhoof, the people who have the lodge on the Kuskokwim River, out of Red Devil, Alaska. They and the kids are flying their plane over for our Fourth of July Party.

Monday, June 29th. I took the loader tracks by Automatic Welding. They're supposed to get the pins and bushings turned in them, and we'll pick them up tomorrow and hook'em back to Dawson. I finally got my back x-rayed today. The doctor said it was only a fractured vertebra and a crushed disk. He said a fraction over the tenth vertebra and I could have been paralyzed, so, am I lucky!

June 30th. We picked up a barbeque grill for the mine at Bill McNabb's today, it sure is a heavy sucker. I got the tracks loaded this a.m., paid for turning the pins and bushings, and we're on our way, hookin'em out to Tok.

July 1st. We got into camp tonight and it was raining cats and dogs. And boy howdy! The hardrock miners had drug a pump on skids up the road, up our hill, and I could barely get up it in 4-wheel drive. It was a mess.

July 2nd. Boy, I got ticked off at the hardrock miners and told them off this morning. They laid a pipe across the road, right by my fuel tank, and ran a hose through it, didn't even bother to bury it or cover it up, just laid it down. Anyway, I went and got them and told them what they had to do. They had to move the pump out of the creek and get it out of the way, and so forth.

So many things went haywire since I left, I don't want to go into them all. But, Dipstick Willie was supposed to change the oil and filter in my dozer and lube it, that's all he had to do. Then he could pan and run the small sluice box in the pit while I was gone. But he took it upon himself to go down and tow the pump on skids up the road and set it right out in the middle of the creek. It rained and the pump almost got covered, then he had to move it on upstream. Anyway, it's a long story.

Here's the story where Dipstick Willie got that nickname, "Dipstick". He changed oil in my dozer and left the dipstick on the track, and then ran over it. He ran over a rock and it twisted that stick and broke it. When I went to get on the dozer, and went to check the oil, the dipstick wasn't there. I asked him about it and he said, "Oh no, I put the dipstick back in." So I looked around down there where he'd changed the oil and I found it, the pieces. I taped them together and wrote on the tape, "Dipstick Willie". I still have it!

I got new rubbers for the shaker plant bars and Bill installed those. Alice and Earl came up today and found a hot spot. They're a couple from Texas we met last winter in Bullhead City, Arizona. It's nice to see them again. They're really enjoying themselves.

Saturday, July 4th. Northern Cat sent their mechanic out today. He and Dipstick Willie worked from 9 o'clock this morning until 7 tonight putting the tracks on our loader. I was still hurting pretty bad and I didn't want to go down and argue with them. Marcene and I have put those tracks on by ourselves, just her and I, in about 2 hours, so it's about an hour per track. They just didn't know what they were doing and when they got all through, the mechanic from Northern Cat came up and said, "Sir, I hate to tell you this, but your tracks are on backwards." I said, "You guys put the tracks on backwards?" He said, "Do you want me to change them around and put them back the other way like they're supposed to go?" I said, "No, I run backwards just about as much as I go forward." I just wanted to get them out of my hair. But it does wear the tracks faster to have them on backwards.

And I'd like to make a note that this is the end of Dipstick Willie. I didn't appreciate him taking all that time milling around out there with the mechanic. But he brought the end on himself. Robert, the Eskimo from Kuskokwim, wanted to work the shaker plant just to get the feel of it, to see what it was like. So I said, "Yeah, okay, if you want to work it we'll let you go up and work about an hour." We cranked up and got started, and Dipstick Willie came driving up in his pickup. Boy, when he saw that Robert was up there on the shaker, he turned around and batted 'em out of Gay Gulch. Later that evening I went down to see him. I said, "What happened to you?" He said, "Well, I've been replaced, that's it." I said, "Okay, no problem, I'll pay you what you got coming."

And this was all happening during our Fourth of July party. We had lots of friends come up. But everybody enjoyed themselves and had a ball anyway.

July 5th. It was nice out today. Our Eskimo friends had to leave to go back to their lodge at Red Devil, and our friends from Texas left this p.m. They panned a little before they left and were happy with the party last night. I paid Bill in full today and he's just a very unhappy person, but he's through here on Gay Gulch.

July 6th. Dave Johnson and Bill Wright came up this p.m. asking questions regarding Gay Gulch. Marcne and I went to Dawson this afternoon and tried to pay Northern Cat, but they didn't have a bill made out. I figure that Northern Cat may be starting in business, but they're on their way out, as far as I can see, with this type of work, and the type of people they're hiring. I like John and Boyd, but their help isn't all that swift.

July 7th. I did about 2 hours dozer work for Hughes-Lang on the road up toward Lone Star Mine this morning. A squirrel got into one of our garbage cans today and almost drowned, he stayed in there so long. It had ice in it, and I can just imagine the little booger just about froze to death too. He was in there with pop and beer and couldn't get out, the plastic can was too slick and he couldn't get ahold of anything. We found him just in time to dump him out and revive him.

July 8th. We went to Dawson, ate at the Downtown Cafe, got grease at White Pass, got bolts, and Marcene stopped by several places. She called Marlene, and Mike's office to ask him to bring me a dipstick for the Case 450 dozer. The weather was pretty nice today, a little sun, clouds, and very little rain. We cleaned up the first 6 sets of riffles this evening. We were running good material, it made the riffles look "yeller", sure looked good to us. I guess most of the "yeller", the gold, came from the bedrock in the bottom of the pit in the old creek channel. Marcene's foot is worse today, so I put her in a chair at the sluice box, setting up on the bank watching the hopper and watching me dump into the hopper, and her motioning to me. We have to keep watching the darn hardrockers' pump, that's in order for the tailings not to cover it up. They're setting down there on the edge of a spring, in a hole down below us, so I got to be real careful with the fine tailings. I'll be glad when they get the heck out of here. The bearing in the shaker started making racket and I guess we'll have to change the bearing in 2 or 3 days. We saw Scotty, with Hughes-Lang, on the road and he said that Dick Gillespie was gonna fix our road, so goody, goody!

Friday, July 10th. Marcene and I are working by ourselves, with no hired help. Marcene went down on the 4-wheeler to talk to Dipstick Willie. She told him that she couldn't work, that her foot was so bad. He told her that he didn't really care, that was alright and just to leave him alone. He was setting in there, holding his little dog.

July 11th. The box ran 5-1/2 hours today, and the weather was good. Marcene talked to Jackie and Ron at the Downtown and they were nice to her. On the way into town we met Tim, with Inglehardt, on his way up to our camp. We also saw one of Crawford's dozers off on its side, it slid off a lowboy. Between Crawford's and Art Fry's, they keep the road on Bonanza tore up all the time. It rained hard this evening.

Sunday, July 12th. Tim came up this p.m. and demonstrated the melting pot, but it's just not the answer for our operation, so he understood, and I did too. I showed Tim the gold, or rather the trash, that the Johnson boys left for us at the bank last fall for our percentage. They left it at the bank for us because they didn't have the guts to give it to us in person. Tim said he had heard about it, but he didn't believe it until he saw it. I promised Ron Johnson that I would show that to every friend, or every person, that ever came to our camp. Gene came up this p.m. for a visit. We went into Dawson and ate with Big O and Lynn tonight and it was sure good food. The weather was nice today, but rained tonight.

July 13th. I loaded the pump for the hardrock miners this p.m., I'm sure glad to get them out of here. They messed up our road again with Klondike Transport's big Cat, it walked right down the road and tore up the hill. I think I'll send them a bill for Cat work, etc. I ground sluiced some today on the south side of the gulch, on claim JDS #3, and moved a bunch of quartz boulders this p.m. Marcene went to Dawson and paid Northern Cat for labor and parts. We like to pay our bills promptly.

July 14th. The riffles looked good today. It was real fine gold, but I guess that's okay as long as it's "yeller". I did a little ground sluicing this a.m., and Marcene worked the shaker today. Marty Tomkins is supposed to come out tomorrow and change the bearings on the shaker plant. He's from New Zealand originally. It was a pretty nice day.

July 15th. It was nice today. Marcene swatted a squirrel off the porch with a broom this morning, he thinks he owns the cabin, we gotta keep him straight. Marty didn't show up today, guess he'll be here tomorrow. We cleaned our gold this p.m. Our bottle is getting heavy. My little camel wheel sure works good, I'm glad I bought it. It beats everything I've ever tried for cleaning gold. We had a rabbit in camp this evening, it won't eat the vegetables, etc., but likes something in the gravel.

July 16th. Marty didn't show today, hope he gets here tomorrow as the shaker bearing is getting louder.

July 17th. Marcene went into Dawson, did washing and called Jadene. I hauled out of the old creekbed paystreak. The oldtimers really worked it extensively. I brought up old burnt wood and logs, and could just picture those poor guys working underground, burning wood to thaw the ground, the smoke and all they had to go through. It was hot today. Marty didn't show up again.

Sunday, July 19th. Marty didn't show again yesterday so we went to Dawson to see him. He got here today, changed the shaker bearings and worked on the motor awhile, and also on the old light plant. We found out that we had put entirely too much grease in the bearings. I didn't realize you could get too much grease in bearings.

July 20th. Last night when we were in town we met some farmers from Iowa. They came out today, panned in the pit and ate lunch with us. We enjoyed having them out. Jim Johnson, Dave's brother, came up to see us and had lunch with us. We ate at the table outside. It was hot today, in the 80s.

July 21st. I'm hauling from bedrock and monitoring the sides. Everything went smooth today, the rocks are washing good. We went to Dawson this a.m. and ate at the Downtown. We picked up old idler rollers from Marty, the old ones for the Komatsu, brought them out to camp and put them on the loader. The generator and voltage regulator don't work on the light plant. I've got to get a voltage regulator. We drove over to see Jim and Shirley on Upper Bonanza Creek, and saw a bear just down by the creek. Also, we stopped by to see Dr. Daunt, and Keirin and his brother. They were panning on Bonanza Creek where the Upper Bonanza bridge crosses over. We stopped by Dave's and got air for a tire.

July 22nd. We went to Dawson this morning and Marcene got herself some nice rubber boots, they were aqua color. I ordered corrugated plastic from Beaver Lumber today for the greenhouse. We ate breakfast at the Eldorado Hotel, and talked with Butch Sealy. The old International light plant is sounding kind of sick, I sure hope it'll stick together for the rest of the season.

July 23rd. Marty came up and took the idler rollers off the loader and pressed the pins out of the support. While he was here, I had him look at the old power plant, it had a broken push rod and spring. So we've got a 5-cylinder International now. He went in and ordered parts from Edmonton. We ordered belts from B.C. Bearing today, got boards for the shaker spillway, and I put the new boards on the shaker.

July 24th. We went into Gertie's tonight and went to the Miners' Ball. Marcene won $200 at Gertie's. We're invited to dinner at Andy's and Maria's on Sunday.

July 25th. We found some good pay on the left side of Gay Gulch this afternoon, close to where the pup comes into the gulch. Marie and John, farmers from Peace River, B.C. came up this p.m. and they're going to spend a few days panning. Boyd, one of the owners of Northern Cat, came out this p.m. He was here 2 hours and ran out of fuel, so he said he'd just charge us for 1 hour, as he had to syphon some fuel out of our tank. I don't know just how much he got, but it doesn't really matter because he knocked off an hour of his time. It's nice to have people like that working for you. It was a nice day today. Marcene's foot was swelling bad this morning, but after a rest it got better.

Sunday, July 26th. We took Maria a watermelon that we had in camp. I went up to the spring to get our big watermelon, and it had been in the water too long. I didn't know you could leave them in water too long, but it had spoiled on the outside, and just the center, the heart we call it, was good. We had a nice visit with Mrs. Hackinson at the Eldorado Hotel, and with Louisa and Marty at the Downtown. We met a nice couple on the road home and they wanted to come up to the mine, so we invited them up to sit by the fire this evening. They're farmers from Ontario, Canada, and real nice people.

July 27th. We had lots of company in camp today. Marlene and Bill McNabb came in tonight, and Fuzzy Springle and his wife Delight, came up and ate supper. People are panning every whichaway. The monitor ran 5 hours today, and it was hot.

Wednesday, July 29th. Bill, Fuzzy and I went to Brown Creek to check on claims over there, and checked on Mike, his son, and his buddy. They were broke down and we helped them get going.

July 30th. Boy, did it ever rain hard today. Parts for our generator came in, but they're the wrong parts. Fuzzy and his wife are still in camp, and Bill McNabb worked the shaker.

Sunday, August 2nd. The riffles look good today. Marlene and Bill were going home today, but Eldorado Creek was so flooded they couldn't get across, the road was all washed out, so they're gonna try to leave tomorrow. Bernie Johnson worked on the road this p.m., building a new section by where their old cabin was.

August 3rd. We went to town this morning, had to pull Bill and Marlene across Eldorado Creek. My darn loader is messing up, the starter switch, or something, we'll try to figure it out tomorrow.

August 4th. We stopped on the trail and visited with Jim Archibald. He sure turned out to be a nice guy. Jim has a unique setup, he has a little dog that watches the sluice box, and every time a big white boulder comes through that little dog chases it all the way down to the end of the box. The dog has seen Myrna, Jim's wife, work the white boulders down the box and he thinks he's working right along with them. They have a solar bank on top of their house overlooking Eldorado Creek and French Gulch. It's quite a landmark that they have up there, they can see up and down the creek for miles.

August 5th. My loader broke down, and I'm waiting on a solenoid and switch from Coneco.

Friday, August 7th. We went to Kathy Fowler's birthday party tonight.

August 8th. The box ran 5 hours today. Marty got the engine for the light plant fixed and the loader going, so everything's running now, we just need the generator and voltage regulator for the light plant. It rained a little this p.m. We still have plenty of water to run as much as we need.

August 9th. Bernie and J.C. came up and brought friends in their helicopter. They're nice and also funny. We went to Andy's birthday party this evening, lots of good food and everything just fine. Davis and Butch came up this p.m., they're trying to find some mining ground. They'll dig test holes on Moose Creek for an option to mine on percentage. That's on the leases over there that Mike and I staked.

August 10th. We had company today. Bernie and J.C. and their friends from Quebec came up, and Bernie did a cleanup through our Denver panner. Zalato and his crew came by this afternoon and fixed the voltage regulator on my light plant. We drove down to see Davis this p.m. to let him know it's okay if he wants to take a backhoe and equipment over on Moose Creek and do testing this fall.

Thursday, August 13th. The riffles looked super, we're back to the old channel, the old-timers didn't get it all. It was cool this a.m., but hot this p.m., and everything's running fine.

August 14th. We cleaned up the front 4 sets of riffles and ran it through the Denver panner. This was our 38th anniversary. We went into Dawson this p.m. and had a real nice party at the Eldorado Hotel. Lots of our friends were there.

August 15th. We picked up 2 guys on the way out to camp this morning. One of them was Charlie Allen from Anchorage. They wanted to see how our mine operated and how we worked. Everyone wants to do it like we do until they get started, then they get greedy and get bigger. I can't quite understand people.

Sunday, August 16th. It started raining this evening, but it's okay, we can always use the water, especially this time of year when it's dry and cool. It's sure nice to hear it on the tin roof of the cabin when everything is so secure. David Peterson, his wife Rosie, and a friend came up this p.m. and we shut down and had a nice visit with them.

Tuesday, August 18th. We went to Dawson tonight, ate at the Midnight Sun and had drinks at the Eldorado with Mayor Peter Jenkins. He bought a round of drinks and was nice. We talked to Wayne Hawk, and he's coming out tomorrow to stockpile and rip bedrock for us.

August 19th. The box ran approximately 5 hours and boy, did we hit a glory hole! About 15 to 18 ounces of gold spooning out of the front 3 riffles. Wayne brought his D8 Cat up and started work around 8 p.m.

August 20th. Marcene got shocked this morning. A big rock fell out of the loader bucket, slipped out and hit the rake, bent the rake, she lost her balance and almost fell off the shaker. It was nice today, but a little cold this p.m.

August 21st. I did some hauling this a.m., on the edge of the old ancient creek channel and it was good for us. I guess the old-timers, 1898 to 1915, didn't think that it would pay to move the material by hand. It was a nice day. We found some nice nuggets after a 4-hour run. We cleaned up this evening and drove into Dawson. We saw Bernie on the way to town. He and J.C. and his sister were flying out to see us, so we went on to Dawson and came right back out. Bernie set down at the original discovery claim on Bonanza Creek and asked Marcene to ride in the chopper with them to camp, so she did.

Saturday, August 22nd. The box ran 4 hours this a.m., the riffles were beautiful. "Yeller"! Wayne brought Norm Pierson, a miner from down in B.C., and his daughter to camp today. They just couldn't hardly believe the gold that we got this a.m. Marcene,

Bernie and I flew over to Brown Creek, but Mike wasn't there, so we called him in Anchorage tonight. He'll be over next week.

Thursday, August 27th. The riffles looked okay today. We started running through the box all the stockpiled material that Wayne put up there, and it's a "duke's" mixture of everything imaginable on Gay Gulch, so we don't expect the riffles to turn yellow right away. We went to Dawson this p.m. to check on parts for the light plant. It was warm today, real nice, but it clouded up this evening and may rain tonight.

We heard that Carl Black was on his way over with a lowboy, bringing the rubber tired loader we'd bought from him, and got run off the road by a tourist over at Chicken, Alaska. That's tough, a real bad break for him. Butch went over to help get his rig out and should be in tomorrow.

August 28th. I'm running general material, and running about 12 to 14, maybe 15 yards at the most, an hour. I have heard that the old-timers used gold witchers, as people use water well witchers. I don't know, but they seemed always to know where the gold was, and anytime we mine and go through where they were, the riffles turn "yeller". We went to Dawson and got the generator and voltage regulator for the power plant, and we met Mike. He flew his Beaver airplane with floats on it over and tied up just up from where the ferry crosses. He's happy with the deal I made with Davis on our claims on Moose Creek.

Sunday, August 30th. It was cold as kraut this morning, and the wind's blowing. Butch brought our rubber tired loader yesterday. We got started about 10:15 this morning and quit a little after 12, it was just plain miserable. So that's about enough for this season, I think. We went to town and ate, but came on home early and drained everything, as it's cold and freezing. We saw Frank Short in town this evening and he forgot where he parked his pickup, he was looking for it.

August 31st. Boy, was it cold this morning! It was 10 degrees at 7 a.m. We went down to the Recorder's Office with Davis and got the paperwork all fixed up on the guys he's bringing over, regarding the claims on Moose Creek.

Thursday, September 3rd. We shut down at noon today for the season.

September 4th. I took the little crusher down to Bud Callison on the Klondike Highway, I'm going to let him use it. Fuzzy came by, brought mail and newspapers from Anchorage, and that was nice of him. Davis came up this p.m., and I guess we'll meet him at the border Sunday morning. We got a check for Carl Black, and we'll send it with Davis when he goes back over.

September 5th. We buckled everything up in camp, took my dozer down to Keirin Daunt's at Skookum Gulch, Gold Hill, and went on into town. We went to see Andy and Maria. We saw Greg Hackinson, and he knew about our gold on Gay Gulch. I met the guys that are over with Davis regarding testing on Moose Creek.

Sunday, September 6th. I stopped at the border and told the guys where to take the equipment on Moose Creek, and where Mike's dozer was to pick up at Brown Creek and bring over to Moose Creek. They're going to do the "switcheroo", and we're going to Anchorage.

Mike Hayden and I took Davis Fowler and a group of his friends down on Moose Creek and did a bunch of testing. We went in about 10 miles down toward the Forty Mile River to see if the ground was good enough for them to work. It turned out to be about $2 to $2.50 a yard, the best we could figure out. I never knew the exact amount of the yardage value, there were too many fingers in the sluice box, too many people panning. There was this one guy's wife that had never seen gold before. I had to make 2 trips into Dawson, one for fuel and another to take Davis in. So there was just absolutely no way to keep track of the gold we actually took out of there. Anyway, the boys were all excited, they'd never been around it before. The one guy and his wife were like kids in a candy store when they saw gold in the pans.

I kept the paperwork on the tests that we did on Moose Creek, and I've got the numbers of the claim posts that we tested by and so forth. While we were in there we converted the leases to claims, and put up the claim posts and marked them, etc. At one time we had to lower 1200 feet of Moose Creek by about 6 feet, we had to go about 1200 feet downstream to get grade to drain water away from the pit that we were digging in for tests. When we finished testing, and as we were moving out, I was the first Cat up on top, and snow was about 4 feet deep just before we got to the Top of the World Highway. I'm sure glad to get out of there and get gone to somewhere where it's nice and warm.

Friday, September 18th. We're back in Dawson and back up to camp. I talked to Pierre Monfet today, he's got his old slouch hat with all the nuggets on it hocked to the bank for $2000.

Monday, September 21st. We left Dawson City this morning and I couldn't bring myself to bring any gold with me. Each one of those people had put up $1000 to go on that little safari over to Moose Creek, and each of them had a little dab of gold. But most of the gang wanted every speck they could gather up. I filed on 12 claims on Moose Creek, and I just hope the ground proves out better when we get a chance to retest it without so many distractions. But I know that we tested enough of the good looking material and it just wasn't where we were, the gold, that is. So much for this season, the geese are going south, and so we should be going soon too. We drove to Tok and spent the night there.

Sunday, September 27th. We had to bring a bunch of pads for the dozer and rollers to Dawson, so we're back. On our way over, just east of the border on that real bad spot by Moose Creek, we pulled a couple from Victoria, B.C. over the bad hill. They had a new Mercury and they had slid sideways in about a foot of snow. They were lost and came through the border after it closed. All we had to tow them with was a small 4-foot piece of nylon rope. The guy said it was too short and small. I told him, "Sir, it's all we have." We pulled him to the top of the hill and followed him for 70 miles into Dawson city. He tried to pay us $50, but we explained to him that up north we just do things like this and don't expect pay for it.

Epilogue

It's 1988, and another season on Gay Gulch. On our way north we stopped off in Bakersfield where we visited our good friends Red Simpson and Bobby Adkins. Bobby wanted to go mining with us. Even though he's a professional musician, we felt that due to the fact we'd known him for quite some time we would give him a shot at working at the mine. Bobby has a brother, Dennis that writes songs for Mel Tillis, and also is a singer in his own right. One of the better known songs that he has written to date is a big one that George Strait had out, (You gotta have an) "Ace in The Hole".

As we left Bakersfield Bobby's hopes were high and he was looking forward to coming up mining with us. We went on back to Anchorage and he was to meet us there.

We took off from Anchorage and went over to the mine by way of Whitehorse, Bobby driving our little '67 Mustang and us driving the 4x4 Ford pickup. We got into Dawson and introduced him around town to all of our friends. It's always good to get back to Dawson City in the springtime, all your old friends want to know where you've been all winter. Of course, with the personality that Bobby has, everybody took a liking to him.

On our way out to the mine we got up to our road at the foot of the hill, and due to the fact that we had so much snow during the wintertime it bent the birch and aspen trees over the road and Bobby got his first taste of work right there. Being from the warm climate, Bobby had a pair of longhandles on and you know what that does to you when you start using a chopping ax on trees. I switched off with him, but even so it took us about 2 hours to get in to the cabin at the mine.

It seemed as if Bobby woke up in a different world about every day, there were so many different things going on at the mine that a professional musician wouldn't be acquainted with, things like raking rocks, etc. It had a tendency to make his arms and hands cramp, and I can see why, because he'd been used to picking bass and guitar. One thing he thoroughly enjoyed doing was running the monitor. It didn't take a lot of effort, but the reason he enjoyed it so much were the times he was able to wash out a big bison head, or a horn, or mastodon tusk, or something that would just really get him excited. Not only that, but the material was always so much easier to run through the hopper and shaker plant after it had been monitored down. So that made it a lot easier on the shaker for Bobby.

I have to tell this little tale on Bobby. One time Marcene and I went into Dawson and left him at Camp to kind of look after things.

When we got back in camp he had all the windows shut, the door shut, and he was setting in a chair listening to country music, and he had the 444 rifle across his lap. I said, "Bobby, why the rifle, and why the door and windows all shut?" He said, "I was 'fraid of the bears!" From time to time we'd see a tree marked by a bear, and sometimes it would be a grizzly. Bobby would have to look it over real good and he took pictures of some of them, but he never did quite get used to all the bears living in that country with people.

He enjoyed going with us to visit the different miners around the area to see how everything else worked, and one thing about Bobby, he never let anything get him down or bother him, his spirits were always up. I remember one day we went over to our claims about 8 miles down on Moose Creek. You have a real steep hill to go off, with switchbacks, and when you get to the foot of the hill you drive off in the creek and go down the creek, slipping and sliding over rocks and stuff. Bobby just couldn't understand doing that, he was so afraid we were gonna break down, or run off in a hole, or something, and not be able to get out. He kept asking me, "Jimmy, how far is it back to the highway? If we break down are we gonna have to walk out of here?" I said, "Well, I don't see any taxis around."

One day on our way back from Dawson City we stopped at Grand Forks, where Bonanza Creek and Eldorado Creek join. At one time there were 15,000 people living there calling Grand Forks their home. They had bars, hotels, restaurants, the whole schmeer. That was back in 1897-98-99, and the early 1900s, but since the dredge went through and wiped out most of the town, there isn't much left to be seen at Grand Forks. Parks Canada now owns the ground in that area and they have it set aside for people to pan for gold for free.

This visit with the folks at Grand Forks that day was our first encounter with a young man, Danny Cozak. Danny would go on to play a part in our mining at Gay Gulch. He was an intriguing guy, he looked like a person that had stepped out of the 1800s. He had a mustache and wore a big black hat, and he had teepee poles on the top of his pickup rack. I thought that was a little odd. Danny asked if he could come up to camp and do a little gold panning. He had some friends there with him, and I said, "Sure, no problem, come on up." When he got up to camp he wanted to know if it would be okay if he set up his teepee, so I told him that'd be fine. I thought it was kind of neat having a teepee setting up at our camp on Gay Gulch.

· Gene Fowler had been negotiating with me to work the left pup on Gay Gulch. He wanted to bring his big equipment up to do some mining there on a percentage, and we could just kind of shut down for the rest of the summer and let Gene have at it with his big equipment. I talked to Bobby about it, and he decided that maybe he'd just go on back to Bakersfield and Vegas, there was no problem, no hard feelings. We asked Danny if he would look after camp while we drove Bobby into Anchorage to catch a flight back to Bakersfield, and of course, he was all for that.

Danny had come north to get away from the rat race in Brooks, Alberta where he worked in the oil fields and was a partner with his dad. He said he was just tired of working 18 to 20 hours a day, 7 days a week, and I could understand that. He said he'd like to have just a little time for himself and he'd never seen such a peaceful place as Gay Gulch in the Yukon Territory.

I talked to Gene at our Fourth of July party, and he'd had a change of mind about working Gay Gulch. He'd found some decent ground that he was stripping down at Fowlerville on Bonanza Creek and decided that he'd stay down there for the rest of the season. So I asked Danny if he might want to work part time with us and he said yes, that would be fine. He wasn't out to make a bundle, so he said, "Sure, I'll work part time with you guys."

Danny worked out real good, he was mechanic, welder, and just a general all around guy. He worked part time for us and also spent a little time working for Jim Archibald down on French Gulch and Eldorado Creek. During the hot days he'd work in his bathing suit at camp. That was very unusual to see a miner in the Yukon working in a bathing suit.

I was always playing tricks on Danny. We had a few fireworks left after our Fourth of July party and I rigged up a tube one day while Danny was working for Jim. It was a little piece of copper tubing, and I stuck it in the ground and aimed it at the fifth-wheel trailer in which he slept. I'd stick these little rockets attached to a stick in that copper tubing, and set 3 or 4 of them off. I got the range right over the top of Danny's trailer. When it come time for breakfast I'd normally holler over, or go over and knock on the door. So the next morning I got up and set the little rocket off, and from then on 'til freeze-up I would do this, and old Danny would come out of that fifth-wheel.

I had never seen a guy walk on gravel barefooted like Danny could since I was a kid back in Tennessee. He had the toughest feet of anybody I'd ever seen. He was the only guy that I knew of that would wear tennis shoes without socks, and I have seen him literally pour rocks and gravel out of his shoes. He'd walk right through the mud, water, sand, or whatever, it didn't matter to Danny.

Everything went good for the remainder of the season, no breakdowns. Danny would go into town with us, and everyone around Diamond Tooth Gertie's would look at Danny, wondering about him because he was so quiet and soft spoken. He just looked the part of an RCMP undercover agent. He had a handlebar mustache, was about 6 foot, and dark complected.

Jimmy Simpson   Epilogue   A VANISHING BREED

We had an early freeze-up that year, and of course, you can't launder rocks and wash gold when you have ice in your sluice box. Danny stayed in Dawson that winter and was gonna "babysit" a house for the banker, Axel Spears. He decided he'd go moose hunting. We figured it was time to go south, so we got everything secured and everything finished for another mining season on Gay Gulch.

I'd like to explain to you one thing about leaving our pit graded out. If you don't leave "dippy-diveys" in the pit, but you grade it out, whether it be steep grade or flat grade, you won't have what they call overflow ice buildup. If you don't grade it out, and you have all these rough spots in your pit, and the ice starts building up during the winter months from the warm springs, you can have yourself a real problem in the spring when you come back to open up your pit. You'll have many, many feet of ice to contend with. When we got back in the spring of '89 for another mining season on Gay Gulch, everything was fine at camp, Danny was with us, in good spirits and ready to go.

After we got our mining underway and used the runoff water, Danny and I decided that we'd go over to Lost Pup, off Henderson Creek. A pup is a little stream of water coming into a large stream, and in the Yukon we call it a pup in the mining circles. We went over and staked a 2-mile lease. You stake a lease and then you have 1 year to do assessment work, that is enough work to figure $200 per claim, and then you have to turn that into claims that year. In other words, you stake 40-acre claims, and a 2-mile lease figures out to approximately 24 claims. So that's between $4000 and $5000 of actual work that you have to put in on those claims in order to just keep them active. Then each year thereafter you have to do $200 worth of work to keep the mining claims active, at least in the Yukon Territory of Canada.

I checked the ground out pretty good on Lost Pup and I was assuming, from the workings of the old-timers, that the ground at one time was a producer. Normally, if you go where the old-timers were working by hand, and you take equipment in, you can do pretty good these days, especially with the price of gold up to where it is.

We had lots of company coming and going the summer of '89, and it's always good to have company. Then there's times when it's just nice to sit around the fire in the evening, put your feet up and relax, and not have to visit an awful lot.

Danny went along with us over to Boundary, Alaska, and met several miners in that district. As we were coming back through Customs we visited with Ron Wilder at Customs, and also Carl Dickerson. Above all, I don't want to forget Ed Zawyrucha and Dave Kobeck, they're with Canadian Customs.

Danny worked part time with us and part time with Jim Archibald again because the water's low at our camp, and we only work 2 to 3 hours a day. Jim and Myrna are working French Gulch, just above Eldorado Creek. Danny pushed tailings for them and ran the D8 dozer.

We had a nice visit from our old buddy Al Oster. He's an ex-disc jockey out of Whitehorse, also a musician, and he also worked for the Canadian government. He now lives in Salmon Arm, B.C. He had a movie camera with him in his pickup, but he didn't have it when he walked up to visit us. I shut the loader down and had a nice visit. Unbeknownst to me, after he talked with us, he took some film of our operation, and he later put it on a video that he distributed throughout Canada. It turned out real good and Al spent a lot of time putting this video together. He had his music and recordings on this video, along with our operation, Queenstakes, and several other mining operators around the Dawson area. We didn't know that we were on the video until we were in Dawson one day, talking to some tourists. They told us that they saw us on a video film that they were showing down at a store in Dawson, Maximillian Books & Gifts. We just about couldn't hardly believe it, but we went and checked it out and sure enough, it was Al Oster's tape.

We ran short of material so we had Wayne Hawk bring his dozer up, and he ripped, pushed, and stockpiled material to give us lots of ground to run for the remainder of this summer and for next spring.

This year was our 40th anniversary. We had our anniversary party at the Triple J Hotel in Dawson, and had so many people come to our party that they couldn't all get in our suite. They had the halls full, and there were a couple of rooms next to us that were all full. Of course, the miners, when they heard that we were going to have our 40th anniversary, came and rented rooms right along the hallway by our suite. It was a party I don't think that we'll ever forget. We just had a ball.

The year of 1989 was the biggest season we ever had, as far as gold production on Gay Gulch. Danny hung right in there with us, doing great.

The year of 1990 just wasn't my year. While in Quartzsite, Arizona, I got a blood clot in my leg. I assumed I had a strained muscle, put a vibrator on it, and the rest was history, I broke the clots loose and they got into my lungs. I made it back to Nashville and checked in at the Madison Hospital for x-rays, etc. I had phlebitis in the leg and the carotid artery was 97 percent closed, so it looked like they were going to have to do something with me.

Dr. Vaughn Allen, The doctor that worked on my carotid artery, came in that first night I was in the hospital after the x-rays and said, "Feller, I don't know what I'm gonna do with you, it's like fighting fire with kerosene. But get a good night's sleep and I'll see you tomorrow morning. In the meantime I'll figure out something." The next day I found out that I was gonna have to have an operation, and they weren't able to operate on me until they'd put a filter in the main vessel that takes the blood back to the heart. The clots were already in my lungs, and they couldn't give me blood thinner at the time for fear of moving the clots.

I was so thankful that I had made it back to Nashville, even though I didn't feel like driving the motorhome, and they got me taken care of. I was evidently at the right place at the right time. At the same time that I was in the hospital in Madison, a suburb of Nashville, Dennis Adkins was admitted to the Critical Care Unit of Vanderbilt Hospital in Nashville.

It was such a warm feeling to have so many nice old friends in the music business come by to see me, or call, while I was there at Madison in the Hospital. Just to name a few, Billy Walker and his wife Betty, Charlie Walker, Mel Tillis called, Howard White, a guy that used to play steel guitar for me, of course Sheb Woolley, and quite a few more that heard about it and called to wish me luck. I got a nice card from all the girls at the Recorder's Office in Dawson City, it was a cute one. They wished me well and a speedy return back to the Yukon.

While I was there in the hospital I finally found a comfortable bed when I left the operating room and got to ICU, but they wouldn't let me take it with me when I got back to the regular room. I even tried to buy the sucker, but I couldn't make a deal with them. It sure was a comfortable bed, but they said they had to keep it in ICU because they can x-ray through those beds and they've got to have them there. I filled some little lockets with gold for the nurses that looked after me at the hospital, but Marcene did more than any of the nurses. She deserves something special, I think.

The worst part of my stay in the hospital was having to lay flat on my back for 7 hours after the filter was inserted in the main vein going back to my heart. I finally got some food after about 4 days and boy, it took me about 4 or 5 meals to catch up. I cleaned the plates of everything on them. Mama brought me up a bunch of food, dressing and Mexican cornbread, and all kinds of goodies.

I didn't know at the time that I'd be able to go back to gold mining in the Yukon, but everything worked out for the best. We had to hang around Ashland City for quite awhile before the Dr. Beck finally released me to go back north. It wasn't until the first of June before I was able to travel, that way he had my blood regulated with Cumedin. I called Danny Cozak in Dawson, he told me the miners still hadn't gotten their water permits for the year. The reason was there was a holdup in the government, something to do with a case pertaining to a dam being built down in Ontario someplace. So, what's new!

It was early June when we got to Whitehorse. I stopped by the hospital there, and they suggested that I see a Dr. Todd. They took my blood test and it was okay. We left Whitehorse and drove into camp on Gay Gulch, got there about 5 o'clock and boy, the cabin looked like a grizzly bear had been inside. What happened, I guess, was the squirrels had gotten in there and they tore everything up. They tore the feather pillows, scattered the feathers all over, we had plastic gallon jars of nuts and candy and etc., and they got into everything, just messed it up something fierce. It took us about 4 hours of cleaning just to get the cabin in shape to sleep.

Due to the fact that we weren't able to be here this spring we couldn't hold Danny up, so he went to work for the Gammy brothers in Dawson, he's running a bulldozer for them. He seems to be quite happy with his work there for the time being. We had to make a fast trip into Anchorage and back, and when we got back to camp the little squirrels were in our cabin again, the little squirts! Needless to say, I declared war on those squirrels.

About the middle of June we drove down to Whitehorse and it took 7 hours to drive down. I had to get my blood checked, and I had to do that each 2 weeks for the rest of the time that we were there that season.

The first of July we went into Dawson and got my blood taken. What they were going to try to do was take my blood in Dawson just before the airplane left, pack it in ice and send it down to Whitehorse. The hospital would call a cab and have it setting at the airport waiting for the plane to come in. I'd pay for that cab to pick the blood up and take it to the hospital to be checked. I'd talked to a doctor in Anchorage and he said they do it all the time in the state of Alaska. The next day we went in to check and, of course, the blood was all out of kilter. I couldn't figure out what was wrong at first and the doctor in Dawson (if he was a doctor, I didn't know for sure, but he was supposed to be) told me to try taking the blood thinner a little bit later at night before I came in. It didn't make sense, so I knew I was with the wrong guy. I said, "Well, why don't we try it just one more time, because it's supposed to work if it's done right." So we took the blood and packed it in ice, and went through the whole rigamarole again. The next morning I called and the results were basically the same. I got on the phone to our daughter Jadene in Nashville, and she said, "Daddy, the problem is that it has to be checked within 4 hours." I said, "Yes, they told me that at the hospital in Whitehorse, and also the doctor in Dawson knew that." She said, "Well, something is wrong and they're not doing it that way." So I called Dr. Beck, my doctor in Tennessee, and he told me basically the same thing. He said what I'd better do was just drive on down there to Whitehorse, a 680 mile round trip, get the blood tested and see how it came out. I did that and it came out right like it was supposed to.

I talked to the girl in charge of the lab and asked her, "What time do you guys close here in the afternoons?" She said that they closed at 4:30. I said, "What if an airplane landed out at the airport at 4 o'clock with some blood to be tested?" I didn't tell her it was mine and she said, "Well, in that case we'd just put it in the refrigerator for the night and test it the next morning." So that answered my question right there.

Ed Rampone and his sidekick Jim came by to see us. Ed's in charge of Immigration in Vancouver, and he comes around to see if the Americans have their work permits, and if all the equipment and stuff that they have in camp has had the duty paid on it. He's a nice guy and a good feller to know. We're always glad to see him come by and try to make him feel at home. They've also invited us to their place out of Vancouver.

About 3 or 4 o'clock one morning a fox was barking and fussing outside our cabin, there was a great big lynx out there that was trying to get to her little pups. Boy, she kept fighting and growling and barking at him. You know, it's odd, we got so wrapped up in watching this fracas I forgot that we had our movie camera there and could have gotten a picture of the whole thing because it was light out at that time.

Our old International generator had been messing up and Gene Fowler told me that he would take care of that problem for us. He sent Don Murphy up with his big generator with a Deutz diesel engine on it, on the boom truck, and Don set it right in place. Don told me that Gene said if I didn't want to buy it at the end of the season to just let him know and he'd stop by and pick it up, no problem. There was no charge or rental for it, and it was awful nice of a feller miner to do something like that.

We went by the Recorder's Office in Dawson and transferred 3 claims on Moose Creek into Dave Kincaid's name. That was because he was so nice and did some assessment work for us there last year. I think it kind of surprised him. He and his wife said, "Well, what's this for?" I said, "It's just thanks for doing the assessment work, Dave."

It's sure nice and peaceful here on Gay Gulch. We may never get rich, but gold isn't everything. Along the middle of July, Marcene and I were setting out in the shade under a tree, and the temperature went from 85 to 90 degrees. It's hard to believe that that kind of temperature can happen in the Yukon Territory, but it quite often does, and at times gets hotter than that.

Dick Hughes, with the Hughes-Lang group, told Wayne Hawk to bring his D8 Cat by our place since he was in the area, and ask if we needed any work done and there would be no charge because we had been nice to them over the years. We let them eat their lunches at our picnic table outside, and in general, we've had real good relations with Hughes-Lang, the hardrock miners. That was something that I appreciated very much.

I've got a little story that I'd like to relate to you about my old buddy, Jerry Bride. He's just over the hill on Seven Pup about halfway up the hill between Upper Bonanza Creek and Gay Gulch. He was in town doing his wash and all he had on was a pair of sweat pants and a sweat shirt, he had already got his washing done and all his clothes were in the dryers. He went in to take a shower, figured by the time he came out his clothes would all be dry. So he came out and not a stitch of clothes could he find anywhere. Someone took them, his socks, his underwear, the whole 9 yards. Jerry said, "You know, I always waited until I got everything dirty before I brought them into town to wash. Man, I don't have a thing to wear!" So we took him a whole slug of clothes, overalls and different things to wear.

We had our first potatoes late this year, the 19th of August, because we got back so late in the season and I didn't get to plant them like I normally do in the springtime.

We had a guy by the name of Arden Danielson come by camp, and we had a nice visit with him. He wanted to buy or lease our claims, and I told him that there might be a way that we could sell him the claims, because I just didn't know for sure yet how things were going to work out with my health. It seemed like it might be a good idea to offer him a deal that I couldn't refuse if he took the offer. Arden left that afternoon and came back the next day and said, "We've agreed to take the claims." So it looked like we had us a deal on Gay Gulch.

Boy, did we ever run into a character on the U.S. border on our way into Anchorage. He went through everything in our pickup, had us take our jewelry off and checked it out and boy, he kept us there for 2 to 3 hours. He went through every envelope and every piece of paperwork, all my diaries, and looked through every nook and cranny. We'd never been shook down like that at the border, but we came through it with flying colors. We found out later the reason for him doing so was because I was wearing a U.S. Customs cap and he thought I was some smart-ass, he was going to show me which way the cookie crumbled, and I guess he did.

We finally got back to Tennessee and even though we missed Arden Danielson on our way through Oregon, we heard from him. He gave us a call and he definitely wanted our claims on Gay Gulch. So we took a plane out to meet with him in Portland to make the deal.

I'd like to add a little tale about a side trip on our way back south. We bought a car just out of Portland and stopped off to see Red Simpson in Bakersfield. We went out to Ethel's, a club where Red plays, halfway between the cemetary and the garbage dump. They come in Cadillacs, Mercedes, ride their horses and there's a hitching post there. Band members from various bands, like Buck Owens's band, Merle Haggard's band, and many, many more, whoever may be in town, show up for the Sunday evening jam at Ethel's. And Ethel has the band do a religious song every Sunday upon closing. I think Merle made a recording, at one time, of a song that Red wrote about Ethel's.

Even though we were out of business on Gay Gulch, we were kind of in the market for other properties for the mining season of 1991, just something to look forward to and keep us busy. I was feeling a lot better and wanted to keep active. In the process of looking around we ran into Al Reisner and his wife Edie in Albuquerque, New Mexico. He had a 1-mile lease on a little pup on Upper Eldorado Creek. He wanted me to do some assessment work. When I converted the lease into mining claims we were to split them. We went by twice to check with him and everything seemed fine, so we went on up in the spring.

I contacted Jim Conklin to take his drill rig out and do some test holes. We went in there and the test looked pretty good, so I hired Jerry Bride to help me stake the claims. We turned the lease into 12 mining claims, did the flagging and the staking, the whole works, and shortly after we got the work done, Al showed up in Dawson and came by our Airstream. When I showed him the results of the test, he kind of flipped out over that, I guess you might say. In other words, he got all excited, he wanted to go up and look over the ground right away. I said, "Well that's fine, we can go do that tomorrow." He said, "No, I'd like to go on up today."

So we were walking up the pup that we had named "Edie", for his wife's sake, and it was slightly up hill. Al got tired, he wanted to rest a bit, so we sat down on the moss and Al said, "Jim, we gotta talk." I said, "What about?" He said, "Well, I owe some taxes and I need to sell one of these claims to you. I need $5000 bad." I looked at him kind of funny. He said, "Now, if you want to lease some of these claims, I'll lease you 1 or 2." Now bear in mind, we had made a deal that we'd go 50-50 on the claims, and he'd even offered to let me build a cabin on whichever claim I wanted to build it on, and I'm so happy now that I didn't go ahead with the cabin building.

Anyway, I told Al that there was no reason to go any farther upstream, and I told him, "You can have the claims, we'll go into the Recorder's Office tomorrow, and if that's the way you are, we'll just go in and get them all squared away in your name." I would like to add that I had paid money up front to Jim Conklin to go in and do the drilling, which was $1000. Al didn't seem all that concerned about it.

Gee whiz! We looked all over the different areas around Dawson for mining ground, and when I say mining ground I mean good mining. It's easy to find marginal ground, and ground where the gold's real deep and you need big heavy equipment to work it with, but we need something that we can more or less play with, or put it this way, work 2 or 3 hours a day and that'll give us something to look forward to. We need some ground that will produce enough to make it worth our time.

This is a little story that comes to mind about a guy we talked to from Calgary by the name of Vic, I didn't know his last name. He'd been up here a couple of seasons and bought some claims from Louie Provonovich over on Bruin Creek. He got Henry Reinink, the driller, to take his drill rig and test the ground on Bruin Creek. The ground was no good, a lot of black sand, but very little fly-speck gold. So, Vic went back to Louie and offered to sell the claims back to him for $1, he'd paid Louie $10,000 for them. Louie said, "No, I don't want them, that's why I sold them to you."

On our way up Eldorado Creek we saw a guy backing a D9 Caterpillar bulldozer. He had backed it up all the way from Indian River, 24 miles into Grand Forks. I asked him if he'd like a drink of water, he was all dusty, and thirsty, and he took a drink. I asked him why he'd backed the dozer all the way from Indian River and he said the transmission was bad and he couldn't go forward. Could you imagine backing a dozer that far, looking over you shoulder all that time?

We had a nice visit with Myrna and Jim Archibald in the Eldorado Restaurant and they invited us up for supper Sunday. When we first came to Dawson, we'd meet Jim on the road and he wouldn't even look at us. It took about 2 seasons for him to speak to us, or nod a little bit. We often wondered what the problem was. We found out that he had his sluice box robbed a few years back and he was just bitter at the world.

Helen Wagner, a lady from Oregon City, Oregon, was in the Eldorado Hotel, talking to Dave Johnson. Her grandfather had come up during the gold rush era, 1890. He had worked Gay Gulch and staked ground on Gay Gulch, right at the mouth, and also up above where our spring is today. She wanted to know who was working the ground now and Dave told her that we were. So we went over to meet her, ate supper and visited with her.

The next day we picked her up to take her to Gay Gulch, right where the hotel used to be at the mouth of Gay Gulch, where her grandfather had left pictures of him standing by his mining claim, and also the hotel. There were also old remains of a sluice box and rock pile that she had a picture of him standing by, on the

Jimmy Simpson   Epilogue   A VANISHING BREED

claim up on Gay Gulch that we used to own. It was so weird, it was the same look today as it was the day the picture was took, as far as the background was concerned. The rock pile still stood up, and stood out.

Her grandfather's name was Mr. Hafstaad, he was from Norway. In later years he moved over to Quartz Creek, he liked that country over there. There's a place called Haystack Mountain in view of Quartz Creek. It just looms up over Quartz Creek and Indian River. He had a will, and when he passed away in 1913, in the will it stated that he wanted to be buried on top of Haystack Mountain. His friends hauled him up as far as they could go with a wagon and then carried him on up. They had to carry him the last 2 miles. They buried him on top of Haystack Mountain with his pick, shovel, and trusty old gun that he used for killing moose. He also stated in his will that the boys buy a keg of beer and enjoy themselves while hauling him up on Haystack Mountain. This was the story that we got from Mrs. Wagner and we sure enjoyed her visit.

In our rounds looking for mining claims, etc., we stopped by to see Lance Gibson at Lucky Lady Placers on Sulphur Creek, and also we stopped over to check on Jim Stanley's things that he stored on his claims just down from Hunker Creek summit. A bear had gotten into his camper and made quite a mess, tore up his sleeping bags and all the groceries. What they can't tear up, they bite into and scatter everywhere, just made a mess of his camp.

We saw Henry, the driller, while driving up Eldorado Creek, and we mentioned to him that we were looking for some claims. He suggested that we go up and talk with Jerry Bride, so we visited with Jerry and talked to him about his claim on Upper Bonanza Creek. He explained to us how he had hand mined it, and that it was good ground.

It's just above Carmack's Fork Creek, also about 1000 to 1500 feet above where the old earthen dam was built in about 1902, or 1903. Until 1967, that big dam held, but it went out in 1967, so for all those years that ground hadn't been mined. Jerry did spend 8 years up there, working it by hand and a bit of equipment, but it's good ground that has been laying there for years, so I thought we'd go ahead and make a deal with Jerry. It seemed that if we could get together and wind up with that one claim, that would be enough for us. During our trip up there we met Vern Trainer, and he seemed like he would be a nice neighbor. Also, Ted Payne would be right next to us and I didn't see any problem with Ted either.

We went by and picked up Jerry, and also a friend of his from Little Blanche Creek by the name of Harvey. Now, Harvey is a character. He's out of Oklahoma, and I asked him, "How do you determine where to dig on your ground when you're mining?" He said, "Well, I get drunk, and which ever way I fall off the stump, that's the way I head my equipment." He goes on a tear every now and then, and most of the time it's now. In fact, every time I've seen him he's been that way, but other than that, he seems like a nice guy.

We rode from Jerry's claim up on Seven Pup, down to Upper Bonanza where we were figuring on buying, and Harvey rode in the back of the pickup. When we got down there he got out and was stumbling around a bit, and Marcene asked him where he'd parked his car. He said, "You know, I don't know." He kept looking around for his car and said that maybe somebody drove it off.

I talked to Henry Reinink, the driller, and he showed me a nugget that weighed about 3 ounces that he'd found on his Eldorado claims just above Grand Forks. He found it digging a shaft the previous winter. He thaws the ground that's permanently frozen with steam, and then he brings his muck up in a bucket on a pulley. Then he runs it through a sluice box in the spring, and that's how he found that big nugget, right there under Eldorado Creek. He's got his shaft now down about 85 feet, and a cross shaft that I think is in the neighborhood of about 70 to 80 feet, so Henry stays busy during the winter months doing it like the old-timers used to do.

We finally made the deal with Jerry Bride on the Upper Bonanza claim, and I contacted Wayne Hawk to bring his D8 Cat up to our new mining claim. He did assessment work and stockpiling material for us. He also leveled off a place for a cabin that we planned to build there, and cut us a road in.

I mentioned something to our old friend John Brown one day, about needing a place to store our things, parts and what-have-you, all the goodies that we had left over from Gay Gulch, had collected for years. So guess what? He came to camp with an Adco building, brought it up on his high-ab winch truck and set it off. He said, "How do you like those apples? No charge. At least I'll know where it is, so don't worry about it, Jim." How do you beat friends like that?

We picked up materials at Bill Bowie's mill, pad blocks and stringers, and all the timbers that go underneath the logs for our new log cabin. You know, building the cabin this time was a lot of work and I told Marcene, "This is hard work!" She said, "Yes, and you're a little older than you were the last time you built a cabin." And especially the one on the homestead that we built in 1957. But we got everything all squared away with the blocks and the stringers, got it set to go up with the logs, and I talked to Warren Schmidt, he was mining up the creek. He gave us a hand putting up the logs.

You know, it seems as if anytime I get in a bind, or really need some help, our good friend Gene Fowler comes through. He sent his boom truck and the operator up, and told the guy to give me a hand and stay as long as need be to get the ridge poles up that go up on top. They were 38 feet long, approximately 18 inches on one end and 12 inches on the other end. We could only put 2 up each day, for 2 days in a row, and then we put 1 up the third day. I tried to pay Gene for the help and he wouldn't take any money. He told me if I wanted to do anything, just give Al, the operator, some money, so I gave Al $500. I was happy to get the work done and Al was also happy.

We finally got all the heavy work done on the cabin, got the heavy ridge poles set up on top, and Warren got finished with his part that he agreed to do. He was going to work for Murray Organski, the Flatlander, over at Sixty Mile, so we got all squared up with him, plus we gave him an ounce of gold for a bonus for being a good hand, and everything. Warren Schmidt is a super nice guy.

The season was winding down and our good friend from Ashland City, Lee Batson, came up for a visit and we showed him around. He's a first class carpenter, good man with a chain saw, does plumbing and all this, so he agreed to help me with the plumbing in the cabin and quite a few odds and ends that we really needed technical people to do, like hanging the cabinets and so forth. In turn, I agreed to take Lee out to the different mines. It worked out good for both of us, I was happy to have him up regardless of whether he worked on the cabin or not. He wouldn't take any money, so I gave him an ounce of gold.

That's a nice cabin that we built there on Upper Bonanza, with a beautiful view up and down the creek. We called it "Hobbit #1". When we had the first ice of the season, it was time to leave. It didn't take us long to get in gear and head south when the ice started showing up. Just below us at Carmack's Fork, a bear was checking out our camp, so we took all the leftover groceries and stuff to Jerry Bride, we didn't want to leave anything to interest the bear. So Jerry was all smiles and happy, and looking forward for the snow to fly.

For the mining season of '92 we weren't in a big hurry getting back to the Yukon, we took our time. We'll have to round up some equipment for our little operation. I'll have to locate a shaker plant someplace, and either a dozer or loader, and this all takes time.

Cast of "Characters"

The following is a song that I wrote about a few of the bush pilots flying out of Kotzebue, Alaska. One note, "homing home" means flying an airplane on instruments to your home base.

When Art Fields flies his Super Cub
He's like an eagle in the sky
He's got so many hours
He couldn't count them if he tried
I don't know where they'll send him
When it comes his time to die
He's too ornery for Heaven
And he's too tough to fry

Chorus:
Homing home to home in Kotzebue
Where the pilots are many
But the good ones are few
They fly all kinds of weather
Never worry about tomorrow
Just homing home to home in Kotzebue

Leon Shallabarger
He's a pilot's pilot
Why, he could write a book
On how to fly
Everybody knows him
From Anchorage to Point Barrow
If you've got the money
Old Leon has the time.

Chorus:

There's a guy that flies real well
Everybody calls him Buck
What he can't haul inside his plane
He'll tie it on the strut
He's up and at'em everyday
Keeping his plane a'flying
He's a guy that don't talk much
But you never catch him lying

Chorus:

There's old "Barefoot" Staley
With a gleam in his eye
He hangs around Kiana
And, boy, can that guy fly
The girls all's used to know
When old Staley hit town

He was a ladies' man
'Til one tied him down
(If you think I mis-spoke "alls", that is a slang, in that part of the country, with the Eskimos.)

Chorus:
>They call old Roger Nordelon
>Kotzebue's hard luck guy
>But that's the breaks, he's got what it takes
>He's got the staying power
>He's up and gone at the crack of dawn
>And he never seems to tire
>There ain't a greedy bone in this friendly guy
>And he don't know when to quit

Chorus:
>There was Archie Ferguson
>A legend in his time
>He was always in a hurry
>But he never was on time
>He kept his plane a'flying
>In his own peculiar way
>He never worried 'bout tomorrow
>He just lived from day to day

Chorus: Homing home to home in Kotzebue

Jimmy Simpson   "Characters"   A VANISHING BREED

(In Alphabetical Order)

I was installing water and sewer lines for **Dave Ahlm** in Anchorage during 1968 by Campbell Lake in South Anchorage. When I'd finished the job Dave tried to give, or trade me lots by the lake for my work. The lots back then were valued about $7500 each. I couldn't take property at that time because I had to have money for equipment payments. In 1979 the Campbell Lake lots available were going for a half million each. We bought our home on Campbell Lake in 1974, a tri-level, for $127,000. We did well on the sale of it in 1978 to Dr. David McGuire.

Shorty Bradley was a man that I won't ever forget. He was an ex-cowboy, ex-Deputy Sheriff of Wrangell, Alaska, homesteader, gold miner, and he spent his last years hunting lost people in Alaska with his trusted bloodhounds. Shorty and his wife Florence were living on their homestead west of Talkeetna at the time of his death. The night that Shorty died, Florence mushed her dog team across the Susitna River to Talkeetna and called me in Anchorage. Florence said that Shorty had told her to call me if he didn't make it through the night. He had given her instructions as to just how he was to be buried. There was to be nothing fancy, just put him in a rough spruce lumber box and bury him beneath the big spruce tree on the east side of his log house. I remember it like it was yesterday, we were to point his feet toward the Susitna River.

Shorty was loved by many, especially the local bush pilots. Two of the better known pilots, Cliff Hudson and Don Sheldon, of Talkeetna, flew people all day throughout Sunday, at no charge, to Shorty's funeral. Don passed away a few years back, but Cliff still runs his bush flight service out of Talkeetna. The last I heard of Florence, she was living in Wrangell. Shorty was truly one of "a vanishing breed".

Jess Carr was head of the powerful Teamsters' Union of Alaska, before, during, and after the Alaska pipeline was installed. In 1967 Danny Thomas and I had a job on 9th Avenue. We had a contract to install storm drain, manholes, catch basin, and all utilities under 9th Avenue, from Gamble to L Street. George Atkinson had the general contract on the overall job, paving, curb, sidewalks, and so forth.

Jess Carr came riding by the job one day with Mr. Aleywine of the #302 Operating Engineers. They stopped by my pickup and Jess told me that I couldn't have my Peterbilt truck on the job without a Teamster driver dispatched from his office. I told him that the truck was mine and I felt I could drive it once or twice a day that we needed to move a piece of equipment. Now I didn't have a problem with Mr. Aleywine, as we were using union operators and, I might add, union pipelayers. Jess Carr told me if my lowboy (Peterbilt rig)

Jimmy Simpson   "Characters"   A VANISHING BREED

was still on the job tomorrow, he would have a picket line on the job. Not wanting to upset the applecart with the other unions, I talked to the laborers on the job regarding working around the clock and stringing all pipe, fittings, manholes, etc., the full length of the job. We finished the last load about 5:45 a.m. and I took the Pete to my yard on Jewel Lake Road and parked it. Jess came cruising by in his Lincoln the next morning, stopped, looked at me and said, "I know what ya did, just don't let me see that rig on this job again."

Some time later, during the summer of '68, he came out to the subdivision that I was developing, Windsor Village, in the Sand Lake area by Raspberry and Jewel Lake Road. I didn't have much time for Jess, and after I listened to his b.s. for a few minutes, I told him that he was trespassing, as the streets and utilities that we were installing would be mine for one year to maintain. In other words, it was private property until the Borough accepted the streets, etc. Until I quit contracting, I never signed a contract with the Teamsters' Union.

In March 1973, **"Coop" Cooper**, one of the snow machine racers that I sponsored, streaked Nome the night before the race. Cooper ran naked from the Board of Trade Bar on Front Street to the Breakers Bar. The weather was clear and 47 degrees below zero. I guess Cooper set a couple of records, coldest weather and the farthest north streaker. The reason Coop streaked was he lost his money rolling dice on a chartered plane en route to Nome. On his arrival at the Board of Trade Bar, I loaned him $100. But after buying a round of drinks at our table and dancing with an Eskimo girl, Coop discovered that the rest of the money was missing from his shirt pocket. Coop said, "I didn't even get a kiss." He looked all over for her and couldn't find her anyplace. I looked at Cooper and said, "Don't ask me for any more money." Then I came up with a plan. I would pass my hat and take up a collection for Coop to streak Front Street. We collected $128 and the rest was history.

"Bedrock" **Bill DeFrang** worked winter months for the Corps of Engineers at Fort Richardson, Alaska. Bill carried large nuggets in his pocket all the time. He'd stop in at my snow machine shop on Jewel Lake Road and show me those nuggets. He kept telling me that they came from Gold Creek, that's 125 miles east from Anchorage, then due north 110 miles on Gold Creek, just off the Big Oshitna River. He talked me into going mining with him. I had the equipment and he had the mining claims, but the partnership didn't work out. There was a little fine gold on Gold Creek, but I found out later that Bill had bought the big nuggets, and he was pulling my leg to get me to take my equipment in there. I figured out that Bill just wanted to get out during the summer months, be out on the creek, enjoying the picnicking and atmosphere on Gold Creek.

In 1953 I met **Jim Denny**, and also **Dolly Dearman**, at Pat Taylor's barbeque in Scottsboro, about 12 miles northwest of Nashville on the Ashland City Highway 12. Jim was manager of the Grand Old Opry at the time. He also owned Cedarwood Publishing along with Webb Pierce. Dolly was manager of Ernest Tubb's Record Shop down on Broad Street. Jim asked me if I had any good songs and I said, "Maybe one or two." He invited me by the Cedarwood Office on 7th Avenue North. This was after I sang a few songs with the local band. Little did I know who this man was at the time I was singing.

Jim was very helpful during my stay in Nashville. He had a booking agency and booked me for awhile. Jim was a true pioneer in the music world. One time I did a session in Owen Bradley's studio. Webb Pierce loaned me his guitar for luck, and Jim called in Grady Martin and paid for Grady himself. Grady was a top session picker in Nashville at the time. The guys out of Springfield that I was recording for made me mad trying to have me sing like, well, rock and roll. I finally got 2 country sides cut and we went over to visit Dolly and Jim at the old Maxwell House Hotel. They had a suite and I got lost in the bathroom. I thought the fridge was supposed to be in the kitchen. I'd had a few.

After we went to Alaska to homestead we kept in touch with Jim and Dolly. I gave a grizzly bear rug to Jim for their new house in 1961, and returned the next winter for the Disc Jockey Convention as "Mr. DJ USA". When I found out that Carl Smith had the bear rug on the wall of his and Goldie's mansion, I come unwound. I talked to Jim, and he went out and got it from Carl, brought it to Tootsie's Orchid Lounge, and threw it on our table. He sat with us, Marcene, me, Bobby Lord, and George McCormack. Bobby was badmouthing Hank Williams's singing, so George sent him on the road. We talked for about an hour about Jim having to fire Hank Williams, and Hank calling him every day 'til Hank passed away.

As a small kid, Jim Denny sold papers on the streets of Nashville and slept in cardboard boxes. I can truly say, and mean it, he was one of "a vanishing breed", because he was a handshake person, his word was his bond. My friend, Jim Denny, has since passed away. Dolly is a beautiful lady who still lives in Nashville. My friend Mel Tillis purchased Cedarwood a few years back. This was the company that gave Mel his first big break in Nashville. Mel was guided by Mr. Denny in his early years in Nashville.

Carl Dickerson was with U.S. Customs up at Top of the World Outpost at Poker Creek. He's since moved back to Eagle Pass, Texas, and is in the import-export business now. He buys and sells equipment used for coal mining and firing their power plants, to the Mexican Government, and he has a good business going. He's got a good connection there.

Jimmy Simpson   "Characters"   A VANISHING BREED

Dieter, the German, is an interesting person in that he is a gold miner part time and fights coal mine fires all over the world. He spends about 6 weeks here on Oro Grande each spring, if he doesn't get a call to fight coal mine fires. He always stops by our place, shows us the gold he gets, and introduces us to his German friends.

During the summer of '82 we had a guy working for us by the name of Rick. He rode over to Dieter's one hot afternoon and, lo and behold, Dieter and his girl friend were mining in their birthday suits. Rick didn't disturb 'em, he turned his quiet little motorcycle around and left'em be.

While working in my snow machine shop one evening in December 1975, a guy came up in a chartered cab. He was an **Eskimo from Kiana**, I don't remember his name, but the story's worth including here. I could tell by his excitement, and the roll of money he had in his pocket that he'd been working on the North Slope pipeline. When the natives have money they like chartering planes, cabs, and buying toys, such as snow machines, motorcycles, outboard motors, 4-wheelers, and guns. When this guy got all through telling me what all he wanted, a new Arctic Cat Panther snow machine, a box of spark plugs, 5 extra drive belts, a pair of mittens, a helmet, a pair of boots, and an Arctic Cat suit, he looked all around and said, "Jimmy, you a gambling man?" I said, "Yes." He said, "Flip'em coin, double or nothing." This guy lost, and after paying in cash, smiled and took off in his chartered cab for a night on the town. I shipped his machine and accessories to Kiana by Weins the next morning.

There was a bush pilot flying out of Nome, and all I ever knew him by was his nickname **"Stinkey" Evans**. He used to stop in and visit with us over at the mine in Utica, and he'd always bring us odds and ends, such as bread and coffee. It was always nice to see "Stinky", and I'll never forget how he would take off from the Nome airport, so loaded that his little Cessna 206 airplane would mush almost all the way down that jet runway before he'd finally get airborne. I asked him one time, "'Stinky', how can you fly like that, flying into the bush and the short strips?" He said, "Oh, by the time I get over to the mines, I've flown enough fuel down so I'm okay. So long as I'm going in, I'm okay, it's the getting off the ground that matters."

In 1953 Marcene and I drove to Creole, Louisiana, looking for **Eddy Farr**, an oil well driller. One rainy night we stopped in a little bar, and asked for Eddy. There were a bunch of rough looking dudes sitting there at the tables drinking beer, and no one knew Eddy, so I asked where the Sheriff's office was. One guy with a big knife on his hip said the nearest Sheriff would be in Lake Charles, 45 miles north. I walked over to the juke box and saw my record,

"Oil Field Blues" and "Ramblin' Blues", and I played both sides 2 times, a nickel a play. Pretty soon these guys asked why I played this oil field song, and I told them it was my record. One of them said, "If you're the singer, bring in your guitar and sing for us." I got my guitar and sang old Jimmy Rodgers's songs, Hank Williams, and so on. After about an hour, the guy with the big knife said, "Who that was you want to see?" I told him and he directed us to Eddy's house trailer. I have many Cajun friends, Jimmy Newman, Doug and Rusty Kershaw are some of my favorites.

Archie Ferguson was a character, and he was a legend in his time. Everybody liked Archie, he flew his airplane like no one else. When he got his first airplane, he had it delivered to Kotzebue, then totally re-did it. He didn't like the way it was set up for hauling cargo, so old Archie re-did his airplane. He played it by his rules in those days.

Archie was flying out of Kotzebue back in the '30s, and a guy came up to him wanting a ride into Fairbanks. The guy had a suitcase with him. Archie was flying mail, freight, everything that he could cram in his airplane. He had that airplane so full, but he took a look in there and said, "Gee whiz, I can't take you and the suitcase." Then he thought about that a minute and said, "I could possibly get you in there with everything else, but I can't take your suitcase. So, take your clothes out of your suitcase and put them all on, everything you can. Stuff what you can't put on in your pockets and get in there, we'll take you to Fairbanks." The guy was wanting to go to Fairbanks real bad, so that's what he did.

At times I think that **Davis Fowler** missed the boat, maybe he should have been a politician. Davis is from a large family originally from Kentucky. The family moved to Arizona when Dave was a young man. I had dealings with all the Fowler boys except Roy, the one in Tucson, Arizona. I did dirt work with, for, and around Bob, Gene, Jimmy, Bill and Davis, and there never was a favor that I needed that was turned down by the Fowler boys. Today, Davis is retired, Bob passed away a few years back, Jimmy is retired and Gene is gold mining on Matson Creek, southwest of Dawson City. In the '50s Davis was partners with "Tennessee" Miller in Kenai, Alaska. "Tennessee" went on to become the most successful contractor in the state of Alaska.

Don Frizzel is a friend of mine for several years. I first met Don when he was manager of White Pass Fuel & Oil Distribution in Dawson City. He was kind and friendly, and treated all people that he dealt with equal, he would thank you for your business if it was $50 or $5000. Don has his own fuel distributing company now, Esso, out of Whitehorse, and is doing well. It couldn't happen to a nicer guy.

Jimmy Simpson   "Characters"   A VANISHING BREED

A real good friend of mine, **Herbie Green**, used to work on the oil rig with me up at Houston, Alaska, about 70 miles out of Anchorage. In 1957 he was about 50 years old, and he drove up and down that highway. He had a dog named Bullet that rode in the pickup with him. Each spring he'd come up to work on the oil rig, and each fall he'd go back down around Bakersfield, California. One fall he was going outside, and he was pulling a little trailer. The trailer hitch kind of broke on him, in between Glennallen and Tok, so he pulled into a shop that was out there and asked the guy if he would weld that trailer hitch for him. The guy said, "No, I don't really have time to do that." Herbie said, "Well, what do you suggest? It's about 90 miles back to Glennallen, and the road is rougher than a cob, what do I do?" The guy said, "That's not my problem."

Herbie went out and got in his pickup. He was talking to Bullet, and they were heading back down the road for Glennallen, instead of the other way to Tok, because it's even rougher on toward Tok. He got to thinking about it, how he'd been ripped off along the highway so many times. He had a 44 laying on the seat of the pickup that he always carried with him. He looked at Bullet and said, "Bullet, we're gonna turn around and go back." So when Herbie found the first turnaround, he turned his pickup and little trailer around and drove back in there. He pulled into that guy's shop, strapped his 44 on his belt and walked up to the guy. The guy said, "I thought I told you I wasn't gonna weld your pickup." Herbie said, "Yes, but the 44 says you are." So he made the guy weld the trailer hitch, and when he got all through Herbie handed him $20 and said, "Now that's just about what it's worth."

I thought I'd inject that tale because it's very seldom a guy gets to pull something like that. The guy in the shop couldn't call the cops on him, of course, he didn't have a phone out there in those days. Every time I pass that shop on the highway out there, I think of Herbie.

In October of '78 we were at the Frontier Hotel in Las Vegas. Barbara Fairchild was playing there along with Mel Tillis. After Barbara and Mel did their shows we went backstage, to the musicians room, and met a guy that really impressed us, **James Gregg**, Mel's bus driver. He introduced himself as **"Radio Red"**. It seems that Mel's brother Richard, gave everybody nicknames, and that one stuck with this guy. Incidentally he was a redhead.

He kept visiting with us, telling us that he lived in Ashland City, which is the town that I'm from back there in Tennessee. It was kind of funny, we'd known Mel for a long, long time, but for some strange reason Mel wasn't showing up. He was back in his personal dressing room and he wasn't coming around. I started to leave pretty quick, and "Radio" said, "No you're not leaving, you're not going anyplace until Mel gets out here." He kept insisting that I stay, and so I did. Pretty soon Mel came out and he looked at me, I was setting on a little barstool there, and he said, "You look so damn big or I'd knock you off that stool." And I said, "What's your problem?" He said, "Nobody walks out on me." He was referring to the time that I was down at his farm last year and a Fish & Wildlife guy showed up. Mel took off with him and left Jadene and me in the kitchen with Judy, Mel's wife. He took off and didn't show back up for awhile, so I just assumed he was gonna be gone for quite a spell and I took off. Anyway, we talked things over, and pretty soon we shook hands and everything was fine, no problems.

That was the time that I first met "Radio Red", and until this day he's one of our dearest friends. He's with a beautiful person today, his wife Duey, and they're living in Reno, Nevada now. I'd like to add that I was impressed enough with "Radio Red" to write a song for him, and about him, about his work that he was doing for Mel. I believe "Radio" drove bus for Mel for about 13 years, that's a lot of dedication.

It was long in August 1973, and we were out in Tennessee. **Fulton Hall**, who's married to my niece, was a sergeant for the Nashville Metro Police, and working undercover for the vice squad. We had driven to Tennessee on vacation in our Winnebago motorhome, towing a Volkswagen dune buggy with rollbars over the seats. Fulton asked if he could use our dune buggy to make a bust, and I said it was okay. The guys Fulton and his partner were making the buy from told them to be careful because "these guys with the vice squad in Nashville are tough". The guys selling saw the Alaska plates and thought the guys buying were okay. Fulton and his partner made the bust, handcuffed the 2 dudes to the rollbar, and in pouring down rain, with Fulton's long hair flowing in the breeze, drove down the freeway to the Davidson County Jail.

Fulton retired in the summer of '92 from the Nashville Police. He told me that not once did he ever have a lawsuit filed against him, or have any bad marks, never got called on the carpet for wrongdoing. He said that he was very fortunate to make it through his whole career, with the undercover work in the vice squad and all, and have come out clean. It's a very thin line the police have to walk to be able to make an arrest and make it stick, without having a lawsuit filed against them.

Mike Hamlin and his wife Ila Jean were staying in our camper park, the Greenbelt Camper Park, in '73 and '74, and in the summer of '74 they were broke and going back to Wisconsin. I talked them out of it, and eventually hired Mike to help me run my snow machine shop on Jewel Lake Road.

Jimmy Simpson   "Characters"   A VANISHING BREED

I first met **Paul Harper** in Anchorage in 1960. Paul played fine fiddle and fronted his own band. He and his band played all the major clubs in Alaska and most of the west coast. I remember one time I was returning to Alaska, it was in January of 1961, and I saw Paul and his band at the Canadian border. He didn't have enough money to get through the border with his group, so I let him borrow $200. I'd like to add that Paul paid me back when he returned to Alaska.

Paul and his band were playing in Fairbanks during the pipeline era, and a foreman with Aleyska Pipeline was in the audience one night. He congratulated Paul on his music. Paul said, "If I could get a job on the pipeline, I'd quit playing tonight." The guy asked Paul if he could drive a water truck and Paul said he could. Paul's career changed that night. I had the pleasure of playing with Paul last year in Wasilla. He has recently retired from the North Slope and is enjoying his life nowadays with his musical friends. Paul is a person that I admire very much.

One night in 1960 **Harrold**, of **Harrold's Rent a Truck** was hauling lumber from Seward, and was down by Portage when a State Trooper pulled him over. The Trooper kept walking around his truck and asking him questions. Harrold finally told the guy, "Hey, if you can't find anything wrong, just let me go." The Trooper said to Harrold, "You can go when I tell you to go." Harrold just put his rig in gear and rolled his bumper and right front wheel up over the rear end of the Trooper's car, smashing it out of commission. Harrold never got through paying for that mistake. But he told me that as he drove up the highway, he said to himself, "I always wanted to do that!"

I first met **Buzz Hoffman** in 1978. He had just come up from Washington to work for First National Bank in Anchorage. I would like to add that all the dealings that I had with Buzz were okay, and everything up front. I traded Buzz a 5-acre tract of ground on Zero Lake in 1978 for a new 33-foot Beach Craft motorhome, and a 914 Porsche car in good shape. He also helped me finance my new Cessna 206 airplane. I was to deal quite a bit with Buzz over the years pertaining to my mining ventures. Buzz founded a bank, Alaska Continental Bank.

In February 1991 Buzz called me in Tennessee to tell me about his brewery that I might like to invest in. The company was Yukon Brewing and Bottling Company, Inc. We talked it over and decided to go along. Things seemed to go along pretty good, then one problem after the other, and it kinda went down the tubes. Buzz told me in '92 that he was sad to inform me, but the company was no longer operating. You can never accuse Buzz of not trying. He now has a company called Banking Solutions.

Jimmy Simpson "Characters" A VANISHING BREED

Jack Hoogadorn is a guy that everyone respects in the Nome, Seward Peninsula, Kotzebue area. We became friends with Jack when we first went up to that country. Jack makes a trek to Nome, approximately 150 miles, every winter. He takes his D4 dozer and pulls 3 Russian sleds (these are old-time Russian freight sleds) hauling supplies back to his camp on the Inmachuk River. Jack has a couple of cabins along the trail and keeps them stocked with food, coffee, and sleeping bags.

On a trip into Nome a few years back Jack decided he would buy him a new dozer, so he called the Caterpillar dealer, the N.C. Company in Fairbanks, 600 miles to the east of Nome. The N.C. Company told Jack to hold tight in Nome and they would send over a salesperson the next day. By the time the salesman arrived the next day, Jack had changed his mind, but he met the guy at the airport to tell him that he'd changed his mind. Jack agreed to pay the hotel bill, meals, and round trip plane ticket for the guy. The reason that Jack changed his mind was that he had sentimental feelings about his trusty old D4 Caterpillar. Also, he went to see Jack Bullock, owner of B & R Tug and Barge, in Nome, and Jack made him a heck of a deal on a D4 undercarriage, tracks and rollers, sprockets and idlers.

There is another story about our friend Jack Hoogadorn that I'd like to mention. Back in 1941, when World War II broke out, he was mining with his brother about 70 miles south and west of his home there on the Inmachuk River. They were digging shafts and testing the ground on bedrock. Of course, when Jack went out there, he pulled a skid sled behind his dozer in order for him to spend the winter out there to do testing.

One morning Archie Ferguson flew over from Kotzebue. It was winter and Archie had skis on his plane to land in deep snow. He brought a message to Jack that he had a notice to go to the Army, he had his draft notice. Archie flew him into Nome. When he got drafted into the Army, it was the first time Jack had been outside to the lower 48 states since coming in with his Dad.

Many years later he went to Seattle again and stayed one night. He said, "I hated it." I wrote a song about him later, it's called "Sourdough Shack", about a gold miner going outside to the lower 48 states; "I want to go back to my sourdough shack, where memories overcome pain."

I first met **Cliff Hudson** in the summer of 1957 in Talkeetna. The road from Anchorage to Fairbanks was just in the dreaming stages back then, so we'd take the train to go up there. It was our first trip on the Alaska Railroad, and in those days the whole town turned out to greet visitors.

Cliff and his wife Ollie so impressed us with their kindness and generosity that we knew they were good people. One time I asked Cliff, "What reason do you credit for your success and longevity as a bush pilot?" He thought about that for a minute, looked over toward Mt. McKinley, and gave me this answer. He said, "Jim, I only fly when I feel it's safe, safety means more to me than money." I guess he really lived by those words, because he surely has outflown most bush pilots in Alaska.

Cliff had a dog that flew with him in his plane everywhere he went. One day, the door was off of Cliff's plane for the purpose of hunting wolves. Cliff didn't have any luck finding wolves, but on the way home he spotted some moose. While circling the moose, about 100 feet above them, the dog got excited and bailed right out of the open door. He fell into the snow near the moose. Cliff brought his plane around and landed on the snow near his dog. From that day on, Cliff would have to carry the dog into the plane. Boy, that dog did not want to go in that plane at all.

I would like to add that this pilot, with all his flights and rescue missions in the McKinley and Talkeetna Mountains, would be the last person to seek publicity. Cliff's sons are carrying a big part of the load today, but Cliff is the same friendly person we met in 1957, a husband, father, a super bush pilot, and most of all, our dear friend.

In late summer of 1957 I had a chance to buy an oil field rigged truck out of Houston, Texas, for $7500. I went to see **Charlie Jett** at First National Bank about borrowing the money. It was a Dart with a 300 Cummins engine with blower, heavy duty trailer with a Tulsa 80 over and under winch, a tail roller on the trailer, also a set of gin poles. Even though I had a load of drill collars and drill bits to haul for Texaco from Houston up to Kenai, Charlie told me that the truck was too large for Alaska. He told me that Harrold's Rent a Truck had the largest rigs required for this country, which were Fords. I found out later that Charlie was taking care of Harrold.

The following year Hill & Hill, an oil field hauling company out of Houston, Texas, received a franchise to haul oil field equipment to Alaska, and went on to play a major role in the development of Alaska's vast oil fields.

Mr. Alfred Karmun, from Deering, was a reindeer herder, and his sons and their families worked with Mr. Karmun herding reindeer on the Upper Inmachuk River. Their herd consisted of about 1650 reindeer, more or less. They butchered once a year and sold the carcasses to various stores around the state of Alaska. Reindeer is a very tasty meat. It's basically the same meat as caribou, except caribou is tougher, the reindeer is domesticated. Also, they sell the horns to Koreans. Koreans come over and help cut the horns off, then grind up the material. Korea is a big market for those ground up horns.

If reindeer get tangled up with a caribou herd coming through, the reindeer will all die because they're used to taking their time grazing. Caribou eat on the run and they'll travel miles and miles in a period of a day. So, needless to say, the reindeer herders have to be real careful when a caribou herd gets anywhere near their herds.

Jack Leakhander made beautiful gold nugget jewelry. He was a very nice, honest man. He later got cancer, and at the end he took his life. Two days before he took his life he told me he was thinking about it, and I tried to talk him out of it. He said, "Well, Jim, I'm spending all of my assets on medicines, doctors, and the government, and I still can't get any relief. I'm just going to spend everything I own, and my kids won't have a thing left." That was Jack Leakhander.

We first met **Dave Lorenson** and his wife Sara in the early '80s. Dave is a heavy equipment operator that has worked in many different countries throughout the world. Dave has mined on several different creeks and bench claims since arriving in Dawson.

There is a true story that I'd like to pass along. Dave staked a lease on the north fork of Henderson Creek along in 1988, and to turn the lease into claims he had to do an enormous amount of assessment work. Dave couldn't afford to do the work within the allotted time of one year, so the day his time ran out he chartered all the helicopters in Dawson for a day so no one else could stake his ground. With deep snow and no road into the north fork of Henderson Creek, the only way to go in was by chopper. Dave couldn't renew his lease, so Sara went with a pilot and she staked the 15-mile lease in her name. They were able to acquire a D8 Caterpillar dozer and other mining equipment and build a road into the head waters of the north fork of Henderson Creek. After all the trouble and heartaches of their venture, the creek proved to not be feasible to mine at today's gold prices.

Dave and Sara are a couple examples of "a vanishing breed", they're always smiling. They are mining today on Cheechako Hill, just upstream from Adams Gulch, on Bonanza Creek. If we need cheering up, we only have to stop by for a visit.

I had hired **George Lott** to run the camper park and I loaned him money to put in a gold nugget jewelry store. He was a whiz at making gold nugget jewelry, but he was broke at the time. He did pay the $10,000 back and made me a nice jade and gold nuggeted buckle that I wear to this day. I also furnished the nuggets and paid him to make up a nuggeted watch and band for Bob

Kirsch, and a beautiful one for Art Fields my partner. I also had him make up one for Hugh Chatham.

In the summer of 1974, we found a large mastodon tusk at the mine at Utica. We shipped it out to George at the camper park. Later, when I went by to see George to pick up the mastodon tusk he said, "Oh, I thought you gave that to me." He had sold it already. One time I brought a plastic gallon syrup jug full of gold down from Kotzebue and gave it to George to clean up for me. He had said, "Boy, I'm a whiz at cleaning up gold." And he was, but by the time I got it back, it had shrunk quite a few pounds.

My old friend, **Big Bob "O.O." Martin** told me, "Son, don't ever let anyone else clean your gold." He's a very respected old-timer here in Alaska. He's a jewelry maker and jade carver, and he used to run the public utilities before the Anchorage Area Borough came into existence. It was called Spenard Public Utilities District in those days.

Buck Matson was a heck of a pilot, and one thing unique about Buck, what he couldn't get inside his plane, he'd tie onto the strut. He'd fly anything, it didn't matter.

In 1975 **John C. "Tennessee" Miller** stopped in to Alaska Sales and Service, the Chevrolet-GMC dealership in Anchorage, on a Monday morning and he wanted to buy 50 crew cab 4x4 pickups for his jobs on the North Slope. After negotiating for about an hour the salesman was happy to make such a sale, but just before "Tennessee" signed the paperwork, he had one more favor and request. You have to know "Tennessee" to understand what happened next. He said, "Boy, there's just one more thing I've got to have throwed in the deal, and this is it, two-tone frontier paint jobs on each pickup by Saturday morning, because I'm shipping all fifty of them to the North Slope then."

The salesman about flipped out when "Tennessee" mentioned this to him, but finally, after contacting all paint shops in Anchorage and putting their own shop on alert, the deal was signed. Alaska Sales and Service couldn't afford not to go along with the deal because of the numbers. "Tennessee" took delivery of his 50 crew cab pickups on time, Saturday morning, and shipped them to the North Slope. The reason Alaska Sales and Service had so many crew cab pickups on hand was that they were "The Rig" for the pipeline and the North Slope.

Tex Noey was a man that loved Alaska. He had an outdoor TV show in the years before and after Alaska became a state. I don't think that Tex ever met a stranger, and if he ever had a problem it didn't show. In the winter of 1972 we ran into Tex at the Iron Creek Lodge on the Alaska Highway. We were involved in a friendly chat when a little dude came in with his little derby hat, suit, and D.C.

tags on his car. Tex introduced himself and said, "What brings you this far north?" The little dude said, "I'm going up to Anchorage to help the Alaska Natives get their Land Claims Settlement Act pushed through. Tex thought about that a minute and said, "I wish you luck, because I have an interest in a bar on 4th Avenue in Anchorage, and I'm sure if you succeed, you will also help make me money."

The Land Claims Settlement Act was passed and the various Native groups were to get in excess of nine hundred million dollars, plus land of choice for all Native people, plus no taxes for 25 years. This Act stopped all future homesteading, and Alaska would never be the same.

Through the years we have dealt with **Norcan Leasing and Sales** in Whitehorse and have found that you can believe Bob Stack, Mo, Clive and the rest of the crew. As a rule, all the miners at one time or the other come in contact with Norcan. In December of '92 Marcene and I were in Yuma, Arizona, looking for a one-ton crew cab dualy pickup. We found the one that we wanted, and just before we signed the paperwork the manager came up and said, "We can't deal with your trade-in because your truck is licensed in the Yukon." He said we'd have to go back to Canada and get paperwork from the Canadian Customs, so I drove off his lot and called Norcan. We talked to Mo and he said they had what we wanted on his lot. We drove all the way to Whitehorse, got the pickup, and left the next day for Tennessee. It was 46 degrees below when we drove through Watson Lake early in the afternoon. We made it to Tennessee in 5 days and arrived at Mama's on Christmas Eve. You know how I feel regarding Norcan.

Roger Nordelon was a bush pilot. He came up to Alaska from Minnesota, and he was into various things out of Kotzebue. He would run the mighty Iditarod Dogsled Race, he flew jade for the Native Corporation up on the Kobuk, flew it out of the jade mine there, and he's just a super nice person.

Louie Peckham is a big friendly guy from Banks, Oregon. I first met Louie after we sold our claims on Gay Gulch to Arden Danielson. Louie, his wife Adele, and friends Dwight and Judy Lanter, went into Lower Brown Creek to mine the summer of 1991. They could barely make it in with 4-wheelers over the thing that was supposed to be a road. Louie purchased the Komatsu loader that we used on Gay Gulch and had a D4 Caterpillar dozer and a shaker plant. They had many problems on Brown Creek, rain, a major forest fire, and the Water Board. He was glad to get out of Brown Creek, with its black sand that was a teaser for gold, just enough to say it was a gold bearing stream.

Jimmy Simpson   "Characters"   A VANISHING BREED

Louie did me a big favor by bringing my wanigan out and to our new claim on Upper Bonanza. The wanigan is a heavy gauge aluminum Adco trailer with bunk beds and big DC3 airplane tires. I loaned it to Bernard Gagnon 8 years ago, and it was nice of Louie to bring it out of Brown Creek for me.

In July of '92 Louie located some ground on Lindall Creek and I went over to look it over with him. I gave Louie and Dwight a hand, did panning in the pit and ran the loader for about 8 hours, and they do have more than teaser gold there, it looked good. I think that for a small operation it will be good for him. Louie and Adele have a little dog, Tarp. One day Tarp was running right into camp, and a black bear was chasing him.

In May of '93 Louie and Dwight helped me get my shaker screening plant set up and going. We ran 200 yards through and I gave them the gold for their help. I gave Adele and Judy gold filled lockets, and Louie gold for retrieving my wanigan from Brown Creek. Louie is a very honest and fair man.

I met **"Tiny" Pettit** in 1950 while working motors on an oil rig out of Robert Lee, Texas. "Tiny" was a drill pusher for Empire Drilling Comany, about 6-foot 3-inches tall, weighed about 250 pounds, and to put it kindly, "Tiny" didn't graduate from the "how-to-win-friends-and-influence-people" school, so I decided to get his attention. I noticed that he would walk over the reserve pit by the shale shaker about 6:30 every morning, across a board that was a 3 x 12. One night I took a hand saw and sawed the bottom of that board almost in two. "Tiny" did his usual the next morning, and needless to say, he took an unexpected bath in the slimy drilling mud. He never found out for sure who did it, as we had 3 crews working the rig, but for the rest of the time that I worked for Empire "Tiny" thought he knew that I was the culprit.

I first met **Jim Prochaska** in Las Vegas in 1978. Jim impressed me to the point that I hired him to go gold mining with us for the next summer. Jim worked out real well for us and we became good friends. Today Jim is a commercial fisherman in southeast Alaska and doing quite well, I might add. We've kept our friendship over the years. He tries to get in touch with us each winter when he comes in from his fishing site.

Joe Ramstead was a nice guy. I worked for Joe in 1960. When I first came into Anchorage from the homestead looking for a job, Joe was nice enough to give me one. The problem in those days was you had to be in the union to get a job with the big contractors, and they wouldn't let you in the union unless a contractor hired you. It was just one of those things.

I fibbed to Joe a little bit when he asked me if I was in Local 302 Operating Engineers and I had said yes. He had a D8 Cat dozer that was stuck down in the swamp, and I mean it was buried. He took me over to look at it and said, "Can you get that Cat out of there?" I said, "Yes, I can get it out." So he told me to go ahead and get it out. I worked on it all day long and finally got it out by cutting logs, and I was working on it all by myself, by the way. I had an ax and some cable. I cabled the logs onto the tracks, and finally got it over to the creek and over to the road about 1:30 in the morning. I'd worked all day long and all through the night to get that sucker out to the road.

Joe came by the next morning all smiles. He said, "You know something? You can go to work now, go ahead and start stringing pipe." He had a go-devil, a sled that you pull down through the swamp, and he said, "Go ahead and string that sewer pipe." It was 24-inch Transite, I'll never forget it. I was by myself and didn't have any help to do it, so I took the Cat and strung the pipe, rolled it all over. I couldn't get down through the swamp, so I had to go down the creek and roll it over to the location where they were going to install the sewer.

Joe came by after I got the sewer pipe all strung down through the swamp there and said, "How come you lied to me?" I said, "Well, Joe, I had to have a job. I was really hurting for work and I figured that was the only way I could get a job, because all these contractors I've gone to ask me if I was in the union. I'd tell them no, and they'd turn me down. I'd go to the union hall and they'd ask if I had a job with a contractor, or someone that would vouch for me to get in, and I'd say no." Anyway, Joe laughed, and said, "You know something, a guy that can do what you've done, well, I'm gonna make a pipe foreman out of you." So, that's where I got my feet wet. I got underway in construction with Joe Ramstead, and it was a good relationship.

Joe helped build part of the Alcan Highway back in '42, and he's been associated with mining at Tin City, Alaska, the tin mine up there, also a gold mine near Manley Hot Springs. He's been into all sorts of things. I highly respect Joe, a dear friend. He's still alive and contracting in Anchorage. At this time Joe's gotta be around 90 years old.

In the early 70s, the pipeline era, there used to be a guy that stopped in my shop on Jewel Lake Road, we'll call him **Raymond**. He was employed by Aleyska Pipeline Service as purchasing agent. He was always jolly when he stopped in for a visit, but this one day he had a long face and seemed a bit worried. He told me that he really had a problem, and I said, "Lay it on me as I have broad shoulders." He said, "Jim, I've really screwed up this time." He was supposed to order one barber chair for each of the 25 maintenance camps along the haul road for the pipeline. When he received the invoice in his office he had made a slight mistake and ordered 25 barber chairs for each of the 25 camps. As Raymond walked out the door, he was shaking his head and wondering how he could possibly explain this to his boss. I never saw Raymond again and I just wonder what he did with all the extra barber chairs.

Marty Rinke is a long, tall, drink of water, ex-cowboy from Montana. He worked out real good for us the years that he worked. Today he is running a loader-forklift combination for a drilling company on the North Slope. We have been friends throughout the years.

Alfe Roberts and his wife Marlene mine on Homestake Gulch, a tributary of Upper Bonanza Creek. They do good with their mining and are in an area where they find lots of prehistoric animal bones. About 4 years ago they found a matching set of mastodon tusks about 8 to 9 feet long, and about 8 inches in diameter on the large end. Alfe has a small screening plant, a 1-yard loader, and a D8 dozer for pushing overburden. Marlene makes gold nugget jewelry and sells to the local stores, and I don't want to forget that she's an excellent cook. They always have a nice garden, and have chickens that lay eggs of all colors. A visit to the Roberts's digs is always a pleasure.

I found a prehistoric miniature horse's hoof on our claim and Alfe gave me the 2 connecting bones for it. It's a prize that we'll cherish from now on. There are so many nice people in the Dawson mining district that it's a pleasure to be associated with them all. My old saying that I'd rather have a million friends than a million dollars is so true. It's people like Alfe and Marlene that make our lifestyle worth it all.

In October of '78 while we were still messing around with Collinsville, we flew out to Las Vegas, checked into the Frontier Hotel, and met **Mort Saiger**. He was the head host and introduced himself to us, as he saw we were wearing quite a bit of gold jewelry. He asked if we had left any gold in our room. Marcene told him it was okay because it was in the attache case under our bed. He immediately went with us to our room to get it and put it in the hotel safe, and told us to always put valuables in the safe.

Mort looks like he just stepped out of Esquire Magazine. He's in his 80s, but looks at least 20 years younger. He was the last Pony Express rider to haul mail in the U.S. He'd pick up the mail in downtown Las Vegas, on horseback, and then deliver it to the Frontier Dude Ranch, as it was called in those days. Many famous movie stars, including Clark Gable, visited there at the time.

That first time we met him, I told him that I had recorded records. Mel Tillis was playing at the Frontier and we were going to go and see him. Mort took me out to his new Lincoln, slipped an opera music cassette into the tape deck, and sang along with it, he had a beautiful voice. Even though I'm not into opera, he really had a great voice. People came by, looked in at us, and Mort just kept on singing. He's a wonderful gentleman. They even named a sandwich after Mort, they called it "Mr. Frontier Sandwich", which is how he was known within the inner circles of Las Vegas.

Mort gave us a Golda Meier coin, and sent one along to give to our dear friend in Anchorage, Perry Green who owns Green furriers. Perry also plays in poker tournaments in Las Vegas. We'd given Mort a nuggeted pin and a nice nuggeted bracelet for his wife Reba, but he added diamonds to it and made himself a bracelet because Reba didn't go in for flashy stuff.

When the Frontier Hotel was sold, around 1991, Mort was let go, of all things. He had only a short time to go to retirement, and he was let go. What a shame, what a waste!

Sam Scardi was a very nice person and a good businessman who owned Alcan Realty in Anchorage. When you finished a deal with Sam you always felt you got a fair deal. I first met Sam in 1967, and he was to play a big hand in our future in real estate. Sam had his office in the Gold Rush Hotel on Northern Lights Boulevard, and the welcome mat was always out. Many people who had dealings with Sam over the years became millionaires and multi-million-aires, but I suppose the one that topped the list was Pete Zamerala who bought, sold, traded, and built on more property than anyone around Anchorage that Sam had dealings with.

Sam called me one night in 1967, around midnight, and said he had a piece of ground listed in south Anchorage, north of Klatt Road. The property was the original Gillys homestead of 160 acres. I went down to his office, and he and I and the Gillys attorney in Los Angeles were on the phone together. I put up a $1000 check as ernest money, and we all agreed that Sam and the attorney would exchange telegrams that the deal was done. I agreed to pay the remaining $24,000 upon closing. I stopped by to see Jerry Bruton, owner of Reliable Builders, the next day and he had already heard about the purchase, but not the price. Jerry wanted to make a deal with me, purchase one half of the 160 acres. I told him I needed to get $25,000 on closing, and he agreed to pay me almost double per acre what I bought it for. I had let him set his price. The attorney that closed the deal for Jerry was Helen Simpson, and she wanted 40 acres. So I let Helen have 40 acres, that left us with 40 acres clear, plus.

In 1980 I traded those remaining 40 acres for the eight 40-acre gold claims on Gay Gulch. Sam sold us his home on Campbell Lake when he moved to Sutherlin, Oregon. Today, Sam owns a beautiful ranch and home just off Interstate 5 in Sutherlin, and is part owner of the country club and golf course in Sutherlin. Sam

Scardi is a fair, honest, and generous man, and this old world needs more people like him.

Leon Shallabarger is a dear friend of ours, a pilot of long standing around Kotzebue, and a very well respected man. One time, there in Kotzebue, Leon had been out drinking a few the night before and had a hangover, he didn't feel too good. His Cessna 185 had 2 ropes tying the wings down to a cable that was latched to the ground. On the tail section, he had an acetylene bottle tied on with a rope to hold the tail section in one position. So, Leon walks out to his plane, cranks it up, warms it up a little bit, taxis out to the runway, and finally gets it airborne. He thought the airplane was acting up a bit, and the control tower called him. They said, "Leon, you've got something trailing behind you." He realized right away it was the acetylene bottle. Leon told me this story, and said, "Did you ever try to land an airplane with an acetylene bottle trying to overtake you as you come down the landing strip? That was hairy!"

Now, here's a guy that's a character, but a nice character, **Frank Short**. He has a partner by the name of Vern Hall. Vern is heavy into fishing in the Kodiak District, and has somewhere in the neighborhood of 4000 people working for him. Frank and Vern make quite a team. Frank is a man of many means and talents; he's an Irishman transplanted to America, and then today, he's working in Canada. At one time he was a place kicker for the Notre Dame football team. He's held so many interesting jobs. He was a diver for the oil rigs in Cook Inlet, and when the Alaska earthquake hit March 27, 1964, he was diving on the bottom of Cook Inlet. Wasn't that a sad awakening! For a few years Frank worked for Red Adair fighting oil well fires all over the world. He later went to work at Ramstead Construction in Anchorage, for an old-timer from way back, Joe Ramstead. Then he got into paving and had his own paving company. Later, he started mining in the Kantishna area near McKinley Park. He and Vern became partners in that operation. In 1980 they moved to the location in the Yukon where they're working today, on Paradise Hill, up Hunker Creek, about 10 miles east of Dawson.

Frank is still an adventurous character. He's got a mining operation now in South America and goes down for the winters to do drill testing. He's getting all set to start mining and producing gold down there. I can say that he is one of the more successful operators in the Yukon Territory.

Al Sly was truly a man of his word, and I like that. Al survived the Bataan Death March and years of torture under the Japanese during World War II. He was top man with the Water Department in Anchorage for many years. When Al looked you in the eye, with his little grin, and gave you his decision there was just no room or reason to disagree with him. Al and Beth Sly were dear friends of ours.

Maxine Smith, the owner of ABM Escrow in Anchorage, has played a very important role in my construction, land development, and mining careers. Maxine has saved me untold dollars, headaches, and attorneys' fees over the years, and she is certainly one of "a vanishing breed". It is so sad that after all the many people Maxine has helped with their many problem, she herself has had to face so many medical problems, her latest being a series of strokes. Maxine is the only person ever to have had full power of attorney on Marcene and me.

Lee "Barefoot" Staley is a very unique person who flies out of Kiana. Everybody calls him "Barefoot" Staley. I've heard various stories, different ones, about how Staley got his nickname, and I don't know for sure which one is right, so I won't venture into that. There is a story about "Barefoot" I'd like to tell. He was flying a black G.I. in from one of the missile sites to Kotzebue and all of a sudden, this dude pushed the wheel all the way forward. He told Staley, "I don't like to fly up high, I like to fly down close to the ground." And, with all Staley's might, he couldn't get that wheel loose from this guy.

He looked around, trying to figure out some way to get this guy to give up his grip on that wheel. At the time, he said, they were about 7000 feet. He didn't have a pistol, he didn't even have a hammer, didn't have tools, or anything to use as a weapon, so he balled up his fist and started pounding as hard and as fast as he could just above the guy's knee. They were at about 1000 feet, or less, off the ground when the guy finally turned loose of the wheel. So, that was a hair raiser for Lee. He got the plane back up to about 8000 feet and called in to Kotzebue to have M.P.s from the base come over to pick this guy up. He found out later that the guy was on dope.

About 3 weeks after the Alaska earthquake in 1964, I got a call late one night. **Standard Oil** wanted me to bring my backhoe down and dig up gas lines the next morning. I started digging in gravel, and I was digging up pure gasoline and gravel. After digging along the 4-inch line for about 80 feet I found the separated coupling. I left my backhoe running and went to A.P.& H. for a Dresser coupling. When I got back I put the coupling on the pipe while standing in gasoline.

As I was just putting the finishing touches and final turns on the nuts, a little dude ran up with a meter. He hollered out, "Shut the backhoe off and get out of that ditch, it's fixing to blow!" I looked at him and told him if he reached for the key to turn the backhoe off I'd warp him across the head with my big crescent wrench. He got

Jimmy Simpson   "Characters"   A VANISHING BREED

all shook up and ran into Standard Oil's office. I finished the repair and backfilled the line, then went and parked my backhoe outside the gate. I got paid for my work and Standard Oil took care of the official with the little meter.

The reason I wouldn't turn the switch off is that if one spark had of occurred I would have went up in flames. I did thank the dude for clearing everyone out while I was in the ditch making the repair. Surprisingly, that was the only break below ground in Standard's yard.

This is a true story about 2 guys named **Swede and Blackie** who were the 2 guys to originally discover gold on the Inmachuk River, right at the mouth of the Pinnell River. Swede and Blackie got into an argument at their camp and ended up making a deal that the first one to reach the Recorder's Office in Nome could file on the claims. These guys split the small amount of food, dried fruit, that they had left and then started out walking through the snow on snowshoes. One guy took his dog along, but the dog gave out in the deep snow about halfway to Nome.

The first one to reach Front Street in Nome was Blackie. He looked back over his shoulder and didn't see his ex-partner back down the street, or anywhere in sight, so he stopped in the first barber shop he came to for a haircut, shave, and a bath. He got to "shooting the bull" and talking about his good fortune over on the Inmachuk River, and needless to say, when Blackie finished with his spruce-up and walked on over to the Recorder's Office wanting to file on the claims, the Mining Recorder said that he was sorry to tell him, but Swede just left about 5 minutes ago. Swede won the race because Blackie stopped to get his haircut, shave and bath. In later years, Swede died a pauper in Fairbanks, even though the claims that Swede staked were great gold producers in their time over the years.

I've known **Danny Thomas** since 1960 and consider him a friend. He and I worked the construction season of 1966 together as a joint venture. That was in Anchorage and we were utility contractors. When we got ready to settle up in the fall, it took us 30 minutes at our kitchen table down on Campbell Lake. Everything was a handshake from start to end and that's the way Alaska used to be.

Bob Thompson, now here was a guy who celebrated his jobs when he got the jobs, not when he finished them. Being a contractor to Bob was a game. One time in 1963 Bob got drunk and about 3 a.m. called Clarence Ablegard from the radio-phone in his pickup, while sitting in Abe's driveway. Abe was in the business of moving dirt and gravel, and did lots of subcontracting work for Bob. Bob asked Abe to come over on Kinik Road to give him a pull, he said he was stuck in his 4x4 pickup. Abe told Bob he'd be over after he

333

made coffee and loaded his dozer on the trailer. Now, Bob was supposedly stuck about 12 miles south of Wasilla, and a total of about 55 miles from Abe's place. When Abe had his coffee, warmed up his diesel truck, and started out of his driveway, there sat Bob Thompson in his pickup, laughing. Clarence told Bob that he was getting a bill for 5 hours truck time, and Bob just laughed it off.

I did a lot of work with, for, and around Bob over the years, and this one job stands out as a doozy. Bob and I had bid on a utilities job in Kenai. Mike Gravelle was the owner of the subdivision, and hired an engineering firm in Anchorage to prepare the paperwork for the bids. When the bids were opened, Simpson Contracting was low bidder. I thought that I had the job, but I ran into Bob on the street and he said, "Guess what, I wound up with Mike Gravelle's job." The next afternoon I went to Mike's office and met Bob in the hallway. Bob said, "Guess what that dirty dog did to me, he sold me out on the Kenai job and gave it to a contractor in Kenai." I said, "Bob, now you know how it feels to have a job dealed away from you." Bob was the founder of Central Alaska Utilities, CAU, the major supplier of water and sewer facilities in the south and east Anchorage areas.

I would later run into Mike on a plane trip to Kotzebue. He was running for U.S. Senator, and was shaking hands and greeting everyone on the plane. He stopped when he got to me and asked if he didn't know me. I didn't stick my hand out, and my answer was, "Yup." Mike was successful in his race for Senator, but I'll keep my opinion of Mike Gravelle to myself.

Mel Tillis played the Frontier Hotel in Las Vegas pretty often there for awhile, and we'd visit with him if he was there and we were too. One time when we were talking to Mel, he showed Mort Saiger a beautiful gold nuggeted and gold coin watch we had given to him. Mort proudly showed Mel the bracelet that his great friends from Alaska had given him.

The watch we had given to Mel was especially beautiful. The reason we gave it to him was that we'd planned on buying a farm from him, overlooking Sycamore Creek, outside of Ashland City, but we changed our minds and bought the big farm across the river from Ashland City. We went by Mel's office in Nashville one day and took the watch by, but Mel wasn't there. We left it with his accountant and told him, "I promised Mel that I would buy his farm, but I found one we liked better, so at least Mel is getting a consolation prize." So that's how Mel came by the gold nuggeted watch.

The winter of '75 Mel, the band, and his brother Richard ("Breadman") were in Alaska and they came out to visit us. I took them to Big Lake, ice fishing. We drove up to Big Lake in our motorhome and everything was cozy. Mel couldn't get over driving out on the lake. Back in Anchorage, I let the guys try out snow ma-

Jimmy Simpson　　　　　　"Characters"　　　　　A VANISHING BREED

chines and everything went fine until Mel ran into a spruce tree. It took me awhile to figure out what he was trying to tell me. He finally got it out, he said, "I b-b-b-broke it!"

We first met **Vern Trainer** and his wife Louise when we started building our cabin on Upper Bonanza Creek by Carmack's Fork. We were planning on using a water tank and hauling water from Dawson. Vern suggested I tie my line onto his system. He has a spring-well combination, a heavy duty pump and big storage tank. I was reluctant at first, but figured it was okay so long as he suggested it. I only had to run 1200 feet of hose and we were in business. We drain the hose when it starts to freeze in the falltime and wait 'til it stops freezing in the springtime to hook back up.

The Trainers have proved to be good neighbors. We usually bring them items when we go to and return from Alaska. They are hard workers and we're happy for them that they're successful miners. Vern and his family used to be loggers in British Columbia. When he first started mining he went over to the Sixty Mile country, then to Victoria Gulch just down Bonanza Creek about a mile or so. Their son Don and his girl friend Pat are there with her son Brent, 9 years old. He's such an intelligent boy for his age. I loaned Brent a small sluice box, and he sold his first gold for $70.

George Tucker was a jolly, shrewd, sharp, but nice businessman with his ever present cigar. He would have 4 to 6 in his shirt pocket every time you'd see him. I first met George in 1957 when he and his partner Ralph Peterson were getting into their oil and gas drilling at Houston, Alaska. George and Ralph had worked at Jonesville Coal Mine just east of Palmer and decided to go mining by Houston. During their strip mining venture they encountered surface gas and got the bug to drill. In those days they were true wildcatters. At the time, there were only 2 oil rigs in the state and one was theirs. They never found the big strike, but I don't know how we would have coped with a high pressure well with the wore out equipment and lack of chemicals, drilling mud and etc. You have to remember, we were 2500 miles from the nearest oil field, in North Dakota, and close to 4000 miles from the fields in Bakersfield.

In the early '50s, George had the Studebaker Agency in Anchorage. He told me one day a real nice guy from Kentucky drove a real sharp '34 Ford in to trade for a pickup. This guy had new spark plugs and points laying on the seat. The car had a miss, and the guy told George that he was going to give the car a tuneup, but just hadn't gotten around to doing it. George believed him and made the deal. Ralph was working in the shop at the time and proceeded to tune it up, but it still missed. Ralph got nosey and pulled the heads off. He found a whittled block of oak wood pounded down one cylinder. It took Ralph most of 2 days drilling and beating to get that oak block out.

George went on to be quite a builder in Anchorage. He would be the first builder to introduce antifreeze in concrete and build a six-story building right through the dead of winter. They just don't come down the pike every day like George Tucker, Cap Lathrop, John C. ("Tennessee") Miller, Wally Hickle, to name a few. They brought dreams with them to Alaska, and made them come true.

Billy Walker came up to Anchorage to see us in the winter of '76. He had some show dates there and we had a nice visit with him. We drove him up to Talkeetna for a snow machine outing, and on the way home we passed by a hippie hitchhiking along the side of the road, carrying a guitar. I drove by him and Billy said, "Jim, are you just gonna pass that poor guy back there on the road?" Here it is, about 40 below outside, so I said, "Oh, you want to pick him up? Well, we'll just back up and pick him up." So I backed up and the guy was glad to get inside the motorhome. Billy looked at him and said, "What kind of a guitar you got there, son?" He had a 12-string guitar, I don't remember the make of it now. Billy asked him, "How come you only have 6 strings on this guitar?" The guy said, "Oh, that's all I can afford, just 6, I can't afford 12." So, Billy's tuning the guitar, and singing in his own pretty way that he always did, and he went through quite a few songs. We got on down the road 30 or 40 miles, and the hippie said, "Hey, man, you know you do pretty good. You ought to try to get on records sometime." Billy never said anything. We drove on in to Anchorage, and he never said a word about being a Grand Old Opry star, and all of his hit records that he's had.

In 1964 **Herb Weir** owned Tips Bar & Dance Hall in Eagle River, Alaska. I was well acquainted with Herb as it was a gathering place for musicians as well as contractors in those days. Just after the big earthquake Herb asked me to haul the steel from a bridge that he'd bought in Whittier, Alaska, to Eagle River from Portage, 10 miles east of Anchorage.

Marcene and I drove the Peterbilt and lowboy down to Portage one night in June after work. We met Herb at the railroad siding there and he proceeded to load the steel with a fork lift. Whether it was the beers that we'd had, or the thought of the horrible road that we had to drive over, I guess I just wanted to load it all on and get the haul over with. I told Herb to put all the steel on, about 3 times the normal load. On the way into Anchorage I blew 3 tires. I think we got in around 2 a.m. After repairing tires and working all day, we proceeded on to Herb's place at Eagle River. Marcene drove my pickup with the radio-phone and she kept calling the weigh station about halfway between Anchorage and Eagle River. When she couldn't get an answer I drove on through, as the scales were closed.

I got to Herb's Tips Bar around midnight and asked him where he wanted the steel unloaded, and he gave me directions to his 2-acre lot. The only thing that I had to unload that steel with was a big pry bar. I finally got it all off and it was scattered all over that 2 acres from the way I had to unload it. We stopped back by Tips and Herb charged us for steaks and beer, and said that he'd take care of me for the trip.

Another month or so went by and we stopped in and paid for our meal and beer again. It was a Sunday afternoon and the band was playing. I walked back to the band and told Tim Perry, the piano player, to enjoy his gig this afternoon, because I was going to Big Lake and I'd be back in about 2-1/2 hours to pick up the piano. He said, "Man, you've gotta be out of your mind." After the business in Big Lake, I stopped back by Tips Bar and backed my pickup to the double door in the rear. I told Tim to get with it, 'cause this was his last number on that piano in Tips Bar. The boys finished the number and they, knowing the story and being dear friends of mine, proceeded to help me load the piano on my pickup. We were almost to the door and Herb came back. He said, "What do you think you're doing?" I said, "Herb, I always did want an old upright piano with a history, so this one will do, and yes, you don't have to worry about 'taking care of me' anymore."

Our daughter Jadene still has this old piano in Tennessee. The "history" of it is that it was in Skagway, Alaska, in 1897, and went to Dawson City, Central City, Big Delta, and then to Tips Bar in Eagle River. Herb Weir no longer has Tips Bar.

Jim West, of Nome, is a very successful business man. Jim came up to Nome from Arkansas many years back. He owns the Board of Trade Bar on Front Street, builds homes in the Nome area, has vehicle leasing, deals in carved ivory, numerous other projects. Jim is a longtime friend of mine and Marcene's, and he always treats us so nice when we go to Nome. He'll tell us to "just take a vehicle and go", and will not charge us for it.

There are some funny characters that I've run into over the years in my gold mining ventures. One of these is **Bill Wright**, they call him "Pig Man", that's his nickname. He's a "Cat skinner", the name for dozer operators, and a good one. He worked for Dave Johnson down on Eldorado Creek a few years back and today he's mining in Thailand. I understand that he went over there with the backing of Dick Hughes, of the Hughes-Lang hardrock mining group. He's now more or less on his own there in Thailand.

Jimmy Simpson   "Characters"   A VANISHING BREED

1898. GAY GULCH IN BACKGROUND WITH GAY GULCH HOTEL ALL OF THIS IS NOW EXCAVATED AND MUCH LOWER.

1898.- FLORA HAFSTAD IN DOORWAY, CARL AND HELEN ON DIRT PILE.

Jimmy Simpson　　　　"Characters"　　　　A VANISHING BREED

1956. JIM OIL RIG AT ALTO, TEXAS

1957.- JIM WITH HIS FIRST DOZER HE EVER BOUGHT FOR HOMESTEADING.

WINTER OF 1957-58.- LOG HOUSE JIM BUILT ON OUR HOMESTEAD.

1958.- JIM SIMPSON ON THE HOMESTEAD WITH FIRST GRIZZLY BEAR HE HAD TO KILL.

Jimmy Simpson "Characters" A VANISHING BREED

1958-59. ZERO LAKE, HOUSTON, ALASKA OUR HOMESTEAD.

1959.- JIM WITH CHUCK ROBERSON (JOHN WAYNE'S DOUBLE) AND HUSKY (QUARTER WOLFE) RAISED AS A PUP AND TAKEN AT BRACKETTVILLE, TEXAS.

Jimmy Simpson "Characters" A VANISHING BREED

1973.- JIM, BILLY WALKER AND MARCENE DURING BILLYS VISIT TO ALASKA.

JIM ON OLD GLORY CREEK AT AUTICA, ALASKA, 18 MILES SOUTHWEST OF DERRING, ALASKA.

Jimmy Simpson   "Characters"   A VANISHING BREED

1975.- AT AUTICA. ART FIELDS W/AL MINTKEN HIS WIFE, DAUGHTER AND ONE OF THE NATIVES WHO WORKED FOR US.

1976.- GOING UP GLACIER CREEK TO STAKE CLAIMS IN JIM'S 6 BY 6 TRUCK, WITH DC-3 TIRES. CLAIMS DIDN'T PROVE OUT. WEREN'T WORTH WORKING.

Jimmy Simpson   "Characters"   A VANISHING BREED

1977.- CROSSING BIG O RIVER GOING INTO GOLD CREEK, ALASKA.

JUNE-23-1977.- KOMATSU - WIDE PAD DOZIER PULLING JIM'S 6 BY 6 OVER CAMERON PASS, ALASKA.

1977.- OUR HOME ON CAMPBELL LAKE

1977.- JIM WITH HIS CESSNA 206 BOUGHT FOR MINING AT COLLINSVILLE, ALASKA.

Jimmy Simpson   "Characters"   A VANISHING BREED

1979.- JIM AT OUR HOME ON CAMPBELL LAKE IN ANCHORAGE, ALASKA WITH SOME WEIGHED UP GOLD.

LEFT TO RIGHT.- WILLIE RUTH PRIMM, LOUETHA CHENEY, DUDLEY SIMPSON, CHARLENE HARRIS, MAMIE HAMILTON, NELLIE SIMPSON, FAYE GOWER, JIM SIMPSON, CLADIE BELL HOLLIS, RAYMOND "BUZ" SIMPSON AT MY PARENTS 60 WEDDING ANNIVERSARY.

Jimmy Simpson   "Characters"   A VANISHING BREED

1982.- AND OLD TIMERS SHAFT ON GAY GULCH IN THE LATE 1800'S

1983.- JIM PROCHASKA WORKED FOR US MANY YEARS THIS PICTURE IS OF JIM WITH CARIBOU AT NELSON LAGOON AREA. ALASKA

Jimmy Simpson   "Characters"   A VANISHING BREED

1983.- LOUETHA CHENEY MY SISTER, RUNNING MONITOR. I'M TAKING IT EASY ON GAY GULCH.

1982.- MARCENE WORKING SHAKER ON GAY GULCH.

Jimmy Simpson "Characters" A VANISHING BREED

1982.- JIM AND MARTY RENKE CLEANING GOLD OUT OF RIFFLE ON DENVER PANNER ON GAY GULCH.

1983.- LEFT TO RIGHT. JIM, MARCENE, TERRA, (MARLENE'S GRANDUGHTER) MARLENE AND BILL, McNABB ON THE PORCH OF THE CABIN WE BUILT ON GAY GULCH.

Jimmy Simpson "Characters" A VANISHING BREED

1983.- OUR DAUGHTER JADENE BY OUR CLAIM POST IN THE KLONDIKE VALLEY.

1983.- SCOTT MAGILL AT MONITOR IN MAY ON GAY GULCH.

Jimmy Simpson   "Characters"   A VANISHING BREED

1984.- BIG RED LEVEQUE WORKING ON BEAR CREEK.

1984.- JIM RUNNING D31S KOMATSU ON GAY GULCH.

Jimmy Simpson   "Characters"   A VANISHING BREED

AUGUST 12, 1984.- FIRST SNOW OF THE SEASON WHILE WORKING ON CABIN ON GAY GULCH.

1984.- OUR DAUGHTER, JADENE AND HER HUSBAND SCOTT MAGILL WITH DOCTOR HOOK.

1984.- GENE FOWLER, DAVE JOHNSON AND BERNIE GAGNON ON GAY GULCH.

1985.- MARLENE McNABB ON GAY GULCH.

Jimmy Simpson   "Characters"   A VANISHING BREED

1987.- BOBBY ADKINS WITH BISON HEAD WE MONITORED OUT OF BANK ON GAY GULCH.

1988. -BILL AND MARLENE McNABB OUR FRIENDS FORM ANCHORAGE, ALASKA.

SEP. 1989.- TESTING GROUND WITH DAVIS FOWLER AND HIS FRIENDS ON MOOSE CREEK, YUKON TERRITORY.

1988-1989.- JIM AND DANNY COZEC AT ACTION JACKSON'S AT TOP OF THE WORLD HIGHWAY ON THE ALASKAN SIDE.

Jimmy Simpson   "Characters"   A VANISHING BREED

1990.- JIM AND JOHN BROWN IN DAWSON CITY, YUKON.

SAM AND BARBARA SCARDI.

Jimmy Simpson   "Characters"   A VANISHING BREED

1991.- OUR 24 X 24 W/8 FOOT HANGOVER FRONT PORCH ON UPPER BONANZA.

1992.- LOUIE PECKHEM - JIM SIMPSON ON LOADER AND DWIGHT LANTER HELPING SET UP JUNIPER SHAKER ON UPPER BONANZA.

Jimmy Simpson — "Characters" — A VANISHING BREED

1992.- LEE BASTON AT JOHN BROWN'S CLAIMS ON SULPHUR CREEK OUT OF DAWSON CITY.

1992.- JIM IN FRONT OF ONE OF JOHN BROWN'S DOZIERS.

Jimmy Simpson   "Characters"   A VANISHING BREED

1993.- RUNNING GOLD WHEEL THRU CLEAN-UP WHEEL ON UPPER BONANZA.

JIM AND MARCENE IN FRONT OF OUR CABIN ON UPPER BONANZA.

Jimmy Simpson   "Characters"   A VANISHING BREED

JIM AND AL OSTER ON UPPER BONANZA.

OUR BANKER IN DAWSON CITY, YUKON PAUL HENDERSON, HIS FAMILY, ELAINE, STEPHEN, KYLEY AND JAMES.

FRANCES AND WC MILLER FROM BATESBURG, SOUTH CAROLINA. A COUPLE OF DEAR FRIENDS WE MET IN DAWSON CITY, YUKON.

Jimmy Simpson   "Characters"   A VANISHING BREED

GRANDAUGTHTERS JENNIFER NICOLE MAGILL AND TIA ELANE MAGILL IN 1998.